MOONFELL WITCHES BOOK ONE

TRIPLE MOON

HONEY GOLD AND WILD

TJ GREEN

Triple Moon: Honey Gold and Wild

Mountolive Publishing

Copyright © 2024 TJ Green

All rights reserved

ISBN eBook: 978-1-99-004795-4

ISBN Paperback: 978-1-99-004796-1

ISBN Hardback: 978-1-99-004797-8

Cover design by Fiona Jayde Media

Editing by Missed Period Editing

This is a work of fiction. Names, characters, businesses, places, events, locales, and incidents are either the products of the author's imagination or used in a fictitious manner. Any resemblance to actual persons, living or dead, or actual events is purely coincidental.

No portion of this book may be reproduced in any form without written permission from the publisher or author, except as permitted by U.S. copyright law.

Contents

1. March, Present Day — 1
2. July, 1664 — 10
3. Present Day — 22
4. Present Day — 32
5. July, 1664 — 45
6. Present Day — 55
7. July, 1664 — 65
8. Present Day — 74
9. July, 1664 — 83
10. Present Day — 93
11. July, 1664 — 104
12. Present Day — 112
13. July, 1664 — 122
14. Present Day — 130
15. July, 1664 — 140
16. Present Day — 149
17. July, 1664 — 159
18. Present Day — 166

19.	July, 1664	176
20.	Present Day	183
21.	July, 1664	193
22.	Present Day	201
23.	July, 1664	213
24.	Present Day	221
25.	July, 1664	231
26.	Present Day	240
27.	July, 1664	251
28.	Present Day	259
29.	July, 1664	270
30.	Present Day	279
31.	Present Day	293
32.	Past and Present	305
Author's Note		318
About the Author		320
Other Books by TJ Green		322

One

March, Present Day

"I think they'll be very pleased with it!" Birdie said, feeling smug as she studied the open-plan living room and kitchen area. "They get their own tower. What could be better than that? I think we've made a good job of tidying it up."

Morgana laughed. "We will also get a modicum of peace. As for tidying it up," she cast her grandmother a sly smile, "I hate to think how messy this place will become. As much as I love my son and Como, I know they will be typical young men. This floor will probably be knee-deep in dirty clothes and unwashed plates the next time we come here."

"It will give Mrs Bell something else to complain about," Birdie pointed out, referring to their cleaner who visited once a fortnight for an entire day with her daughter. The house was so big, they tackled parts of it at a time. Magic kept it clean in between the visits. As far as Birdie was concerned, though, nothing beat a proper, manual cleaning. "Although, of course, we know that she will love fussing over them. As will I." She was so excited about the prospect of Lamorak, her great-grandson, and Giacomo, her great-nephew, arriving that she had barely slept. It was an unexpectedly warm day in mid-March, but the room was chilly, and with a word of command, the logs in the grate erupted into flames. "Perfect."

"Now that I'm here, I'm wondering why *my* bedroom isn't in one of the tower rooms." Morgana walked to the east window, leaning her hands on the stone sill as she looked out of the arched, Gothic window. Her long, dark hair was loose over her shoulders, the grey streak curling around her chin, and her black dress hid her slim form. "The view is amazing."

"I know why mine isn't. The stairs would play havoc on my knees. And it's too isolated up here for me," Birdie pointed out. "Even though I'm more youthful now. Besides, I love my room. It's an oasis of calm."

Before Christmas the witches had performed a banishing spell on a Fallen Angel, and there had been unexpected consequences. The Goddess had reduced her age by twenty years, taking her from being an infirm 89-year-old who could barely see or walk, to a vibrant sixty-something. However, that didn't give her the energy of a teenager—thankfully. Age brought its own rewards, like wisdom and knowledge, and the unapologetic need to do what she wanted without caring what others thought.

It was Sunday morning, and the two witches were on the top floor of the southeast tower that overlooked the orchards and the front of the house. The tower was part of Moonfell's original Gothic building, and over the years had been extensively renovated. It emerged from the second floor of the house, with another two floors above that level.

When the young men had stayed with them over Yule they had been given their pick of rooms, seeing as they had declared that they wished to move in permanently over the summer, and both had chosen the tower. There was a bedroom and bathroom on each floor, and the top floor contained a comfortable lounge and kitchen that they had opted to share, decorated in the fashion of the house, with dramatic colours and oversized furniture; a fusion of Gothic and modernity. Totally self-contained, it was perfect for their needs.

Birdie joined Morgana at the window and gave her a brief hug, knowing how nervous she was about Lamorak moving in. Morgana hadn't always had the easiest relationship with her son, but it seemed to have improved over Christmas, so that was something. "They're only here for a couple of weeks, so it's a good way to judge our success, don't you think?"

Morgana nodded, her gaze distant, and it was obvious that she wasn't really seeing the garden anymore. "We need to introduce them to the bees. We never did it at Christmas."

"It was too cold. They were hibernating. This is the perfect time." Birdie smiled to herself as she surveyed the gardens that were springing into lush life again with the advent of spring. Ostara was a week or so away. The view also afforded a glimpse of the Waxing Moon Gate to the east, the Full Moon Gate to the south, and the tangle of paths and planting around them.

"It will seem so quiet here after university halls. All that hustle and bustle, plus the pubs and restaurants. They're bound to be bored. I can't see them wanting to stay here for long."

"Good grief, Morgana. We're in London, on the edge of Richmond Park, not deepest, darkest Peru! Storm Moon will keep them entertained. It's hard to be bored around shifters—and magic! They wanted to come!"

"I know, but..."

"No. Let's not second guess. I certainly do not expect them to live here forever, but even if they only stay a year, isn't that something to look forward to?" Birdie bit back her impatience with Morgana. Sometimes she forgot to enjoy the present because she was so focussed on the future. "What time are they arriving?"

"Late this afternoon. About four, I think."

"Excellent. We'll head to the bees at dusk."

Morgana's eyebrows shot up with surprise. "We're doing that *today*?"

"Why not? Sooner the better. It doesn't do to disappoint the bees. Besides, I'd like an excuse to stroll through the orchard." Birdie walked away, leaving Morgana to her thoughts. "I'll prepare everything now. And stop worrying!"

Birdie headed down the stone stairwell, past the doors to the bedrooms, and on to the second floor of the main house. She had another reason in mind for the bee ceremony. She wanted to start their Ostara celebrations early, and had found the perfect spell to help welcome spring to Moonfell. She had newfound energy since she had been gifted a few extra years, and spring, a season of new beginnings, seemed an excellent time to give thanks and weave her own sense of renewal together with that of the coming season.

As the coven's High Priestess, it was her role to plan their ceremonies. *Well, most of them, anyway.* For the last few years, Morgana and Odette, her two granddaughters who also lived at Moonfell, had picked up her roles as she had been unable to perform them. Consequently, Birdie now delegated leading some rituals, as the three witches all had diverse magical abilities, and it seemed silly not to use them appropriately.

Taking a deep breath of satisfaction at the future unfolding before her, Birdie absorbed the sights, sounds, and scents of Moonfell as she walked down the richly decorated hallway. She had never lived anywhere else, and her soul was deeply entrenched in the estate. She had only been a teenager when the house declared its intent that she would be its guardian. It was hard to explain how that had happened, but every guardian experienced the same thing, more or less. It was a type of *knowing* that just struck one day. Sometimes it happened in dreams, sometimes during a spell or while gardening, or even just reading in a quiet room in the house. The house decided, and then informed you. It also let the current guardian know who the future one would be, too. The house, with its own innate magic instilled by generations of witches, instinctively knew who to choose, and when Birdie died, Morgana would take over. The guardianship had skipped a generation, her two sons and her sister's children completely bypassed. However, it was a wise choice. Morgana was steadfast, level-headed, and a skilled witch, but Birdie sometimes feared the responsibility would isolate her too much. With luck, Odette would continue to support her. Someone always did.

Birdie was suddenly struck by how hushed the house was, almost expectant. She patted the wall. "Not long now...then you'll wonder what has hit you," she muttered under her breath.

Not that their recent months had been uneventful. They had dealt with a demon-summoning witch who had been imprisoned in their other tower. The house's magic had contained him when he tried to attack them and the shifters guarding him. Several members of the Storm Moon Wolf Pack had stayed there for a few nights after the demon attacked them to recover from their injuries. Birdie hoped that nothing like that would happen again any time soon, but it had been fun to work with Maverick and his pack again.

The bright gleam of sunshine through the window at the end of the hall beckoned with its promise of burgeoning life, but she still had much to do before she could stroll through the garden. Quickening her pace, she descended the stairs to the first floor and entered the library that housed their enormous collection of journals, spell books, history books, and magical treatises, along with many other varied titles. Her research was spread out on a table that lay under one of the huge, arched Gothic windows that overlooked the interior courtyard. The centre of the collection was a slim volume about bee lore, the myths surrounding it, and associated spells, written in the seventeenth century by one of her ancestors called Caleb Masters. She knew very little about him, other than he seemed to be fascinated by the bees that had lived in the orchard before the house had even belonged to their family.

It was valued more for its illustrations than its content. Caleb was a fine illustrator, and he had sketched and painted the hives, bees, sections of honeycomb, and the orchard itself. The hives looked different now, but nevertheless, the other illustrations demonstrated the continuity of the house.

One spell had caught her attention. It recommended a ceremony in which the members of the household reintroduced themselves to the bees at the spring equinox, binding themselves to the growth of the hives and the garden. To Birdie, at least, it was charming. For as long as she could remember, this had never been observed in her lifetime. *Not surprising*, she reflected as her gaze swept over the vast array of family histories in the library. *There were far too many spells and rituals to do them all.* With every generation, the manner of honouring the seasons changed. Only the yearly Yuletide protection spells had survived the five hundred years of Moonfell history.

The good thing about this particular spell was that Caleb recommended it be cast on the new moon before Ostara, and the new moon was that night. A time to set intentions for the month ahead. Birdie consulted the spell's ingredients, made a note in the margins, tucked it into the pocket of her long cardigan, and headed to the still room.

Odette, at thirty-one, was the youngest permanent resident of Moonfell. She observed the narrow path she had cut through the long grass strewn with bluebells in the orchard.

Over the winter, although the grass hadn't grown much, the bluebells and crocuses had sprung into life, almost obliterating the main path that led from the lawn to the beehives in the centre of the tangled, wizened fruit trees. Pink and white blossoms were already emerging, a mix of apples, pears, plums, and damsons, and all, despite their age, were heavy croppers.

She cast aside the old-fashioned scythe that she had used, peeled off her gardening gloves, and rubbed her sweaty hands on her jeans. Despite using gloves, she could feel tender skin at the base of her thumb from where she had wielded the gardening tool. The sharp scent of earth and young growth was rich, and she breathed deeply, savouring the warmth from the sunshine on the back of her neck that felt like a tickle. However, the tickle persisted, and she absently rubbed her skin as she turned towards the hives that basked in the unexpected heat of early spring.

Half a dozen hives were spread under the trees in the centre of the orchard, and the deep thrum of bee song added to the drowsiness of Odette's surroundings. The hives were painted in shades of pale yellow or green so that they blended in with their surroundings, and the witches had freshened up the paint over the previous weeks. It had taken longer than they expected. The centre of the orchard, as was its wont from time to time, would prove elusive to find, as if the bees had willed it so. The phrase *hivemind* kept circling Odette's thoughts.

"It's all right," she said out loud. "I won't cut any more grass. I just wanted an easy path to find you. Not that it will help, I'm sure. When you want to stay hidden, you're remarkably stubborn." She pursed her lips, hands on slender hips as she studied the few bees that had emerged from their winter hibernation. "We'll be back later. We have new members of the household to introduce to you, so you better not hide then!"

The buzzing intensified, and for a moment, Odette swayed, dizzy with their hypnotic song. Unable to control an overwhelming need to sit, she rested cross-legged in the long grass, the cool earth beneath her. Closing her eyes, she concentrated, as if she might understand what the bees were saying. Their murmured song intensified until it was all she could hear. The sounds of bird call and the creak of branches vanished, and spring sunshine painted a golden glow upon her closed eyelids.

Odette was used to this state. Her magic encompassed a type of knowing beyond her own mind. She saw to the truth of things, whether she wanted to or not. Secrets could not hide from her for long, even if she tried to block them—or if people tried to block her. It wasn't mind-reading, though, and the revelations seemed to come when she least expected them; when she was relaxed, perhaps, or engaged in conversation about something else entirely. It was a heightened perception, really. She had learned to live with it, and she had certainly learned to keep secrets—some of them, at least. Often, insights would emerge as she painted in her studio, as if the paintbrush were a conduit to the hidden realms. Or the moon gates would reveal glimpses of the past, like they had at Yule.

Her breath slowed as the murmur of bees filled her up until she thought she might overflow with the sensation. Then suddenly an image entered her mind, and she saw a collection of hives that were very different to the ones they had now. The wood was silvery with age, the trees that surrounded them weren't quite as gnarled as the present, and it was later in the year...late summer, perhaps. Ripening fruit hung on twisting branches, and the deep green leaves made a cave of the orchard. A breathy, uneven sound disturbed the silence.

Crying.

A whirlwind of emotions hit Odette so hard that she took a sharp intake of breath. Someone was so panic-stricken, so overwhelmed that he or she could barely think straight. This person was drowning in fear, and Odette ached to help whoever it was. She waited, hoping that her vision would change to show the figure responsible, but annoyingly, the sound started to fade, and in desperation, Odette tried to force it. It was the worst thing she could have done.

Abruptly, the normal sounds of the orchard returned, the golden glow receded, and all trace of the unbidden images vanished as if it was a dream.

Two

July, 1664

Eliza Wildblood finished reading the letter from her Uncle Lester, and was so cross that she balled it up and threw it across the room.

"That man is useless! He's a beef-witted buffoon, and if he were standing in front of me right now, I would hex him!"

Her younger brother, Ansel, bent to scoop up the letter and smoothed it out so he could read it. "Honestly, Eliza, you should calm down."

"How? We have hardly any money, and magic alone will not keep this house standing."

Ansel rolled his eyes. "It's hardly falling down."

"It will if we can't make decent money!" She paced across the room to the windows, skirts flouncing around her. "The work we do for the peasants doesn't pay much, and I am sick of wearing old clothes. And no," she said, rounding on him before he could speak, "I don't want to keep casting spells to make dresses. We need material and money to pay a seamstress. What is the point of being here if I look like a peasant, too!" She flung her arms around to encompass Moonfell, the grand, Gothic manor that was their ancestral home.

She and Ansel were in the small parlour on the first floor that overlooked the front of the house. It was her favourite view, because it contained the Full Moon Gate and the sprawling orchard that looked lush with verdant greenery in the midsummer sunshine. *At least*, she reflected, *the garden was thriving, unlike the family*. It had been a very hard few years. The Witch Trials had swept across the country and Europe, and the residents of Moonfell had been forced to be extremely circumspect with their magic. They had retreated behind the walls, keeping to themselves, and only helping those who they knew to be firm allies. Unfortunately, those had been few.

Consequently, they had lost all of their influential customers they had been accumulating ever since Sibilla Selcouth's time. All the lovely, landed gentry with their deep pockets and even deeper obsessions that required a little magic to help them. Heirs, money, influence at court, good health, gardens that dazzled their visitors, and protection spells to keep them safe. The witches of Moonfell had offered all those things at one point or another, but not for close to thirty years—decades before she was born. She had contacted a few descendants of their old customers but had heard nothing, and she decided it was too risky to pursue. Their accumulated wealth was quickly dwindling.

Eliza was twenty-three years old, with responsibilities far beyond her age, and those included looking after her younger brother, Ansel, who was twenty-one, and their fifteen-year old sister, Jacinta. Their mother had died six months previously, and her useless Uncle Lester, her mother's younger brother, was in Europe, pretending not to be a witch, and making his living as an English tutor. Her mother's last words had been to promise her to be careful about using her magic for customers again, even though King Charles II had been restored to the throne, and the Puritans no longer had any influence. *Well, very little.* Over the last couple of years, the country had thrown off the dour, grim lifestyle they had endured following the Civil War, and the king had ushered in a new era of frivolity.

Her mother, Virginia Wildblood, the old High Priestess of Moonfell, had remained cautious, however, and Eliza had respected her wishes, but now that she was dead, she was free to pursue her own agenda. Her mother, always prone to drama, had become increasingly so in her elder years. Although Eliza was sad about her death, she also had to admit to feeling a little relieved. The last few years had been hard as her mother had become increasingly difficult. Her paranoia had grown, and her spells became ever more convoluted. Now, surely, it would be safe to find new clients, perhaps to open Moonfell's doors—discreetly—to new business. Theatres were booming, women could act now, and the court, by all accounts, was filled with music and dancing. Yes, there were religious divisions, but when weren't there? They would navigate those just like they always had.

"Ansel." She turned to look at her brother. He was slim-built, tall, with a shock of dark hair just like hers, inherited from their father who had left Moonfell years before. "We need to start finding customers again. Ones that can pay. Either that or we need to work—proper jobs."

Ansel was still reading their uncle's letter. "He's staying in Lisbon, then. Well, I suppose if he has good employment, and feels safe…"

"But what about us? He said he'd come home after Mother died, but he didn't and never will. Neither will Aunt Angelica's children. Our cousins have forsaken us!"

"Can you blame them, after what happened to their mother?"

Angelica, her mother's older sister, had almost been arrested after being accused of witchcraft, and it was only by magic, ironically, that she had escaped and fled to Ireland, where she and her family lived very different lives in County Cork. It had been a terrifying time. They should have stayed at Moonfell, where the strong protection spells would have kept them all safe, but some members of the family railed against it, saying it felt like a prison. *Prison!* Moonfell was never a prison. It was a sanctuary.

"We're better off without them, anyway," Ansel continued. "The house is ours. Well, *yours*, legally and magically. That counts for a lot."

The house was always passed to the firstborn, whether male or female, but the house itself chose its magical guardian, and that had fallen to her, too. She sensed it on the day she turned sixteen.

"I'm serious. We need customers! It's time to re-join the world."

Ansel threw himself into the nearest chair. "You make it sound as if we never go out."

"We go to the market to sell vegetables and chickens, and treat the folk in the villages and farms, but we need more than that. We need money. Proper money." She studied the room's faded furnishings again, and noted the general air of polite abandon. She could glamour it, of course, but that didn't change the root of the problem.

All three of them spent most of their time in the garden that fortunately provided them with an abundance of fruit and vegetables. They had chickens, two cows, and the bees, of course, so they had milk, eggs, and honey to sell, too. In any spare time they had, they painted, kept diaries, and wrote silly plays to amuse themselves, as well as practice their magic. Ansel should have apprenticed himself to a skill by now, but their mother had been so terrified of witchcraft accusations that she had kept him at home.

"I have an idea," Eliza said, hoping Ansel wouldn't think it was madness. "We'll go to the theatre."

"Why?"

"Because we need to meet the landed gentry, and that's where they go. Especially The King's Playhouse. It's the king's favourite theatre, and it's where King's Company perform. We'll go and mingle."

Ansel pursed his lips, looking incredulous. "You just think we'll waltz in there and meet a duke who'll offer us a magical job?"

"Of course not. We're going to talk pleasantries, eavesdrop, cultivate friendships, and then find a duke to offer us money."

"That's dangerous and foolhardy, and sounds remarkably simplistic."

"Have you a better suggestion?"

He ran his hands through his hair. "Spells for wealth."

"I cast them all the time, especially at new moons. I have also checked the records of all the landed gentry that we worked for, trying to decide how to rekindle our contacts. The ones we had the strongest connections with are dead. I sent letters to another couple, but have heard nothing."

Ansel's eyebrows shot up. "You kept that quiet."

"I didn't want to get overly excited, or give anyone false hope. They haven't replied."

"The thing is, our skills were only considered after everything else failed—well, for most people, anyway. And we relied on word of mouth. It will be hard to get that again."

"Exactly. We're starting at the beginning again, so that means we need something else." Eliza took a breath, wondering how her next suggestion would be received. "We know someone at the Playhouse, not very well, admittedly, but it's a contact, and she knows what we can do."

"You're talking about Nell. She's just an Orange Girl."

Orange Girls sold oranges to the theatre audience, and were scantily clad, by all accounts. They also carried messages backstage to the actresses. *Assignations*. Everyone knew what they did. It was common gossip.

"Not anymore. She's been given a few small acting parts, and they're getting bigger. She's good, apparently."

Ansel frowned. "She's ambitious. I'm not sure we can trust her."

"We helped her. She owes us a favour." Nell had a mother who drank too much, and a sister who was constantly in trouble. Her mother ran a bawdy house, and when she had fallen ill, it was Virginia who had helped her. Eliza remembered going with her into central London, and feeling overwhelmed by the crowds, but she'd met Nell. She was feisty and spirited, and they had got on immediately. "She'll remember me, I'm sure. We had to see her mother a few times. She was always there." Plus, the place itself was unforgettable. A cheap house filled with prostitutes.

"Even if she's acting, she is still a peasant."

"But she mixes with the right people. I was hearing it only the other day at the market."

"I'm not convinced. You do know that theatres' backstage areas are sometimes little better than a brothel? Most of the actresses are prostitutes. Nell might be, too."

Eliza's frustration and rage at their circumstances was building. They needed to be bold. To leap into the unknown. "I don't care. If the bees agree, will you come with me?"

"They aren't soothsayers." He rose to his feet. "I'll come and listen."

"*No!*" Ansel could communicate with animals, an unusual family magical ability inherited from one of the first witches who lived at Moonfell, and she did not want him influencing the bees. She could communicate with them well enough in her own way. "You will interfere. You can talk to them on your own."

"I can't influence them!"

"I'm not risking it." Eliza knew she was being petulant, but didn't care. "I shall see you later. Check on Jacinta, please. She's suspiciously quiet."

The heat was suffocating when Eliza left Moonfell's cool interior to cross the garden. The summer had been indifferent up until a few days ago, and now the heat was like a furnace. It was a relief to enter the orchard and walk through cool greenery beneath the trees, accompanied by the somnolent buzz of the bees who were busy foraging in the shade, but there wasn't a breath of wind, and when she reached the hives, she was hot and sticky. She pulled her long, dark hair free of her ribbon so that it coursed down her back. She had hoped the walk would calm her down, but if anything, she was more incensed, and by the time she arrived at the hives she burst into tears and collapsed in the grass.

This was not how her life was meant to be, she was sure of it. She should be casting spells and making money, and wearing fine clothes and eating fantastic food. Then she realised how shallow that sounded when she was surrounded by the magnificence of Moonfell, and cried even more.

What was she doing? She was selfish and vain. She owned more than most people ever would. If the roof developed leaks, and the soft furnishings had moth holes, what of it? Magic would help. *At least that was something they would never be short of.*

This was a beautiful place, gifted to her family for good and generous deeds that she did all the time. They were good witches! They helped people. She should be happy. However, there was no denying that they needed more. Her ancestors had invested well, but the way their fortunes were going, it wouldn't last forever. Unfortunately, some family members had presumed it would, and had been a little footloose with their investments.

Plus, if she was honest, she was bored.

She sat up, brushed her tears away, and faced the hives. Even they looked a little worn. The bees, however, were industrious. They buzzed back and forth, wings jewel-bright in the shafts of sunshine, and for the most part, ignored her completely.

"I need your help, bees. I need advice." She waited until the murmur quieted, and then outlined her worries and her plans. "Is it a good idea?"

A few moments later, a bee landed on her hand, and she held it up to her face to see it properly. It traced a dance on her skin, a sunwise circle, round and round three times before it flew off. It was a sign.

Yes, the bees approved.

For the rest of the afternoon, Eliza considered which night would be best to go to the theatre and what she could wear, as she anxiously waited to see how Ansel fared with the bees himself.

She had spent her time in the garden with Jacinta, trying not to appear too anxious in front of her younger sister. Not that she should worry, though. At fifteen years of age, Jacinta was smart and already controlled her magic well. Plus, it was obvious to anyone with eyes that Moonfell needed work done and they needed money.

When Ansel finally appeared, they were in the kitchen organising their dinner, a simple omelette and vegetables.

"How did you get on?" Eliza asked, wiping her fingers on her apron.

"We need to make them an offering, and I have just the one. We can do Great-Uncle's old spell. The one that offers a binding."

Jacinta, lips and chin stained with raspberry juice, her hair knotted and wild, asked, "We're binding ourselves to bees? What for?" She looked between them. "You're up to something. What?"

Ansel nodded at Eliza. "Your sister has come up with an intriguing way for us to make more money."

"I didn't think that you were worried about that."

Eliza glared at Ansel. "I'm not *worried*. I'm just aware that what we have won't last forever. I asked the bees if they approved of my idea. They did. With caveats, clearly."

"The binding spell." Cinta wiped the juice off her chin and smeared it over her cheeks instead. Eliza despaired that she would ever become a lady. "Elaborate then, brother."

"It will strengthen our connection." He grinned at Eliza. "Tonight."

"We *have* a connection! They're our bees! Well," she qualified it hastily. The bees truly belonged to no one. "You know what I mean! What does that have to do with my plan?"

"Patience, dear sister." Ansel reached into the bowl of fruit and fished out a peach. "As you know, they approved your suggestion, and they have promised to help our endeavours with a little bee magic."

Eliza narrowed her eyes. "I have never heard of such a thing before. Is this something new?"

"Something *old*. Something Great-Uncle Caleb discovered when he went on his travels. You know he was obsessed with the bees."

"Like you."

"I'm not obsessed. I'm respectful, as we all are. You know, they are very wise. Uncannily so. They even remember him."

"How? That was years ago. They can't possibly be the same bees."

Ansel smirked, which made him look rakishly charming. "Bee memories. They pass them down, you know. It's sort of like a collective memory. The hivemind. They work as one and remember as one."

Eliza wasn't scared of much, except abject poverty and losing Moonfell, but the bees were unnerving. It was as if they had power to rival her own. "Well, I suppose that's even more reason to keep them happy. What do we do?"

"We search Caleb's papers. I know what we're looking for, because I read them a while ago. Unfortunately, it's not the most optimal time of year, but it's what they want. If you stop filling your face with raspberries, Cinta, we can gift them to the bees."

"We have plenty."

"Not the way you're eating them."

Eliza looked around at the partially prepared food. "Dinner can wait. Let's go to the library now."

The library was a grand room, designed by one of their relatives, but unfortunately only a small portion was filled with books. The rest was lined with shelves waiting to be filled. It had tall windows capped by high Gothic arches that overlooked the inner courtyard, and a narrower raised level was accessed by a spiral staircase. One day it would be breathtaking, but right now it was draped in shadows and dust—except for the family grimoires, of course, which were looked after with reverence.

Ansel headed unerringly to a shelf in the centre of the room, leading them past Sibilla Selcouth's grimoire that was wrapped in a linen cloth. Eliza had looked through it, but had been warned not to damage it. It was 140 years old and spelled with protection, but even so, they treated it gently. The grimoire they used most often now was one started by her mother. The Wildblood Grimoire, bound in dark, reddish-brown leather. All three siblings, however, had started writing their own grimoires, too.

"Here they are," Ansel said, full of confidence as he lifted out a bundle of papers, carried them to the table, and fanned them out. "We should really bind these properly. He died before he could do it, and he spent so much time on them, it would be a shame not to."

Eliza smiled. Her brother could be very thoughtful—sometimes.

"This is the one," he said, extracting a couple of pages and scanning the contents. "We need to make offerings at dusk. And it's a new moon. It might not be Ostara, but the new moon will help."

Cinta folded her arms across her chest, her superior expression muted by the smear of berries. "What will this binding do?"

"Bind us to the bees, so that their magic will help us. If we want wealth and success, they will court it."

"Binding always makes me suspicious," Cinta complained. "They will help us do what, exactly? You still haven't told me!"

Eliza knew the excitement that this would cause. "We are going to the theatre to find rich clients—but we'll be subtle, of course! We're not shouting about magic and spells!" She mimed sealing her lips to her sister. "There are still religious zealots and Puritans lurking in the dark like rats in the sewers. We must be careful not to alert them."

Cinta's eyes widened with surprise. "The King's Playhouse?"

"Yes, of course, but perhaps we'll try all of them. This is not going to happen overnight. Before you ask, you are too young to come with us." Plus, Eliza didn't want to expose her sister to the greedy eyes of the men who would be there.

Cinta shrugged. "That's fine. I'd have to get all dressed up, anyway. I'd rather stay here. Perhaps I can cast my own spell to help you. Help us!" Her gaze raked the room, lips twisting with distaste. "The Goddess knows we need it. Perhaps you should find a husband, too."

A weight settled over Eliza. She was late for marriage, and even later in having children. "There are reasons for that, as you well know. I must first trust who I marry. They will have secrets to keep."

"But we know people who will keep them," Ansel pointed out. "Men who like you, if only you weren't too worried to entertain the thought. One in particular is very sweet on you—"

Eliza cut him off before he could continue. "I will not be drawn into that conversation now, because I *do* have other things to worry about. Like this spell. So, let's get on with it."

Three

Present Day

Morgana frowned at her twenty-one-year-old son, watching him shovel chocolate cake into his mouth as if he hadn't seen food in months. "No one will steal it, Lam. Slow down!"

"But it's so good," he said, once he'd swallowed. "Have you put a spell on it?"

"It's made with a little love, that's magic enough." Giacomo, her second-cousin or something of the sort—he was her great-aunt Horty's grandson—was sitting next to Lamorak, equally absorbed in eating, and having little interest in anything else. "The same applies to you, Como."

He grinned at her, revealing chocolate in his teeth. He was a year younger, dark-haired and dark-eyed, much like his Italian father, and he'd inherited his stocky build too, looking quite different to Lamorak, who was tall with light brown hair and pale skin. "Sorry, Morgana, but Lam's right. I could inhale it."

"I think you already are."

Both young men, behaving like teenagers, were sitting at the wooden table in the dining end of the main kitchen in Moonfell. It was an enormous Gothic room, with huge windows looking over the north side of the grounds, and it was furnished dramatically, just as Morgana liked it. The tiles were black, the cupboards and work surface were made of dark wood, and the stainless-steel appliances gleamed. However, it wasn't austere. It was warm and lived-in, with jars of herbs and well-thumbed recipe books stacked on shelves—along with her kitchen grimoire, of course. Like most kitchens, it was the heart of the house.

The boys had arrived only half an hour before, and after dumping their bags in their rooms and declaring themselves very happy with their living arrangements, had promptly asked for food. *And so it starts*, Morgana had thought, reflecting on the fact that she would need to buy three times as much food as usual from now on. She had forgotten how much they had eaten at Christmas. It was a good job that she loved cooking. Besides, she had years of mothering to make up for. Lamorak had lived with his father for most of his young life, so this was something that she would relish.

Morgana checked the time, noting the thickening twilight. "Well, you had better finish up. We'll be heading to the orchard soon."

Lam wiped his finger across his empty plate and licked it. "For our introduction to the bees?"

"Yes. So comb your hair, please. You look as if it hasn't seen one in weeks."

Como snorted. "Do the bees care about our hair?"

"It's a sign of respect! You can't just rock up looking like you have fallen out of bed. This is a proper ceremony." She ran her hands down her dark green dress, admiring the smooth velvet and lace. It had been her mother's and had a distinctly seventies vibe that she rather admired. "Wear a shirt, too, rather than a t-shirt."

"A tux, perhaps?" Como asked sarcastically.

"We'll have one somewhere." She laughed as his eyes widened in horror. "You'd be surprised what we have tucked away in our many cupboards."

"I have no objection to wearing tuxes in the right place, but not in an orchard!"

"I really don't think the bees would mind. As I said, first impressions count."

Lamorak leaned back in his chair. "Are their consequences if we disappoint them?"

"If you're very rude or insulting they might sting you, but seeing as you won't be, I really wouldn't worry about it. Although, perhaps you should ask Birdie that. She's been doing far more research on the subject than I have, and it's been years since we've made such formal introductions."

"Because we're moving in permanently in the summer?" Como asked. She nodded, and he continued, "So, visitors don't need an introduction?"

She collected the plates and headed to the sink. "No, although we always keep them apprised of our news. It's been a long time since we had new residents. You, though," she said to her son, "were introduced as a baby a few days after we'd informed them of your birth. That's another requirement. Births, deaths, and marriages."

Lam grimaced. "They sound like a council office."

Amused, she said, "I wouldn't tell them that. Enough chat. Go and get ready or Birdie will hex you if we're late. She's already out there, setting up."

They scooted out of their chairs and headed to the door at the back of the kitchen that led to the narrow rear stairway, very different to the grand one in the entrance hall, leaving Morgana musing on how much they had to learn about the house and its ways.

Not just them, though, she reminded herself. It had been years since any of them had taken part in such a ceremony. A new moon ritual would be fun too. She always loved celebrating the moon cycles. Once the bees had been attended to, and it was dark, she would head to the New Moon Gate in the north and cast her own spells. She wanted to foster a closer bond with her son, and it was the perfect time. She wouldn't leave Como out, either. Potentially, he might find it hard to settle in Moonfell. His mother, Jemima, had never liked the place, resenting the fact it had chosen Birdie over her mother, Horty, to caretake the house. Not that her resentment had passed to Como, though. He'd had a great time at Christmas.

Shaking herself out of her revery, she stared into the deepening twilight. New moon magic was already building, and she had a momentary flash of concern. Spells could manifest strongly at the new moon, and she wondered whether this would affect their bee ritual. She shrugged it off, though. *What could possibly go wrong?*

"Where were you when you had the vision?" Birdie asked Odette after lighting the last candle-filled lamp beneath the trees with magic.

Odette pointed to a spot beneath an apple tree. "There. It felt as if the crying person was right behind me, but I couldn't turn to see the figure. I couldn't even tell if it were male or female. No doubt all will become clear at some point."

"No doubt," Birdie said, echoing her sentiments, still distracted by the coming ritual. "It might be inconsequential, too."

"True. It might have just been the strength of the emotion that left an impression. Only the Gods know what other scenes these trees and bees might have witnessed. By the way, Birdie, this looks lovely."

Birdie nodded with satisfaction as she appraised the scene. "Thank you. It should work well."

A dozen old lanterns filled with candles were either placed in the grass or suspended from tree branches, and a line of witch-lights bobbed along the newly scythed path, disappearing into the cool shadows of the orchard. Incense coiled around the hives, and the faint murmur of bees blended with the creak of the branches, although the bees were returning to their hives with the onset of dusk. In another month there would be many more of them, and the air would be thick with bee song. It was so tranquil, and yet, spring energy was stirring. Birdie thought that if she sat here quietly enough, she might hear the grass growing, leaves unfurling, and petals opening.

She caught Odette's eye. "This orchard gets under your skin."

"I know. It feels stronger than usual today, too. As if it knows what we're going to do. It's spring magic—well, almost."

It was another couple of weeks until Ostara, but the earth had started waking with Imbolc. Birdie opened the small wooden table she had brought with her and set it on the grass, then pulled a bottle of mead from her bag, and a cut glass chalice. "Can you open the bottle, please? I thought mead would be better than wine. I've brought sugar for the bees, too. A little gift." She placed the goblet on the table with her other altar equipment that included a jar of the previous year's honey. "My spell suggests toasting with the hives' honey, so that we bind ourselves to the bees, and," she reached into her bag and withdrew another jar, "our homemade damson jam."

"From the orchard's fruits. I love it. I can't believe we haven't done this before."

"It's always such a busy time though, isn't it? Bear with me while I find Hades."

Hades was a large Savannah cat who was also her familiar. He'd arrived in her teens when she first found out that she would be Moonfell's guardian and had never left. She cast her awareness out, speaking to him in her mind. "Where are you, Hades, my friend? You need to be here, too." Suddenly, she was seeing through his eyes as he eased through the prolific bluebells. A bird erupted out of the grass and vanished into the trees. "You're hunting!"

"Merely a diversion on my way to you."

"You're incorrigible."

"It's in my nature. You should be grateful I'm not a goat or a pig. I would destroy the garden."

"You most certainly would not."

Hades laughed. A strong, purring rumble that started deep in his chest. *"I'd like to see you try to stop me."*

"Do not tempt me."

It was harmless banter. They rattled back and forth like the old friends they were. She would never, ever harm Hades, and he would never harm her. He was an old, mysterious being, and even after seventy-odd years together, she still hadn't discovered his past. He wanted to remain an enigma.

"Are you close?" she asked.

Then she saw herself through his eyes as he emerged from behind one of the hives, her white hair aglow from the candlelight, and her long, red dress puddling around her feet. She looked rather regal, even if she did say so herself. She blinked and snapped back into her own awareness. "There you are, you old rogue." Voices carried to them, and before Hades could answer, Morgana, Lamorak, and Giacomo arrived. Birdie had only seen them for a few minutes when they arrived, as she was already heading to the grove. The two boys looked so large in the gloom, both much taller than herself. "Excellent timing!"

"Not without some effort," Morgana said, raising her eyebrows. "They had to change. At least the path stayed true. It clearly didn't want us to be late, either."

"Wow!" Lam said, eyes wide as he observed the magical scene. "This is quite something. I feel Titania is about to emerge from the gloom with Bottom."

"Let's not encourage the arrival of the fey," Morgana chastised him. "This garden causes enough trouble on its own."

"As long as I don't end up with a donkey's head," he muttered.

Birdie couldn't resist teasing him. "I don't think even my powers are that great, although I wouldn't put it past the bees."

Odette tittered. It was a wonder she hadn't planned a prank. She always loved to tease. Maybe she was planning on something that she was keeping quiet.

"How many hives?" Como asked, eyes narrowed as he looked around.

"Half a dozen," Odette told him. "There were three originally, but Sibilla added to them and since then, that number has never changed. When you're here in the summer, you can learn to look after them. We all share the responsibility."

"This place is...odd," Como finally said.

"Odd things are always the best," Birdie told him. "Gather next to me, and let's begin before the light disappears entirely."

She finished preparing the altar, aware that the twilight was manifesting odd shapes and shadows beneath the trees. She expected Hades to join the witches who were all lined up, facing the closest hive, but he stayed back, tail swishing in the long grass.

"What are we supposed to do?" Lam asked, shuffling nervously.

"Follow my lead, stand up straight, and be confident. The bees hate slovenliness. We will have a general introduction and blessing, and then I will introduce you to each hive." Her stare quelled further interruptions.

Birdie faced the hives, arms outstretched in supplication. "Dear bees of Moonfell, guardians of the orchard for generations, we join you tonight, on this the new moon and the cusp of spring, to introduce you to the newest members of the household and to reaffirm our connections to you. Will you consent to our presence?"

If Birdie was honest, she wasn't quite sure what would happen. The ritual suggested a moment's silence, and advised that if the bees weren't interested, they should get ready to run as they would swarm to drive them away. She very much doubted that would happen, as she had already advised them of her plans earlier. Nevertheless, a faint trepidation fluttered though her as they waited.

The bees' murmuring vanished, leaving behind a deep well of silence. Nothing stirred. Not a blade of grass, or a branch, or a breath of wind. Finally, a few bees exited the hives, and Birdie clutched her skirts, preparing to run. However, they weren't swarming; instead, they settled in a line on top of each hive facing them, as if to witness the ritual.

Good grief. They were actually watching. The hairs stood up on her arms as wild magic swelled in the dusk. She could not mess this up.

Moistening her lips, she ploughed on as if it were the most normal thing in the world. This was so formal compared to their general interactions. She dipped her head, acknowledging each hive. "Thank you, you are most gracious. I am Thea Cornelius, High Priestess of the Moonfell Coven and Guardian of the Grounds. I come here tonight to renew our bond. Morgana, my granddaughter and future Guardian of Moonfell—" Morgana gave a light, dipping curtsey, "and Odette, the youngest member of our coven," Odette followed suit at the mention of her name, "share with me the care of the estate. We affirm our commitment on the auspicious new moon before Ostara. May our futures continue to grow together." She paused as the bees buzzed in response, a warm, fruity murmur of what seemed like approval, and taking it as a good sign, waited until they had fallen silent again. "However, we have two new members of the family who will join the household in the summer, and we would like to introduce them." She turned to the boys, sure of herself now. They, however, looked frozen in shock. "This is Lamorak Blake, Morgana's son and my grandson, and Giacomo Santini, my great-nephew and grandson of Hortense, my younger sister." Both blinked like owls, swallowed, and nodded. "They intend to pursue their magic. They will reside in the southeast tower, and will learn to look after you in the summer."

She was aware of the bees' glittering eyes that seemed to follow her every move. It was unnerving. Still nothing moved beneath the trees, the orchard waiting in unnatural silence as if they were a tableau frozen in time. Perhaps they were. Maybe she would find that either no time had passed, or it would be dawn when the ritual had finished.

Birdie lifted the mead. "We honour you and reaffirm our bond with mead, made with the gift of honey from your hives." She poured a measure into the goblet, sipped it, and passed it to the others, reassured as they passed it down the line, each taking a sip. "With jam, made from the fruits of last year's harvest." She had set the jam on small crackers, and each witch took their offering. The sweet flavours exploded on her tongue. She lifted the bowl filled with sugar, a spoonful of which she would place on each hive as she escorted the young men around the hives. "With sugar to sustain you, and our unreserved respect and regard." Now for the peculiar charm she had found to end the first part of the ceremony. "*Bee-eye bright, bee-wing's flight, let this charm our house unite. Honeycomb's gleam, bees' delight, let this spell bring dreams to light.*"

As her words drifted beyond the hives and into the deeper orchard, a golden light carrying the scent of flower blossoms and a shimmer of pollen seemed to suffuse around them for the briefest of seconds before vanishing again, renewing her connection to the land and the garden. She blinked as if waking from a heady dream, and glancing around, saw her family doing the same. The bees, however, shining like amber jewels atop the hives, watched impassively, the wink of candlelight making them shimmer. She felt enthralled, and battling for mastery of herself, said, "Now for our gift. Everyone."

She summoned her coven to her like obedient dogs, and they walked around the hives, depositing a spoonful of sugar on each one as she introduced Lam and Como. The witches uttered a few words in hushed tones. Birdie rarely felt out of her depth, but she did now, and she knew she had woven a more powerful spell than she intended. The bees continued to watch them, their regard like a weight on her shoulders. Not unpleasant or unfriendly, just expectant, as if something else might happen. It was with relief when they reached the last hive, and after completing their final offering, they all stepped back. Unbidden, Morgana and Odette cleared away the table and extinguished candles, and she knew they were as unnerved by the experience as she was.

Birdie nodded once more at their audience. "Thank you for your time. The household otherwise continues as always, and we will update you with our news."

The murmurs of bee conversations started as they walked away, the witch-lights blinking out behind them, leaving the orchard in inky blackness as if twilight had long passed, and no one said a word until they were back at the house. It was only then that Birdie realised she had no idea where Hades was.

Four

Present Day

"What on Earth just happened?" Odette said, not speaking until they were all back in the kitchen where it felt safe, protected by the robust stone walls. Not that she had felt threatened by the bees, just unnerved. "That ritual should have taken half an hour, and we have been in the orchard for nearly two!"

"*Two?*" Lam exclaimed, checking the time on his phone and comparing it to the large clock on the wall. "That's totally freaky."

"Did we get lost on the way out?" Como asked, eyes wide as he stared at the three female witches. "It didn't seem as if we had."

Birdie clucked with derision as she headed to the fridge. "Of course we didn't get lost. I think time got away from us, that's all." She extracted a bottle of white wine, then selected a bottle of red from the wine rack, before heading to the cupboard for glasses.

Morgana caught Odette's eye, her expression guarded, and her long, grey streak seemed brighter than usual against her dark hair. "I think the bees cast their own spell, which is very peculiar. I quite liked it, although a little warning would have been nice. It's a good job I put the Beef Bourguignon on low or our dinner would be burnt!"

The kitchen smelled wonderful. Rich scents of beef and herbs such as thyme and rosemary wafted around the kitchen, and Odette realised how hungry she was. A slow-cooked casserole was one of Morgana's staples for when they were busy. Not that she cooked for them all the time. Very often, Odette would fix herself something simple in her own small kitchen in her suite of rooms. She always had breakfast there. Deciding to help, Odette placed deep, earthenware bowls on the table while Morgana organised the food.

"Peculiar is one word for it, Mother. I would call it outright weird!" Lam reached into the cupboard for Birdie, who was struggling to reach the shelf, taking out five wine glasses and placing them on the counter.

Birdie patted his cheek. "Thank you. But you must get used to weird around here. Besides, it's not weird, it's magic. Although, I will concede that tonight was altogether not what I expected."

Odette accepted a glass of the chilled white wine and sat at the kitchen table, leaning left cheek into left hand. "It was more intense than I expected. Weightier. It felt as if the entire orchard was listening. The birds, the mammals, and insects—not just the bees. The atmosphere felt a little like when I was there earlier this afternoon." She cast back to the crying she'd heard, and the powerful emotions she'd experienced that had reminded her of her own heartbreak. "Time was layering there. Generations. Or maybe just one from a long time ago." She'd been gazing into the pale, yellow liquid in her glass, but now she looked up and found everyone staring at her. "It would explain why we slipped an hour."

"No way!" Como exclaimed, face wrinkling with disbelief. "You can't just lose an hour! The ritual just took longer than we thought. By the time we'd said our hellos to all the hives, of course it took longer than expected. Then the walk through the orchard. I could feel magic, though. The air hummed with it." He grinned, making him look younger than his twenty years. Still so boyish at that age, and yet not, in that peculiar way of early adulthood. "I'm getting used to my air magic now. I'm more sensitive to its vibrations."

Lam sat next to Odette, kicking out his long legs beneath the table. Now that he was getting older, his face losing his boyish features, Odette could see Morgana in him. Her high cheekbones and studied gaze. "Of course you could feel magic, you idiot! Granny cast a spell."

"Birdie, thank you!" She glared at Lam, and he smirked. She hated being called Gran or Grandma. She forbade it, saying it made her feel old. "Actually," Birdie continued, "It was a charm, far lighter in design, and a ritual, of course, as I explained. But it was more powerful than I expected. I must examine dear Caleb's papers again."

"Caleb?" Como asked.

"Yes. The witch whose papers I found the charm in. Old, of course."

"How did you find it?" Odette asked, curious.

"A spell, cast to help me find anything on bees. As you can imagine, there were quite a few books on beekeeping—several rather lovely ones—but not that many spells, which surprised me. Anyway," she shrugged, "it's done now. I sensed no ill will. I dare say we shall see how things unfold in the coming days or weeks."

"That long?" Lam asked.

Morgana, busy cutting crusty bread at the counter explained, "Spells can take a while to work, so you can't always tell the outcome for weeks. Really, Lam, you should know that!"

"It's quite hard to keep up with things when I'm working on my degree! University doesn't really allow much alone time. That's why I need to be here. To immerse myself in it. I feel," he paused, nose wrinkling, "disconnected from my magic. I think that's why tonight was such a shock."

Odette frowned. "Even after you were so involved in the Yuletide spell?"

He nodded, his eyes hooded with disappointment. "It was fantastic for days. I could feel it, like it wanted to burst out of me. And then, well, life got in the way. I've tried, I really have!"

Como plonked in the chair next to him, as if his body was suddenly far too heavy to support. "Same here. That's why I'm here for Easter rather than at home. I know my mom is a brilliant witch, because she helped that shifter guy recently. But she just won't talk about it with me! In fact, I only found out about that by accident when she warned me that there were shifters in Salerno."

"What shifter guy?" Lam asked.

"Maverick something?"

Como looked to Odette for confirmation, and she nodded. "Maverick Hale, the Alpha of the Storm Moon Pack. We had issues with a demon-summoning witch, and he needed to find his brother." Not wanting to cause issues between him and his mother, she said, "Jemima was incredibly helpful, but I guess she has her reasons for keeping her magic to herself." *Like pure and simple resentment.* Both young men looked disappointed by their lack of progress, and they needed to cheer them up. "But look, both of you—you are always witches, never forget that. Your magic is just a bit rusty right now. We'll work hard on that over the next couple of weeks. As well as making sure you revise, too." She looked over at Birdie and Morgana, who were dishing up their meal. "Perhaps we should set some daily intentions, or easy little habits. Nothing too onerous. Things you can continue over the next few months before you're back in the summer."

"Exactly," Birdie said, carrying the plate of fresh, crusty bread to the table and a bowl of steaming casserole. "I'm looking forward to it. It's always good to refresh the basics. I'm very glad you weren't here for the demon, though. It would have terrified you."

"It terrified *us*," Morgana pointed out, placing more bowls on the table.

Lam had been about to tuck in, but now he looked at the three women. "You met a demon?"

"I wouldn't say *met*," Odette said, stifling a giggle. "It's not like we had formal introductions. However, we fought one and sent it back to its own plane. The shifters and our other friends were very helpful. We couldn't have done it without them, actually. The drive still has our trap scored into it."

Como nodded. "I saw that! Wow. You three are unexpected."

"Don't get too excited," Birdie said, as she and Morgana finally joined them. "Life here is generally quiet."

"But we can meet the shifters?" Lam asked, cocking an eyebrow. "They sound great."

Odette smiled. "Your mother is their healer. Yes, let's head there sometime this week for drinks."

Lam, always a little standoffish with his mother, looked at her with renewed interest, and Odette smirked. It was high time Lam learned a lot more about his mother's abilities, and she was very happy to help.

"If we can just return to the bees for one moment," Birdie said, topping up her wine glass, "I'll head there tomorrow, just to make sure everything's okay. For some reason, Hades is being elusive, so maybe he's hanging out with them. He's not telling me why, though." A frown marred her features.

"But he can be elusive, right?" Odette asked.

"Yes, of course." She wafted her hand airily. "It will be fine."

Odette, however, was not convinced, and neither was Morgana by the look of it. Both, however, knew better than to pursue it—for now, at least.

"Great. So that's it for tonight?" Como asked. "No more rituals?"

"Not for me," Odette said. "It's the new moon, so I may do something simple in my own room, but that's all."

"I'm heading to the New Moon Gate," Morgana confessed, "but that will be private, if that's okay?"

"Of course, dear," Birdie said, not prying. She beamed at Lam and Como, her mischievous expression taking years off her. "In which case, I shall join the boys in their rooms and instruct them on new moon spells and intentions." She beamed at them. "No reason to delay our lessons. We'll have candles and tarot cards, and a blazing fire. It will be wonderful."

If the boys had hoped for a lazy night watching TV, they hid it well. That suited Odette perfectly. Everyone was busy, which allowed her some space. Odette hadn't been completely honest. Her simple ritual was less to do with the new moon and more to do with her strange experience that afternoon. With luck, the new moon would add some clarity, and for that she needed silence. If the New Moon Gate had been free she would have gone there, but she had another destination in mind that should work just as well.

As soon as Odette finished her meal, she headed for the attic that covered most of the original house. It was a cavernous space, and she loved it. For her, it was the heart of the house. The place where their ancestors resided. Paintings hung on the roughly finished walls, a mix of old and new, mainly painted in oils, but some modern ones were painted in acrylics, and there were also pencil and charcoal sketches. Huge wardrobes, drawers, and wooden chests contained old clothes, again from a mix of time periods. It was rare for anything to be thrown away in Moonfell. Well, anything of significance; otherwise, they would drown in ephemera.

Odette made her way through the twisting space, past broad support beams and stone walls, carrying her candles and incense, and eschewing the chairs scattered throughout the space before sitting on an old wool rug on the floorboards in the centre of the attic. She turned the electric lights off with a whispered word of command, lit her white candles, and let the flickering light dance across her closed lids. Silence settled around her. Whatever else may be happening in the house, she could hear none of it.

She sensed the ancestors gathering, their spirits aflutter like moth wings.

Air stirred against her cheeks, and she wasn't sure if it was them or the wind finding gaps to wriggle through. She didn't often come here at night, and wondered if the place always felt like this. Goose bumps rose along the nape of her neck, but taking deep, calming breaths, she centred herself, becoming one with the air.

Images flooded her mind. Picnics, moon gates, parties, whispered conversations, midnight spells. They raced in and out so quickly like a turbulent tide that she could barely grasp them, but she stuck with it, unable to even sense her limbs now. She focussed on the feeling she'd had that afternoon. The frustration encompassed within the soporific heat and murmuring of bees, as the golden light played upon her eyelids. Suddenly, she was there again, and the feeling this time was stronger.

The orchard spread before her, the pale, silvery wood of the hives knee-deep in grass. Bee song was wild and joyous, and dust motes danced on the air. A section of grass was squashed, and in the centre of it was a pulsing heap of clothes emitting deep sobs. After what seemed like endless moments, the heap arranged itself into the form of a young woman. Her midnight black hair tumbled about her face, and slender, white hands pushed it back to reveal a heart shaped face with hazel eyes, currently red from weeping, and a distinctive widow's peak. She looked desperate, and very young.

The shock of recognition was enough to send Odette back to her body, and with a thump she felt the rough carpet beneath her and the flutter of wind on her face. She opened her eyes in shock. The candles were guttering, wax spilling down their sides, as shapes fled to the darkness.

Ignoring them, Odette struggled to her feet on partially numb limbs and found the painting she was looking for. Eliza Wildblood was the crying woman in the orchard.

But why was she seeing her?

Lam's head was spinning by the time Birdie left his and Como's living room on the top floor of their tower. She had talked for hours about moon phases and spells, waxing and waning energies, and then digressed to the moon gates, their positions in the garden, and their symbolism. They hadn't had a chance to talk about tarot cards, although the pack sat tantalisingly ready on the coffee table.

He waited until he heard Birdie's footsteps fade as she walked down the stairs, and then released his pent-up frustration. "Bloody hell! I don't know whether I'm coming or going!" He was seated on the Persian rug in front of the fire, and he flopped onto his back and stared at the moulding on the ceiling. "And I'm shattered!"

Como laughed. "This is what we came here for, you fruit loop. I thought it was brilliant. Birdie knows so much. Although, of course, I've already forgotten most of it."

Lam lifted his head to stare at him. "You took notes!"

"You'll thank me later. And of course there are those." He pointed at the stack of books on the coffee table.

Como was also sitting on the floor, leaning against the tan leather chesterfield sofa. *That was something, at least.* They didn't have to live with the jewel-bright colours spread throughout the house. This was a man's room. Dark blue and charcoal grey with leather accents and richly coloured Persian rugs. Although, now that he thought about it, how did they get that sofa up the narrow tower stairs? He had enough to think about already. That conundrum could wait.

Lam rolled onto his side and propped up on one elbow. "I'm supposed to be revising."

"Just a bit of light bedtime reading, then." Como reached for his wine glass. "This is what you wanted. We are witches, and our families are steeped in witchcraft. Look at this house. Our rooms!" He flung his arms wide and grinned. "It's fucking amazing! We need to know how to use our magic properly. I don't want to dabble. I want to use it as well as Birdie and the others. So here we are, up in a tower in crazy old Moonfell, learning our craft. Just to put it into context, Lam, you twit, we've just had private tuition from the High Priestess herself. You need to forget she's Granny." Como lowered his voice and leaned closer to Lam. "The Goddess gifted her twenty years of her life back. That's insane! Just take a moment to feel this place. To take stock. That's part of being a witch, you know. *Reflection*. We are in our very own Hogwarts!"

Lam sat up as the enormity of it sank in. He took so much for granted. Had resented his mother for years, although that was stupid. He had chosen to live with his father. She hadn't rejected him. If anything, years ago, he sensed the enormity of his magical inheritance even then and shied away from it. It was only over the last twelve months that he felt like he'd been missing out. It was like an itch beneath his skin that longed to be scratched, but he could never find the right place.

He studied the room, not having had a good chance to really inspect it. It was a huge, square space with a vaulted and ribbed ceiling. The walls were mostly plastered and painted, but sections had been left exposed, highlighting the huge blocks of solid stone that emphasised the solidity of the massive building. The mouldings were carved into leaves and flowers, and every now and again a mischievous face peered out from behind the leaves. A small but modern kitchen took up one corner, and a table and chairs were positioned under one of the enormous Gothic windows. A couple of bookcases laden with all manner of reading material were positioned between the windows, along with a TV and music system. Beyond the windows lay Moonfell's mysterious garden. In the lamplight and candlelight, it was magical. Not that he could ignore Moonfell's magic. It was a constant, if subtle, presence.

In the silence that had fallen, he felt the weight of it. The years, the knowledge, the experiences. And here he was on the top floor of a Gothic tower. He suddenly couldn't wait to explore everything. More than that, he couldn't wait to make his bedroom his own. A place to sink into his magic, including in this room, of course, with Como.

He gave Como a rueful grin. "Hogwarts! I hadn't even considered that." He exhaled heavily and reached for his glass of wine. "You're right. I'm just tired, especially after the whole bee thing. It was weird. Did you see the light?"

"After the charm? Yes. I don't know where it came from."

"The bees themselves, I'm sure of it. It drifted from the hives."

"I thought it came from the trees, actually. Like falling pollen, but then I thought I'd imagined it. The air felt turbulent."

"There wasn't a breath of wind."

"I know." Como grimaced. "That's what I don't understand. It's like I said earlier; I'm more attuned to it, but don't really interpret it well."

"At least you experienced *something*. I'm still struggling to master whatever magic I have."

"You know what you have. Fire, and earth too, I suspect. You're going to sculpt."

"Which reminds me that I need to organise my workspace in the stables tomorrow." His mother had promised him space in the stables for his sculpting. It had been too cold to set it up in the middle of winter, and they were short on time then, but now he could clean it out. Suddenly, the thought of having both the space and the time to indulge his passions lifted his spirits. He rose to his feet. "I'm heading to my room. I need to unpack and sleep. I've got loads to do tomorrow."

Como nodded, dark eyes shadowed in the firelight. "Fair enough. I'm staying up to enjoy all of this."

However, when Lam arrived in his room, the last thing he wanted to do was sleep. The room was as opulent as the living room above him, and as imposing. It felt decadent to have such a huge bed all to himself, and he was beyond relieved to see it wasn't a four poster, but a clean, modern design. The room was again decorated in dark blue, but this time with accents of burnt orange, the colours complimenting his fire nature. He'd never really considered furnishings before, or decorating, but it was something he couldn't ignore here. The whole house was an assault on the senses. It demanded your attention. Your opinions. No doubt once he'd lived here long enough, he'd cease noticing it so much.

Once he'd unpacked his clothes, showered, and cleaned his teeth in his equally Gothic bathroom complete with a large shower and claw-footed bathtub, he sat in the middle of the bed, contemplating his coming days, and trying to ignore the fact that he would have to speak to his mother more often. She kept a respectful, if loving, distance from him, and that was his fault. He'd cultivated a standoffish air, but he couldn't afford to do that any longer. For a start, she didn't deserve it, and secondly, he really wanted to master his magic. *But why hadn't she joined them tonight?* He had expected she would, but instead she had cast spells at the New Moon Gate. He wasn't sure if he was relieved or not.

He brushed it off. He had essays to complete and final exams to revise for. He was studying for a Bachelor of Arts in Literature, and he had no idea what he wanted to do with it. However, his secondary subject was art, and as he'd said at Christmas, he was finding that far more interesting than his main subject. It had crept up on him, much like his magic had, over the previous year. He'd started carving small pieces of wood, but metals were calling to him now. First, he needed to finish his degree before he could truly explore it.

He could set his laptop up on the table under the east windows. The house would sweep him up in things, but perhaps if he spent the morning studying, he could indulge in magic and sculpt in the afternoon. Then he could study again at night, as he usually did—when he wasn't in the pub. Although, there was Storm Moon to consider. That was one thing he had definitely missed out on with his father. He may be a very cool musician, but he wasn't the healer for the pack of shifters that lived virtually on their doorstep. Plus, his mother, Odette, and Birdie had banished a demon. *A demon.*

The creeping feeling that he was on the wrong path hit him with unexpected force now. He had been for years, and he'd pushed the niggling sensation aside, but not anymore.

Resolute, and with Birdie's voice in his head talking about candles and moon magic, he jumped off the bed and voiced his intentions aloud. "I will master my magic, especially *fire* magic. I will make amazing sculptures, and I will be in tune with this house." As he announced each intention, he used his magic to light the candles placed around the room. This was the new moon, a time when intentions would grow and take root. "I will learn the mysteries of this house, and I will no longer be a stranger to its magic. I will also make things right with my mother. And..." He paused, thinking there must be something he was missing. By now, candlelight flickered in corners and reflected in mirrors, and he sensed the house was listening. He better make this good. "And I will master another type of magic. I don't know what yet, but I can do more, and I will learn more! So, house," he extended his hand with a flourish, "I am here to learn, so if there's something you need, I'm your man!"

The candle flames blazed a foot in the air, and he muttered, "Bloody hell!"

That was a sign, right? The house heard him. He waited, feeling foolish, as if the house might applaud him, too. *Idiot.* Nevertheless, as the flames settled back to normal, he knew it all felt right. Leaving the candles safely burning in their glass jars, he turned the lamps out, clambered into bed, and fell asleep in seconds.

Five

July, 1664

Ansel, as much as he tried to hide it, was very nervous when they arrived on Bridges Street where the Playhouse was situated.

It was Friday evening in the heart of London, and it was teeming with the wealthy, merchants, and the very poor. It was a seething mass of humanity. It also didn't help that he was hot and bothered, and felt as trussed up as a pig on a spit. He had his finest clothes on, but at least he didn't have to wear a ridiculous, enormous wig. That was reserved for rich men. Besides, he had excellent hair, unlike some of the men around him. The unfortunate truth was that wigs hid a multitude of problems, especially syphilis sores. Ansel did not have to worry about that.

The carriage was a short walk away, driven by their gardener, Jem, who doubled as their groom, and he would meet them later to take them home again. Ansel adjusted his long coat and breeches, self-conscious of the fact that a glamour spell made their clothes look far better than they really were, and in line with the latest fashions. He didn't particularly care in general, but if they were to make the right impression, they had to blend in. Their normal disregard for convention wouldn't do. His sister was equally well dressed, although not as provocatively as some. There was an eye-opening display of cleavage on show, revealing the creamy skin of the ladies with their painted faces.

He took a deep breath to steady himself, and then wished he hadn't. The stench of the London streets was powerful. Effluent, horse dung, and sweat. A far cry from the clear, fresh air of Moonfell. But the place had life! He had never been this far into the centre of London, and he didn't know where to look first.

"Stop looking so nervous," Eliza reprimanded him. "We look the part. We are the part, in fact. Our family loves the theatre. Who here will know us, or care? Anyone can come to the theatre!"

"A few here may know our mother. Admittedly, it would have been a while ago, but it's possible."

"We won't mention her at all, yet. And," she added, as if either of them could forget, "the bees will help us."

They had performed the binding ritual a few nights earlier on the new moon, and it was an unnerving experience, even for Ansel, whose strongest magical ability was that he could understand the emotions of animals. The bees' magic was unearthly, and it had crept under his skin, enhancing his already well-developed power that had manifested when he was eleven. Back then, it had happened so gradually that he didn't even notice it. It was as if his body was trying to shield him, allowing him to learn how to manage it. He innately knew when to tune in and when to let it become background noise, just like the chatter of people around him. In the past few days, however, he had found it hard to control.

"Are you okay?" Eliza asked him. She stared deep into his eyes, knowing the toll the binding had taken.

"I'm okay. Let's get in there. We need tickets."

Eliza hooked her arm through his, and he led them through the crowded entrance and into the foyer, and after fighting his way through to the front, bought seats for the second tier.

"Couldn't we get closer?" Eliza asked.

"No. Besides, these will give us a good view of who's here." He nodded towards a man with an enormous wig and heavily laced shirt. "Like Lord Villiers, for example."

"The king's friend? How do you know it's him?" Eliza turned slowly, trying not to be obvious.

"I heard his name mentioned. He's dressed very grandly."

"Does that mean the king will be here?"

Ansel smirked. "Not planning on an introduction tonight, are you?"

"Of course not! But we do need to find Nell later."

The King's Playhouse had three levels, and as they climbed the stairs, Ansel was aware of the stares that his very pretty sister was getting—and the men weren't being subtle about it. If he was honest, he was very distracted by the women there too, and was receiving his own fair share of attention. However, they were there for Nell. He just hoped they could find her after the performance.

Cinta had her own ideas for spells to help the family make money, and they had nothing to do with finding Nell Gwyn, or binding themselves to bees.

As she had grown older, she had explored her magic and found she was skilled with elemental magic, water in particular, but she was also talented with elemental air. She was determined to develop them both, wanting to be as powerful as her older sister, the designated guardian of Moonfell.

Eliza was an earth witch, but had a particular affinity with knowing what people needed, too. She was also a healer, and skilled with herbs. Ansell, of course, had his abilities with mammals, insects, and birds, but was also skilled in the kitchen—which was fortunate, because neither Cinta nor her sister had many skills there. However, Cinta was keenly aware that she needed to help them. They tried to shield her from their money issues, but their lack of funds was obvious, and there was no doubt that they couldn't continue as they had been at Moonfell.

Cinta had long been fascinated by the idea of a familiar. No one in Moonfell had one, unless you counted the half a dozen cats on the grounds that killed the rats and mice, and the odd bird, too. She didn't. They gave her dead rodents, not advice. Familiars were animal spirits who could guide witches through the spirit realm or help with magic...or so she believed. Unfortunately, familiars had also been an obsession with the witch hunters, having been equated with the devil. Now, however, with the Puritans gone and Charles II on the throne, all that horror was behind them. *Almost.* Consequently, Cinta had decided she wanted a familiar. Someone who would guide her and her family, especially in the tricky situation they were now in. It sounded comforting.

There was a summerhouse by the large pond that was heaped with cushions and rugs, and it was her favourite spot on the grounds. Most afternoons she would head there to practice magic, and recently try to connect to an animal spirit. So far, she had failed.

She was determined not to fail again.

The summerhouse was cool in the late evening, and the sky flamed with rose gold as the sun set, leaving the summerhouse in shadow. Cinta faced east, the sky inky black over the garden, a few early stars already pricking the night sky. After cleansing the space with the smoke from a bundle of sage and placing the lantern behind her, she sat with crossed legs on a floor cushion, and knowing she would feel the cold, even on a hot night, pulled a shawl around her shoulders.

Unlike the other times she had tried, she had prepared a potion that had been recommended in her mother's grimoire. Something that would allow her mind to travel. Mugwort and valerian. She swallowed the bitter brew, and quickly settled her mind, her practice over the previous days paying off. However, no visions came to her, and no spirits manifested.

Feeling reckless, she pulled another spell out of her pocket. Something far older, written in a crabbed hand that she had found in another grimoire after spending hours searching for inspiration, eyes aching with need. It promised to produce a creature of the elements, "*Made of the very Air, Fire, Water, or Earth that underpin all magick.*" Not entirely sure what that meant, but knowing it promised a spirit that would guide and advise, she ignored the warning to only use with great care and assembled her ingredients. A candle for Fire, salt for Earth, the smoking sage bundle for Air, and Water from the pond.

"Fine!" she muttered into the increasing darkness. "I will find a familiar, despite your efforts at thwarting me!"

She felt guilty as she uttered the words of the spell, because she hadn't said anything to Eliza or Ansel of her plans. Not because she thought they would disapprove, but because she wanted to surprise them. However, a slight niggle in the pit of her stomach warned that she might be out of her depth here. *Moonfell will protect me.* Throwing caution to the wind she cast the spell, her voice growing in strength with every iteration.

Power gathered around her, crackling with energy, and forking like tiny lightning bolts. *This was actually working.* Wind swirled around her, and she stepped out of the summerhouse to stand on the lawn, feet planted firmly, arms raised. "Come to me now! Bring me your wisdom. Your power. Your strength."

Something coalesced in the darkness. Something earthy, rooted in ancient knowledge, and twisted like roots dragged from the earth. The scent of leaf mould, dankness, and mystery.

In the centre of it was the flash of amber eyes.

The play was bawdy and funny, and Eliza enjoyed it greatly.

Nell, even though she only had a small part, was brilliant, drawing the eye like bees to pollen. She looked nothing like the young Nell she remembered, who had been dirty and wore scruffy clothes, although with her impish grin, even then she had beauty and fire. Eliza half suspected she had a little bit of witch in her, too. That night, dressed in an assortment of costumes as she paraded across the stage, she looked magnificent. It was a funny play, and the audience roared with laughter.

Eliza tried to find the familiar faces of clients who had visited Moonfell for help, but it was pointless. Their association with the rich had ended years before, and even if a few had continued to see her mother, she would have been too young to remember. The theatre boxes were filled with the very rich, but there was no sign of the king that night.

When the play ended, they headed to the stage door, where Eliza rapped on it, amplifying it with a little magic. A large man in rough work clothes answered, eyes raking over them, and lingering a little too long on her modest cleavage. Giving him a beaming smile, she said, "We're old friends of Nell. Can you let us in?"

He laughed, revealing stained and broken teeth. "Everyone's friends with Nell."

Suspecting she'd have to resort to glamour, it rolled off her, and still smiling, she said, "You'd love to let us in. Me and my brother."

A glazed look fogged his eyes, and he stepped back. "Follow the corridor around the back. The dressing rooms are at the end. You can't miss 'em."

The backstage area was full of people bustling up and down a warren of narrow passages and stairways, and manoeuvring around props and clothes. The lead actress's room was hard to miss. People already gathered around it, and laughter filled the corridors. The night had been a success, so everyone was celebrating. A few gentlemen were here already. Old and young men in their huge wigs and embroidered frock coats, leather boots polished until they gleamed, all fawning around the lead actress's dressing room, and several more speaking to the other women in the production. These were the men they wanted to meet. Or their wives. Although, she couldn't deny that there was a distinct air of seediness about the whole place. Eliza wasn't naïve. She'd heard the rumours about actresses. Many were prostitutes, and from the way some of them were speaking to the hovering men, there would be more than one assignation later that evening.

She focussed on finding Nell. She wouldn't have her own room, and after asking a few people, they spotted her laughing with the other actors in a cramped communal dressing room as they took off their makeup.

"They're not shy, are they?" Ansel noted, eyes sweeping over some of the scantily clad women as they removed their costumes.

"Don't get any ideas," she warned him.

"I can't help it. Look at all that flesh!" The Orange Girls were backstage, too and they giggled at Ansel, one winking as she brushed by him.

Eliza grabbed him by the elbow and propelled him into the room. "Forget them. Nell! How are you?"

Nell had been mid-conversation with a woman her own age, but she stopped and turned, frowning with confusion. She was pretty, with a thick mane of chestnut hair and pale skin. Her eyes flashed with wit and intelligence, and it was obvious she would make something of herself. Eliza could see it as clear as day. Nell smiled. "I remember you. Eliza, weren't it? You helped my mother." Her accent had changed, too; not as coarse as it had been.

"Well, my mother did most of it, but yes, I helped."

"You were good with her, I remember. It weren't the easiest place to be."

The girl next to her interrupted. " 'Elped with what?"

"Me Ma was sick, and Eliza here helped her get better, with herbs and things."

Eliza's eyes flashed a warning not to say too much. They had only ever presented themselves as cunning folk, but she didn't want rumours, even now. "Just simple poultices and old herbal remedies."

"Oh. You a 'ealer, then?" the girl asked.

"Yes, we both are. Were. My mother died recently." She gestured to Ansel, who was taking very little notice of the conversation, flirting with the other actresses instead. "My brother, too."

Nell's eyes softened. "Sorry to hear that. So, what are you here for? Not me, surely?"

"Yes, we are, actually. Can we speak outside?"

She rose to her feet. "We'll find a quiet corner somewhere."

Eliza dragged Ansel with her, and in a few minutes they were in the corner of a props room, with no one else around. "Thanks, Nell. I know we haven't seen you in years, but, well, we think you can help us."

Nell folded her arms, pushing her breasts high in her cotton undergarments. "If I can, I will."

"There are a lot of wealthy men and women here, and if possible, we'd like a few introductions. Years ago we treated lots of influential people...had connections. We've lost them all." She hesitated. "We had to be careful. Simple treatments could be twisted into something else."

Nell's jaw tightened. "Puritans and Witch Hunters. Miserable knaves. They are not welcome here. They made life hard for a lot of people—us included." She smirked. "But there's always need of a bawdy house, even for the Puritans, despite what they say otherwise."

Ansel laughed. "Men's needs never change."

"Don't I know it." Her eyes lingered on Ansel's handsome face.

Eliza cleared her throat, summoning Nell's attention. "I gather that you know several influential people now."

"The rich lords and ladies? I know a few. Villiers is here most evenings. He's taken quite a shine to me. He's a bit of a rogue, too. Him and the king are always falling out."

"He's here tonight," Ansel confirmed. "We saw him out the front."

"You want an introduction to him?"

Eliza's heart pounded. "You wouldn't mind? We're not planning on touting for work straight away, of course. We just need to get to know people who may need the type of help we can offer."

She left it deliberately vague, but Nell leaned closer. "There was always something a little extra about what you did. I saw it. Could feel it." She lowered her voice. "I have no problem with magic. It's a gift, and it will be my pleasure to help. I won't forget your kindness to my mother, or my sister." She rolled her eyes. "Who is still causing a lot of trouble. Enough of 'er, though." She studied their clothes. "You look good. Rather than me introducing you here, come to The Red Dragon. It's a public house round the corner where we all gather after a performance, especially on a weekend. There'll be a lot of drinking, and lots of fun. There'll be more than Villiers there, too. The only thing is, many of them use doctors, not healers. I'm not sure you'll get much interest."

"Don't introduce us like that," Eliza said quickly. "Say we're just friends who love the theatre. That's a start."

"Fair enough. What do you say? The Red Dragon, then?"

Ansel answered for both of them. "Sounds excellent."

Six

Present Day

"Hades, where are you?" Birdie stood in the dappled shade of the orchard, hands on her hips. "Honestly, this isn't funny. I'm worried!"

The orchard was beautiful in the early morning sunshine, although it was brisk. Dew gathered on the long grass and settled on the bluebells and lingering daffodils, and the gnarled grey trunks of the fruit trees were like ghosts unfurling skirts of blossoms. However, other than a passing appreciation of it, her sight was cast inward, trying to see through Hades's eyes.

Usually, she could slip into his mind easily once he heard her call. *Was heard the right word? Felt, perhaps?* Anyway, normally she need only reach for him, and he was there. He was unnervingly absent now, as if their connection was broken.

During the bee ritual, he had watched with the bees rather than being with her. He hadn't expressed disapproval at their ritual, or raised any concerns, so his actions were curious. Maybe as an animal—of sorts—he felt being with the bees was his place. The bees, after all, had lived in the grounds for centuries. Perhaps Hades had too, in one form or another. She had long suspected that his present incarnation as a Savannah cat was one of many. Neither had he followed her home. Again, nothing unusual there, but now she thought about it, she was sure he might have even left before the ritual was complete. *Had he been there at the end?* The event had been so unlike what she'd expected, she had been a little flustered, and that was quite embarrassing. She was no ingenue. She was the High Priestess.

Birdie took a deep breath in and out, kicked off her wellington boots to wriggle her feet in the earth, and endeavoured to ground herself. Being Moonfell's guardian came with a few extra abilities, such as an awareness of the house and gardens. Most of the time, it was in a state of wild, joyous balance, magic coursing through the grounds like a vigorous blood supply through a body. It was now so natural to her that she didn't even notice it. It meant that if she couldn't find her granddaughters, if she focussed, she could detect their magic wherever they were in the grounds. She didn't often use it, feeling it was intrusive, but it might help her find Hades.

Unfortunately, she had to conclude after several minutes of searching that he wasn't there. However, there was a shift in the house's energy. The bee ritual must have stirred things up, and maybe Hades felt it more than any of them.

Rather than panic, Birdie headed back to the garden. She was in no mood to see the bees right now. She needed to fortify herself for their next encounter. However, she had barely reached the outskirts of the orchard when Odette met her on the path, looking as if she hadn't bothered to brush her hair. It was a wild mass of untamed curls, and wearing her old boots, jumper, and jeans, she looked half feral. No wonder she'd fallen in love with a wolf-shifter.

"Good grief, Odette! You're never up this early. Are you okay?"

Odette didn't bother with a greeting. "I know who I heard in the orchard yesterday. It was Eliza Wildblood."

"Eliza?" The name sounded familiar, and she blamed her worry for Hades that it took a while to click. "Oh! The witch who helped Charles II?"

"Yes, the very same."

"How do you know?"

"I went to the attic last night, trying to trigger the vision again. It worked. I saw her face this time, and she was young. Much younger than she looks in the portrait."

Birdie's heart raced with excitement. "You're sure it was her?"

"She's so distinctive! Her hair was dark, and she has that widow's peak. Oh my, Birdie. She was so pretty. Like Vivien Leigh in *Gone with the Wind*! And she was almost as mad as Scarlet was when she yelled at Tara."

"Not at Tara! She loved Tara, but I know what you mean." *Gone with the Wind* was one of Birdie's favourite films, even though she found the petulant Scarlet a wilful madam. "Do you know what had upset her?"

"No. But I *felt* it. I saw her desperation." Odette looked quite desperate herself. "I was so shocked when I recognised her that I lost it again. I'm really cross with myself!"

"Don't be. At least we have a name now." Birdie slipped her arm through Odette's as she steered her back to the house. "I wonder why you're seeing her, though. You know, I feel a shift in Moonfell's energy. That bee ritual has mixed things up." She tutted, annoyed with herself. "I don't know why I feel compelled to do these things sometimes."

"I thought it was a lovely ritual." Odette squeezed her arm to reassure her. "But there's no denying that it all felt quite odd. It was so intense last night. Do you think you've set something in motion?"

"Yes. Does that sound stupid?"

"Yes and no. I saw Eliza before the ritual, so something else must have set that off. It could be completely unrelated. Maybe it was just the heat of the afternoon. It was unseasonably warm for March, and it seemed to be late summer in the vision." She laughed it off. "I'm just weird sometimes."

"Wonderfully weird, and I wouldn't have it any other way. Time will tell, I guess."

"But," Odette prompted her, "you said you felt a shift in energy. What kind of shift?"

"That's just the thing. I don't know exactly. It's just different. Plus, I still can't find Hades."

Odette stopped walking and faced Birdie. "He's gone?"

"Yes. I can't feel him at all." All her fears came rushing back. "That hasn't happened for years."

"It has happened, then?"

Birdie laughed. "A long time ago. He said he needed to be elsewhere for a while. He didn't explain, and I didn't ask. He was back within a few weeks."

Odette's lips twisted in a half smile. "Well, that's odd. Did he need a holiday?"

"I didn't ask. We respect each other's privacy. If he'd wanted to tell me, he would have."

"But he did tell you that he was leaving. Odd that he hasn't now then."

Birdie pushed down her rising anxiety. "I'm trying to remain rational. It's Hades! He's an ageless familiar who can certainly look after himself. It's fine."

"Of course it is. Tea is what we need right now, and breakfast. I'm all out of sorts being up this early. Let's see what Morgana has in the kitchen."

"Good grief," Morgana said to Lamorak when he entered the glasshouse at just after eight on Monday morning, "I didn't expect to see you for hours!"

He looked bright-eyed and alert, and she reasoned that Birdie must have fired his enthusiasm the previous evening, while she had been casting her spell at the New Moon Gate. Or maybe that was too negative. He *had* wanted to come to Moonfell of his own volition.

"Why not? I have things to do!" He grinned, and she had a sudden urge to ruffle his hair as if he was a child again. "And not enough time to do it!"

"Like what?" She reached for her secateurs and headed down the gravel path, Lam following her.

"Organising my studio."

"Ah! We've cleared out the section in the stables we agreed on at Yule, but thought you'd want to organise it yourself. A few of the tools you requested have arrived and are still in boxes."

"What did you do with the broken crap in there?"

"It went on the bonfire we used to banish the demon, so it served a purpose." She reached the raised bed filled with tender herbs and started to take some cuttings.

"Was it really hard? To banish the demon, I mean?"

"Very. I won't bore you with the details, but the damn thing was a stubborn bastard." She finished snipping the lemon balm, placed the cuttings in the trug, and finally looked at him. He regarded her silently, lips pressed in a thin line. "It was touch and go for a while, so yes, it was very hard."

He expelled his breath in a huff. "I can't even imagine it."

"Trust me, you don't want to. Summoning, controlling, and banishing demons is not in our regular tool kit. We had to do lots of reading on the subject. It was nightmarish."

He leaned against the next raised bed, arms folded across his chest. "I didn't know you could do things like that, or even got involved with that kind of magic. And the whole Fallen Angel thing! I don't know whether I'm impressed or horrified. Actually, I'm both! You could have died!"

"Yes, we could have. A shifter almost did. I nursed him here for days." Lam was clearly trying to make sense of the magic they used as he came to terms with his own. "Please don't think that kind of thing is normal. Well, not for us, anyway. In general, we make herbal teas, potions, candles, and balms. I help women with their pregnancies, Odette paints, and Birdie...well, she looks after this place—with our help, of course. It's not all action. Not of our doing, anyway." She turned away to continue collecting cuttings. "But when friends need help, you can't turn them away."

"If we'd have been here, me and Como, would we have helped?"

Good question. His expression was earnest, eager even, but fear lay under it. "Would you have wanted to?"

He swallowed and then nodded, eyes not leaving hers. "Yes, of course, although I'd have probably crapped myself. Does that make me mad?"

She laughed. "No. I'm glad to see that you're not being too gung-ho about it. We'd have welcomed your help, but you'd have been under strict instructions, and will be if anything else like that happens. Understood?"

"Completely."

Some young witches tended to think they were invincible, so it was a relief to see that Lam wasn't behaving like that. She hoped Como would be the same. "It's good to have you here. I'm sure it will be a fun couple of weeks as you get to grips with things. No demons either, hopefully." She winked at him. "There won't be."

"What are you doing now?" He nodded to her cuttings.

"I have a few tisanes to prepare, and fresh herbs are so much better. Especially if you pick them early."

"I thought everything in here was poisonous," he said, looking around suspiciously as if a plant would attack him.

"Not everything! Some things. It's a greenhouse, like any other. Things either over-winter here or stay in here all year round. This is lemon balm. Quite harmless! That is basil." She crushed a leaf and held it out to him. "It smells delicious. In a few months, there'll be lots of it outside. We could sow some more seeds today."

"Who's it for?"

"Clients mostly, but for us too, of course. Herbs make great spell ingredients." She pointed to the long bench against the wall that separated the glasshouse from the kitchen. "Grab some secateurs and come and help me."

For the next few minutes, Lam did nothing except ask lots of questions, trying to understand the nature of their days. "Do you call yourself a witch with your clients?"

"With some, who are familiar with the paranormal world. With others, I just present myself as a herbalist." She smiled. "Witchcraft is not seen how it once was. Lots of people are very open about it. Our degree of power is quite unusual, though. I'd rather not mention it to those who don't understand. Although, some suspect, I think," she added as an afterthought. Her clients were always respectful, but a few looked as if they would like to ask lots of questions but didn't. She treated all sorts of people, not just women with fertility issues.

She helped with chronic injuries, depression, and unbalanced energy fields. Fertility issues were her specialty though, which she loved because she felt it connected her to Sibilla, the first Moonfell witch.

Lam, however, was looking increasingly distracted. "Can you hear that? I've been hearing it on and off since I woke up."

"Hear what?" Morgana had the radio on, but had turned it down when Lamorak had arrived. "The radio?"

"No. Something else. A sort of chatter." He stood looking towards the partially open door that led into the kitchen garden. "No, actually a buzzing sound."

"Have you been listening to music loudly? You might have tinnitus."

"No!" He rolled his eyes. "Well, not that loudly, anyway." He shook his head, and smacked his hand against his head. "It's so annoying."

"It might settle down, but if not, a healing spell will help, I'm sure. Have you had breakfast?"

Lam was still distracted, continuing to grimace and shake his head. "A black coffee was it."

"That must be it. You need breakfast. Follow me, and bring the herbs!" Morgana was looking forward to cooking for her son again. She had mounds of bacon and eggs, cereal, fruits, yoghurt, and bread available. She was determined that this visit would be a success. "Where's Como?"

"Still snoring like a pig when I passed his room."

"Ah. I'll cook extra, just in case."

Morgana mentally started to plan her day as they entered the kitchen. *Cook breakfast, make tisanes, prepare for the week's clients, and if she had time, follow up on her new moon ritual, which had turned out to be more intense than she had expected.* Her spell had felt portentous, but that sounded ridiculous. She did moon spells all the time. Then she needed to cook for everyone this evening.

"Lam, will you be eating with us tonight?" she asked as they entered the kitchen. "I'm cooking a beef curry."

"If the alternative is beans on toast in our kitchen, yes. And then Storm Moon? Please!"

"I suppose we could. Monday is always a bit quieter in there, so it should work out fine."

Besides, she was very curious to see what Como and Lam made of the shifters. *With luck*, she thought a little selfishly, *it would make her far more interesting than her ex-husband.*

Como woke with a start and sat up abruptly, sleep still fogging his thoughts, wondering what had woken him, and where the hell he was.

He could have sworn he'd heard a thump. Light leaked around the closed curtains, sending a streak of sunshine across the rugs and polished floorboards, but the rest of the room was gloomy, the heavy cotton curtains blocking out most of the light.

Of course. He was at Moonfell.

He flopped back on the bed and stared at the ceiling, the thumping noise still resonant in his head. *Maybe it had been a dream.* He'd had such strange ones all night long, but the details of them escaped him now. He had a vague recollection of being chased through dense foliage and twisting paths, but he wasn't sure where. *Moonfell perhaps?*

A guilty feeling flooded through him as if he'd done something he shouldn't, but the only thing he'd done the night before was prowl around the tower, and then explore Moonfell's second floor, unable to sleep after Birdie had left and Lam had gone to bed. He'd felt energised by talk of magic and moon spells, and he couldn't forget the weird bee ritual. The palpable sense of magic had been like a caress on his skin.

He'd explored every inch of their tower sitting room and then his bedroom, familiarising himself with every cupboard, book, corner, and crevice before exploring the rooms closest to the tower on the second floor. He found opulent bedrooms, bathrooms, small sitting rooms, and reading nooks, decorated in all manner of styles, all filled with arcane objects, unusual furnishings, and interesting art. He couldn't for the life of him fathom why his mother hated it here. At this moment in time, he didn't want to leave. The thought of going back to university was a drag.

And of course, he'd practiced witch-flight. Knowing that he needed to be very familiar with where he was flying to, he had flown from his sitting room to his bedroom, then the great Gothic kitchen on the ground floor and back again. Just thinking about it gave him goose bumps. It was brilliant. He had wrapped air around him like a cloak, and felt as if he had become one with his element. It was both the most natural thing and the weirdest thing he'd ever experienced. Plus, he no longer felt sick, which was a huge bonus.

Perhaps he felt guilty because he'd explored Moonfell's rooms. Not that it was forbidden; it was his home, and Birdie had encouraged them to look around. He shook his head, unable to shake the feeling. *Coffee and breakfast would solve everything*. It wasn't until he was out of bed and had opened the curtains that he saw the pile of leaves and cut grass on the rug at the end of his bed.

Weird.

There was no trail of leaves from the door, the windows were shut tight, and he was sure he hadn't brought them in from the orchard last night. But he had drank a few glasses of wine. *Had he flown to the orchard and forgotten?* No. He might have had a few glasses, but he wasn't that drunk. Then he saw a few stray leaves leading to the bathroom. When he reached the door, he stopped dead.

Something was in his bathtub.

Seven

July, 1664

As far as Eliza was concerned, the night had been a success.

She and Ansel had been introduced to lots of theatre folk, rich and poor, and plenty of landed gentry who loved to be seen with members of The King's Playhouse—especially the pretty young actresses. There had also been a couple of very wealthy ladies who had flirted outrageously with the actors, too.

"You know," Ansel said, adjusting his cuffs and straightening his jacket as their carriage pulled through Moonfell's gates, "I could probably find us a wealthy benefactor, too. I had a fair bit of interest." He lifted his head and tapped his chin. "This handsome face had fans."

"Would you be prepared to be a lady's lackey, escorting her across town night after night—and maybe more? I think not," she said, amused. "You would be at their beck and call, and would be cast aside when the next best thing came along. I can't see it, dear brother. Besides, we're not that hard up."

"Yet."

"And won't be. Tonight was a good idea. Not everyone is enamoured of doctors. Many value the old ways, and know that using leeches is just quackery. They simply have to trust us. We'll go more regularly now, and cultivate friendships." Then she stopped, head cocked as they entered the grounds and the gate receded behind them. "Something is different."

"What do you mean?"

"Here at Moonfell." She stuck her head out of the window and inhaled deeply. "The energy has changed."

Ansel stuck his head out next to her, lifting his nose like a dog. "Smells fine."

"It isn't a smell, fool. Feel!" She rapped on the roof. "Jeremy, stop!"

As soon as the carriage halted, she jumped to the ground and opened her awareness, rolling it across the grounds. It was unmistakable. A palpable change had infiltrated Moonfell, like the cold breath of winter dispelling the muggy night.

Jem tipped his hat to the back of his head and looked down at her. He was only a few years older than she was, and knew all about what went on at Moonfell. His parents had looked after the house and grounds for years, and they had played together as children. She trusted him with her life. "You all right, Lizzie? You look like you've seen a ghost. You haven't, 'ave yer?" The starlight illuminated the stubble on his chin and his strong jaw as he looked at the house and back to her again.

"No, but something feels off. Can't you feel it, Ansel? Focus!" Her brother was very good with some magic, but surprisingly dense at other times. She stared into the gardens while she waited, trying to decide where the strange change in energy had emanated from.

"I feel a chill," Jem confessed, slipping off the carriage seat to stand next to her, "which is a bit odd on a night like tonight. Aren't your protection spells working?"

"Of course they are. I check them every month."

Ansel was next to the horse, Hercules, hand wrapped in his mane as the horse pawed at the ground. "I can't feel anything, but he can. He feels a darkness spreading." He nodded to the west. "From that way."

Eliza shivered, sudden fear for Jacinta coursing through her. "You carry on to the stables, Jem. We'll walk. Have a look in the house, please, for Cinta?"

"Of course, but," he looked down at her, eyes glinting with worry, "be careful. Magic or not, if something has found its way in here, it's because it's powerful."

"Then you be careful, too," she said, realising she had never felt fearful in Moonfell in her whole life. "You still carry the amulet I made you?"

He pulled the small bag from under his shirt, hung on a leather cord. "Always."

"If you find Cinta, stay with her, please." He nodded, and without another word, set off up the drive. She turned to Ansel. "We'll head west then, to the moon gate first." Eliza called on her magic, so that it sparked on her fingertips. "I don't know whether to use a witch-light or not. I don't want to alert whatever it is to our presence."

"It's a something, then?"

"Well it's not a nothing!"

"Sorry," he said, lowering his voice. "This is weird. I never thought we'd be hunting something in our own grounds."

Eliza took a deep breath, sorry that she had snapped. "I'm sorry, too. It could be that Jacinta has cast a spell that has just unbalanced the place. There might not be a *something* at all." She stepped off the drive and onto a path that wound through the shrubs towards the pond. "We'll go this way."

She quickly gave up on her idea not to use a witch-light. For all her familiarity with Moonfell's gardens, at night, surrounded by dense shrubs, especially the unusual topiary that had grown very large and that now towered over them, she felt threatened. However, the half a dozen witch-lights she cast overhead didn't make it better. If anything, the long shadows made her more nervous.

Ansel broke the uneasy silence that had fallen. "The animals have quieted. They're uneasy, too."

"Look!" Eliza pointed at the summerhouse across the pond, aglow with candles. "Jacinta must be there. By the Goddess! What has she done?"

It was at times like these that she wished she had witch-flight, and she started to run. Ansel caught her arm. "No. Steady, Liz. No point throwing ourselves into danger."

"But Jacinta!"

"If we're hurt, we can't help her. The animals are even quieter here." He hesitated, head lifted as he listened. "They're scared."

Heart hammering in her chest, they advanced around the pond, keeping to the west side. The garden felt oddly sterile, and yet... She paused, feeling a pulse of strange, wild energy. Instinctively, she knew something was there. *Something elemental.*

She gripped Ansel's arm, halting him. Her lips were dry, and her tongue felt glued to the roof of her mouth. Moistening her lips, she shouted, "Jacinta! Can you hear me?"

When no one answered, she crept onwards, power crackling in her palms, and Ansel followed suit. The summerhouse was now only a short distance away. Cushions and rugs were heaped on the floor, and Cinta's own Book of Shadows, mostly blank pages as yet, was open in the middle of them. Her sister was enthusiastic, keen to embrace her magic.

Eliza's gaze, however, was quickly drawn to the area in front of the summerhouse, where Jacinta stood surrounded by...what? *Energy?* Her arms were outstretched, and her hair streamed in a spectral wind, skirts ruffling around her.

"What has she done?" she muttered under her breath.

Spell ingredients were cast upon the floor, and a candle flared with an unnaturally large flame.

Ansel held her back. "Don't get too close. Is she possessed?"

"I don't know." She could feel the energy now, like bites across her skin. "Jacinta. Turn to look at me. Are you all right?" *What a stupid question. Of course she wasn't.* Her body was lit from within.

But her sister turned nevertheless, a strange, fey light in her eyes. Eliza gasped and stepped back. Earth and fungus were clotted in her sister's hair, moss clung to her skin, and when she spoke, it wasn't her voice. It was ancient, cracked with age and power. "*Do not fear for Jacinta. She is still here. I have inhabited her form.*" She threw her head back and took a deep breath. "*So, this is what it feels like to have a body. It is both limiting and invigorating. So small, and yet, so...*" She examined her hands as she twisted and turned them. "*Delicate. Fragile. I could snap so easily.*"

Eliza's gut twisted. She had feared it was some kind of demon or spirit, but the wild, primal energy made her dismiss a ghost straight away. She was also pretty sure it wasn't a demon. Another option presented itself. One that chilled her blood. "What are you?"

"*You do not know?*"

"I suspect. I would like to have you tell me, though."

Jacinta grinned, revealing teeth caked in earth. "*You do not trust yourself, witch?*"

Eliza knew the power of names and words, and did not wish to give this creature any more power than it already had. However, she reasoned, she did not know the creature's personal name—if it even had one. Perhaps knowing that would swing the power her way. "You are an elemental. Earth, I suspect, from your current appearance."

A cracked laugh broke free, like earth fracturing in a dry summer. *"Well done, witch. I am an elemental earth spirit as old as time, from the dark deep where life springs and returns. I create and I destroy."*

Eliza's first instinct was to run, but she had a million questions, and forcing her fear down, she asked, "Why are you here?"

"Your sister wanted this. Wanted to help you. But I do not help humans."

"Then return to where you came from and release Jacinta."

"Not yet. Not when I have so much to see. To feel. I may even like this place far too much to return." Her head twisted unnaturally to look behind her, and Eliza winced as Ansel gave a sharp intake of breath. *"There is magic here. Powerful magic that may enhance my own. I may choose to stay."* Malevolent eyes narrowed as she stared at Eliza. *"We shall see."*

"This is not your home, and there is no place for you here. You must leave."

"No!" The earth cracked between Jacinta and her siblings, and the elemental stepped back and was swallowed by the night.

A couple of hours later, Ansel found his sister and Jem in the tower spell room, where they kept all their magical ingredients and the Wildblood family grimoire.

As soon as the elemental vanished, they tried to track it. Unfortunately, it was quickly obvious that it was impossible. Jacinta, despite her physical form, had disappeared. Instead, they gathered up Jacinta's magical workings, and Eliza returned to the house. Ansel had stayed to communicate with the animals.

It was distinctly eerie wandering through Moonfell, knowing an elemental creature he didn't fully understand was lurking there, somewhere. He had tried to communicate with the many creatures that made Moonfell their home in an effort to understand what was happening, but they had retreated to burrows and nests.

It was a relief to be back in the house. Jem and Eliza looked expectantly at him, but he shook his head. "The animals are hiding. Even the night hunters have gone. I would have thought they would be comfortable with an elemental earth spirit roaming the garden, but it seems not."

"Because," his sister said, hand on the grimoire she was studying, "it is not where it should be, or have such a form. It is unnatural." She had changed out of her elegant evening gown, and was now wearing a simple linen dress. The elaborate hairstyle that Jem's mother, Lucy, had helped her with was now half tumbled down her back, and her eyes were wide and bleak. "I have no idea what could be happening to Cinta. Even worse, I have no idea how to banish it."

"You will find a way," Jem reassured her. "I know you will. You are Eliza Wildblood, High Priestess of Moonfell."

Ansel gave a hollow laugh. Jem adored his sister, thinking Eliza the greatest witch that ever lived. Seeing him now, the way he stood protectively close to her, Ansel saw what he'd missed before. Jem loved her. Suddenly, with unexpected clarity in this moment of drama, Ansel knew that if Jem had the nerve, he would ask her to marry him. He shoved that thought away to mull over another time. "We are a coven of two. I doubt we are strong enough to tackle an elemental. What was Cinta thinking?"

Eliza lifted Cinta's Book of Shadows. "She was compiling her own spells, a collation of several from older grimoires. I recognise a few. Many seem to be focussed on finding a familiar. Did she mention her research to you?"

Ansel took it from her, flicking through the pages. The early spells had been so neat, but that soon descended into scrawl with scribbled notes, little pictures, and the odd ink blot. "No, not a word. We talked about magic, obviously, and I know she practiced a lot, but she never mentioned this."

She held several sheets of paper out, covered in earth and candle wax. "I found this amongst her things, all screwed up. She must have thought it was another spell to find a familiar. It even has a warning on it."

"Perhaps," Jem suggested, "she had an idea it wasn't, which is why it's not actually in her spell book. It seems secretive."

Ansel shuddered as he read the spell. "It's dark. The words drip with it. She must have been desperate. I can't believe we even have such a spell."

"We have worse. It's wise to know dangerous spells as well. We just choose not to use them. It's also useful if magic is used against us. Attack is as important as defence." Eliza looked at Jem and then to Ansel. "I presume she was trying to help us. No wonder she didn't want to come to the theatre. She's been working on these spells for weeks." She flopped into a chair and leaned on the table. "And I thought I'd been so clever at keeping things from her."

"She's fifteen, not five!" Ansel, too nervous to sit, paced to the windows and looked out at the garden. It had taken all his nerve to walk through it, knowing the earth elemental was out there, somewhere.

"How can the elemental have hidden her so effectively? She's still flesh and blood."

Jem sat opposite Eliza, pulling the Wildblood grimoire towards him. "I don't even really understand what it is, although I know you weave elemental magic. Is it something like that?"

Eliza shrugged. "Yes and no. Elemental magic uses the energy of air, fire, earth, and water. They all have distinct qualities. But there are spells that suggest you can harness elemental magic and call it into form. I suppose you could argue that a dryad is an earth spirit, and sylphs are air spirits. Supposedly, we are now cut off from the Otherworld, and those spirits are no longer in this world, but that was not a dryad. My understanding is that it has its own shape, and that was not what we saw tonight."

Ansel nodded. "What we saw had to use Jacinta. But how did a fifteen-year-old who is only just learning magic drag that from the earth?"

Eliza shook her head. "I can only suspect that she drew on the garden's magic, but it's how we get rid of it that concerns me most."

He studied the original spell again. "If she can summon it, we can banish it."

He just hoped he sounded more confident than he felt.

Eight

Present Day

"Are you sure you weren't in the garden last night?" Odette asked Como.

He looked pale beneath his olive skin, his thick, dark hair unruly. "No! I'm not senile!"

He wasn't lying; she would have been able to tell, and he was genuinely spooked. "Did you leave a window open, perhaps?"

"So that a bloody great bird could bring a bunch of twigs and sticks into my bathroom? That look like some creepy stick doll? Odette! Seriously?"

"I'm trying to find a logical solution."

"You're trying not to freak me out. You're failing. I'm not a child, so stop worrying."

They were in Como's bathroom in the tower after he had manifested in the kitchen with a whirl of air just after Odette and Birdie arrived. He had managed to land on the kitchen table, fortunately before it had been laid for breakfast, and although he had tried to subdue his panic, it was obvious—to Odette, at least.

So far, Birdie, Morgana, and Lam hadn't said a word. Birdie had taken one look in the bathtub and started prowling the rooms, hands hovering over every surface, while Morgana examined the weird stick poppet. Lam just muttered, "Fuck," under his breath.

Como straightened his shoulders. "Could a ghost have done this?"

"The ghost of creepy poppets? Sure, why not?" Lam said sarcastically. "Or the Ēostre bunny has come early."

"*Stronzo*!" Como huffed. "I am trying not to freak out that something was in here while I was sleeping!" He swore profusely in Italian, and his accent became stronger with every passing minute.

Lam frowned. "*Stronzo?*"

"It means asshole, you English imbecile."

"Screw you! I'm trying to make light of it. It's called English humour, you Italian moron!"

"There is nothing *funny* about this!"

Odette had thought that Italians being voluble and loud was an exaggeration. It turns out, it wasn't. "Deep breath, Como, and slow down. I won't be able to understand you if you keep talking at breakneck speed. And stop insulting your cousin. He doesn't mean to be an arse."

Lam glared at her and gave her the middle finger. She sniggered. While they had expected Como and Lam to liven things up, this wasn't what she imagined. Although, to be fair, the entire situation was very worrying.

Como was still ranting. "Would you be freaked out if this was in your bathroom? Now I'm thinking that my dreams were even more weird than I thought."

Odette stared at him. "What dreams?"

"Last night! I dreamt I was being chased through a wood. Maybe a garden. It was dark, confusing. I felt lost. Threatened. And then I thought a thump had woken me. I'm cool with magic, but not with a haunted bedroom."

"It's not haunted," Morgana said, standing up, but leaving the twig poppet in the bath. "We have many weird things in Moonfell, but the ghosts of our dearly departed are not one of them." Odette wasn't sure she agreed with that after feeling the fluttering of spirits in the attic, but she knew what Morgana meant. They didn't walk the halls like in a haunted mansion. Morgana continued, "We cleanse the place regularly and I can assure you, we cleansed this tower very well before you arrived."

"Then what brought *that*? Is it really a poppet?"

Odette exchanged a wary look with Morgana. The twig doll was a couple of feet long, filling the bottom of the bath, and made from a bundle of twigs bound into a stick body shape. Cord bound its parts together. The head was a woven ball of little twigs and dried grass—blind and dumb. Most of the twigs were old and brittle, but a couple were fresh, with a few deep green leaves.

Before Odette could answer, Birdie did. "No. It's not a poppet. There is no spell attached to it, no binding magic. It's something else." She stood at the bathroom door, seemingly unruffled. "I think it's an offering."

"To what?" Como asked.

"Or who?" Lam said, darkly.

"I don't know. Yet."

Como shuffled nervously. "Is it connected to my dream?"

This was a question Odette was surer about. Could feel the truth of it. "Yes, but I'm not exactly sure how yet. You must have connected to something…or something has connected to you. We need to find out what. Potentially, it's connected to Hades, too."

Birdie's wise old eyes locked with Odette's. "Perhaps it's connected to Eliza, too."

"Eliza?" Como frowned. "Who is that?"

"She's a witch," Odette explained, "who was considered one of our most powerful. She's also a little notorious, because she advised Charles II."

"The king?" Lam gaped. "How did she manage that?"

Odette shrugged, perplexed. "To be honest, I don't know the details. I presume it was a matter of introductions by landed gentry. Queen Elizabeth I had John Dee as her magical advisor—and he was pretty open about that. He was called the Queen's magician. But he was a man, and therefore also seen as a man of science. Witchcraft, especially practised by a woman, was viewed quite differently. I guess, however, Charles decided he needed a magical advisor, too. Of course, Eliza never had an official title. That would have been far too dangerous. The Witch Hunts were still rumbling on."

"However," Morgana warned, "we don't know how much she actually advised him or not. It's been whispered down through generations. Her role might have been overexaggerated."

Como gaped, mouth dropping open. "You haven't checked?"

Birdie clucked. "Do you know how many ancestors have achieved all sorts of interesting things in their lifetimes? Lots! We can't possibly read up on all of them. Many of them did not write diaries!"

Lam remained persistent. "Why mention her name? What does she have to do with this?"

Feeling as if she'd been overly secretive, Odette said, "I heard crying in the orchard yesterday, and last night I investigated in the attic. I saw that it was Eliza."

"A vision?" Morgana asked, hands on hips. "You never said!"

"I was going to tell you all at breakfast—before Como arrived with such fanfare."

"Then perhaps we should do exactly that." Morgana shooed them out of the bathroom. "Let's eat, and then we decide what we do next."

***

Birdie was feeling cranky, although she was trying very hard to hide it.

This was supposed to be a lovely few weeks of introducing the boys to Moonfell and getting them settled, and now the house was throwing conundrums their way. She was determined to get to the bottom of it quickly.

Smearing her toast with a generous amount of butter and honey to fortify herself, she asked Odette, "Was there any clue at all as to what made Eliza cry?"

"No. I was so shocked to recognise her that I lost the vision again. It was really annoying. It didn't help that there were lots of other memories fluttering around up there."

Lam was about to shovel a mound of bacon into this mouth, but he paused. "What do you mean, fluttering?"

"I could sense them, like moth's wings on my cheeks and in my hair. I get like that sometimes, and the attic has so many personal items there that it can be quite strong." She shrugged. "I've grown used to it."

Perhaps, Birdie mused, it was better they had this issue now. Better that Lam and Como understood that the house was odd, and magic had consequences. Like the bloody bee ritual that she was convinced had caused some of this. "So," she said authoritatively, "let's discuss timelines. Odette heard crying by the beehives before the ritual. That was mid-afternoon. The vision was of the orchard in summer, correct?"

Odette nodded. "Yes. There was ripening fruit, the leaves were dark green, and it had that summer feel."

"Good. And the later vision, at midnight?"

"Not that late, but same timeframe in the vision. I saw her from a different angle. She was younger than me. Early twenties, perhaps?"

"Someone make a note," Birdie said, "to check her date of birth, and we'll try to work out the year. So, after the first vision, we had our bee ritual. I think there was extra magic there that came from the bees. As yet, that is to be confirmed. After that, for me it was an uneventful evening of educating these two about moon spells and cycles. Odette went to the attic. Anything else happen?"

Odette shook her head. "No. I tried to connect again, but couldn't. I'll head to the moon gates tonight. One of them might show me more. I just need to work out which one. Hopefully, the garden will guide me."

Birdie nodded. "Morgana, you went to cast a new moon spell. Anything happen at the gate?"

She stirred her tea, not looking up immediately. When she did, she met Birdie's eyes for a moment before glancing away again. "Well, the spell I cast seemed to take well. You know, the usual things, flaring candle flames, a breath of wind. All quite normal, actually."

"And the spell?"

Morgana kept it vague, which worried Birdie. "Just that the boys should settle in well and enjoy Moonfell. You know, a new intention, new beginning spell. Very new moon orientated."

Birdie tightened her lips. There was undoubtedly more, but she wouldn't push for details now. "Okay. So one new moon spell, one vision."

Lam wagged his fork in the air. "I cast a new moon spell, too. You inspired me, Birdie. It seemed to take well. I had a whole flaring candle thing, too." He fell silent, as if summoning up courage for what he would say next.

"Go on!" Birdie fixed him with a piercing stare.

"I basically said I didn't want to be a stranger to the house and its magic, and that I wanted to learn its mysteries." He faltered as all three Moonfell witches stopped eating to look at him. "Then I said I would be happy to learn new magic if the house needed it. *Shit*. Was that a mistake?"

Birdie massaged her temples. "Not a mistake, as such, just perhaps a little vague, and therefore troublesome. A spell, cast well, will work, but if you're not specific in your intent, it can bring things you don't expect." Lam looked frozen with panic. "It's okay. The house is our friend. Let's just think about it later. Anything else before I move on?"

"I have tinnitus or something. My ears feel a little buzzy."

"Is that new?"

"It started this morning."

Morgana intervened. "I thought it was low blood sugar."

Or the spell is already manifesting. "Let's hope breakfast rectifies it." With a tight smile, Birdie turned to Como. "Giacomo, any new moon spells from you?"

"No, but I was so excited at being here that I explored the tower and part of the second floor, and then practiced flying. Only in the house, though!"

Odette's lips twitched with amusement. "You were very inspiring, Birdie. I think that's wonderful."

Birdie decided to rise above her jibe. "That is my aim, always. Well done, Como. Your flying is clearly improving, even though you did land on the kitchen table. Practice makes perfect. So, to come back to our twig offering..." The twig figure was propped on the kitchen counter, looking harmless, but how had it arrived? She chewed thoughtfully on her toast, the honey giving her a boost of energy. "The twigs could have come from anywhere, but most likely our orchard. But why are there fresh leaves as well as old ones, who made it, and how did it get in the house?"

"You're missing events on the timeline," Morgana reminded her. "Como had vivid dreams and woke up because he thought he heard a thump in his rooms, and Hades disappeared at some point after the bee ritual. Did you cast any spells last night, Birdie?"

"Yes, actually, I did. I asked for guidance on finding Hades, and asked the Gods to keep him safe." She played with the toast crumbs on her plate. "I also asked that the boys learn our Moonfell ways and enjoy themselves."

Morgana's eyebrows shot up. "So, three new moon spells last night, one bee ritual, two visions, one vivid dream, a thump, and one missing familiar. That's a busy twenty-four hours. Plus, of course, a new moon, a potent time for manifesting."

"And," Odette chimed in, "you can feel a shift in the house's energy."

Birdie sighed. "When you put it all like that..."

"We need a plan," Odette said. "I will endeavour to find out more about Eliza. I'm sure the library has information. I can try the moon gates today, but I always have more success at night."

"I'll help," Como said. "I have time before I need to revise. Besides, I can't concentrate with all this happening." He flashed them all a grin. "It's actually quite exciting."

Odette nodded. "I may be able to help you with your dream, too."

Morgana started clearing the plates. "I have tisanes and potions to prepare, but I can help later. Maybe I'll search the gardens. I can visit the bees, too."

Lam looked sheepish. "I was hoping to set my studio up, but I could help after that?"

Morgana smiled. "Setting up your studio is important. You can help me search the garden later, if you want, and if needed, we can all help in the library this afternoon."

"I will scry," Birdie declared. "It's my favoured medium for finding things. It may help me find Hades. Then this evening we will go to Storm Moon. I think we'll all need a break after today. Maybe we should eat out, too. Save you having to cook, Morgana. We'll have a busy day."

Plus, she had ulterior motives. Shifters had hunting skills, and they might be able to help find Hades.

Nine

July, 1664

"How do we banish an earth elemental?" Eliza asked, despair creeping through her. "What if it's already too late?"

She had barely slept she'd been so worried about Jacinta. Every time she closed her eyes, she saw her sister's face contorted into the elemental creature. *What if they could never separate them? What if the elemental had dragged her beneath the earth and suffocated her? Or did the elemental being need to breathe at all?* When she did finally sleep, her dreams were of being hunted in Moonfell's gardens, the thick summer vegetation clawing at her and dragging her to the ground. Even now, in the early morning sunshine that poured through the kitchen windows, the dreams haunted her.

"Stop it," Jem said, snapping her back to the present. He must have woken earlier than usual for him to be at the house already. "I can see the panic in your eyes. You need to calm down and be rational."

"I tried that. It didn't work."

"Last night you were tired and overwrought, and you acted on instinct. Now you need to focus." He lifted the pot off the range and poured boiling water over some fresh herbs in a teapot. "Drink this. It will help."

She inhaled the scent of lemon balm and lavender. "Calming and uplifting. When did you learn about herbs?"

"I tend the garden, remember? I'm a man of many skills. And I've been around witches my whole life."

She regarded him over the rim of the cup. He was of average height, with broad shoulders from working outdoors, looking after Hercules, and being their general help around the house. His brown hair was streaked blond by the summer sun, and his tanned skin made his blue eyes look even brighter. He was like a brother to her, and yet lately, she had begun to think of him as more than that. "Thank you. I know you are. I take you for granted."

"No, you don't. You're always kind and thoughtful. You always have been. Stubborn, mind…" He grinned, teasing her.

"Sometimes I have to be." Like when standing up to her mother in her increasingly paranoid years. "Where's your mother?"

His eyes flicked to the garden beyond the windows. "I told her best to stay away today. I hope you don't mind."

She heaved a sigh of relief. "No, I'm really pleased about it. Thank you. I should have thought to say last night." Jem's mother, Lucy, was a big-hearted, plump woman who was like a second mother to Eliza and her siblings, except far more stable. She and Jem lived in the village, a short distance away. Jem's father had died a few years earlier. Like Jem, Lucy knew all about the family's magic, and they both followed the old Pagan traditions. Eliza hated to think she might be attacked by the elemental. "We need to set a trap for it."

"I can set animal traps, but elemental ones? Not so sure about that."

"A magical trap, not just elemental, but yes, easier said than done."

He poured his own drink and sat opposite her. "Say you do trap it, what then?"

"We send it back. Ansel was right. If Cinta could summon it, there must be a way to banish it."

"I thought you said it wanted to explore? It might be harmless."

"Harmless would be manifesting without inhabiting my sister. Besides, that thing was dark with a ruthless power." She shuddered, remembering the wild magic it exuded. "You know I use earth magic. Tap into its stability and strength. I've always found it comforting. Grounding. But what I saw last night..." The image of her sister's possessed face filled her mind again, and she realised how utterly exhausted she felt. Her sleep had been both too brief and never ending. "I need to scry. I think that using my obsidian glass, something forged in the earth, will allow me to see it. Then I'll work a spell that reverses what Jacinta cast." The scrunched-up paper was on the table, and she reached for it and smoothed it out again. The sight of her sister's handwriting sent another rush of guilt through her. "She copied this from somewhere. If it was part of a series of spells, that might help me."

"Was it your mother's?"

"Maybe, but I don't recognise it." She stood, resolute. "I'll head to the tower room and start now. Or perhaps I should search Cinta's room first. By this afternoon I want to have a spell ready to try."

"So soon?"

"I'd rather try it in the light than the dark. It's out there, still." She nodded to the garden. "It casts a shadow."

"Ansel is already out there again," Jem told her. "I saw him leaving as I arrived. Perhaps I should be with him. I want to help!"

"I'm not sure you can. Besides, he'll be trying to communicate with the animals here. That might give us some insight. Neither of us can help him with that." Ansel's power was unusual, and even he didn't master it all the time.

"I'm strong. You can draw on me if you need to." He looked so earnest.

"I can't do that, although that's a generous offer."

"Why can't you?"

"It's important to protect yourself, psychically. You have had no practice at doing that. You'll be completely unprepared. I won't risk it."

"But you won't drain me, I know you won't."

His trust in her took her breath away. "I won't *want* to, but if the spell needs more, I might draw from you too much and not even realise it at the time. I won't do that. Besides," she squirmed, uncomfortable at what she was about to admit, "you've never seen me practice magic. You might hate it. It might even scare you. You might think me a freak."

He blinked, his clear, open expression clouding like a storm, and she realised she'd hurt him. "I would never think that. I've seen you cast small magics. I can even feel it. I love what you do, and wish I could do it, too. If I wasn't comfortable with it, do you think I'd still be here?" He shook his head. "I thought you knew me better than that."

She took his hands in hers before he could step away. They were so big, warm, and solid. Just touching him made her feel grounded. "I'm sorry, that was thoughtless of me, but the small magics are very different to what I'm proposing to do today—and you didn't see that elemental creature last night. I value your friendship, Jem. I couldn't bear to see you scared of me. And of course it's tempting to draw on you. Just holding your hand now makes me feel stronger..."

"So do it." He changed their grip, wrapping her fingers within his own, eyes locking on hers. "I trust you."

"I don't trust myself."

"You should do."

He was so close now that their bodies were almost touching, and she had to tip her head back to look at him. She had never been this close to him before. He was intoxicating. She could see flecks of amber in his blue eyes, and the attraction she'd recently felt for him exploded into desire. *Could he see her need for him?* The thought terrified her, making her feel exposed.

Reluctantly, she pulled her hands away, and already felt diminished. "I'll think about it. I promise."

A smile played around his lips. *He knew.* "Good. In the meantime, let me do something else. I can help you lay spell traps around the garden. I know it like the back of my hand. As well as you do."

"All right, but I need to decide what to do first."

He picked up her empty cup, moving to the sink. "What about last night? Your success after the play? How long do you think it will take for anyone to ask for your help?"

Eliza gave a dry laugh. "I'm not even considering that. It could take a long time. I was thinking of going to the theatre again tomorrow, though with all this happening..."

"But it's a good idea, one you should capitalise on. Hopefully, we can rescue Cinta soon."

"If we don't, and someone turns up asking for my help, the elemental might choose that moment to attack in some way." The thought was horrifying. "It's too risky."

"How would it attack someone, and why?"

"I don't know! That's what's so awful about this." *By the great Goddess, this was all too much. Her mother's death, their lack of money, and now this.* "I'm going to the spell room. I need to get started."

"You haven't even had breakfast!"

She walked to the door. "I don't have the time."

"Then I'll bring it up to you."

Eliza knew better than to argue. Besides, he had a glint in his eye now, and a smile that threatened to break at any moment. She felt his eyes on her as she left the room, and knew something had changed between them, and despite the awful situation, she had a spring in her step as she mounted the stairs.

Ansel sat beneath the yew hedge that made the Waxing Moon Gate in the east of the garden, surrounded by a circle of salt to ward against the elemental that might appear at any moment.

The garden, so familiar to him, now felt unnervingly foreign, and the general air of growth and abundance that existed at this time of year now felt unfettered—even chaotic, as if all the rules of nature had been exaggerated. He noticed small changes as he walked the paths. Some familiar plants that he passed daily had grown quickly overnight, and nodding blooms had proliferated. The yew hedge, dark green in its summer glory, had tips of bright green emerging, as if it was spring again. Everything was unbalanced.

It had affected the wildlife, too. The night before, everything had shied away from him; now, it was riotous. The grounds resonated with bird call, butterflies were rampant, and the foxes boldly raced through the garden. Normally this would have excited Ansel, but now he was worried. He sensed panic in the creatures, as if they detected the abnormality of what was amongst them. He had walked the entire garden, his protection spells strong in case of attack, and had noted the change had affected everywhere...all except for the bees in the orchard. They had remained steadfast, unhurried. He needed to think about that, and therefore needed a quiet space.

The yew hedge was his favourite place in the garden. It cradled life, and yet also provided order with its neat, clipped form. The parterre garden beyond it was a graceful mix of form and function that soothed his soul. And of course, the hedge harboured a lot of wildlife. Birds, insects, and mammals.

He sat cross-legged on the bare earth, toes wriggled into the ground, and knowing he was fully protected, closed his eyes and slowed his breathing. He slipped into his meditative state quickly, blocking out everything except the wildlife. Ansel's particular skill did not allow him to talk to animals, but he could discern their emotions. Thoughts was too strong a word. If he was especially lucky, and the conditions were right, he could sometimes see through their eyes. The sharp-eyed glare of an owl, the predatory stare of a fox, the dark branches beneath the hedge as seen through the eyes of a hedgehog. However now, as the general hum of life flowed around him—feeding, nesting, hunting, and building—he sensed that underneath all of that, everything was unsettled. On edge. He focussed on a family of mice close by, and immediately detected their almost frantic behaviour.

But why weren't the bees affected? The elemental being had left them alone, or the bees' own strange powers had blocked it somehow. *If he could find a way to leverage that...*

His eyes flew open, alerted by the chaotic scattering of the wildlife, the scent of decay, and the wild, dark presence of the elemental earth creature. Far closer than he expected, he yelped in shock. Cinta, body caked in earth, leaves, and moss, her dress smeared with dirt, stood outside the circle, a gleam of madness in her gaze.

"You!" He wanted to run, such was the sense of panic the elemental caused, but he steadied himself, trusting that he was safe, and stubbornly remained seated. "If you harm my sister, I will kill you. On this, I swear."

Its eyes flashed scornfully. "*You cannot kill me. I am everywhere and nowhere.*"

"Not right now, you're not. You're right here."

"*Only just.*" It cocked its head. "*But you know that. I feel you as you reach for me.*"

"Not for *you*. I'm reaching for the garden. The animals."

"*They are me.*"

He scowled. "No, they aren't. They have their own business. Their own concerns. You should not be here. You are upsetting the natural law. The garden feels wrong!"

The creature darted forward, snarling. It transformed his sister's face, and something else could be seen behind it. The elemental's true form. Ansel couldn't help himself. He flinched backwards, remembering at the last moment not to break the circle. The creature tested the edge of it and fell back in shock, a horrible guttural roar emerging from its mouth. "*What is this abhorrence?*"

"Things that do not concern you. You cannot break it."

The creature's voice changed again, it certainly wasn't Cinta's anymore, grating like stones scraping together. "*I will find a way. I am the natural law. They all know it. They bow before me.*"

"They flee from you." Ansel felt surer of himself now. He had wondered if salt would work against an elemental being, especially one of earth. It was reassuring to know that it did. "You know you don't belong here, out in the light. Leave now, before more harm is done."

The elemental didn't answer, instead staring at the trees and walls that comprised the garden's boundary. "*That is what traps me here.*"

Their protection spells. She—*it*—had obviously tested those, too. "Yes, and you can't break them." *I hope.* "As I said, leave now, while you still can."

"*No. My will is my own. Although,*" it looked up, shielding its eyes from the light with earth-caked hands, and stepped into the deep shadow cast by the hedge, "*the light dazzles me. It is too hot.*"

He was desperate to keep it talking. Hating the light and the warmth was a weakness he could exploit. *What others did it have?* But before he could question it again, it literally stepped into the hedge and vanished. He didn't wait, instead hurrying back to the house using the brightest, most sunlit paths he could find. He ran up to the tower spell room and found Eliza at the table under one of the windows, spell books stacked in front of her.

"I have a plan," he said, breathless after charging up the stairs. "I've seen it again. It hates the warmth and sunlight. That's where we need to trap it. Somewhere bright." He updated his sister on their conversation.

She rolled her neck, easing kinks, and pushing her hair back. She looked girlish today without her fine dress and jewellery, her hair unkempt. "The salt circle kept it out?"

"Yes. Which means it will also keep it in." He nodded at the texts. "Have you found where the spell came from?"

Her jaw tightened. "An old grimoire that I found in Cinta's room. Not a family one, but one that had been added to our collection. She had ripped the page out of it, which is frankly terrible. When she recovers, I will have words with her about it. But mother had written something similar in her own grimoire, and I wonder if she had found the same spell. Her fear of the Witch Trials drove her to make some strange spells, Ansel. She was prepared to conjure forth anything that might help us, if threatened."

He sat next to her. "Is that what that spell was? To save us?"

"I think she thought so. She was not of her right mind, however."

"She didn't discuss it with you?"

"No. She spent hours in her rooms, you know that, and I had long dismissed her ramblings." She picked up the spell they had found by the summerhouse. "Cinta used the old one though, not mother's; I'm sure of it from the way it's damaged. I am working on a way to reverse it. I cannot believe that our mother made her own version. She was never one for this type of magic before."

"Fear does terrible things." Ansel, horribly, had been relieved when his mother had died. Her instability had become more and more worrying. Moonfell felt far less dramatic without her intense presence. "Do you think we can reverse the spell?"

"Perhaps." Eliza leaned back, looking weary. "Everything feels unsettled to me. I think it's affecting my concentration."

"It feels even worse out there." He further described what he'd experienced. "There are lots of places that have full sun. I'll find the perfect spot. Somewhere that will align with the elements."

"It all must be right. The time of day, the direction, all of it. Jem has offered to help."

Was it his imagination, or did a faint blush creep up her cheeks?

"How?"

"By lending us his strength."

"He doesn't have magic."

"But he has heart and determination, and there are only two of us. We need him."

Ansel reluctantly agreed. As he walked down the steps, deciding to return to the bees, he had another idea. Cinta had been trying to find a familiar. Something that offered advice from the spirit realm. She might have had the right idea.

Where she had failed, he would succeed.

Ten

Present Day

Lamorak couldn't believe that he could use such a large area as his studio. It was amazing, and it would be even better once he had it set up exactly as he wanted it.

It was situated at the end of the stable block, in the newer extension that had been added in the 19th century. It had brick walls and floors, with windows on the three sides. Those were big, metal-framed ones painted black that offered intriguing vistas of the garden. There was a sink and a counter on one wall, a couple of wall cupboards, and a large cupboard that ran from floor to ceiling. An old chaise longue upholstered with dark blue velvet was in the corner, catching a pool of sunshine, and he saw himself relaxing there after sculpting. Double wooden doors opened onto a small, courtyard-style garden. That too was brick-paved and edged with plants, and a couple of paths led into the grounds.

He realised that there was no area of Moonfell that was left untended. It all had a purpose. Every part of the garden was planted and designed; placed strategically around the grounds were sheds, summerhouses, arbours, benches, tables and chairs, composting areas, and moon gates, of course. Everything had evolved from thousands of hands and thousands of ideas. The house was the same. Lots of rooms filled with unusual objects, over-the-top décor, and interesting furniture. It was an assault on the senses. And yet, everything worked. Even the garage and old stables were attractive, though also functional and organised.

Fortunately, the large area in the centre of his room was clear and ready for his art—whatever that would be. Stacked in the corner were old bits of metals and wood, and delivery boxes lay on the countertop. He tore into them, finding blow torches, tools, soldering equipment, and carving instruments. Basic ones, for now. He eyed the walls. He needed racks to display them, so everything was at hand. That meant he needed plywood and hooks. He could drive into Wimbledon and stock up there.

His thoughts were as busy as his hands as he unpacked and planned, moving furniture to accommodate his ideas. It wasn't until he took a breather that he realised he needed a kettle and a small fridge in there, too. *Would that be too cheeky?* He could even work outside when the weather was good. He smiled as a tight knot in the centre of his chest started to ease. He hadn't even noticed he had that before. *Was that because his magic had been locked up and unused?* He rubbed his eyes. Moonfell was getting to him. He was being weird and fanciful.

Then he noticed the buzzing again.

Time slowed, the air around him feeling syrupy and heavy. The buzzing became chatter. *Whispers, perhaps?* He spun around, half expecting to see someone lurking outside his windows, but there was nothing except a blackbird on the top of a topiary shrub carved into the shape of a stag, the tines of its antlers rising majestically. The blackbird stared at him, and the pounding in Lam's ears intensified. Shocked, he stepped back, nearly falling over the broom, and it was as if he'd broken a spell. The bird flew off, and time seemed to shift again.

I need some fresh air.

Through the rear window that looked to the west, Lamorak caught a glimpse of water and the edge of a wooden structure. It looked like a good destination.

It took longer than he expected to reach the area. So many paths intersected and diverged in different directions that he ended up going the wrong way a couple of times. Finally, a brick-paved path brought him to the edge of the long, oval pond. The morning had cooled, and a fresh breeze sent tiny waves across the water, rustling the reeds and aquatic plants that edged it. Low clouds covered the sun, and he was glad he'd worn his jacket. He hadn't explored this area of the garden, and when the glint of a large moon gate caught his attention, he set off towards it.

Up close, he marvelled at its design. The twisting bands of bronze, rich with patina, invited him to explore the sinuous curves. It was cool under his fingers, as smooth as silk, perhaps from hundreds of Moonfell witches' hands. This hadn't been the gate he'd been at for the Yule spell, but it called to him more than the south gate. *Because of the metal, perhaps.* He leaned his forehead against it and heard whispers again. He cursed under his breath. *What the actual fuck? Was this place playing tricks on him? Or was this a result of the new moon spell he'd cast?*

Hand still clutching the bronze gate, he looked at the summerhouse, gloomy with the increasing clouds, and saw a slink of shadow close by.

"Hades!"

The bushes rustled, and he set off in pursuit.

Como huffed as he surveyed the hundreds of shelves filled with books. "Where do we even start?"

"Where the oldest are kept, of course." Odette led the way across the library, spelling lights on as she walked. It was gloomy, especially with the gathering clouds outside.

"Of course! The upper level." Ever since Morgana had shown him the mezzanine floor at Yule, he had longed to explore it further. He bounded ahead of Odette, reaching the level before her. "Will her grimoire be near Sibilla's?"

"Possibly." She shrugged. "I'm not sure. We've never had cause to look for it before. If we can't find it, we'll use a spell. If I'm honest, I quite like searching the non-magical way. That way you find all sorts of unexpected things." She gave Como an impish grin.

Como never considered the ten-year age difference between them. Odette was so informal in her jeans and jumper, always with unruly curls and bare feet, that she seemed elfin to him, especially with her slight build and teasing humour.

"Last one to find it has to buy the first round tonight." She winked, cast a spell at his feet making him lose his balance, and raced ahead of him.

"That's unfair! You're a sneaky shit, Odette!" He raised his hand to cast a spell at her.

"Be careful! Don't forget the precious books up here. I'll point you in the right direction, though. We need—I think—this section." She gestured to an area on either side of where Sibilla's grimoire was kept.

Untangling himself, he swore revenge later. "What's her surname?"

"Wildblood."

"Are you for real? That's a name?"

"Yes! Cool, isn't it? I'm not sure how many generations had that surname, though. I guess we start broad and narrow it down."

For a while they worked in silence, Como extracting book after book, some containing mundane things like room designs and lists of expenses. "Is any of this catalogued?"

"Loosely. As Morgana no doubt told you, the older and the more important grimoires and books were placed up here. Although, important is subjective, isn't it? I figure being King Charles's witch qualifies. I'm trying to work out where her grimoire could be chronologically. Eliza lived roughly one hundred and forty years after Sibilla, so that's what? Six or seven generations? Maybe more. Shorter life spans back then, usually. A few things are kept together, age-wise."

"Well, these aren't grimoires. They're about the house, but I guess if you wanted to read a history of how this place has developed, it's very important."

Como reached for a book bound in dark red leather, and found a pentagram stamped on the cover. The name *Virginia Wildblood* was inscribed in curly script on the flyleaf. "Odette! I've found a Wildblood!" He squinted and cast a witch-light above it. "There's an inscription on the flyleaf. '*Moonfell is wild with magic, the elements are unbound, but in my blood it finds symmetry, and knowledge to confound.*' Bloody hell. That's impressive."

"And a little dramatic." Odette stood next to him. "Perhaps even boastful! What's written beneath it?"

"Something about keeping her maiden name, as it was better suited to her magic. Interesting. So she married and didn't take her husband's name. She sounds headstrong for the time."

Odette winked. "Just like her surname. I like her more with every passing minute!"

Como turned the page. "Yes!" A simple family tree took up most of the space, written in tiny letters. He jabbed the page. "I spy Eliza's name. Born 1640. That must be her, right?"

"Well done! I guess that leaves me buying the first round, then. Is this Eliza's grimoire as well, though?"

Como continued to skim through Virginia's book while Odette searched the shelves. "I don't know as much about magic as you, but there are some odd spells here. Look at the titles. '*To capture darkness.*' '*To trap fire.*' '*Drawing down a dark moon.*' '*Enchanting magpies.*' '*To catch laughter.*' What the hell?"

"She sounds experimental."

"She sounds like a fruitcake." Como experienced a trickle of unease and put the grimoire aside.

"They might not be as bizarre as they sound."

"Maybe I'll study them later after I've fortified myself." *With alcohol.* "I presume I can take these to my room?"

"Of course. Just treat them gently." Odette straightened up, holding half a dozen leatherbound books of various sizes, and quickly flicked to the opening pages. "All Wildbloods. May as well make ourselves comfortable. Bring that one, too."

Odette led them to a couple of chairs in an alcove with a reading lamp on a round table, and dropping into one of the chairs, crossed her legs beneath her. Como envied her agility. If he tried to sit cross-legged with his stocky build, he'd dislocate a hip.

Placing Virginia's grimoire on the table, opened to the family tree, he reached for a slim green volume. "This belongs to Ansel, and he is...Eliza's brother!"

"Younger or older?"

"Younger. He's not much for making notes, though. There are spells in here, but nothing elaborate."

"Not all spells need be complicated. Perhaps he shied away from it, if his mother was a bit dramatic. The simplest spells are also sometimes the best. Clarity of intention is our most powerful tool."

"That's an interesting suggestion. About Ansel, I mean. There are quite a few spells about animals and insects." He spotted an interesting title. "*'To control full moon surges.'* This is a potion, I think. It talks about simmering times."

Como realised that all this deserved further investigation, just out of pure curiosity. Although, his urge at Christmas to explore Moonfell's history re-exerted itself. He could already tell it would be easy to lose himself down a rabbit hole.

"Well, this grimoire," Odette said, tapping a black leather cover, "belonged to Annabelle Wildblood."

Como referred to the family tree again. "Virginia's mother, therefore Eliza's grandmother. She's the daughter of Ichabod Wildblood who, according to this family tree, married into the family. Annabelle's mother is Beatrix Masters. I have no idea who her parents were, but she must be a witch."

"Ah! I have Beatrix's grimoire, too. That makes her Eliza's great-grandmother." Odette's face wrinkled with consternation as she also studied the family tree. "So, Annabelle married Daniel Goodheart, but kept her own surname and passed it on to Virginia. Daniel wasn't the witch, and Annabelle, Virginia's mother, was?"

"Exactly. Or Daniel could have been, just not a Moonfell witch. There's no reason why she couldn't have married a witch. Eliza's father is Harry Vincent." Como laughed. "No wonder Virginia kept Wildblood as her surname. It's far more dramatic than Vincent."

"Poor man. I wonder if he was upset about it?"

"Ooh! I've found it." Como opened an oxblood red grimoire, and spotted Eliza's name scribbled on the flyleaf. He quickly flicked through the following pages. "Now, this one is packed with spells."

"Any notes, diary entries, observations?"

"Give us a chance!"

Odette studied the family tree again. "We're missing a grimoire. Eliza had a younger sister called Jacinta."

"Maybe it's still in the cupboard?"

A few minutes later, Odette returned to this side. "Nope. Not there."

"Not a witch, perhaps?"

"Unlikely. Maybe it's stored elsewhere."

"Does it matter?"

Odette drummed her fingers on the arm of her chair. "Maybe not, but seeing as Eliza was crying over something, it would be good to link their histories and spell books together."

"Perhaps she shared Eliza's grimoire?"

"No. Her family members each had their own, just as you do." Odette's strange, far-seeing gaze returned, and she fell silent for a moment. It was uncanny how still she became. She stood up abruptly, hands opening like a book, and cast a spell. "*Jacinta's book, hidden well, hear the words of this short spell. Show your place and glow with light, guide me to your secrets bright.* Como, help me see if it's stored elsewhere. We should see a light, like a glowworm, showing us where it is."

Giacomo scanned the shelves on the mezzanine, and then the lower level, until they both came to the same conclusion. "It's not here."

"Or there isn't one. Or maybe," Odette said, eyes narrowing, "it was destroyed or hidden for a reason."

"Hidden by a spell?"

"Perhaps." Her eyes flashed with intrigue. "A mystery. Oh well, something to think about. Now, let's focus on Eliza." She returned to her chair. "I think she was in her early twenties when I saw her. That would make the years somewhere between 1660 and 1665. Was Charles on the throne then?"

"I think so." He used a search engine on his phone to confirm. "Yes. 1660. When did she start working with him?" Como started to search her grimoire, looking for dates and names. "She has dated some of these spells, and references moon phases with others. Outcomes, expectations. I'll need to study it properly, though. Her writing is so cramped, and there are so many spells."

"Good. At least we know roughly the timeframe. I could take our search back a couple of years, in case she was younger. Are there any dates of death in Virginia's grimoire?" She picked up the book and studied the family tree again, her eyes widening with surprise. "Ah. Virginia died in 1664. January. So Eliza might have been crying about her death."

"Or the death of a cat? Or a broken heart?"

"Those are also possible causes. No other dates of death, though." Odette turned to the end of Virginia's grimoire. "Wow. The latter spells are a mess. They look hurried. Chaotic. I think I'll study this further, if you check Eliza's."

"Will do. There's no family tree in Eliza's or Ansel's grimoire." Como sat back, studying Odette. "I know you see to the truth of things, and that you can see people's real thoughts and emotions..."

"Not thoughts," Odette said, correcting him. "I don't read minds. It's so hard to explain. I just feel the truth, or see to the heart of the matter. Sometimes it's very obvious, but at other times, it's more subtle. And," she started laughing, "I sometimes see hidden magic, if it's strong enough. I recently saw two Nephilim's hidden wings. It was astonishing."

Como blinked. "A Nephilim? The son of an angel? Really?"

"*Two* of them! Really." Her mischievous nature exerted itself again. "Their wings are magnificent, as are their muscles!"

Como experienced a wave of dizziness again, as if the floor moved beneath him. "The biblical Nephilim who are the sons of Fallen Angels? I thought that was myth."

She rolled her eyes. "You really should know better, Como. They existed, and some still do. And before you ask, yes, they were involved with the Fallen Angel we exorcised. Believe me, it all got much worse, but it should be over now."

Como had so many questions, he didn't know where to begin. "I need to sit down and have a proper chat with you."

"I'm more than happy to enlighten you."

"Will I meet one? A Nephilim, I mean?"

"Probably."

He huffed and leaned back, the grimoire heavy on his lap. "This is not straightforward, is it? Stepping into a magical life."

"Not always, but it is rewarding."

He considered his other pressing question. "You can't read objects? Like this grimoire?"

"Psychometry? No. It's more emotive than that. It would be handy though, and probably exhausting." She smiled. "This place will all seem far less strange in a few weeks. Until then, let things soak in."

"I haven't got many weeks though, just a couple." His frustration at his urge to soak everything in and immerse himself in Moonfell surged again. "This place gets under your skin. All the weird objects, and the pictures, and the funny passages that I stumble into, and the quirky little doors that lead to unusual little rooms. I don't want to leave."

"I know how it feels. It's a good sign, though, that you feel like that. Obviously, the house has accepted you. You'll be back in the summer, so enjoy the end of your university life—*really* enjoy it. You need your degree because you'll still need to earn a living at some point. You're studying history, aren't you?"

"Yes, in Naples. I'm focussing on the Italian Renaissance. Art, literature, da Vinci, and the political figures, like the Médicis."

"That sounds fascinating!"

"It is, to be honest."

"Then don't let this place distract you. There'll come a time when you want to work, even if you work from here. Your research skills will stand you in good stead. Plus, this house isn't going anywhere! You have your whole life ahead of you. You don't need to rush."

He nodded and blinked, as Odette's features seemed to shift and become owllike, her eyes fixed on him. In a flash, the vision vanished again. "Thanks, Odette. You're very wise."

"In the meantime," she tapped the stack of books, "we need answers."

He held out Eliza's grimoire. "Swap. I'll take Virginia and Ansel. I feel quite invested in her crazy spells. You should have Eliza's. You already have a connection to her."

If Moonfell's history contained a few unstable witches, he wanted to know about them.

Eleven

July, 1664

On Saturday afternoon, while Eliza was still deep in her exploration of spell books and only a partially drafted spell written in her own Book of Shadows, she heard the heavy toll of the bell down by the main gate that was now locked because of the elemental that roamed the garden.

Rising to stand at the window, she looked across the grounds, wondering who would be calling on them. Within moments, Jem rode down the drive on their horse, Hercules, bareback from what she could tell. Heart in her mouth, Eliza hoped that the elemental wouldn't appear out of nowhere and attack him, or try to leave. Abandoning her studies, she hurried to the ground floor and out the main entrance.

By the time she arrived, Jem was cantering back, and spotting her, he nudged the horse in her direction and dismounted. "There was a messenger at the gate. Had come from the Playhouse, apparently. Impatient, too. Didn't like having to wait. I tipped him. He delivered this." He reached into his shirt and pulled out a small envelope. "You have a letter."

"It must be from Nell." The paper was of thick, cream stock. Expensive. A red seal was over the fold. Heart pounding, she said, "It looks official. What do you think it is?"

"I have no idea! Open it."

Not sure whether it would be good news or bad—although why it should be bad, she had no idea—she ripped it open and found a short letter with a scrawled *EG* at the bottom. "It's an invitation to the public house after the performance again tonight. Nell has someone she wants us to meet."

"So soon? Does she say who?"

"No, she's frustratingly vague. It must be someone important, though, or why the rush? I knew we'd make an impression!"

"But tonight?" Jem frowned. "I thought you'd be casting the spell then."

"No. We need sunshine. The elemental is strongest at night, in the dark and cool. Ansel met it again this morning."

"Was he hurt?"

"He's fine, although it was a shock. It gave him some interesting insights, though." A spasm of concern rocked through her. She had pushed her sister to the back of her mind, focussing on banishing the elemental, but now his description of how she looked, and how the elemental was mistreating her body made her wince. Her hands flew to her cheeks. "He said Cinta looks terrible, though. I'm taking too long to find a solution, but if I get it wrong, and we make it worse, or it just vanishes with Cinta…" She trailed off, horrified. "It doesn't bear thinking about."

"You've only been working on it for a few hours. Don't be so hard on yourself!"

Eliza had been so sidetracked by the unexpected visitor and the invitation that she'd barely taken any notice of her surroundings, but now her concerns came crashing back. She hadn't been outside for hours, and the change in the garden struck her forcibly. It was another hot day, and the atmosphere was oppressive. Usually on days like this, the garden slumbered in the heat, but not today. The ivy that grew up the walls of the house had proliferated, and shoots snaked across the borders and onto the paths. The lawn at the front of the house, deliberately kept long in the summer, had been looking dry, but now was lush green and almost knee-high—a proper summer meadow. The cows were in the middle of it, skittish. And the moon gate… She tucked the letter in her cleavage and hurried to it. The south moon gate, officially called the Full Moon Gate, was made of layers of stone and slate, supporting an ancient honeysuckle. It had grown so much overnight that it hung over the gate, almost obscuring it, and it raced across the ground, tangling in the long grass.

She turned to Jem who had followed her. "It's too much. It's unnatural."

"I know. I presume the elemental caused this?"

"Yes, unfortunately." Eliza was in tune with the grounds, and she felt the strain of the change, and the edge towards autumn. She groaned. "Of course. Earth is associated with winter. She—*it*—is hurrying us towards it."

"Why?"

"I think it's just what it does. If there is an underlying purpose to this, I'm not sure what it is."

"If there is one, it's that the house and land will be overrun with vegetation. Ivy can tear a building down, Liz."

Together they turned to look at the house, and from a distance it appeared even worse. The ivy that had clambered so gracefully up the stonework now cavorted across lintels and windows, and was almost at the roof. Potential images of it pulling the chimneys down, or punching through windows and growing into the house were horrifying.

Eliza gave a shallow laugh, and under the blazing sunshine felt she might faint. "So, here I am, worried that if we continue the way we are, that we'll run out of money and I'll have to sell off bits of Moonfell, when now the real worry is that it might not even be standing at the end of the week!"

Jem stepped between her and the house, gently holding the tops of her arms. "There must be spells you can use to stop it. Or surely the house's protection spells will help? This is an attack, of sorts."

"But I don't think the house will see it as such. Our spells are to stop an obvious attack and repel malignant spirits and other such malevolence. This is insidious—and elemental—and we use elemental magic to weave spells. Besides, it's *everywhere*! I can't possibly cast a spell across the entire garden on my own!"

"Don't think about that now. Focus on a small part—one step at a time."

She took a deep breath, once again Jem's steadying presence and firm grip clearing her panic. "Yes, I can try to countermand something small."

She stepped away from Jem, running through a few spells that she knew well. Making plants flower and new leaves grow were the type of spells they did when they were young, but they were still hard to master, as the witch was manipulating a natural cycle of growth. Now she was trying to stop growth commanded by an elemental creature.

The honeysuckle that draped the Full Moon Gate had a sweet and overpowering scent. Close up, she could actually see tendrils growing before her eyes. Focussing on them, she cast the spell most likely to work, commanding it to stop. Nothing happened. She tried another spell, one that was designed to put the plant into a winter sleep. Again, the plant continued its creeping growth. She was just about to cast another spell when the elemental figure emerged from beneath the moon gate, almost exploding under her feet.

Eliza shrieked and fell backwards, thudding into Jem, and they both tumbled to the ground.

Jacinta loomed over them, looking monstrous. There was barely any sign of her skin now. She was covered in moss, her nails were caked in earth, and her fingers resembled roots. Her shoes had vanished, and her feet looked more like claws. Her dress was in tatters, and her hair was knotted and wild. She thrust out her hand, and roots shot out of it, wrapping around Eliza's feet.

Instinctively, Eliza blasted it with fire. At the same time, Jem, struggling beneath her, fought free and dragged her backwards. The creature shrieked and the earth cracked, roots shooting out of the ground. Eliza blasted them again and again, making them shrivel and recede, her magic instinctive as she fought back.

By now, she and Jem were back on their feet, retreating to the house, but the creature kept coming.

Jem shouted, "You have to attack her!"

"I can't. It's Jacinta!"

"She's not there anymore."

His words were like a dagger to her heart. "She is! She's my sister!"

"And she's about to kill us!"

The creature seemed to loom larger, towering over them. *So much for the bright sunshine being a deterrent.* Roots and branches lashed towards them again, and with no other option, Eliza blasted the elemental backwards with wave after wave of power, sending balls of pure energy crashing into it. With an Otherworldly howl that made plants explode around them, the creature tumbled end over end into the long summer grass and vanished.

***

Ansel was in the middle of the orchard, close to the hives. Here all was calm, and the unnatural bustle that marked the rest of the garden was absent.

He approached the bees cautiously, bringing them up to date on their news, and advising them of what had happened to Jacinta. Their response gave nothing away, and he had no idea if they knew or not, or even whether they cared. Their easy connection the other day had gone. Wondering if they had done something wrong, he said, "I'm going to spend some time here. It's the most peaceful part of the garden. Is that all right?" He felt foolish for asking, but he had to honour the bees. Feeling that there was no objection, he settled himself into his next job.

The murmur of the bees was soporific, and safe within a salt circle again, he sat cross-legged, sipped his potion prepared using mandrake and wormwood, and closed his eyes. He knew all too well about what familiars were of course; they had been demonised by the Puritans and the Witch Hunters, but they were nothing to do with the devil. They were spirit advisors who came in many shapes and forms. To his knowledge, his ancestors didn't have familiars, but why should he know? No doubt they would have kept very quiet about it in more recent times, and he hadn't spoken to his uncle, aunt, or cousins for years.

Jacinta's spell book had described her endeavours, and Ansel was pretty sure he knew why she had failed. She had tried to force it. Familiars should come to you. They could not be forced to appear, or be commanded. His own experiences with the garden's creatures had demonstrated similar things. He had learned to wait. To open his mind up to higher wisdom. To accept what he could not control. And he had to relax, something his sister never did. She was always *doing*. Pushing thoughts of Jacinta aside, and wondering if he would ever see her again, he let the murmur of the bees and the soft sounds of summer fill him up.

The outside world vanished, as did any sense of time. He appealed to the Gods. *Send me help. My sister is lost, and Moonfell is under attack. I know I'm not clever enough to stop this. We're alone.*

He was swallowed by a vastness he could barely comprehend, and suddenly the edge of his self slipped away and he became part of something enormous. Amorphous presences seemed to slide past him, and he was surrounded by a magical, honey-gold colour. He felt more at peace than he had done for years, and a part of him wanted to carry this feeling forever.

The honey-gold colour receded, leaving him with a view of the orchard, but he was higher now, seeing auras of the trees and the bees and the fruit. Everything glowed, especially the bees that looked like tiny golden stars, buzzing in and out of their shimmering hives like constellations.

Shocked, he realised his body was below him, and the protective circle around him was a shimmering white light. *His protection spell.* As his consciousness reasserted itself, he realised he was not alone. A huge barn owl with amber eyes sat on the branch next to him. Majestic. Imposing. Ancient and wise. Ansel felt he was tumbling into his huge eyes until it blinked, and a deep voice resonated in his head.

"Ansel Wildblood. Finally, we meet."

Ansel's composure vanished and he stumbled over words he didn't know he could say in this state. "*You're actually here! Hello! What do you mean, finally?*"

This was his familiar? A beautiful owl?

"*We have been destined for a while, but it has been difficult to catch your attention. You block effectively—even me.*"

"*I block? Oh, when I shield from the animals. But you're not an animal, as such.*"

"*No, but nevertheless, your psychic defences are strong. That will be useful for what is to come.*"

"*You mean banishing the elemental?*"

"*Amongst other things.*"

"*Such as?*"

"*One thing at a time. I need to show you the garden. Beyond the orchard you will see the full extent of the creature's malevolence.*"

"*I can travel like this?*"

"*With me, and on your own with practice. You have skills you need to master, and much untapped potential.*"

Ansel experienced a surge of excitement at the prospect of learning magic from his familiar. "*I am very grateful for any help. Thank you. But if we're going to work together, I need your name.*"

"*Hades.*"

Twelve

Present Day

Morgana arrived at Storm Moon's long copper bar, just as Vlad, the Assistant Manager and wolf-shifter, strode through the door that led from the staff offices and kitchen.

Vlad, full name Valdemar Rasmussen, was a blond, blue-eyed giant from Denmark. He had been recently promoted to the role, and had settled in well. He had a dry sense of humour, and was calm and even-tempered compared to some of the more hot-headed shifters. When turned into his wolf, his thick fur was white-blond, and stood easily as high as Morgana's hips.

He caught her eye and grinned. "Morgana! A social call, I hope!"

"Of course! We've brought my son and cousin to meet everyone. Well, anyone who's here, of course." She turned and pointed to one of the booths against the wall where the whole coven was sitting.

He headed behind the bar to serve her, as the other bartenders were busy serving customers. "A family night out, then. I can see which one is your son. He looks a little like you—around the eyes."

She smiled, thinking it a compliment. "I've always thought they're his father's eyes."

"No, there's a bit of you there, too. It's the weight of his stare, and that's all you." He took her order, and then asked, "What have you said about us? They look worried."

He and Como were staring around the room as if the place might bite. She kept her voice low. "They've never been in a shifter bar before. They're very excited."

"They do know we're not about to shift out in the open and give them a show, right?"

"Of course." She laughed at the prospect, thinking it might make Storm Moon an even more popular venue.

Although it was Monday evening, the place was still reasonably busy, but they had missed the after-work crowd. It was now close to nine in the evening, as they had stopped to eat at a Thai food restaurant down the road first.

He passed her a glass of red wine while he pulled the pints. "Are they staying with you now? I remember you mentioning them."

"They're here for a few weeks, but then they head back to university after that to finish their degrees. Come the summer, though, they'll live with us."

Vlad smirked. He knew all about Moonfell and its effect on people. "They like it there?"

"Love it, which is good, but things are a little off right now."

"Aren't they always?"

"No! We can go months without issues. The last bit of trouble we had was all *your* fault."

"Blame Maverick, not me." He finished pouring the drinks and placed them on a tray. "I'll bring these over for you and say hi. Maverick is upstairs. Want me to call him?"

"No, not if he's busy. We just thought they should come here, especially considering my connection to the pack."

"I'll let him know. Most likely, he'll be down soon anyway to see how things are."

"How are things with him?" Maverick Hale, the pack Alpha, had a tricky time a month or so before when he discovered the truth surrounding the death of his parents. The witches had helped, and the experience had reinforced their ties to the pack.

"He's good. We have niggles with the North London Pack, of course, but nothing we can't handle."

He towered over Morgana as they walked across the room, and he placed the tray on the table and greeted the young men. Both handled themselves well, but there was no doubt they were trying very hard not to look intimidated. *Wait until they meet Maverick.*

Vlad didn't hang around, and Morgana joined the coven at the table.

Birdie reached for her gin and tonic. "I'm glad he's calling Maverick down. I want to ask him a favour." Birdie had sparkled ever since Yule, when she'd regained a few youthful years. Today, however, she looked flat and preoccupied, especially after her attempt to find Hades by scrying had failed.

"You think Maverick can find Hades," Morgana said, realising why she wanted his help.

Lam frowned. "Really? If he's not here, and he's a familiar, will he even have any scent to pick up?"

"Hades has a physical body! His scent will be all over the grounds."

"So, how does that even work?" Como asked. "I thought familiars were spirit-only."

"Some are, some are not. You've seen Hades. You know he's real!"

"To be fair," Odette said, "I understand their confusion. He's been your companion for years and hasn't aged a day."

"He's magical." Birdie looked a little tearful. "I miss him. It feels like a part of me is missing. I'm sure that bee ritual is behind it all."

"I thought I saw him this afternoon," Lam said. "I was exploring the garden after tidying up my studio, and I saw a shadow streak into the undergrowth by the pond. I ran after it, but it vanished. I guess it could have been any animal. I was just a bit overexcited, I think."

"I was hoping for a great breakthrough after reading Virginia's grimoire," Como admitted, "but so far, I haven't picked up on anything. Except the fact that I think she was a bit cuckoo."

Morgana had heard some of the excited chatter about finding the Wildblood grimoires, but in the end had been so busy with making potions, tisanes, and balms that she hadn't fully concentrated on what Odette and Como had found. The talk in the restaurant had been about Lam's studio, which he was very excited about, and background on Storm Moon and the pack.

"It was a difficult time in the 1600s," Odette said. "The Witch Trials were devastating. I would imagine that Virginia was very scared. By the time Charles II came to the throne, the atmosphere was very different." Her eyes glazed. "Can you imagine the wigs, the over-the-top dresses, silk stockings, and fanciful shirts? And buckled shoes! The divide between rich and poor would have been enormous. I ended up getting sidetracked," she admitted. "I searched for images of what they wore, and the attitudes of the court. I think, after the effects of the Puritans—did you know they banned Christmas? —that no wonder the whole country went mad with theatre, colourful clothing, and ridiculous extravagance. It must have been like living under a rock for years." She huffed. "How depressing! Thank the Gods they restored the monarchy. At least there's something to be said for a bit of life and fun!"

Morgana leaned her chin on her hand. "It's amazing, isn't it, what a change of character at the top can do. It must have felt like a breath of fresh air."

"Charles was very naughty, though," Odette said. "He had many mistresses, and I think thirteen illegitimate children. His lovers all overlapped, of course, and they all knew about each other. They were very beautiful from what I can gather, and he was also very generous to them."

"In what way?" Lam asked.

"They were given grand residences, his children were gifted dukedoms or some such, and they were provided for with a large allowance every year. He wasn't mean with them at all. His children of course weren't legitimate heirs to the monarchy, but they did quite well out of it all."

"As did his mistresses, by the sound of it," Birdie said. "And Eliza? How does she fit into all this?"

"I'm not sure yet. She was young, I think early twenties when I saw her in my visions. I suspect I saw Eliza crying over her mother's death, but that's pure supposition. She died in 1664, which would make Eliza twenty-four then. She had a younger brother and sister, Ansel and Jacinta. We've found Ansel's grimoire, but nothing of Jacinta's. There was an uncle and aunt, too, but so far we haven't found their grimoires, either. We'll keep digging, of course. Eliza's grimoire is quite big. I've started reading through it, but the language makes it hard going. I've doubled back on some things and become sidetracked with little notes. I've presumed that the earlier part of the grimoire is when she was younger, but although some of it is dated, not everything is. I've had to make leaps in my guesswork." Odette squeezed Birdie's hand. "As for how this connects to Hades, I have no idea. It might not."

"And we still have no idea how this relates to the weird, stick-doll thing, either," Como added. He shifted in his chair, fingers gripping his pint glass. "I'm not sure what I think about sleeping in there tonight."

Morgana exchanged a worried glance with Odette and Birdie. They were all concerned about that. Morgana said, "I think it's wise not to, until we know what's happening. We have lots of other rooms that you can sleep in, on either the second or first floor. Of course, if you want to move out of the tower completely..."

"Or," Lam countered, glaring at her, "I can stay in Como's room, too. Or we all do. What if whatever it is, arrives tonight as well? I like the tower. I want to stay there."

"So do I!" Como pouted like a child. "It's really cool in the Hogwarts tower. But seriously, my dreams were weird, and something actually thumped! That twig thing is real!"

Morgana suppressed a smile at the name, 'Hogwarts tower.' The resemblance hadn't struck her at all, but Como clearly had a vivid imagination. However, they couldn't ignore the fact that something had manifested there. "Birdie, is this down to new moon energy? There were a lot of spells cast last night."

"We're always casting spells! It's what we do. I scry, Odette paints magical images and sees things, and you are constantly brewing magic in the kitchen. All of that is completely normal. The house is magical. There has been a trigger."

"But it can't have been the bee ritual, because Odette saw Eliza crying before then!" Lam said.

Birdie was like a storm cloud. "Then it was something else!"

Odette straightened her shoulders. "The bees made it happen. We might not have done the ritual then, but I was setting up the area by the hives. They are responsible for me seeing Eliza. She was distraught and had gone to them for help. It was hot in her time, just like it was yesterday when we had that unexpected spring heat. We aligned for a moment."

Como snorted with disbelief. "That suggests the bees wanted you to see it for a reason. I know the bees have power, but that stretches it for me. What if it was just like at Yule, when the events overlapped?"

"Holy shit!" Odette said, mouth gaping open. "What if she did the bee ritual?"

The table fell momentarily silent as they all pondered Odette's suggestion.

"That would work," Morgana finally said. "We're connected by the same ritual."

Lam frowned. "Where did you say you found the ritual, Birdie?"

"In the library. It was in one of Caleb Masters's treatises on bees. He was a little obsessed."

Como nearly choked on his pint. "I know that name! I've seen it today! You did too, Odette."

Odette looked confused, and then she groaned. "He was in that Wildblood family tree. The details escape me now, but I think you're right."

Morgana felt a rush of excitement. "They knew about it. It would have been an almost contemporary document to them."

Birdie looked smug. "So I was right. It is the ritual."

"It's more than that." Odette ignored her grandmother's smug smile. "Something significant occurred because of it."

"Something that has affected us now," Lam agreed. "Why did they need a twig offering to some kind of deity, though?"

Before anyone could answer, the door by the bar opened, and hearing voices, Morgana looked up to see Maverick and Arlo enter the room. Spotting them, they crossed to their table, and Maverick sat next to Morgana at the end of the banquette seat, while Arlo pulled a chair over and sat at the end.

Arlo grinned, reserving his biggest smile for Odette, his ex-girlfriend. They had been at odds for years, but now seemed to be getting on again. Arlo was a charming, mixed-race shifter with dreadlocks and a lean, muscled physique. He shook the young men's hands. "Hey, guys. A Monday night visit! This is unusual!"

"But a welcome one, of course," Maverick said. "Your son and cousin?" He shook their hands as Morgana introduced them, weighing them up with his alpha stare. "Welcome to Storm Moon."

Maverick, tall, broad-shouldered, and slim-hipped, had an easy grace and a long stride. His shoulder-length, dark-blond hair had a slight wave to it, with a tousled, rockstar look that suited his well-worn jeans, black t-shirt, and boots. Maggie Milne, the DI of the paranormal team, was right. He did have a rockstar swagger. It suited him. And he was a ferocious wolf. Huge, with massive paws and a powerful jaw. When he chose to unleash the full power of his alpha stare, most people had to look away, shifters included. Morgana had experienced it, and it had taken all her magic and willpower not to cow down in front of him. *Animal magnetism* could well have been a phrase made specifically for Maverick.

Arlo, his best friend and Second in Command, was a little easier to be around, and certainly easy on the eye. "So, you two have joined the coven?" His eyes twinkled. "You have a lot to live up to if you're going to be as good as these Triple Moon lovelies."

Birdie snorted. "Triple Moon lovelies! What are you after, Arlo? Have you been on the gin already?"

"Can't I compliment my three favourite witches?"

"Do you know any others?"

"I don't need to. These three," he leaned in addressing Como and Lam, "are seriously kick-ass witches. Your mother, Lam, has saved us from death on several occasions."

Morgana laughed with a flush of pleasure. "You are, of course, exaggerating!"

"I am not. Xavier was close to death just recently. You saved his life. And mine."

"You shouldn't go falling through glass windows then, Arlo."

He winked. "It was sort of fun, at the time."

"Well, that's why we're here," Como said, "to learn from the best. You met my mother, Maverick. In Italy? Jemima."

"Oh! You're her son!" Morgana wasn't sure if she'd imagined it, but she could have sworn a flash of guilt, maybe alarm, crossed his face. It was gone in seconds, though. "She was really helpful. You don't learn magic from her?"

"Not really. Not like I will here."

For a while they chatted easily, catching up on general pack news and the boys' plans, and then Birdie said, "Actually, it's not just a social call. I have a big favour to ask."

Maverick didn't hesitate. "No problem. What do you need?"

"Hades has vanished, and I was hoping your fantastic sense of smell could help find him." She gave him the background of what had happened.

"We can come tonight, if you want. I can round up half a dozen of the pack. They'd love to explore your grounds. Me too, actually."

"At night might be tricky. The garden is unusual."

"I know all about that, and we can wait until tomorrow if you prefer, but the sooner we track, the better the outcome. *If* we can track him, of course. Hades is no ordinary cat."

Arlo nodded. "He totally freaked Hunter out, but I know he'll help, too." He cocked his head at Maverick. "Tommy, Monroe, Domino, Hunter, and us two. That should be enough. If we need reinforcements, we can ask a few others."

"It's a big garden, and I don't want us hunting alone. Let's make it eight, and then hunt two to each quarter."

Birdie didn't hesitate. "Perfect. Thank you."

Thirteen

July, 1664

Eliza had been badly scared by her encounter with the elemental creature. It was more powerful than she had realised, and to be honest, she hadn't expected it to attack her.

"I think it was trying to kill us," she said to Jem, as they cleaned up their injuries in the kitchen.

Both were scratched and bruised. The horse had run off into the grounds, and they had decided to find it later. The last thing Eliza wanted was for Jem to meet the creature on his own. She just hoped Hercules would be okay. But worse than any of that was the sight of her sister.

Jem applied a salve to his scratched arms. "Why though? Just out of spite?"

"Because I tried to countermand its magic. It only attacked when I cast a spell on the honeysuckle. It knew!"

"So it can travel very quickly across the garden using earth as a medium? Interesting."

"But why use my sister's body? Surely it doesn't need to." Eliza cupped her face in her hands, trying to block out the memory of her sister's warped form, but with her eyes closed, it was worse. "Is it somehow dragging her through the earth, too? Her lungs surely are full of soil. Did you see her hands and feet?" She sobbed, collapsing in a chair. "She's not human anymore."

"But that's magic, right? If you banished the creature, she would go back to normal." His hand rested on her shoulder with a comforting squeeze.

"Would she? I can't see it. And how can I banish it? I can't even stop its magic."

The windows were now curtained on the outside by sheets of ivy, making the house's interior as dark as night. Very soon, the garden would be lost under the chaotic growth that strangled everything. The whole place felt wrong. Even the animals seemed wilder. It was as if it was reverting to some kind of wild wood.

She gasped and sat up, blinking away her tears. "By the Goddess. That's exactly what's happening!"

Jem frowned. "What is?"

"The grounds are becoming a wild wood. It's reverting everything to its natural state. That creature will try to pull down the perimeter walls, and then work its way out from there. What if it calls upon other elementals? What if it tries to bring forth an army of them?" She stood on shaky legs. "My sister is still a witch underneath it all. Her magic still courses through her veins. Perhaps the elemental needs it."

"Surely it has enough of its own magic?"

"But it was Cinta who summoned it."

Jem finished dressing his cuts, and paid full attention now. "Because before it was trapped, unable to leave its natural state."

"Exactly. Which means it's out of its natural state now, and that's why it needs Jacinta. It doesn't change anything, though. We still need to trap it and send it back, and that will be hard considering it can move through the earth."

"But it couldn't penetrate Ansel's circle."

"No. That was sacred space." Eliza started pacing, and the sting of her injuries faded as she considered the issue. "Ansel said the orchard has not been affected. That must be because of the bees. But what is it that's so special about them?"

"Perhaps Ansel will know. Shouldn't he be back by now?" Jem asked, worried.

Eliza tried to control her fear. "He's clever. I have to trust that he'll be fine. I'm sure he's doing something important."

"What about tonight? That invitation."

"How can I go now?"

"I think you must. What if you're going to meet someone important who could change your fortunes? Not turning up could be a disaster. Plus, you said you haven't got a spell ready yet, and at night she's stronger."

"But to leave here could be a disaster, too. I might not get back in. Ansel could stay, of course. We could try and work out a way for me to get in using magic. If I go, we need to find the horse."

Jem folded his arms, his jaw clenching. "You are not going to the Playhouse alone. They're predators, and you're very pretty. Absolutely not. I'll go with you."

You're very pretty.

Was it shallow that was all she could think of? She blustered. "I'm not, and I'm a witch. I'll be perfectly fine alone."

"You're going to cast a spell on someone if they try to touch you? If you turn up alone, it will give the wrong impression. You know it will. I don't care that you'll be meeting Nell. Anything could happen."

He was right, of course. The men who crowded the theatre leered and pawed over the actresses, and their greedy eyes showed their thoughts only too well. She was about to protest regardless, but checked herself. *Of course she couldn't go alone. She was trying to build up a reputation, not sell herself.*

"All right. That's a fair argument. Are you sure you don't mind going? We have clothes to fit you. Ansel is not as broad about the shoulders, but we have other options. I can glamour both of us, so our clothes look smarter. It worked last night." However, as the snaking movement of growing ivy outside the window caught her attention, she gave a despairing laugh. "What am I thinking? The way we're going, I won't have a future."

"Of course you will! You will find a way, and I will help. We're going tonight. Let's just hope that Ansel has discovered something to help. Now, come on. Help me find Hercules, because no horse means no carriage, and I'm not walking all the way to Covent Garden."

Ansel had never experienced anything like spirit-walking before, and he wasn't sure if he wanted to again.

It felt dangerous; in fact, it *was* dangerous. If he did the wrong thing and severed the silvery cord that attached his soul to his physical body, he would die. Only Hades gave him the strength to do it.

"*Relax,*" Hades instructed. "*You did this without me, remember.*"

"*I sat on a branch above my body. This is different.*"

"*It's the same. You're just travelling further.*"

They were still in the orchard, the golden stars that were the bees traced patterns below them, but the edge of the trees was marked with a murky green line, and once they were in the main garden, Ansel saw the true effect of the elemental. It was as if a black mist had settled over the garden like a miasma. The orderly plants that he was so familiar with had been replaced by unruly growth, and as for the animals, they appeared as sparks of dark red light. He understood enough about auras to know they were angry. Bewildered.

"*What has it done?*"

"*It has called forth the garden's untamed side and unleashed it, and it's gaining momentum. Your boundary is all that contains it.*"

That was clearly marked by the shimmering light that pulsed around their grounds, and also visible, but very faint, were the shimmering lines that connected the moon gates to the house. But areas of the boundary were being tested. The light was muddy in places. The sight was awful, but also instructive, because Ansel could now clearly see the magic that encompassed the garden.

"*We need to connect to it,*" he murmured. "*Tap into the family power.*"

"*You are its power.*" Hades was shimmering next to him, his eyes like amber orbs. "*Don't forget that. You and your sister, year after year, have helped reinforce the spells. It is a well you can draw on. There it is, testing the boundary again.*"

A black shape was on the north side of the garden, much darker than the surrounding murky mist, and Ansel tried to move closer. Hades stopped him.

"*No. Keep your distance for now. It will see you on this plane, too. Until you are surer of yourself, we watch from here.*"

"*If it breaches the boundary?*"

"*It won't...yet.*" Hades was annoyingly calm.

"*Why didn't you appear to Jacinta? If you had, this wouldn't have happened!*"

"*Because she didn't call me. Besides, I was waiting for you. I am your familiar, not hers.*"

"*Why didn't another one appear?*"

"*You know why. She is young, immature. She isn't ready.*"

"*Surely that's exactly why she needs a spirit guide.*"

Hades swelled in size until he dwarfed Ansel, reminding him that an owl was a bird of prey, and not to be taken lightly. "*You think we have time to appear for everyone's whims and fancies? We are busy and cross worlds all the time. This plane is dangerous, and we don't just answer humans. There are others to consider.*"

Ansel was all too aware now of Hades's sharp, curved beak and enormous talons, and his eyes that seemed to peer into his very soul. "*Sorry. I'm scared for her. Scared for us. Look at Moonfell! Look at the house!*" He realised that he had taken Moonfell for granted, and he couldn't afford to do that anymore. "*What do I need to do?*"

"*The moon gates and the bees will give you the power you need. I will help you. You bound yourself to the bees. It should help save Jacinta. She was involved in the ritual?*"

"*With the bees? Yes. They asked me to do it. It was uncanny. Like an instruction that lodged in my head. Have you any idea why?*"

"*The bees know things that even I cannot see. Perhaps they foresaw danger and took precautions. They have been on this land for a long time. As long as the orchard has existed, and longer than the moon gates.*"

"*So they want to protect it, too.*"

"*This is their home, just as it is yours.*"

Ansel absorbed the news. The orchard was like an island in a stormy sea; it sat alone, bathed in golden light. But perhaps the orchard wouldn't sustain itself against the elemental's prolonged onslaught, either. He now understood the danger they were in. The elemental wasn't just a threat to Cinta. It was a threat to all of them.

"*Can the elemental get in the house?*"

"*No. It is too solidly constructed, and soaked in magic that it cannot breach. But like the boundary...*"

"*It could collapse under enough pressure.*" Ansel spotted his sister and Jem heading towards the horse, skittish in the area by the pond, their auras bright against the gloom. His sister's was golden like the orchard, but Jem's was a bright blue. "*The horse looks unsettled.*"

"*They were attacked. It ran off.*"

"*What?*" Ansel was horrified. "*When?*"

"*While you were in the orchard. Fear not. Your sister fought well. Unfortunately, the elemental has seen them again.*"

In seconds, the elemental's dark energy flashed from the boundary and appeared behind them, striking with lashing roots. They were totally unprepared, and the attack threw them both to the ground.

"*We have to help!*"

"*I will help. You will watch.*"

Hades flew towards them, and Ansel, despite the warning, followed him. Hades's talons raked through the air and gripped the unsuspecting creature that was focussed entirely on Eliza and Jem. He seized it by the shoulders and dropped it into the lake. Water churned, and waves exploded upwards in vast jets. The elemental erupted out of the lake, carried by the water, but Hades was ready, and he again grabbed it, dunking it into the water again.

The horse raced around the pond, screaming in terror. Even from a distance, Ansel felt its fear. While Hades kept the elemental busy, Ansel headed towards the horse, desperate to calm it. Not even sure he could do what he needed to, he landed on its back, laced his fingers through its mane, and sent soothing words and thoughts. He'd half wondered if his presence might terrify the horse even more, but fortunately, his connection held, and it calmed under Ansel's touch.

"*Don't be afraid, old friend,*" he murmured.

As if their hearts now beat as one, Ansel led the horse calmly to the stables. The scent of hay and dung was strong, but it was also comforting, and the horse settled in its own stall. It was only then, with the drama over, that Ansel gave a thought to his own safety, and envisaged his circle beneath the tree. It was as if he'd given a signal to his subconscious.

In seconds, he was back in his body.

Fourteen

Present Day

Lamorak, ridiculously he knew, felt a little wary of the shifters, and irrationally jealous.

They seemed to know his mother very well, and all of them had an easy camaraderie with the Moonfell witches. For some inexplicable reason, Lam had assumed that the three women were isolated, locked in the grand house with only each other for company, and their occasional clients.

Yule hadn't done much to change that. Only family were around, and they hadn't visited Storm Moon at all. In fact, they had barely talked about it. Of course, he knew they'd exorcised a Fallen Angel because Birdie had become younger, but even that hadn't been much discussed because of the excitement of the Yuletide spell and Sibilla's gift. Storm Moon was a shock. It was a cool and edgy bar, and bloody Maverick Hale was a force of nature. They all were.

Lam pouted, not too proud to admit that he should add *intimidated* to his list of emotions regarding the pack. And here eight of them were, all lined up on Moonfell's drive, half-naked and bristling with muscle and barely concealed aggression. Not with him, of course. Just in general.

Fuck. They were wolves.

Maverick was the consummate alpha. Commanding, hard-eyed, and dangerous. It oozed from him, and Lam could swear he saw a yellow gleam in his eye. Monroe and Tommy were enormous units, as well. Tommy was as hairy as a bloody great Yeti, and Monroe, black skin gleaming, looked like he should be a wrestling star. He also, Lam noted, flirted with his mother. Worse, she seemed to like it. Vlad was like some Nordic God, with his flashing white teeth and ice-blond hair. Arlo, also ridiculously cool with his dreads and charming smile, looked completely at home in Moonfell, and was chatting quietly with Odette. She looked livelier than he had ever seen her. And then there was Hunter. Cocky did not even come close to describing him. He was ripped, lean, and good-looking, with a sarcastic Cumbrian charm. Not that Lam was charmed at all. He was irritated. Hunter winked at him as if he knew exactly what he was thinking and grinned. And then there were the two women. Cecile had a killer physique, with legs that just went on and on. She looked at him like he was an ant. Domino was shorter, sexy, and bristling with attitude.

Yes, he was seriously intimidated. But he was also fascinated. He had never seen a shifter before—*to his knowledge, at least*—and had certainly never seen one shift. They were all poised, half naked, and brutally confident.

However, Lam, as much as he was trying, couldn't fully focus on what was going on. The strange buzzing he had experienced earlier had returned. It was as if there was a low level of noise underneath everything else. He glanced around, confused, convinced he should see *something*... In fact, he was sure the noise was intensifying around the shifters. *Was that normal?* Como, his mother, cousin, and grandmother all looked perfectly fine.

He tried to focus on the conversation, but the buzzing sound was distracting. And he could feel an owl watching him. He couldn't explain how he knew; he just did. It was somewhere in the cedar tree at the side of the house. Plus, he was aware of movement all around him. A constant scurrying that made him restless.

What the hell was the matter with him?

Maverick had always wanted to hunt in Moonfell's grounds, so searching for Hades was the perfect opportunity.

Although, he didn't want to hunt to kill. He wanted to hunt out its mysteries. However, standing on the drive where they had recently banished the demon, with barely a sliver of moon above them, he wondered if that was wise. He hadn't even shifted to his wolf, and already he sensed thousands of eyes on him, and hundreds of years of magic spreading across the garden like a spider's web.

He turned to Birdie who stood close by, hands twisting nervously together. He had never seen her worried—not like this. Worried about a spell perhaps, or banishing a demon certainly, but not this kind of vulnerability. She had been good to him, and wanting to reassure her, he said, "If he's here, we'll find him."

"I don't doubt your skills, Maverick, but something is horribly off. What worries me is that you'll either find him dead, or find evidence of something...odd, and then what do I do?"

"We'll find a way." He meant it, too. He knew he didn't need to repay Birdie and her coven for helping him a few weeks earlier, but he wanted to.

The seven pack members who were with him were all in varied states of undress, ready to shift. Vlad and Cecile had joined Arlo's original selection, and had already paired themselves up. Monroe and Tommy would hunt together, as would Hunter and Domino. Maverick was hunting with Arlo.

He was aware that Como and Lam watched them intently. He suppressed a smile. They were nervous, but excited too, clearly fascinated at being with the shifters. Maverick wondered if Como knew Maverick had slept with his mother, but he didn't seem to, and he certainly didn't detect any animosity. He'd honestly never expected to meet Jemima's son. Not that it would have changed anything. He'd have slept with her regardless. *Oh, well. Another secret among many. What was one more?*

"I'm still not sure," Morgana said to all of them, "that you should be alone out there."

Hunter shrugged. "Come on, Morgana. It knows some of us after last time. Plus, we come in peace. Doesn't that mean anything?"

"Just be careful."

"Always!"

Domino snorted. "That's bullshit!"

He gave her a lazy grin. "Good job you're with me, then. You can keep me in check. Or I can take you to the wild side."

Maverick internally rolled his eyes. Hunter and Domino's flirting was becoming unbearable; or rather, Hunter's was. He wished Domino would just let him off the hook and shag him already. There was enough sexual tension to cut with a knife.

"Perhaps," Como suggested, "we should come with you? A witch per team?"

"You'd slow us down," Arlo said kindly. "You're best waiting here. Have you got anything with Hades's scent, Birdie? It would be good to refresh our noses."

She handed over a blanket covered in cat hair. "He sleeps on this a lot."

Maverick passed it around, scenting cat and something else. He knew he was a familiar, and that meant he had a kind of spirit energy. *Could they even hunt that?* "Right. We'll split up as discussed. Start at the house, work our way out. If you find anything, howl. And if anyone finds anything unusual, summon the rest of us before you do anything!"

"The energy here has changed," Odette warned him. "It shifted during the new moon. We cast a lot of spells, especially in the orchard. Things there feel different."

Maverick nodded. "I feel it, too. Don't worry."

They had separated the garden by moon gates. West moon gate to north. North to east and so on. He and Arlo were covering the west to north area by the pond. Unwilling to wait any longer, he stripped, shifted, and loped into the darkness, Arlo at his side.

Hunter was searching the east to south quadrant with Domino, and that comprised the orchard.

Although it was tempting to rush headlong into the garden, they took their time, sweeping methodically out from the kitchen garden, even hunting through the glasshouse that was ripe with rich scents. It was easy to find Hades's trails, but they were at least twenty-four hours old. The scent reminded Hunter of his encounter with him only weeks before. The cat was uncanny, and like nothing Hunter had ever come across before.

Although Domino was Head of Security, Hunter knew the garden better after living at Moonfell for a few days the previous month. He led the way to the east moon gate and shifted back to human, and she followed suit. Tempting though it was to linger on her naked body, he kept his attention on her face. "This is the Waxing Moon Gate, roughly the edge of our quadrant. The gates are the oldest parts of the original Moonfell. They even predate the house, the witches think."

Domino, slender and athletic, was confident in her nakedness, like all shifters. "I can feel it. It has a different quality. Is Hades as old as the house?"

"Arrived in Birdie's teens. Whether he was here before is another matter. She doesn't know."

"You met him, right? You said he was odd?"

He nodded. "Yeah. Animal, but not animal. He felt so old, but I guess that's familiars, right? Ancient spirits that cross boundaries between worlds."

"So, in theory, he's just crossed again. I know Birdie said he wouldn't just go without telling her, but maybe he had an emergency."

"Like a familiars' meeting."

She smirked. "Idiot. And his body?"

"Probably resting under a hedge. You know, suspended animation."

"That sounds even more ridiculous. I presumed his body would go with him, but what the hell do I know?" She stared to the south, and the edge of the orchard. "If everything started there, that's where we should go."

"We are supposed to be logical."

"What does your gut tell you?"

"The orchard."

"Let's go, then. We can always come back here."

Hunter led the way again, nose to the ground as they tracked back and forth along the gravel paths, grateful the garden wasn't resisting him, and aware the animals were giving them a wide berth. But where the garden had been easy to navigate, the orchard was less forgiving. They seemed forever stuck on the outskirts, unable to find their way to the centre.

He shifted, crouching on haunches as he sniffed the air. "This place is messing with us."

"I agree," Domino said, shifting too. "But I scent Odette and the others that way. It's strong, and closer to the house. There must be a path."

This time, they had more success. A scythed path of grass snaked into the interior, and a trace of magic guided them. After several minutes they found the hives, silent in the darkness. Contemplative. It felt, bizarrely, like hallowed ground, and Hunter had the strongest feeling that the bees knew they were there. Not that they were afraid of him, of course. Bees did not fear wolves. Hunter found the strongest scent of Hades yet, to the rear of the hives. Domino gave a short, soft yip as she followed a trail to the south. Instead of becoming stronger the scent faded, and forced to retrace their steps, they ended up back by the hives.

The grass to the rear was barely disturbed, unlike the front where he could scent the witches, and see the remnants of their spell. Candles were still in jars, suspended beneath the trees, and incense seemed caught in the long grass. This is where Hades had watched. Hunter sat in the exact same spot, as if watching echoes of the ritual. *Where had he gone?*

Hades's tracks led them here, and yet no tracks led away. His scent strengthened the memories of their last encounter. It was like falling into a well of experience and knowledge too fathomless to comprehend.

So how could such a strong individual just vanish?

Birdie's worry had swiftly been replaced by anger. "Something has done this to him. Hades would never willingly go!"

She was trying not to shout seeing as they were all gathered in the middle of the orchard next to the silent bees, but it was hard when all she wanted to do was rage and throw things. Particularly at the hives. Half of the pack were still wolves, the other half human now. The wolves prowled the area, investigating scents, while the others talked about the endless possibilities.

"He *is* a familiar," Arlo said, as if she was old and senile, "so he can surely turn into his spirit form at any point."

Magic gathered at Birdie's fingertips. She loved Arlo like a son, but right now she wanted to strangle him. "Why won't you listen to me? He wouldn't just go! Something made him. The ritual did it, I just know it. I knew I hadn't seen him at the end of it, but I doubted myself, like an idiot. He never followed us home." She glared at the hives and then thought better of it in case the bees could tell, and instead glared at the trees.

"I think," Morgana suggested, staring at Birdie meaningfully, "that we should discuss this elsewhere. We'll disturb the bees."

Fuck the bees, Birdie thought. Instead, she nodded. "Yes, let's head down the path."

Safely gathered a short distance away, she questioned Hunter and Domino. "So, his trail headed south?"

"Came from the south," Domino corrected her. "He'd come from the lawn at the front of the house, and the south moon gate. I can tell by the way the grass is crushed which direction it was."

Birdie nodded. "I remember."

"You're sure he didn't express an opinion on the ritual?" Maverick stood, legs wide, feet planted in the earth and arms crossed, and she wished she was half her age. *Dear Goddess. He was magnificent.* She focussed on his words reluctantly.

"Yes. I didn't actually consult him on it, to be honest, but that's not unusual. I just said I had something lovely planned for the boys. I even said I'd found an old ritual, but I didn't see much of him that day. He loves being outside, and the weather was unseasonably warm."

"And still is," Tommy pointed out. "Can't yer feel it here? It's like early summer, not spring. It's cold enough to shrink me nuts in the main grounds, but over here it's bloody tropical." He gyrated his hips as if to prove it, and Birdie averted her eyes. She hadn't seen so much flesh in years.

Cecile feigned gagging, her French accent strong with disdain. "Good grief, Tommy. They're like swinging coconuts."

"And a huge palm tree, right?"

"You're comparing your dick to a palm tree?"

"You started it."

"Enough!" Maverick roared as the group tittered. "Stop swinging your tackle, Tommy. This is not one of your parties."

Tommy just grinned and winked at Birdie. "Just a bit of fun. But I'm right. It's warmer in here than out there."

Odette agreed. "I thought it was just warmer under the trees, but now that you mention it, Tommy, it does feel like more than that. It feels like remnants of my vision, actually."

"The one of Eliza?" Maverick asked.

"Yes. She was by the hives too, but it was full summer then. I could almost feel the heat."

Hunter cocked his head, eyes narrowed. "Can your visions leave aftereffects?"

"Not normally. Not in a physical capacity, anyway."

Como had been silent up until now, like Lam, both looking overwhelmed in the presence of shifters, but now he said, "So, this one has left an actual trace behind. An echo of summer. That must be significant."

The others chattered excitedly, all the shifters now back in human form, but Birdie wasn't listening. The word *echo* resonated with her. *Had the ritual been an echo of one cast before? Or more likely, had it resonated somehow across the years with one cast before?* In theory, that shouldn't be possible. They cast spells all the time that had been used before, the Yuletide protection spell one excellent example. Good spells were used time and time again without consequences—except for perfecting them, of course. *Was that it? Had she perfected it? Or did it resonate for a completely different reason?*

Morgana's hand on her arm made her focus again, as she asked, "Birdie, are you all right?"

"No. Er, yes, sorry. I have an idea." And then she had another thought. "Maverick, while you're here, can I ask another favour?"

"Of course."

"A strange twig doll appeared in Como's room. It looks old, and we have no idea how it arrived, but now I'm certain that it's connected to Hades's disappearance. Perhaps you could scent it, maybe see if it came from the garden?"

His eyes gleamed with excitement. "Of course."

Fifteen

July, 1664

Eliza was not happy at having to go to The King's Playhouse again. Under any other circumstances it would have been fine, but with the garden suffering under some kind of enchantment, it was the worst possible time. And yet, she couldn't refuse the offer.

Even the unexpected news that Ansel had found Hades, his familiar, had offered her little comfort. That was another reason for not leaving. She had endless questions that had been barely addressed that evening. Ansel had arrived back late, and she was already bathing for the theatre. She would worry about that later.

The Playhouse was full once more. They had timed their arrival for the end of the show, intending to blend in with the crowd and soak up the atmosphere again. She felt on edge, brittle even, as if one wrong word would shatter her. It was so raucous after the silence of Moonfell, and the conversations were shallow and bawdy. She tried to keep the look of distaste from her face, and was incredibly grateful that Jem was with her.

"God's breath," he murmured. "This place is filled with all manner of nightmares."

"You don't like it?"

"I don't like the way the women eye me as if I'm meat, and the men watch you the same way. I can't believe you thought to come here alone."

"It's just people having fun," she reminded him, as much as herself. "It's harmless. A way of letting off steam. We keep ourselves too locked away."

"I'm in the public house plenty in the village. It's nothing like this. But you're right. They're people just like us, trying to get by, and by the look of some of them, they have a hard enough life. It's not for me, though." He nodded as a line of men passed, dressed in the finest silks, linen, and lace, strutting like peacocks, their elaborate wigs curled and perfumed. "Maybe I should adopt that look." He lifted his head and stared down his nose at her. "Do I look suitably haughty?"

She giggled. "Yes, but it doesn't suit you."

"It will if I keep practicing. Your hand, my lady." He extended the crook of his elbow, and she slid her hand in place, trying not to flush at Jem's close proximity.

She wasn't naïve to the ways of men and women. At 24 years old, she'd shared a few secret kisses with the baker's son when she was younger, and they fumbled in the barn when he visited the house once with a delivery, murmuring sweet promises in her ear, but then he had promptly married a young seamstress, and that had been the end of that. She wasn't sorry. She would never have married him. She wasn't sure she would marry anyone. Being the sole mistress of Moonfell seemed far more fun. And yet, Jem had a way of looking at her. Perhaps she should do as these women did. Find a rich lover who would save Moonfell with his money. She eyed the dandies as they walked, finding fault in all of them. *Too foppish. Too aloof. Too ugly. Too fat. Too vain. A sneer of disdain that spoke of cruelty.* No. She'd have none of these. It was love or nothing. The women weren't much better. Their faces were painted, eyes calculating as they scanned the crowd. False laughter rang loudly. However, there were some true beauties in the crowd, too. She must stop judging if she was to provide a service for any of these people.

The public house was busy. Men played dice, jeered, and teased each other, beer was slopped on the floor, and the tables and chairs were rudimentary, but the actors and actresses from the theatre and their admirers were all in another room, the one they had frequented the night before. She nudged Jem to follow the dandies and couples down the corridor.

"It's quite a warren," Jem noted as he entered the next room that was far better furnished but just as busy.

With drinks in hand, they circulated, nodding politely, aware they were being watched and assessed. She greeted several people with a nod, recognising them from the night before. Everyone watched each other, but there was genuine pleasure there, too. Even more than the previous evening, she felt everyone's relief at being able to enjoy themselves without censure, and no doubt this had been the case for the last few years that they had been locked away, with only the occasional visit to the poor.

When Nell eventually arrived, she and Jem had relaxed considerably, cheered by wine, although Eliza only allowed herself very little. It was the drink of choice as soon as Charles II ascended the throne, but women of a certain class rarely drank—in public, at least. Here, it didn't seem to matter in the slightest. Nell arrived at her side in a cloud of perfume and kissed her cheek. Her dress was extravagant, and Eliza realised what she had missed the night before. Nell clearly already had a wealthy and influential lover.

"You made it, then," Nell said in greeting. "I wasn't sure my note would give you enough warning." She eyed Jem. "This isn't your brother."

Eliza introduced him as a friend, unwilling to tell her about his role in their house.

Nell lowered her voice, although with all the noise it was hardly necessary. "It seems a few of my acquaintances have heard of your mother. Wildblood is not a common name. They've heard of Moonfell, too."

"Well, I suppose such a large house gains attention." Suddenly tense, and feeling as if all eyes were on her, Eliza asked, "Is that a problem?"

"You living in a great big 'ouse? I should think not. That place has a reputation. An even bigger one since no one outside your family has been there for years. The minute you left last night, a few people started to ask questions." She adopted a sing-song posh voice. "Were you *that* Eliza Wildblood? Where is Virginia? Was the house really as unusual as everyone said?" She sniggered. "My girl, if you think you have been forgotten, you are clearly mistaken."

"But I have contacted people—"

Nell cut her off. "The wrong people. There are others who have heard the name 'Wildblood' whispered at ailing bedsides and recommended to women with *problems*. I saw your house once. The high walls, the broad trees, the shadowed drive, a glimpse of a tower. All very mysterious. They," she nodded to the people around them who now seemed to be showing more than a passing interest in their conversation, "will always want to be associated with someone who lives in a place like that, with reputations such as yours. I must admit, I had no idea until last night that the Wildbloods had been as influential in the upper classes. But why would I know, living in a place such as I do, with my mother running a whorehouse?"

"Eliza hasn't got a reputation," Jem said, interrupting. "You're exaggerating."

"It's all right." She tapped his arm, giving it a squeeze as she did so. "They're just whispers. Everyone knows the value of keeping some things quiet."

"We keep to ourselves, for obvious reasons." Eliza's jaw clenched, and she now wondered if she had done the stupidest thing ever by coming here. But this was what she had wanted. *Reputations, though, could kill.*

"Well, you shouldn't keep to yourself anymore. You need to come here more, go to other theatres. Make friends. Invite them to tea. Cultivate rich female friendships." Nell winked. "You, like me, are a survivor. We have to use the gifts given to us. Who would have thought that I should be onstage after my upbringing?" She leaned closer. "I wasn't content with being just an Orange Girl, and neither will I be content with being just an actress. God gave me wit, beauty, and grace for a reason."

Eliza needed Nell's spirit, and she threw her shoulders back and lifted her chin. "You're right, Nell. You're braver than I."

"It ain't bravery. It's survival. You look pale. Smile, my love. Villiers is here tonight. He wants an introduction."

Jem gasped. "The king's friend!"

"My friend, too." She glanced across the room. "There he is. Come on—and smile!"

Villiers was a robust-looking man with calculating eyes, somewhere in his thirties, so several years older than Nell and Eliza. He was dressed in the finest clothes, and it was clear he admired Nell. He gripped Eliza's hand and brought it to his lips with a flourish. Jem's reception was polite but distant. "My dear Eliza. I had no idea when I saw you last night that you were from Moonfell."

Heart pounding, Eliza plastered a smile on her face. "Why should you? We are not important enough to garner attention."

"And yet Moonfell draws attention whether it wants to or not. So many rumours abound about it. Or did. I quite honestly thought it empty now because I heard so little of its occupants, and yet, here you are." His eyes glittered with intrigue. "You may not know, but I was brought up in Charles I's household. It is why I know the king so well. Your grandmother, Annabelle I believe her name was, performed many services years ago for several women of the court. Their ladies' maids, too. Discreetly, of course. I was of course much younger then and privy to the chatter of the ladies who visited. They ignored young boys running around. With her daughter, too. Virginia?" Eliza nodded, and his eyes shone with amusement as if he knew all about the services he spoke of. "I never met them, of course. I trust they are well?"

"I'm sorry to say that my mother died several months ago, and my grandmother died years ago. I have only a faint memory of her."

"My condolences. Nell here suggests you are looking to continue the family business?"

"That's correct. My mother and grandmother taught me many herbal remedies."

Nell interrupted. "Her healing skills are excellent, Charlie."

He smiled. "Fascinating. I'm sure there are many who would be grateful for your help. Not all like to use doctors. They do bore one so with talk of humours and leeches. The king, however, is a great advocate of science. He granted a Royal Charter to the Royal Society a couple of years ago. He is most keen to extend scientific knowledge. He may not be so enamoured of herbs."

He said it so disdainfully that Eliza retorted, "And yet herbal remedies have been around for thousands of years. Mr Culpepper published his book with extensive research on the use of herbs. I have a copy and consult it regularly."

"Do you? You can read?"

Eliza had been looking forward to meeting Villiers, and yet now, all she wanted to do was slap him. *Maybe hex him*. However, if she made a good impression, she might be introduced to his numerous, wealthy friends. "Yes, I can read and write. It is essential if I am to record my remedies and note the needs of my patients. I make sure to keep up to date with all advances in medicine, although I may not agree with all of them."

"Madam, you are most refreshing. May I be permitted to call upon you one day? With Nell, of course."

Eliza gathered her wits that had scattered at the suggestion. "Of course. Although, we are having some minor work done right now. As soon as it's complete, I will be delighted to entertain you at Moonfell."

If she could even get inside the grounds once she arrived home.

Ansel was in the spell room in the tower, the windows open to catch the slight breeze, lanterns and witch-lights illuminating the grimoires and jars of dried herbs. The place was chaotic, as if Eliza had rummaged through everything whilst investigating the spells and ingredients earlier.

He was finally back in his body, and very pleased to see that Hades had also taken physical form, and was twice the size of a normal Barn Owl. He was perched on the windowsill, hooded eyes grim, preternaturally still as he watched Ansel try to organise Eliza's notes, and they continued to converse by thought alone. Well, Hades did. Ansel spoke aloud.

"It looks as if she has started to formulate a spell that will reverse the one Cinta used. It's convoluted, though. Messy."

"She will refine it, I'm sure."

"But we need it now, and it's not ready."

"Neither are you. You need better preparation to tackle the elemental creature. It is strong and grows stronger the longer it is here. Especially now it has begun to manipulate the garden."

"Begun to? It already has full control, surely." Ansel stuck his head out of the window. "Look at it. It's wild and unkempt, and I'm not ashamed to admit that I don't want to walk in it anymore. I feel it will swallow me up. I can't see the entry gate from here, but I dread to think what it will look like!"

"Whether you want to or not, we must help Eliza get back in. Only together can you fight the elemental."

"I know." He was already marshalling spells for protection and attack, and of course, he had Hades. "Are you the guardian of the Underworld?"

Hades laughed, his beak opening to reveal its sharpness. *"Nothing so grand."*

"So why the grand name?"

"It amuses me. Besides, you couldn't possibly pronounce my real name. I wouldn't want you to, either. Names have power. Just know that it is long and old."

"Does that mean you're old?"

"It depends on your definition. My life, such as it can be called as I am spirit, has lasted millennia."

Ansel felt dizzy at the prospect, and staring into Hades's large, unblinking eyes, he felt insubstantial. "Then I must be very honoured to have you here. Why me?" Then another question formed. "You said we had been destined for a while. Since when?"

"*Why you? Because I sensed something in you, and I have worked with others in your lineage over the years.*"

"You have?"

"*Centuries ago. And not just your family, of course. There have been many others. To answer your second question, it would be months ago in your measurement of time that I needed to contact you, but as I said, you block effectively.*"

"So, you contacted me to do what?"

"*To deepen your magical knowledge. To learn spirit-walking, for example. You do it naturally. It is like your ability to hear animals. Some witches are naturally gifted. Jacinta's abilities lie elsewhere. However, this conversation is not helping her.*"

"I'm just curious," Ansell said, feeling frustrated. "I'm trying to understand it all, and I can't."

"*You will, in time. Now we have more urgent things to focus on.*"

"Can you help us banish the elemental?"

Hades stared over the garden, gimlet-eyed. "*I can, but it will be hard, and I cannot guarantee your sister will survive. The creature has dug deep, like the roots of a mountain. It will not go easily.*"

"You mentioned the power of names earlier. Will it have one?"

"*Of course, but learning it will be hard.*"

"But can we? Can you? If we discover it and use it as a command in a spell, then surely we can banish it more easily."

"*Perhaps, but I have other suggestions. We need to craft a doll to bind it, and it has unfortunate ingredients…*"

Sixteen

Present Day

Maverick recoiled as he sniffed the twig figure. "That is no ordinary wood."

"Isn't it?" Birdie asked, alarmed. "Why not?"

"It stinks of pain."

"Pain!" Lamorak snorted. "What the hell kind of comment is that?"

Maverick was easy going—up to a point. Being challenged by a cocky young man certainly pushed his boundaries. Out of respect for Morgana, he restricted his response. "Pain has a scent that I am very familiar with. Have even been responsible for, on occasions." His eyes kindled with an orange flame and Lamorak stepped back. It was clear that Lamorak had a problem with the Storm Moon Pack. He was both defiant and wary, and it was an odd combination that came from feeling threatened by their presence and needing to exert his own masculinity. He would get over it.

Odette said, "Shifters have an excellent sense of smell, Lam, and as paranormal creatures with almost super-sensory perception, they detect layers of meaning. Much as I do, sometimes."

"What do you detect?" Arlo asked her.

"Strangely, I feel nothing. That in itself is ominous." She folded her arms as if trying to shield herself from it. "I touched it when we found it yesterday, and it was like touching a void."

"You didn't tell me!" Birdie said, annoyed.

"I've been trying to work out why, and I can't. Plus, I've been distracted by searching grimoires!"

They were all in the Moonfell's huge kitchen, some seated at the table, others lounging around the fire. The shifters were semi-clothed, ready to shift again, and Morgana had supplied them with drinks. The temperature had dropped outside, and the scent of snow was in the air. *Except for in the orchard.* Maverick would think about that later.

The twig doll looked fragile, as if it would break into pieces at the slightest touch, the wood tinged with grey. But it was as hard as nails. "I can't feel a void, but however it was obtained came at a cost."

Hunter leaned against the counter, coffee in hand, watching the exchange with interest. "Did a spell make it appear in Como's bathtub?"

"We don't know," Birdie admitted.

"I just heard a thump," Como said. "It woke me up. I'd been having strange dreams about being chased through a wood or a garden. Moonfell, perhaps."

"We are yet to understand what it means," Odette explained. "We haven't had time."

"But I think it's an offering, rather than a poppet," Birdie said. "I cannot feel any type of binding on it, so I find it curious you speak of pain, Maverick. A binding would cause pain."

"Many things will cause pain." He sniffed the twig doll again, closing his eyes this time, as he tried to fall into the scent it produced. Something else was there. His eyes flew open, searching out the keenest nose in the room. *His Head of Security.* "Domino, what do you make of this?" He led them inside the glasshouse for quiet and privacy.

"It's creepy," she admitted. "It looks like it might come to life at any moment."

"A bit fanciful for you."

"That's Moonfell. I'm used to hunting at night. Love it, in fact, as we all do, but the magic in these grounds gives it an added layer of mystery." Her eyes gleamed in the low light. "I thought anything might appear. A gnome, or an imp. Is that madness?"

He laughed. "Yes. But the feeling that I was being watched by hundreds of things was...interesting. So, what about that?"

Domino closed her eyes and buried her face in the twig doll. "I sense pain, too. Anger, even. And a very faint trace of Hades."

He grinned. "It's an old scent, though, right? As if it's been in a box for years gathering dust and must."

"Yes! That's exactly what it smells like! Do you think it has been in a box?"

"Maybe, but where?"

"If we can track the scent, we might find out. We'd have to follow the scent of pain, though." Domino shook her head, dark hair falling over her face as she bent over the twig doll. "How odd does that sound?"

"It makes life interesting. You didn't detect anything on your travels earlier?"

"No. But we headed to the orchard before covering all of our quadrant, and then we summoned you."

Maverick considered their options. He and Arlo had more ground to cover too, and no doubt so did the others. "I wonder if there's a spell to enhance the scent."

Odette had grave doubts about trying to enhance the scent of something they knew little about, but Birdie was desperate, and she had to admit that she was curious.

"Let's place it in the trap in the spell room," Birdie said to her and Morgana.

"No." Odette knew that was wrong. "We use the garden. That's where all this is happening."

"It appeared in Como's room. Maybe we should try there," Morgana suggested.

The twig poppet may be a void to Odette, but she was sure of where the spell should be cast. "No. I feel it. If you're worried, we'll set up in the devil's trap that's still on the drive."

Morgana groaned. "Do we have to?"

"It's spelled with all sorts of protection. It will save time."

"Bad memories?" Como asked sympathetically.

"Very," Morgana answered dryly, leaving much unsaid.

Vlad, the blond, blue-eyed Dane, asked, "Can we watch? I'd like to see more Moonfell magic."

Tommy laughed. "I can tell you weren't with us last time, right Monroe?"

"Be careful what you wish for, Vlad."

Vlad gave him the finger. "I saw what happened in the carpark! Besides, the witches wouldn't do it if it wasn't safe, right?"

Odette lied. "Of course not. We must if we're to find out more about it. It's related to Hades's disappearance, Como's dream, and maybe it's about Eliza, too. The spell might even help me gain greater insight into it."

Birdie was holding the poppet now, chewing on her lower lip as she studied it. "I felt so sure it was an offering rather than a poppet, but now I'm not sure *at all* after hearing Maverick's news."

"Why did you think that?" Maverick asked.

She shrugged. "First impressions. It's far bigger than a poppet normally is, and a poppet is usually solid. Either a cloth doll, or a clay image that you can put pins in or bind with string or ribbon, or sew a binding into, of course. Whereas an offering to a deity can be crafted using natural objects such as twigs, flowers, or moss. Of course, the type of wood used can also offer another layer of magic. Importantly, there's no evidence of a binding here. Nothing around what I presume is the head, or the limbs. It's very unusual. My other thought was that it was nothing to do with witchcraft at all, and that it's just an old garden ornament. A decoration that was placed on a bench or a wall. A seasonal decoration, perhaps. That, however, seems nonsensical. Why has it manifested if it's not magical in the slightest?" She huffed. "So annoying. But you detecting pain..." She shot Maverick a perplexed look. "Well, that changes everything. You're sure it's not Hades that's in pain?"

Maverick's eyes softened. "As sure as I can be, but it is faint, even to me and Domino, and no offense to my pack, but she has the best nose on the team."

Odette took the poppet. "Let's see what secrets it holds."

In fifteen minutes' time they had gathered on the drive, the cold night feeling all too reminiscent of the events only a few weeks earlier. The unseasonable warmth had vanished, and typical March weather had returned. There was a distinct nip to the air, and her coven, new members included, were well wrapped up in coats. Most of the shifters were in their wolf. The coven had chatted about their spell options, discussing whether they could combine a finding spell with one to magnify the scent, but in the end decided against it, fearing the combination might have unintended consequences. If they needed to cast more spells later, they could.

Hades's absence was now weighing on all of them. He was a familiar part of the garden, and even though he wasn't Odette's familiar, she could normally detect his presence close by. He was part of the fabric of Moonfell. The word 'fabric' struck Odette as being very apt. The whole place was shaped by time and circumstance, choices made by their ancestors and whoever had owned the land before, the warp and weft of their decisions the backdrop to their existence. This current mystery was one layer of many.

Standing once again on the edge of the double-circled pentacle, candles marking the perimeter and the five-pointed star, she had another of her startling epiphanies. As if fine sheets of tracing paper were layered over each other, she suddenly saw images of the garden—old plants, new plants, trees as saplings, hedges before they were topiaries, sheds that weren't there anymore, benches that had moved, and the unchanging moon gates. Shadowy figures walked the paths, and she saw four seasons race across the garden like a sudden storm—snow, leaf fall, spring bulbs, and the heavy, full flowers of summer.

And there she was.

Standing on the garden path, hands clenched, face creased with fury, the garden around her as wild as a tropical jungle, was Eliza. Her hair and her long skirts flapped in a vicious wind, and lightning forked overhead. The heat struck Odette like a blow, and she staggered back, feeling strong arms wrap around her, a broad chest at her back, and warm breath on her cheek.

Arlo's voice, as smooth and sweet as honey, said, "I've got you."

She sagged against him, feeling like she'd returned home. *By the Goddess, how she'd missed him.* However, her stumble and his touch shattered her vision, and the garden, very much in the present, took shape in front of her. "*No!*" She reached forward. "Come back!"

But Eliza had gone.

Odette turned, still supported by Arlo, and she reached up to cup his face. "Thank you. I'm okay." She saw the rest of the group watching her, eyes wide, especially Como and Lam. The wolves lifted their muzzles, sniffing and growling, as if something bad was in the garden, but nothing untoward was. In fact, the garden welcomed her back, like an old, comfortable cloak settling around her shoulders. "I'm okay, honest. Just a very strong vision. It was incredible."

Birdie hurried forward, concern etched across her face, and she took her hands. "You feel cold. You need tea and chocolate."

"No, I'm fine, honestly. It was actually quite beautiful." She was aware that Arlo's arms were still around her, and gently stepped free of him, feeling horribly cold without him close. "I was thinking about how this place is shaped by what's happened in the past. It's like fabric, the warp and weft making the pattern we see now, but it tripped a vision. I saw images of past gardens layered over each other, and then I saw Eliza. Right over there." She pointed to the gravel path that led from the drive to the house. "The garden was wild. Like a jungle. And it was so hot. There was a storm. Everything was so intense!" She took a breath again, steadying herself, and she reached into her coat pocket for the sweets she often carried. "I feel energised. We're on the right track."

Lam had been staring down the path, but now he asked, "Did she see you?"

"No. It was a flashback. She didn't know I was there."

"Any clues about the poppet?" Maverick asked. "Did you see it?"

"No, but I had a side view of Eliza, and it was hard to see her hands. There was no one else in sight. The garden was abnormally overgrown."

Domino stepped closer, hand gentle on her arm, a yellow gleam kindling deep within her eyes. "Sorry, this will be weird." She leaned in and sniffed along Odette's neck and collar. "Petrichor."

It was a word used to describe the earthy smell associated with rain. "You can smell the rain? The storm?"

Domino nodded. "Strong vision."

Now Odette was keener than ever to cast the spell on the poppet. *If Domino could smell that, what more could they find?*

Giacomo took his place around the trap, reassured that they would not be summoning any demons, and stood on the sign for Air on the pentagram, thinking his place in the coven was meant to be. *Five witches, five points.* Lam stood on Fire, Morgana on Earth, Birdie at Water, and Odette on Spirit. The doll lay in the centre of the space, while the wolves ringed the circle.

They hadn't set up an altar. Birdie would lead them. She, Morgana, and Odette carried their wooden staves decorated with arcane symbols. Como felt the weight of responsibility settling on his shoulders. He had a role to play, and he needed to do it right, especially with the shifters watching.

"This will be simple," Birdie instructed, now settled in High Priestess-mode. "This is just to magnify the scent. As soon as we're sure nothing malignant is happening, I will break the circle so the shifters can get closer. Okay, Maverick?"

He nodded. "Perfect."

Maverick was not what Como had expected. He'd thought he would be an enormous, muscle-bound chauvinist who liked to boss people around, and while he was undoubtedly muscular, he wasn't as big as Monroe or Tommy. Instead, he exuded a quiet confidence. His pack were deferential, but not cowed. They questioned, but only once. Plus, Domino, the hot, dark-haired shifter, was his female Head of Security. *Interesting.* Maverick even listened to the witches, including Lam, who was bristling with annoyance. Como hid a smirk. Lam always tended to exude superiority. He could not get away with that here.

Como decided he liked Maverick. Admired him, even. All of them, in fact. Storm Moon would likely become his regular haunt, and he couldn't wait to see the bands they booked. Como looked away as Maverick stepped out of his jeans and shifted to his wolf to join his pack.

Birdie started the spell. As Morgana and Odette reiterated the words, he and Lam did too, lending his power to theirs, and with a thrill, felt their power magnify. Birdie directed it all at the twig poppet and issued a word of command. They fell silent as a hazy light appeared around it; Birdie extended her hand as if calling the scent forth. A dark, greenish-black cloud formed and drifted higher, and Como inhaled as the wolves lifted their noses, a couple whining and pawing at the ground. They must be able to scent something, even with the poppet still inside the protective circle.

Suddenly, one of the twig poppet's slender branches twitched, then another and another. In seconds, shoots erupted from its legs and arms, and it jerked upright and ran across the circle. Como stayed put with the greatest effort as the weird, twisted doll struck the protective circle and bounced back. It set off again around the circle like a headless chicken, blind and dumb, hit the boundary, and fell back again. It was horrible to watch, even though it was just twigs. It seemed so alive. Then the fresh green shoots multiplied.

Birdie didn't hesitate. She uttered words Como didn't understand in what sounded like middle-English. Something guttural and commanding. The fresh green shoots shrivelled and died, and the poppet collapsed instantly.

Lam spoke first. "What the fuck was that?"

"The source of all pain," Birdie said ominously, cutting the protective circle with her athame and letting the green miasma out.

The wolves gathered around it, inspecting it from all angles, and sniffing cautiously. Maverick, easily identifiable by his size, howled, eliciting a chorus of responses, and the wolves divided into pairs and scattered across the garden.

Seventeen

July, 1664

Eliza travelled back to Moonfell on the seat of the carriage with Jem, rather than in the carriage itself, talking about their meeting with Nell and Villiers.

She was hopeful and fearful all at the same time, curious as to what gossip abounded about Moonfell, and how much was rumour opposed to truth. *All of it, probably.* At least she hoped so. She gazed upon Moonfell's walls with gratitude. Home. Safety.

Or it had been, until now.

Thick strands of ivy wound about the wrought iron gates that were rarely locked, shifting and writhing as if they were infested with rats. *Perhaps they were.*

"'sblood!" Jem said, swearing. "This is a fiddle-faddle. We'll never get through that."

"Yes, we will!" Eliza stood on the seat, shoulders thrown back, glad the road their entrance was on was a distance from the village and that no one was around. She was so annoyed that she ceased to care what Jem would think, and blasted it with fire balls, one after another, her fury growing as the writhing mass seemed to just shake them off.

"Save your magic!" Jem laid a hand on her arm. "You know that won't work."

"It made me feel better."

"Really? Because you look furious."

She turned on him. "This is our home, and look at it now! That damnable creature has made it a nightmare!"

He reached for an axe under the seat. "We came prepared, remember? Summon Ansel like you agreed."

Sulkily, she said, "I doubt the axe will work, either."

"It might now that you've imbued it with magic." He tutted. "Come on, Eliza. You could well have another meeting with Villiers in a few days, and need to save your sister. Those should be motivation enough."

Jacinta. Eliza imagined her cavorting in that horrible way in the garden, covered in earth and moss, like a half-rotted doll. She extended her hand into the air and shot sparks high over the wall. Ansel should be watching from the highest tower for her signal. Perhaps he and the mysterious Hades would have a solution.

"What do you think of Hades?" she asked Jem, watching him shrug off his coat and loosen his shirt before swinging his axe to limber up.

"I don't know what to think. He seems as unnerving as the elemental. Are you sure we can trust him?"

"No, but he helped earlier. He picked the creature up!" The memory of the elemental creature landing in the pond was still fresh in her mind. It had brought them enough time to race to the stables and secure the horse, and then she had placed a myriad of protection spells around it. "I think I may bring Hercules into the house tonight and take him into the inner courtyard. I'm not leaving him in the stables. Not now. He'll be terrified." He was already shuffling nervously and pawing at the ground. "Maybe I should have brought the cows in, too. What if the growth that has accelerated the garden does the same to them?"

"Then it would do the same to all the other animals too, and there's no evidence of that. It's just the plants."

Slightly reassured, she assessed the gate, wishing they had brought a ladder with them. At least then they could have clambered over the wall. Or perhaps lodged the horse in the village with a friend. That, however, seemed defeatist. Something must affect the plants. If fire didn't, maybe freezing them would work. Or maybe Jem had the right idea with the axe. She could cast a spell to cut like a knife.

She paced, impatient with herself, and urging Ansel to hurry. She had spent time that afternoon thinking about several spells that may help, but the evening with Villiers had distracted her. Her thoughts were scattered, and the so-called rumours circled like a murmuration of ravens in her head.

Focus.

As soon as he saw the cloud of orange sparks over the gate, Ansel headed outside, while Hades exited through the tower window.

The intervening hours had not been kind to the garden. Ivy hung like ropes around the house and snaked across the grounds. Weeds proliferated in garden beds, hedges were twice the height they should have been, and flowers had run rampant. The scent of roses and lavender was almost overpowering. Beneath all of it was the thick scent of earth, so dense that it infiltrated the house. The humidity had soared too, and even at night a fine sweat beaded his brow. The animals were what affected him most, though. He sensed their distress and confusion at the arrival of the elemental. It might have been a natural spirit, but it wasn't where it should be, and it had inhabited a beloved resident of Moonfell.

"Is it close?" he asked Hades as he swooped overhead.

"No. It is testing the boundaries to the east. It still has not affected the orchard yet."

"Then if we're cut off from the house, we head there. It will be our refuge." He hoped the honey-infused potion he had brewed that evening would be as effective on larger plants as the small test was earlier. It had taken hours to brew the recipe, and he only had enough for the gate area, so his trial was small. His reasoning was that the bees must be responsible for the orchard, so maybe their honey would repel the growth. Hades had agreed.

Scanning the way ahead, he found the drive was still the easiest way to get to the gate. The lawn they let grow during the summer for the cows had also doubled in height, and he couldn't even see the cows now. Fortunately, the drive was not long, although edged with thick shrubs it provided plenty of cover for the creature. *No time to worry about that now.*

Hades landed on an outer windowsill. "I will distract the elemental as I did earlier. You focus on the gate."

Tucking the pots safely into his pack, Ansel sprinted down the drive, leaping over clusters of roots and thick limbs of ivy, and ducking beneath overhanging branches. His witch-lights bobbed overhead, and rather than illuminating his way, they caused long shadows to dog every footstep.

Suddenly, the elemental creature reared up in front of him, and roots tangling around his feet, he fell over. Jacinta was now unrecognisable. Her hair was matted, and her nails were long claws. Even her eyes blazed with an unnatural light. But Hades was already there, and screeching, he plucked the elemental up and carried it away. It fought Hades too, trying to bind his wings with whipping branches, and he fought back by snapping at them with his razor-sharp beak. Ansel had to trust he could cope, and hacking at the roots with a knife, he ran for the gate again.

He heard repetitive, dull thuds and swearing coming from the other side. "Eliza! Are you there?"

"Yes!" Her voice sounded muffled. "Are you all right?"

"Not really, but I have a plan." He grasped the thick, fibrous ivy and pulled himself up, slashing the branches back as they snaked around his wrists. When he reached the top, he peered over. Jem was hacking at the ivy, trying to free the gate so they could pull it open, but as fast as he hacked, the ivy grew back. Eliza looked up at him, mouth agape. "You made it!"

"With help. Brute force seems to work better than spells at the moment."

"Really?" Jem looked up at him, wiping sweat from his eyes. "Not here it isn't!"

"Admittedly, it doesn't last for long!" He reached into his pack and extracted a bottle of the potion. "It's not as much as I wanted, but it should be enough to free the gates. I have a bottle for both of us. Are you ready to catch it?"

Eliza held her skirts out, and he threw it and an accompanying charm written on paper wrapped around a brush down to her.

"What's in it?" she asked, looking at the golden liquid.

"Honey, amongst other things. I'll tell you later. I'll tackle this side. You need to daub it over all the growth, especially the thickest branches, and say the charm."

"But what does it do?"

"It shrivels the growth—but not for long. We have to be quick!"

The ivy was in danger of smothering him, so working quickly, he untangled himself and dropped to the ground. He could still hear Hades screeching as he fought the elemental creature.

Using a coarse brush of badger hair, he painted the potion on to the thick, gnarled stems and leaves, chanting the spell as he worked. They blackened and shrank back as if burnt, and buoyed by his success, he quickened his pace. In a few minutes, the sound of Jem's axe became louder and louder, and there was a break in the greenery through which he saw Eliza's pale face. In another few minutes, he was able to pull one of the gates back, and Eliza pushed the other side open. Jem, already on the carriage, urged the horse into the grounds.

With a hiss and a slither, the ivy tried to escape onto the lane, and as anxious as he'd been to open the gate, Ansel now closed it just as quickly. The shrieks and curses of the elemental drew closer, and Ansel and Eliza heaved the gates shut together.

"Get in, now!" Jem shouted.

But the carriage wheels were already wrapped in thick vines.

"It's too late," Ansel instructed. "Leave the carriage here, and ride to the house."

Eliza started to protest, but Jem agreed, already freeing the horse of the harness. "He's right. I can ride with you, Eliza. What about you, Ansel?"

"I'll run."

Eliza's attention was now on the garden. "Look at it! It's so much worse!"

Exasperated, Ansel said, "The house, now! There's no time to waste."

Jem pulled Eliza up behind him, and they raced up the drive. As the thick ivy wrapped around the gates again, Ansel knew there would be no way out again. If they didn't defeat the elemental creature, Moonfell would become their mausoleum.

Eighteen

Present Day

Morgana stepped inside the circle, avoiding the murky green miasma that still hung in the air, and examined the twisted twig figure. Her skin crawled at the unnatural sight.

"Holy shit," Lam said, next to her. "It actually came to life. It's like something out of a horror film."

"Is it possessed?" Como asked, sounding impressed more than horrified.

Ignoring both of them, she crouched, Birdie and Odette at her side, all keeping a safe distance, and prodded it with her staff. "Well, whatever you said worked, Birdie. I didn't catch the command, though."

"It's a spell I've used before and found a long time ago. Before you were born." Birdie's attention, like hers, was fully on the poppet.

"It's useful against natural objects that appear possessed. It's harsh. I essentially destroyed the living wood."

"*Non ci credo*!" Como muttered. "I was right!"

"Is he?" Morgana sat on the ground, ignoring the cold stone, and looked at Birdie. "Are you sure?"

"Probably a poor choice of word. I don't understand what this is." Birdie smiled at Como. "I understand your reasoning, though."

"I might feel it," Odette said, prodding the poppet with her staff, too. "If I touched it again, I might not experience the feeling of a void this time."

"No!" Birdie's voice was sharp. "Not yet."

"What did you mean," Morgana asked, "when you said it was the source of all pain?"

"Living wood grows as we expect. It roots, it grows in the spring, rests in the winter, and seeks sunlight, water, and nutrients. But it doesn't become animated. It doesn't run around! I think this was once something else. Something older, darker..." She looked around at the garden, her expression bleak. "I think something very bad happened here, years ago."

"Do you think Hades was involved?"

"Why else has he vanished?"

Morgana exchanged a worried glance with Odette. "Then it must mean the effects of this are still ongoing, somehow."

Birdie shook her head. "Not necessarily. This is an echo, perhaps. Just like what you suggested happened in the orchard, Odette." She sat back, like Morgana, on the drive. "This is so frustrating. I'm going to scry again, but I'll use these twigs to help guide me."

"Bloody hell!" Odette said. "That's just as dangerous as me touching it!"

"Not true! I will see, not experience."

"Sometimes that is just as powerful," Morgana reminded her.

"Set the circle again," Odette instructed. "I'm going to touch it and see what happens, and then I'm going to settle at one of the moon gates. Either south or east, because they're closest to the orchard. It's poor logic, I know, but there's so little to go on!"

Lam interjected, "What about the scent you pulled out of it? It's still there! The scent of pain! I don't know about you guys, but that's horribly ominous. What the fuck does that mean?"

Morgana huffed at him. "Don't swear at your great-grandmother!"

"I wasn't swearing at *her*! I'm swearing at the situation. You three might be used to all of this, but to me, this is seriously fucked up. Twig dolls should not run around like we're in a cartoon! It should not manifest out of thin air in Como's bedroom, and it should not be in pain!"

Despite the situation, Morgana smiled. "You're quite right on all those things, but there are deeper mysteries in this world. Things we still don't understand fully. Things we might never understand. But we need to try. Witchcraft is a journey of discovery, but we walk that path respectfully."

"What has that to do with pain?"

"Well, trees and plants are living things, and they experience pain. Scientific research suggests such a thing. They obviously feel on a level we cannot detect. It could be the same for this. I don't know why it's presenting so strongly, though. Unless…" she hesitated, unwilling to voice the idea that had just occurred to her.

Birdie levelled her gaze at her, a knowing deep within her eyes. "I think we're thinking the same thing, my dear. Go on."

Morgana swallowed as goose bumps rose across her skin. "I think it's an elemental spirit. An earth spirit, somehow made into form and substance."

Birdie nodded, gaze settling on the twigs, her slender fingers grazing her bottom lip. "Yes. An elemental creature that found its way here.

Giacomo, do me a favour and go and collect a large jar from the stillroom—something with a stopper. We are going to capture *that*." She nodded towards the miasma.

"We should seal this in something, too," Morgana said, hoping it wasn't about to leap into a parody of life again.

Odette had inched towards the twigs, face scrunched with concentration as she examined it. "There's a sticky substance on this. Particularly the parts scorched with your spell, Birdie. By the Gods! I think it's blood."

"Blood magic?" Lam asked.

Morgana shook her head, confused. "Why didn't we see it earlier? It would have coated the twigs. Neither did we detect magic at all."

Birdie groaned. "Because it comes from the twigs themselves. That's the only explanation."

Morgana could barely believe what she was hearing. "You think the twigs contained blood? That doesn't make sense!"

Birdie gripped Morgana's wrist with surprisingly strong fingers. "It isn't natural, Morgana. This is an abomination, and someone made it happen. Enhancing the scent has somehow...activated it. Even if only briefly."

"As much as I hate to say it," Odette admitted, "that *thing* came from this garden, and we need to find its source. I just hope the wolves are having success. But we need to understand it, too. You said, Morgana, that witchcraft is about exploration. I need to explore this, and you two know it, too. I'll be okay. Let's face it, nothing might happen."

Morgana felt they were stepping into something dark and dangerous, but Odette was right. The path they were now on couldn't just be sidestepped. They had to follow it. The garden that had always seemed so welcoming, a place she knew every inch of, now seemed threatening as shadows stretched and lengthened towards them as the candles flickered in the breeze.

Birdie squeezed Morgana's wrist, whether as a warning or a comfort she wasn't sure, and then releasing her hold, she nodded reluctantly. "All right, Odette. When Como returns, we seal the circle, and you try it. But we remain here together. I want to be close to you."

Odette nodded. "Thank you."

But there was no joy or relief in her response, only a grim acceptance of the task that lay ahead.

***

Odette sat on a blanket on the ground, the twisted limbs of the poppet within reach, and took some deep, calming breaths. Birdie and Morgana flanked each side, while the boys sat opposite.

This was turning into a big night for them, a night no one had anticipated, but they couldn't delay. The situation was becoming more bizarre by the moment. Not that Lam or Como looked worried. They looked excited. So was she, if she was honest. This was so unusual.

"I'm ready," she announced. "Don't rush to rescue me if anything happens, even if I faint."

"Don't tell me what to do, missy," Birdie said caustically. "If you faint, I'm hauling it away from you. Now be careful!"

Ignoring her grandmother, Odette turned to Morgana. "Make her wait!"

Before anyone could object further, she reached forward and clasped the poppet.

Immediately her surroundings vanished, and she rushed headlong into a vast, dark pit. She was suffocating. Earth was packed in around her, and she could feel it up her nostrils and down her throat. If she screamed it would fill her lungs. It pressed against her skin and eyes, and she feared she'd never see sunshine again.

No. Not her own. Whatever was attached to the poppit was enduring this horror.

Forcing herself to be calm, Odette separated herself from the situation, trying to maintain some sense of rationality. *It's not me. Not me.*

Beyond the suffocating feeling, there was something else. Something ancient and unfathomable. And it wasn't afraid of the earth. It welcomed it. As Odette's breathing steadied, she revelled in the joy of her surroundings. It's cool comfort. The mix of decay and burgeoning life, the cool scent of stones that were the ancient bones of the earth, and its dark beauty. With the knowledge came a certain freedom.

The constriction of earth vanished, and Odette ran through wild greenery. Thick roots, whipping branches, unfurling leaves, and the sense of controlled chaos. And glee. A destructive, malevolent glee.

There was shouting and yelling coming from some distance away, and despite her efforts to see who was responsible, it was impossible. With aching limbs, she continued to race, slipping easily between earth and greenery, root and branches, and every now and again, she experienced a flash of fear.

Her cavorting ended abruptly as icy bands encompassed her, and Odette found herself back in her own mind again, the poppet inert in her hands.

"What happened?" Morgana asked, twisting to look at Odette's face.

She took a moment to compose herself, breathing in the sharp, cold, fresh air of the spring night. "I was alive, sort of, as something else. A creature with limbs and thoughts and emotions. I can't quite work it out, but I think you're both right." She turned to Birdie. "I was in its consciousness, and it liked the earth, was comfortable with it, and seemed to command growth. I need to filter out the range of things I was feeling, but essentially, it was ancient. I think it was an elemental creature, and I'm pretty sure it was here in this garden." She described her vision.

"An elemental *earth* creature," Birdie corrected. "Someone must have summoned it. Did you see or feel Hades?"

"I'm sorry, no. However, I do think someone was trying to control the creature." She'd also felt fear, and Odette was sure it wasn't the elemental's, but she wanted to work out what that was about before she shared her thoughts.

Maverick was used to the scent of fear, either his own or his pack's as they faced something terrifying like the demon, but scenting pain was unusual—in these circumstances, at least.

He had killed animals before—for food, not pleasure. He tried to do it quickly, but as his jaws clenched tight around his victim, or ripped cleanly through a tender throat, there was always a flare of pain, no matter how short-lived. He'd sensed it as an adult, and as a young teen he'd scented his parents' pain that had resonated around their dead bodies. It was sharp and ugly, and horribly sad, as well.

This pain reeked of being trapped, of panic, and mixed in with it all was anger and destruction.

Arlo paced a short distance away, zigzagging across the grounds like Maverick, nose down mostly, hunting trails in the earth. Occasionally Maverick lifted his muzzle to scent the air, but quickly returned to the earth again. Cold stone, green plants, bulbs, the scent of badger, insects, cat. They hunted a long time, until they reached water. He paused overlooking the large pond, scenting frogs and mud. He loped along its edges, heading for the summerhouse, and immediately sensed the strange miasma.

He yipped, drawing Arlo to him, who growled as soon as he reached his side. They focussed on the immediate area where the scent was more pungent, and eventually found a patch of soft earth, looking as if it had been recently disturbed. He shifted to human, as did his Second in Command.

"It's the same scent, right?"

Arlo nodded. "Want to dig?

"I suppose we should. Perhaps summon the witches first?"

"You know," Arlo looked over his shoulder, eyes narrowing, "I thought we'd find this by a moon gate. They're like sentinels for this place. They certainly act as anchor points for the house's magic. That's what Odette told me, anyway."

The west moon gate, its twisted bronze ribbons contorted in the darkness, was a short distance away. "There might be something there, too, for all we know." Maverick crouched, brushing his hand across the earth. The disturbance was slight, and positioned behind a tree it would have been hard to spot. The summerhouse was a short distance away. "Why here?"

"It must have significance. At least the garden isn't blocking us." Arlo's lips curled in wry amusement. "Maybe that means it approves. It can send you in circles, you know."

"So I gather. Did you explore here much when you were with Odette?"

"With her, yes, but rarely alone. It was usually in the day, too. It was good to be out in my wolf in daylight. A rare treat."

Maverick understood that. Because they lived in central London, they couldn't shift in the day, even in the large grounds of Richmond Park. There were too many visitors and staff. "Perhaps now that the witches know us better..."

"And you've got over your hatred of them," Arlo reminded him, eyebrow cocked.

"That too. Perhaps they will let us shift here. Not hunt as such, just be in our wolf in the daylight. I'd like that. I'll ask Birdie later. Unless you want to ask Odette? It hasn't escaped me how close you two seem to be."

Arlo laughed. "Now who's hunting something else? Just friends, Mav."

Maverick didn't push it, instead staring at the disturbed earth again. He'd been putting it off, but couldn't anymore. "You better call the others."

Arlo shifted to his wolf and howled.

It took a good ten minutes for everyone to arrive, and Maverick and Arlo used the time to explore the area, searching around plants, tree roots, the pond edge, and even the summerhouse.

When the rest arrived, Maverick shifted back to human and showed them the disturbed earth. "There's nothing else here. Just this." His eyes narrowed as he noted Odette's pallor. "Odette? Are you okay?"

"I touched the poppet. We're all now sure that it's an elemental creature of earth. A spirit that found form. I *was* it, for a brief moment."

"What did you sense?" Arlo asked.

"Many things. I'll tell you later." She looked around at the gathered wolves. "Did anyone else scent anything like this?"

They all shook their heads, taking turns to sniff what Maverick had found.

Domino shifted to her human shape. "I agree, Maverick. It's the same as the poppet. We found nothing in our area. Are you going to dig?"

He shrugged and looked at Birdie. "I'd like to. What do you think?"

"Can you scent Hades?"

"No." Her face fell, and he wished he had better news. "We'll keep searching the garden, though. I can keep going for hours yet. I'm sure the others can, too."

His pack nodded in agreement, and he knew they were relishing the chance to further explore Moonfell.

Birdie nodded. "Thank you. Let's see what that holds, first. Just be careful."

Maverick didn't need to dig for long. He and Arlo proceeded carefully in their wolf, nosing through the earth and raking it back until it was high behind them. With every pawful they moved, the scent became stronger, until a robust metal box was exposed.

Feelings of intense pain, anger, and terror hit him like a blow, and both wolves fell back, howling their shock to the stars.

Nineteen

July, 1664

Their home and garden looked so much worse than Eliza expected, and despair swept through her once she finally started to recover from the nightmare race to the house.

Hercules was now safely in the inner courtyard with a bale of hay, and she, Jem, Ansel, and Hades were gathered around the wooden table in the kitchen, all looking ghoulish in the candlelight. The rustling of the ivy outside made it hard to concentrate, and she felt as if a veil of shadows had been thrown over the house.

"You know," she said, thoughts scattered, "we should make a proper herb storage area in the next room. Move the scullery. That way we don't need to keep going up to the tower room."

"You're thinking about re-arranging the house now?" Jem asked, wide-eyed, his collar loose, and his jacket over the back of the chair.

"I'm thinking that I want everything to hand, right here! The spell room can be repurposed. In addition, if I am to receive guests for appointments, I need a room that's respectable."

"Again," Ansel said, shooting Jem an incredulous look, "we have a few problems to overcome first."

"And we will! I'm just planning ahead. I know there are other things to address first. I refuse to think that this elemental creature cannot be beaten!"

Jem leaned his head on his hand, the other cupping a glass of their homemade ale. "You're avoiding the issue."

"Just for a while. It all seems so huge!" Hades, a spectral owl that flickered in and out of her vision with the candlelight, was sitting on the deep stone windowsill, and he fixed his large, round eyes on her and blinked slowly. He was spectacularly unnerving. "Can he hear me?"

Ansel nodded. "Every word."

Now that her heart rate was returning to normal, her thoughts finally marshalling themselves into some sort of coherent whole, she saw how dirty and scratched Ansel was. Soil was under his fingernails and smeared across his face, his shirt was torn, his hair was raked in all directions, and scratches ran up his forearms. "You look terrible."

"Have you seen your hair? You don't look much better."

A glance at her reflection in the window showed he was right. Her hair had fallen from its pins and tumbled down her back, thick ringlets tangled with twigs. *How had that happened?* She wanted to go to bed, sleep for hours, and pretend none of this was happening. But she couldn't. She was Moonfell's High Priestess.

She drew herself upright, took a large sip of wine, and straightened her shoulders. "Right. We have work to do. Tell me about Hades."

"He's my familiar."

"Something I don't know!"

Ansel smirked. Eliza was on the backfoot, which was most unusual, and she could tell he was enjoying it. "I decided to do what Jacinta was doing, but I knew I could do it better. You know Cinta. She has no patience. I set up in the orchard, the quietest, most protected space, and emptied my mind."

"So easy for you." Her turn to smirk.

Other than a glare, he continued unperturbed. "He was there within minutes. I spirit-walked. We travelled over the grounds together."

"Yes, yes. You told me earlier. He rescued us from the elemental." Realising she sounded churlish, she nodded at the owl. "Thank you, and for tonight, too, of course. But where has Hades come from?"

"The spirit world. He doesn't have an address."

"You are being very trying."

"So are you."

"Ansel!"

He shrugged, eyes dancing with mischief. "He's my familiar. He's been trying to get through for a while, but because I block out the animals, I blocked him, too. When I opened my mind, there he was!" He smiled at Hades. "I feel we are already old friends."

Eliza had so many questions that she wasn't sure where to begin, but she knew most of them could wait. "Can he help us rescue Cinta?"

"He thinks so, but it will be hard. We both came up with the honey spell."

Jem leaned between them. "It was effective. What made you think of that?"

"The orchard," Ansel explained, "is untouched by all this madness. I saw it when I spirit-walked. It remains an island of golden light in the midst of this murky greenness. I don't know why, or how. Hades seems to think that the ritual we did will offer some protection to Cinta."

"Our bee binding?" Eliza asked.

"Yes. Cinta's bloodline binds her to the house, but Hades thinks the spell binds us to bees too, and they have been on the land for a long time. We all know bees have their own power."

"It would be helpful," Eliza said, exhaustion making her sarcastic, "if they would just swarm the elemental and drive it back where it came from. Can they?"

"I suspect they would have done so already if they could," Jem said. "They certainly haven't shown the slightest inclination to do so now."

"What if we provoke them?" Jem asked.

"Absolutely not," Eliza said, aghast. "Such a thing would have terrible consequences."

"Aren't we experiencing terrible consequences already?"

Eliza slapped the table so hard it stung her palms. "We never provoke the bees."

Jem held his hands up in surrender. "Just a suggestion."

"You should know that. You tend the garden."

"Desperate times, Eliza."

"Not that desperate." She turned to Ansel. "Tell me more about the honey spell. Can we make more of it?"

"Of course. We have jars of it in the pantry, and plenty of ingredients, but it doesn't affect the elemental. We need its name, and..." he hesitated, shooting Hades a nervous glance. "Are you sure?" Hades nodded and Ansel exhaled. "We need pieces of the creature."

Eliza recoiled. "*Body parts*? You know it's Cinta!"

"The roots and branches that it uses like whips? That's not her."

"We don't know that."

"Regardless, we need them. Hades says that to send it back where it came from, we must fashion a poppet. We must bind it, and then drag it from Cinta like the parasite it is."

"Will she survive?"

Ansel swallowed, but he didn't break eye contact with her. "We don't know."

"And how exactly are we to take bits of it? It's more likely to take bits of *us*!"

"We have to try."

"How?"

"We lure it out with something it wants."

"Which is?"

"Freedom."

Incredulous, Eliza asked, "How do we offer that?"

"We create a break in the boundary."

"By ending our protection spells? That's risky."

He pinched his finger and thumb together. "Just a small section."

"Even trickier! Those spells have been there for a long time, and they are connected everywhere! To the moon gates, the house, us! If we break them, putting them back will not be a quick affair. They are complicated spells. No. I hate that idea!"

Ansel shot Hades an impatient look. "I told you she wouldn't like it!" He turned back to her, persistent. "In its place, we put a trap, hidden in the earth. It steps on it and can't move."

"But that means having a break in it so it can enter. You've seen how quickly it moves. Sealing the break behind it will be hard."

"Unless it erupts under it." Ansel's eyes gleamed with excitement.

"What's to stop it from leaving the same way?" She sagged back in the chair, realising how physically and mentally exhausted she was. "It won't work. It's an elemental and can move in too many ways. Hades must know that."

Silence fell, the rustling ivy sounding like rats in the walls, and Eliza had the paranoid impression that it was actually listening to their conversation. *Could it?* She dismissed the thought, fearing she was going mad. She needed to sleep, but was worried she would wake up to find that the elemental was too strong, and that the ivy had broken into the house and was trying to smother her.

Then she had an idea. "We need to work with elemental correspondences. You were on the right track, Ansel."

"I was?"

"In what way?" Jem asked.

"When Ansel said that we use daylight and sunshine against the elemental."

Ansel huffed. "But I was wrong. It's as strong then as now."

"No, it's not. It's still strong, and still dangerous, but not *as* strong. Earth, Air, Fire and Water are all balanced, normally. Right now, Earth is out of balance. We need to bring Fire, Water, and Air back to balance." She stood, suddenly full of nervous energy. "Feather and incense for Air, Water is itself, obviously, and flames for Fire. Trying to ground myself with Earth is a mistake. Somehow, we need to use the other elements against it."

"But," Jem argued, "there is no way that you could make the other elements as strong. No way! You would be consumed by it. So would all of us! Surely the elements don't battle each other. They complement each other."

"Plus, even if you do," Ansel said, "it brings us back to the same issue. We need parts of it. I will use myself as bait. When it attacks me, you must then attack it. Jem is best with the axe. Just don't hack bits of me off!"

Jem nodded. "Which means I must make my swings accurate, because when I start, it will flee."

Eliza had been only half listening, mulling over their options with the correspondences. "We must utilise the garden. It is already arranged on compass points, the moon gates aligning with them. No wonder the elemental spends so much time in the north. It is associated with earth, the new moon, and midnight. Fiddle-faddle. And it appeared with the new moon too, or at least close. Its opposite is fire in the south."

"Summer and noon!" Ansel added.

"Exactly. Those will be part of Moonfell's spells."

Jem looked between them. "So, the plan is to use the south moon gate at noon. We were there only today. That's where she attacked!"

"We were there later. It doesn't matter anyway. I will work spells there to strengthen it, and as I said, use symbols of the other elements."

Ansel had fallen silent, head cocked, but now he said, "Hades will offer up some feathers. They will have extra power. He is spirit, too."

"But he's not actually there," Eliza pointed out. "I can only see him as some shadowy half-creature."

As if to prove her wrong, three beautiful, tawny feathers materialised out of thin air, and floated down to the table. Ansel picked them up with a flourish. "You said?"

They were magnificent, and as real as any feather she realised, when she took them from him. Soft and silky smooth, yet full of magic. "Thank you, Hades. It won't hurt you to use them?"

"He says no. They must be part of the binding spell, in the poppet that we fashion. As for the spell, that is something we both should work on."

"In that case," Eliza declared, "let's sleep, and hope we wake refreshed. And hope there is a house left for us to wake in."

Twenty

Present Day

Fear lanced through Lamorak, as the bloodcurdling howls of Maverick and Arlo were continued by the pack.

The noise around the large hole by the pond was so visceral that he felt it through to his bones. Their feelings were strong enough that he felt them, too, and could suddenly differentiate between every single wolf, all displaying varying degrees of shock and surprise. Maverick's emotions were particularly powerful, overriding his pack's.

Commanded by an emotion he couldn't understand, Lam reached out mentally, urging calm, and trying to soothe. He directed it at Maverick, knowing he would convey it to the others. Lam laughed at himself, incredulous in the midst of it all. *What was he doing? As if he could influence a pack of wolves.*

He darted forward, far quicker than the other witches, and reached into the earth to see what the issue was. He suspected a body, and didn't want his mother to see that, and certainly not Birdie.

Morgana shouted, "Lam, stop!"

"It's okay! It's a box." The metal glinted under the damp, rich earth, and he tentatively brushed the dirt off it. It was tarnished, but the witch-light overhead revealed runes and sigils etched into it. "I think it's spelled. I'll dig it up."

Como landed next to him, lying on his stomach, while Morgana and Birdie loomed overhead. Odette was checking on the wolves.

"I'm worried about you touching it," Morgana said.

"Well, unless you can levitate it out," he replied sarcastically, "I'll have to! Besides, I've already brushed dirt off it."

She snapped back. "I meant use a spade!"

He twisted to look up at her. "I'll be fine."

Como snorted, voice low in his ear. "You heard the wolves, right?"

Lam ignored all of them and completed clearing the dirt to reveal a box that was larger than he first thought. About the size of a boot box. Roots were wrapped around one end of it, and he moved them using magic. Finally, he was able to grip it properly and pulled it free, placing it on the ground next to him while he regained his balance. Immediately, Birdie and Morgana bent to examine it.

"Fuck!" Maverick said forcefully. "That's a small box to pack such a punch. And *you* have some explaining to do."

Shocked, Lam found Maverick looming over him, his *junk* far too close for comfort, and looking very intimidating in his stupidly buff nakedness. The other shifters changed back to their human shape and stared at him too.

Lam knew exactly what Maverick was talking about, and he stood up. "You heard me."

"Yes, I fucking heard you. How?"

"I don't know. Seriously," he stressed, as Maverick's eyes narrowed, and their feral yellow gleam kindled like a flame. He stepped back. He couldn't help himself. "Your howl triggered something in me." He struggled to explain. "I could distinguish between every single one of you. You weren't scared, but you were shocked, and you felt a kindred sorrow for the pain. I felt it in here." He thumped his chest. "Right to my core. It was this huge flash of insight. I swear, I didn't do it on purpose. I responded instinctively. I couldn't help it."

Maverick tapped his head. "You were in here, like you had a megaphone."

Arlo nodded, shoulder to shoulder with Maverick. "I felt it, too."

Odette intervened. "What's going on?"

As the shock of finding the box wore off, and his anger rose at Maverick's attitude, Lam's thoughts cleared, and with a jolt, he realised he could feel the owl watching him again. With crystal clarity he homed in on it, sitting high in the branches of a willow on the far side of the pond. It was shrouded in darkness, yet Lam stared at it, feeling its curiosity. *I can't help it*, he said in his thoughts, feeling helpless. *I don't know how I'm doing this.*

The owl didn't move, it just watched him, as if waiting for something, and for mere seconds, Lam saw himself through its eyes. He swayed, dizzy.

"Lam?" Odette said, stepping in front of him. "What are you looking at?"

"The owl over there in the tree."

Hunter snorted. "How can you see that? I can barely make it out."

"I can *feel* it. That's what led me to it." He turned to see Hunter looking amused. "What's so funny?"

"You are, mate. You look like you've seen a ghost. I heard you, too, you know. But only in my wolf."

Lam was aware of a growing silence as Birdie, Como, and his mother suddenly became aware of the conversation. But the buzzing noise he'd been hearing on and off all day intensified, and he realised it was the scurrying of insects. *Holy shit.* "I can't feel your emotions now, if that helps."

"And now?"

Hunter abruptly shifted to his wolf, and shockingly large, looked at Lam, eyes dancing with amusement. The bastard was laughing at him. Lam could *feel* his mirth. But he could also feel his curiosity, his danger, and he was willing Lam to deny it.

"Yes! I'm glad this is amusing you! And no, I won't deny it!"

Hunter shifted again, and his laugh broke the mood. "Fookin' hell. He can read animal minds. I'll call you Doc D from now on!"

Morgana gasped. "Lam? Is it true?"

"Yes, maybe. Minds no, emotions yes. *Fuck*! I don't know!"

Birdie took charge, the metal box cradled in her arms. "Back to the house, now. All of us!"

Birdie had a lot to deal with, and she wasn't sure if she was enjoying having so much to process and organise, or whether it was just really annoying.

Most people were now in the large green lounge on the ground floor that overlooked the east terrace. The group was scattered around the room, either singly or in clusters, spread across the enormous, squashy sofas and armchairs. The fire was blazing, the lamps were lit, and they all had drinks. Mainly alcohol. By the Goddess, what a few hours it had been.

This is life, Birdie! she reminded herself. Better than languishing in her rooms, bent double with arthritis and half blind with cataracts. *Although, more normality would be appreciated.* A missing Hades, two young witches with more enthusiasm than sense, a spelled twig doll, a suspected elemental spirit, a buried metal box, a brooding alpha, and an amused bunch of shifters left a lot to sort out. *At least they were all dressed now.* She'd found it hard to concentrate with so much flesh on display. Earlier she'd caught Como ogling Domino and Cecile, and fearing for his safety—and furious at his lack of respect for the women—had given him a stern glare that only made him smirk. *Men!* Fortunately, they had both been amused, although Cecile whispered something in his ear that made Como stutter, turn red, and promptly walk away.

Birdie exchanged a rueful glance with Cecile now, and topped up her glass of wine. "I'm so sorry about Como earlier. You would have thought he'd never seen a naked woman before. To be fair, all that skin is distracting, even to an old lady like me."

Cecile smirked with typical French aplomb. "It's okay. I'm hot, he's a man, and he'll get over it. It's the wild wolf that some men want to challenge."

"That and your pert breasts. What did you say to him earlier?"

She leaned close to Birdie's ear. "I told him the pulse in his throat called to me like a mouse calls a cat. And then I sniffed him. I think he got the point. Either that or I gave him a boner." She grinned revealing white even teeth and two prominent canines, and then headed to the chaise longue in front of the windows, draping herself over it.

Birdie had taken a liking to Cecile after the days she'd spent in the house a few weeks before. She may be aloof, but she was also amusing, loyal, and hardworking. No doubt maintaining her place in a male-dominated pack would be tricky. Right now, however, what concerned Birdie more than Como's wandering eye, or even the metal box, was Lam. He sat apart from the others, deep in thought. Morgana, sensibly, was giving him space, and was in the kitchen with Monroe preparing snacks. It seemed his spell the previous night in which he had asked for more magic was already bearing fruit, and the unusual ability to communicate with animals was now blossoming; Lam didn't look too happy about it. Maverick certainly didn't. He eyed Lam suspiciously, as if he was eavesdropping on his thoughts all the time. At least the other shifters seemed more amused than annoyed, thanks to Hunter. He and Tommy were joking about it right now.

Hunter said, "I wouldn't want to know what was in your head! It'd be all food, sex, and destruction."

"Yer a cheeky shite," Tommy shot back. "I quote poetry to myself in quiet moments. 'I wandered lonely as a cloud, that floats on high o'er vales and hills!' Proper stuff. He'd learn a thing or two off me."

Hunter snorted. "You are so full of shit. Did you read that on a beer mat?"

Cecile interjected. "It is nothing compared to French verse. Baudelaire was a genius. *Pour n'être pas les esclaves martyrisés du Temps, enivrez-vous; enivrez-vous sans cesse! De vin, de poésie ou de vertu, à votre guise.*"

"Which means what?" Tommy asked.

Cecile raised her glass. "Time to get drunk! Don't be martyred slaves of Time, Get drunk! Stay drunk! On wine, virtue, poetry, whatever!"

Tommy smirked. "I can drink to that, but it's not Wordsworth!"

Birdie was glad of their humour, and ignoring their continuing banter, decided it was time to examine the metal box. It was on the side table next to a chair that looked out of the long run of doors to the garden. "Lam," she called to him softly, not wishing to disturb the others. "Shall we open it?"

As if summoned from a trance, he blinked, nodded, and pulled a chair next to her. It was a large room and they were away from the others, so she decided to keep it that way. Odette was talking to Arlo, and she let her be. Lam needed her.

Birdie smiled at him, remembering how it felt to be so sure of yourself one minute and then doubt so much the next. "I thought we'd do this together. You dug it out, after all."

"Maverick found it."

"Of course, but you grabbed it fearlessly."

"I was a bit bull-headed. I just wanted to get it done."

"You're so like your mother. That bodes well."

"It does?"

"Of course. She's the next High Priestess of Moonfell. It needs a bold leader." He gaped at her. "You didn't know?"

"No!"

"The house has spoken, and it chose well. Well, it didn't speak as such, but you know what I mean."

"I think so. That's cool, I guess."

"It's an honour. How's your head?"

"Fine. Now, at least. When I go outside it's not so good. I think it's getting worse." He stared anywhere rather than at her.

"More acute?"

"Yes."

"There are ways to control it. We'll have a long chat tomorrow. Don't worry!"

"I'm not sure Maverick will forgive me."

"Of course he will. It was just a shock. Plus, he's the alpha. He's probably got all sorts of secrets tucked up there. No wonder he's worried."

"I can't read minds!"

"I'll reinforce that to him. Although, he heard your voice. From the little I admittedly know about this, I believe that is unusual. Perhaps it was the urgency of the situation."

His serious gaze, so like Morgana's, settled on her. "I did honestly just want them to calm down."

"Personally, I find this very exciting, because I have never known a witch in our family with these abilities. You should be excited, too. Now. Let's tackle this first." She lifted the box onto her knees, giving it a gentle shake. Nothing rattled inside.

"You're not going to put it in a circle?"

"No. I've examined it, and it will be fine. Sometimes you can overthink things. I aim not to be ridiculously jumpy in my old age. You proved that by just getting on with it. Not always to be advised, of course…"

"And if you're wrong, and the elemental jumps out?"

"You better get ready to run!" She laughed, trying to bolster her own mood. "Right, let's check these runes first. Do you recognise them?"

"No. I don't know them at all."

"These are Elder Futhark runes, used for writing, magic, and divination, and were first designed by Northern Germanic tribes two thousand years ago. This one that looks like a trident is called *Algiz*. It means elk, and represents protection and defence, acting as a sort of shield. It also offers a connection to the Gods. This next one is interesting. It is called *Eihwaz*."

"Like a cock-eyed 'Z.'"

"Yes. It means yew tree and stands for perseverance, personal power, and endurance." A weight settled on Birdie's shoulders. "They must have struggled to contain this creature. It would have been a battle of strength, and perhaps wit. This one that looks like an 'M' is *Ehwaz*. It's commonly used on talismans because it denotes magical protection. And this last one is *Teiwaz*."

"The arrow."

"Yes. Tyr is the Sky God. He is a warrior, associated with leadership, balance, and victory. And," she added reluctantly, "self-sacrifice. Of course, it could mean sacrificing many things. Freedom, choice, comfort, or even your life."

"So, not necessarily bad?"

"Not always. They are placed around the one in the centre, and this one," she said, glancing at Lam to find him watching her intently, "is what I think describes what they faced. The 'H' denotes *Hagalaz*. It means hail or stone, and is associated with uncontrolled forces, disruption, and the wrath of nature."

His pupils dilated as his breathing quickened. "That sounds pretty scary."

"It does, doesn't it?" Birdie sipped her tea, a soothing blend. She had wanted to keep a clear head for opening the box.

"And the weird sigil?" He tapped the front side of the box, just under the clasp.

Birdie traced the shape with her fingers, double checking she had deciphered them correctly. "The 'X' is *Gebo*. Gift. It is associated with oaths, generosity, and family. It is laid over *Perthro*. A vessel or cup. It denotes truths, secrets, and change. The final symbol, 'O,' means *Othala*. Property, but it can also denote ancestral homeland and spiritual journeys. I don't know why, but it feels like loss to me."

"As in death?"

"Maybe. Of course, these are the most basic interpretations. More in-depth meanings could be there. I think we know enough for now, though."

Mouth suddenly dry, Birdie sipped her tea again. This quiet time of reflection and analysis was exactly what she needed. A moment of calm in the madness of the last twenty-four hours.

Odette's voice broke her thoughts. "You started without us." She stood, arms crossed over her chest, a line between her brows.

"Just taking a moment with Lam, as you did." Arlo did more for Odette's mood and mental balance than she might care to admit. "How are you?"

"Fine. How's the box?"

"Interesting." The shifters had fallen silent, and Birdie realised that Como, Morgana, and Monroe had returned too, and all were watching her and Lam. She stood up, reconsidering her earlier intentions. "Let's open it outside."

Pulling a thick cardigan around her shoulders, Birdie stepped onto the terrace and placed the box on the wrought iron table as Morgana turned the terrace lights on. The harsh light made the damage of time all too obvious. Rust edged the lid and clasp, and she used magic when she struggled with the catch. It seemed they all held a collective breath when, using a word of command, she flipped the lid open, and it crashed against the table with a clatter.

No one flinched, much to their credit, and nothing untoward emerged. There were no rushing spirits or the twisted limbs of twig dolls.

Inside was a bundle of dark, oiled cloth.

Twenty-One

July, 1664

It was mid-morning by the time Ansel felt even remotely ready for the coming battle, and it would be a battle, there was no doubt about that.

He, Eliza, and Jem had woken early, refreshed and eager to get to work. The first thing they had done was secure a way out of the house, using the three elements to counter earth. That alone had taken an hour to work successfully, but finally the front door—the quickest way to the south moon gate—was complete. Sigils for the three elements, woven with spells, had been etched into the frame, and a perpetual flame burned safely on the threshold. It was a gentle spell, designed not to arouse the creature's anger. It was the first lasting success they had experienced controlling the growth, and it buoyed their spirits.

Ansel had then used spirit-walking to fly over the house and gardens, and found the elemental once more in the north, attempting to rip down the wall with roots and branches. So far, it held in place. But the garden was a disaster. Rampant greenery smothered everything. Walls, outbuildings, the stables, paths, and even the outer edges of the pond were impossible to reach. The summerhouse was a green heap, invisible beneath thick foliage.

Fortunately, the south fared better. The meadow grass was long, but no extra growth seemed to be advancing, except along the edge of the drive, where the shrubs had grown extravagantly large. The orchard remained bathed in its golden glow. Hades had not accompanied him, instead venturing to his own spirit plane, endeavouring to find out more ways to trap the creature. Ansel had known him barely twenty-four hours, but already suspected that Hades would reveal very little of himself. He was male, that was as much as he could discern for sure. So far, however, he was proving useful, and Ansel knew his own magic would grow stronger the more he saw of him.

When he joined Jem and Eliza, Jem had just finished whetting the axe blade. "That would cut a thick branch with one blow," he said, satisfied. "Especially with the magic you have added, Eliza."

"So, we are ready, then?" Eliza had a basket next to her, filled with beeswax candles, feathers, and a chalice for water. Her hair was tied back in a long plait, and she wore her plainest linen dress with short sleeves. The house was as hot as an oven, the ivy serving to trap the heat in. "Ansel, how goes it out there?"

"As bad as you can expect. We are on the way to becoming an ancient forest. The elemental is engaged at the north wall, but the south looks better than the north."

"Good. Then our thoughts on this were correct. Do we wait for Hades to return?"

"I think he will be there when we need him. Let's set up. But you two need more layers of clothing, or your arms will be ripped to shreds. You should wear one of my shirts and breeches, Eliza."

She grinned. "Oh, what liberty! Yes, please."

Jem looked askance, but then recovered quickly. "Yes, I think that is a good idea."

Ansel wanted to ask if he was excited at seeing his sister's shapely form in trousers. After all, that is why the female actresses now played men on occasions. Any titillation would cause excitement at the theatre. However, he thought better of it.

"You won't need your basket," Ansel added, nodding to her supplies.

"Why not?"

"Because we won't have the time or space. I just need to draw it in, and then we attack. The rest can wait."

Ten minutes later, under the blistering hot summer sun, with noon rapidly approaching, they gathered by the south moon gate, the honeysuckle rampant and heady with perfume, ready to do battle with the creature. Ansel had his sharp knife for self-defence, but dreaded having to use it. He would be wrestling with his sister, after all. The plan was that while he acted as bait, holding the creature as secure as he could, Jem would hack at it, and Eliza would aid with magic, collecting the wood at the same time.

"We should set up under the moon gate," Ansel suggested. "For a start, it's cooler under there, and the area is already partly ringed off."

Forcing their way through the undergrowth, they found that the area beneath the stone gate was like a cave, and almost plant-free, the bare ground parched from the dry weather. The scent of honeysuckle was almost overwhelming, and sweat trickled between Ansel's shoulder blades.

"Not much room to swing my axe," Jem noted grimly.

"Good! I don't want to lose a limb."

His sister shook her head. "I cannot see this working. The area is too tight."

"We'll make it work! Jem, you need to stand just beyond the gate. Use your shoulders to hold the honeysuckle up. If it comes up this way like it did yesterday, it will knock you off your feet. You too, Eliza."

"What about Hades?" Eliza asked, once they were in position.

"I'll find him." Ansel closed his eyes, finding it helped him connect to his familiar more easily. "*Hades! It's time.*"

The steady beat of wings filled the silence, and in seconds Hades was in his thoughts. "*I am here.*"

"*Have you found anything to help us?*"

Hades's large amber eyes filled his spirit vision. "*I'm getting closer, but go ahead, call it now. This is only the first stage, after all.*"

Ansel opened his eyes to find Jem and Eliza watching him. "He's here. I'll call it."

Using the spell they had decided on, Ansel attacked the honeysuckle with a combination of fire and the blade spell, turning air into a weapon. He sliced through the honeysuckle, slashing and burning at the same time, both dreading and hoping for the elemental's arrival. He didn't hold back, and within seconds the creature erupted beneath him.

It knocked Ansel on his back, showering earth over him, its attention solely on him. It was as if a boulder had fallen on his chest. His sister's face, a grim parody of what it had been, leered down at him. Dampness enveloped him, and the fetid stench of fungus filled his nostrils as Jacinta's clawed hands wrapped around his throat. Whipping branches flailed around him, striking the underside of the gate and sending small stones flying like hail. Rather than throw it off as his instinct screamed at him to do, he wrapped his legs and arms around it, and tried to wrestle it beneath him. He felt rather than saw his sister trying to pin it down, too.

Jem acted quickly, and three loud clunks resounded in swift succession. The creature hissed and screamed, trying to attack Jem. Ansel clung on. It was mayhem in the enclosed space. He and his sister wrestled around on the ground, trying and failing to avoid being whipped by lashing roots and thick green stems that tore his skin, splashing his blood everywhere. The creature's mouth gaped open wide, revealing blackened teeth. There was nothing of his sister left in that face.

Jem bellowed as roots tried to trap him, but he was relentless, twisting and swinging brutally. Hades materialised, his huge wings making the space even more confined, trying to distract it from Jem, and giving Ansel words of encouragement. Sweat and blood poured from Ansel as he clung on.

With horror, he felt the ground open underneath him as the creature tried to escape. He fell into a pit of soft earth that swallowed him up to his shoulders, and he could barely breathe. The creature pulled him from below, but Eliza and Jem gripped his wrists.

"It's going to tear me in half!" Ansel yelled. Well, he tried to yell with the scant breath he had left.

Then Eliza did something unexpected. A flash of magic passed from her to him like a flame, running down the entire length of his body, suffusing both of them with a golden light. A resounding rumble rocked the earth and the moon gate, and the creature released its hold and vanished.

"She's gone!" Ansel was desperately trying to pull himself up, his chest compressed by earth, as his vision started to black out.

Jem gripped him by the shoulders and hauled him free, and Ansel slithered out like an earthworm. None of them spoke as they regained their breath and composure. They were all injured, their bodies smeared with blood and dirt and sweat. But they couldn't stay there. The creature might return for revenge at any moment.

"Did you do it?" Ansel asked, lifting his head slowly and waiting for his dizziness to clear.

Eliza pointed to a pile of withered roots and branches. "Oh, yes. Time to make our poppet."

Eliza felt as if she'd wrestled a boar.

Every part of her body ached. She had cuts and grazes everywhere, despite Ansel's breeches and jacket. Their healing balms were soothing, but she feared the cuts would take a while to heal. They weren't natural. The two men looked just as bad, but despite their injuries, they were successful. A large pile of pale, yellow roots, clammy to the touch, lay mixed with thick green shoots and sap-filled whip-like branches on the kitchen table.

"I hope this is worth it," she said to them.

"There's enough there to make several poppets," Jem noted. "I've got to be honest, that felt really satisfying."

"But it hurt her," Eliza said, feeling sick. "Jacinta, I mean."

Ansel rubbed his chest. "You don't know that. We should be pleased. That thing feels pain."

"That thing is our sister."

"Not all. In fact, only a small part of her is left now. You must see that."

Eliza didn't want to admit it. When she looked into the elemental's eyes, she had seen only dark, inhuman pits. She had tried to connect to Jacinta as she grappled with it, trying to find a spark of her somewhere inside the creature, but all she'd found was darkness. "I think we've lost her."

"Hades says not."

She looked at the spectral owl, sitting on the huge iron range, amber eyes glowing like the eternal flame at the front door. "How can he know?"

"He says a spark of her spirit remains."

"But her body is a wreck. Where will her spirit go?"

"He says it's possible her body will survive." Ansel's lips pinched into a thin line, and she saw the doubt in his eyes. "He's not sure."

Eliza wanted to cry, but she refused to. *Not yet*. Whether Jacinta survived or not, the elemental must go. "How do we make the poppet? Like any other, I presume?"

"Yes, but it must be large, Hades says, the size of a small child. And we must bind it using the three remaining elements."

An idea formed as she stared at the mass of roots and twigs. They had more than she had hoped for. "We'll make three, one for each element."

It took shape in her mind. Flaming strands of fire magic would bind one, and the heat would burn through the damp, cold earth, to weaken the elemental. The next would be bound with smoke from a collection of a dried herb bundle—sage, rosemary, and angelica—and also the feathers to represent air. The final one would use water...saltwater, perhaps. Or seaweed. She had dried seaweed in the tower. That would contain the boundless energy of the sea. River stones too could be used in some way, and water plants. Something from their own garden that would break earth. Yes, powerful magics to bind a powerful earth elemental, and then perhaps all three could be bound together. It needed more thought, but she felt she was on the cusp of an excellent spell.

"But then what do we do with them?" Jem asked, disturbing her thoughts.

She squeezed his hand. "I'm not sure yet, but I'm getting closer. Unless Hades has an idea?" She couldn't keep the sarcasm from her voice. She was still unsure of his motives, although there was no denying that he had helped them so far. She should be pleased that Ansel had found his familiar.

Ansel shrugged. "He is not a witch, but he says we must remember our binding with the bees."

The orchard was still not affected by the elemental. Maybe that had something to offer, too.

Twenty-Two

Present Day

"Why is a book buried in the garden?" Odette asked. "It's weird. Unpleasant, even. Does it contain something terrible? And perhaps more importantly, do you shifters still scent pain?"

The slim, leatherbound volume lay on the table, on top of the oilskin cloth that had protected it, the group gathered around it. It was clearly preserved with magic, barely showing any signs of aging. No one had touched it yet. Birdie had gently teased the oilskin wrapping off it so they could see it properly.

Arlo shrugged, meeting her eyes. "I don't feel it now. I think maybe I felt it in the soil?" He looked to the others as if for confirmation.

"Aye," Hunter agreed. "It looks pretty innocuous. It was the earth around it that carried the pain."

Birdie clucked. "Things don't get buried in spelled boxes because they're innocuous. I can't feel anything malevolent, though. I'm going to open it."

"Wait!" Morgana restrained Birdie's hand. "Let's try a few revealing spells on it first."

They were all so jumpy, Odette thought. Spooked by odd scents, visions, and a missing familiar. *What had happened to cause this emotion?* They were always normally so level-headed, not prone to flights of fancy, and yet, here they were, looking at a simple spell book as if it might explode. And there was no doubt—for Odette, at least—that it was a spell book. She was also convinced that it was Jacinta Wildblood's, too. She just knew it.

However, after a few minutes of speculation and spellcasting, the book was declared safe, and needing to get a first impression before anyone sullied it with their energy, Odette picked it up. As she'd told Como, she didn't read objects, but her skill at seeing to the truth of things came in many varied forms. Her overriding emotion was sadness. Of dreams lost, hopes dashed, and magic unfulfilled.

"Well?" Birdie asked, watching her anxiously.

"It's not good news for whoever owned this book. It embodies unfulfilled promise." She turned the front cover and confirmed her suspicions. "Well, now we know why we couldn't find Jacinta's spell book. This is it."

"She's dead?" Como gasped.

"Of course she's bloody dead," Lam said, rolling his eyes. "It would be a miracle for her to be alive now!"

A ripple of laughter ran around the shifters as Como glared at Lam. "I meant, you wanker, did she die young?"

"A very interesting question," Birdie said, supporting him. "Odette?"

Odette placed the book on the table and turned the pages slowly, as everyone crowded around. "I have no idea if she died too young, but something significant certainly happened. I mean, why bury this otherwise? She was a few years younger than Eliza, but no dates of death are recorded for any of them."

"There aren't many spells in here," Morgana noted, "but she's interested in finding a familiar. That seems to be the main subject of the spells."

Maverick frowned. "You read the writing quickly."

"I'm familiar with Middle English. We have many spells from that time period. It has its own rhythm, and is easy to understand when you get used to it."

"Ugh!" Cecile said, grimacing as she squinted at the page. "Does that say Dead Man's Bells? What is that?"

Odette laughed. "It's an old-fashioned name for foxgloves. Many flowers and herbs were named after their appearance. It's poisonous, so I can see the connection."

"I love the old names," Como said. "They're colourful and interesting."

"And dragons' teeth?" Cecile asked, pointing at another.

"Vervain," Birdie explained. "A powerful herb with many magical qualities, used here I suspect for its properties that enhance psychic abilities and dream states. It would help her search the spirit realm for her familiar."

"But does the book help us find Hades?" Hunter asked. "If she was looking for familiars, did she summon him?"

"Hard to say," Odette admitted. "I don't see that, and Hades hasn't told Birdie that, but things are far from certain right now. We can examine the book in greater detail, and compare it to Eliza and Ansel's, her siblings. Something may jump out at us."

"In the meantime," Birdie said, picking up the oiled cloth as her attention swung to the shifters, "you should all go home. I'm tired, and I'm sure you are, too. If you still want to help, why not come back in the morning? You can have the run of the garden."

"I'd love that," Maverick admitted, "and so would the pack. We were only just saying earlier how little opportunity we have to be in our wolf in daylight. Maybe I'll chat to Lam then, too." The pack broke into excited chatter as Maverick cocked his head at him. "I'm curious about this magic of yours."

Odette stopped listening, because she'd spotted something falling from the oiled cloth. Delicate things that seemed to glitter. She reached forward and touched her fingertip to one. "Wings," she muttered. "Honeybee wings."

"What?" Arlo asked, leaning so close she scented his musk. "Have you found something?"

She reached the tip of her finger higher to show him. "Look. And there are more of them. They're in the bottom of the box!"

They had barely given the box a second glance once they had removed the oiled cloth package, but now she picked it up to examine the fine layer of wings on the bottom.

"What does it mean?" Arlo asked.

The scent of honey seemed to settle around her, and she heard a melodious bee song for a few seconds before it vanished, but it was enough to leave her with a sense of wonder. "I don't know, but we have now learned something else. The bees were involved."

Giacomo returned to the tower sitting room with renewed vigour once the wolves left Moonfell.

He would not be afraid of sleeping in his room, or this tower. He had been given a message that led them to find Jacinta's spell book, and he would not run away now.

Birdie was worried about his decision, but Odette had gazed at him with her far-seeing eyes and said, "Yes, I think you should sleep there. You may find out more."

The question was, did he try a spell to encourage vivid dreams, such as using vervain like they had mentioned earlier, or did he just sleep naturally? A cup of soothing chamomile tea might help. Generally, herbal teas were not his preference, but here at Moonfell, it seemed appropriate. He needed to fall into step with its rhythms.

"Do you want tea?" he asked Lam as he entered the room.

"No. I want whiskey after that. Have we got some?" Lam threw his jacket on the couch and dropped onto it, spreadeagled.

"Have the wolves traumatised you?" Como asked sarcastically.

"Just that bloody Maverick! It's not like I had control of my actions!"

"Quite honestly, if your voice appeared in my head, I'd freak out, too!" He reached into the cupboard and extracted a bottle of single-malt whiskey. "You're in luck. We have been blessed with spirits and wine."

"Good. Make it a large one. Please," he added, belatedly remembering his manners. "I don't understand anything of what's going on. The doll, the book, the bees' wings, the fucking wriggling poppet...any of it! I especially don't understand why I can read animals now—well, their emotions."

"You did ask the house to give you more magic last night," Como reminded him, pouring a generous amount of whiskey and handing him the glass. "Or did you forget that?"

"I didn't expect such fast or unexpected results!" He gulped his drink down and winced. "Ah! That's the business."

Como returned to the kitchen for his own drink, and then sat opposite Lam. He was proving an interesting roommate. "You don't really believe in magic, do you?"

"Of course I do! My entire family are witches!"

"I mean, you didn't really believe that your powers, or theirs in fact, were as tangible as they are."

He didn't answer for a moment, instead taking another sip of whiskey. "Maybe not, actually. What does that say about me?"

"That you're an idiot."

"Thanks, *stronzo*!"

Como laughed. "Well, seriously, even after Yule?"

"It seemed like a dream afterwards. It's all very real though, isn't it?"

"It's not putting you off staying here, is it?"

"No! If anything, I'm more determined to get my head around it all. Everything is so tangible here. And the shifters, well…" He huffed and took another large sip of whiskey.

Como couldn't disagree. They had an air of danger and unpredictability, and yet he knew that was stupid. They were fully in control of their shifts. *But that feral gleam in their eyes, and those heightened senses… And their size.* "Birdie glared at me for staring at Cecile and Domino, but I couldn't help myself. They're seriously hot! And naked *a lot*! Like, *naked* naked!"

Lam snorted. "There's only one type of naked!"

"You didn't look at the hot girls?"

"Of course I looked! I'm not dead. I just didn't stare like a pervert."

Como flushed at the thought of what Cecile had whispered to him. He'd surely have dreams tonight, and it wouldn't be about poppets. "I'm Italian. Well, half-Italian. I love women! *Love* them. And I love having sex with them. I have needs!"

"I don't want to know! And English guys have needs, too! Just because you're Italian doesn't mean you have the monopoly on lust." Lam smirked. "What did Cecile say to you?"

"She sniffed me and said something about cats and mice. I couldn't concentrate. All my blood rushed to my dick and I had to leave the room." Lamorak exploded with laughter, and Como laughed, too. "It wasn't funny at the time! It has a will of its own sometimes."

"Well, seeing as we'll be seeing a lot more of the shifters, get it under control!"

Como decided it was time to change the conversation. "I think the poppet appearing in my room must have been sent as a clue. It led us to Jacinta's grimoire and the bee wings."

"Those bloody bees. Why you?"

"Why not me?"

"Because you've just arrived, like me!"

"So?"

Lam sighed. "If anyone was going to send anything about Hades being missing, why not send it to Birdie?"

"Because... I don't know."

"What if it's to do with your room? I mean, who lived in your room. Or even this tower!"

"You mean one of the Wildbloods could have lived here?"

"Why not?" Lam asked, sitting upright with renewed enthusiasm. "The poppet is clearly connected to them and some kind of event that happened at that time. This tower is also part of the original building. One of them could have slept in your room."

Como now wished he hadn't drunk chamomile tea, and considered putting whiskey in it. "So, the ghost of whoever it was delivered it to me? No, wait, that doesn't make sense. Someone dug it up from the garden! It wasn't like it was hidden in the walls." He rubbed his temples. "This is so weird. Do you think Jacinta died young?"

"I don't know, but why bury her book on its own? Surely if you wanted to get rid of it, you'd bury it with her."

"Interesting. Why the scent of pain? Which, by the way, is just gross."

"Because something bad happened here. Really bad. I think Birdie, Odette, and my mother know that too, and they just don't want to admit that wonderful Moonfell has a murky past."

Como frowned at Lam. "You're being unfair. They are very honest about this place's checkered past, and the oddities of previous inhabitants. But you can't blame Morgana for trying to shield you. She wants you to stay here. You must see that."

Lam shrugged. "I know. Look, I'm a bit fired up, and I can't sleep yet. Why don't we search your room?"

"For what? Ghosts?"

"I don't know! Hidden panels or something. Something that might tell us who stayed there."

"After four hundred years!"

"It's possible. Plus, I'm prepared to sleep in your room with you, just in case. On the floor with my quilt."

"I'm wondering if I'll have those dreams again of running through lots of thick greenery. It was like a jungle. No, a wild wood." And then he had a thought. "I saw something in the library earlier. There were plans of rooms and layouts, right where we found the Wildbloods' grimoires. What if it says who slept in my room?"

Lam stood decisively. "Let's check it out."

Morgana sat in silent contemplation in front of the fire in her living room, barely aware of her surroundings. The balance of magic had shifted in Moonfell, and strange energies were manifesting that she couldn't fathom.

She jumped when Birdie appeared. "I thought you'd gone to bed."

"No," she said, sitting opposite her and placing a tray on the table, "I saw the shifters out and made us a hot toddy. It was cold outside. It gave me a chill."

"Thank you. That's a good idea. Are you feeling okay?" Despite her grandmother's seeming robustness, she couldn't help but worry about her health.

"Of course!"

Her short answer didn't invite more questions, so Morgana took one of the glasses and sipped it appreciatively. "Delicious. You've put honey in it."

"It seemed appropriate, seeing as the bees seem to be involved in all this." Birdie nodded towards Jacinta's spell book. "I think the elemental that Odette saw attacked Jacinta. I think it became her, or why else was blood in the twigs of that poppet? It's horrific. I don't think I've seen anything so awful for quite some time."

"Do you think she summoned it?"

"Accidentally, yes. And I think Hades was involved, too."

"Why wouldn't he have told you?"

"It was a long time ago. Why would he? Perhaps he was embarrassed, or maybe ashamed?"

Morgana shook her head. "Why would he feel like that? He might have helped stop it."

"Of course, you're right. I'm leaping to unfair conclusions." She looked up and smiled as Odette joined them. "I was hoping you'd still be up. Hot toddy for you, too."

Odette gave a weak smile as she picked up her drink and settled next to Morgana on the sofa. "I can't sleep yet. I take it none of us can?"

Morgana shook her head. "We need to work this out. I have so many possible scenarios whizzing around my head." She took another sip of her drink, and fortified, said, "Let's be logical. Hades has vanished, and we're convinced that the bee ritual did it. If not, it's an incredible coincidence. Then the poppet appears. And it's no ordinary poppet. It has blood in its twigs, and it came to life. It was buried over Jacinta's spell book. Why protect the box with so many sigils and runes?"

"Maybe it was a kind of memory box, and it was respectful," Odette suggested.

Birdie huffed. "Perhaps. It certainly wasn't to keep us out. But why wasn't the poppet in it? And who took *that* out of the ground?"

"Because someone needed us to find it," Morgana said, sure she was right. "And who else but Hades would need help right now?" She sat up, all tiredness vanishing. "We've already said that the bee ritual must have been used by the Wildbloods. It was part of their relative's collection of bee lore. When we used the bee ritual again, we triggered something connected to that time, and the bee ritual has trapped Hades somehow. He's stuck in some elemental plane, or something of the sort."

"Why?' Birdie asked. "And why not give the poppet to me? Plus, if he's trapped, how can he get the poppet?"

All three witches were leaning forward now, eyes alive with intrigue, magic palpably building, and silence fell as they considered their options. Morgana loved these times, sitting with her coven and mulling over magical riddles. It was fair to say that she didn't enjoy the current circumstances, however.

Odette finally spoke. "He must have helped. He's a familiar, he can't be killed, so he's out there somewhere, and maybe he's found another spirit from that time. Perhaps he's found Jacinta? Or Eliza?"

"But to what end?" Morgana asked, knowing they were missing something fundamental. "Are Eliza or Jacinta the only ones who can help him? And if so, why?"

"Well, if we're going to throw them in, we may as well suggest Ansel, too!" Birdie said, frustrated. "Plus, that ritual could have been done lots of times over the previous years."

"I saw Eliza," Odette reminded her. "She is linked to this. I saw her in the orchard and in the main garden, and the place was overrun with plants. And I sensed the elemental. I inhabited its presence." She leaned forward and squeezed Birdie's hand. "I'm not wrong, and we're in danger of overthinking this."

"What if we miss something?"

Morgana snorted. "We're missing plenty. Jacinta is connected to the earth elemental in some horribly sad, tragic way—likely it infected her, as we've surmised. If the garden was overrun like a wild wood, it was either because the Wildbloods wanted it like that, or the elemental caused it." She sipped her hot toddy, hoping for inspiration. Then she had a horrible thought. "What if the bee ritual awoke the elemental, too? What if that has trapped Hades?"

The colour drained from Birdie's face. "Then he's engaged in an epic battle for his soul. What if it's trying to inhabit him?"

"You mean his cat body?" Morgana asked.

"No." Odette was abrupt. "His body isn't real. He doesn't age. Perhaps Hades is stopping the elemental from getting back in, and it has to overcome him."

"Maybe he sensed that and went willingly," Birdie said. "That would be so like him."

"Or perhaps," Morgana suggested, "somewhere in the murky middle lies the truth." She lifted her head and looked at the door. "The boys are here."

Como burst inside, followed by Lam. Both looked excited as Como announced, "Jacinta used to sleep in my room! I think her ghost found the poppet!"

Twenty-Three

July, 1664

While Eliza worked in the spell room, gathering her ingredients and perfecting her spells, Ansel and Jem constructed the dolls, leaving a pile of twigs yet to be used. By late afternoon, they were ready.

When she rejoined them, Eliza decided to keep the remaining twigs safe, and placed them in a sturdy wooden box, protected by spells.

"It's stupid, I know," she said to Jem and Ansel, "but I feel like they might come alive and attack us."

"Without will to direct them?" Jem asked. "Surely that is impossible."

"I thought an elemental taking over our sister would be impossible, and yet we battled it this afternoon and have the scars to prove it."

The featureless twig dolls should have appeared innocuous, and yet they seemed to brood with malevolence. Maybe it was the ivy-induced darkness and the flickering lantern flames that made them seem so threatening, or perhaps it was just plain common sense that urged her not to trust them.

"After all," she continued, "we are using them because they are part of the elemental. They contain its power. Its essence. They provide a bridge from us to it."

"And vice-versa," Ansel pointed out. "I think you're right. The poppets could attack us, under the right circumstances. We need to bind them as quickly as possible." His hands flew to his neck that was already bruised from his fight earlier. "I can still feel its fingers around my throat, and its weight on my chest."

Eliza agreed. "Then we shouldn't delay. As you pointed out earlier, brother, we have a well of power to draw on, and I am going to use the moon gates and call upon the elemental power they contain. They will provide a very strong binding. We should not wait any longer. We must get this done tonight. I would prefer to use the gates at the corresponding times for full effect, but instead we must press on. At least we can cast the water spell at sunset. That, at least, will be correct."

"Then let's use the south gate now. There are hours of daylight left yet, and the day is still hot. We just must make sure not to harm the plants."

"I have no intention of touching them at all," Eliza told him. "I think the fire spell will be the easiest, too." She looked around the kitchen. "Where is Hades?"

"He is trying to find the elemental's name."

A spark of hope flamed within her. "He really thinks he can?"

Ansel grinned. He had such faith in Hades. "He lives in the spirit realm and has many contacts. Others who act as familiars. He told me that time has little meaning to them."

"He travels through time?" Jem asked, eyebrows shooting up in surprise.

"No, I don't think so. It's just that his plane does not measure time. Not like ours."

"So, he cannot go back and save Cinta?" asked Eliza.

"Well, I didn't ask," Ansel admitted, "but surely he would if he could. Our time still moves linearly, even if his does not."

Eliza decided not to pursue it. She had enough to worry about. "Then we must hope he has success with its name. I have already found a few spells that could work, should he be successful."

"Really? Where?"

"In our mother's grimoire, of course." The section she'd found them in referred to binding people to one's will. There were spells to control the mind, love, affection, to bind someone to do one's bidding, and other dark subjects. The spells made her flesh crawl, and to her knowledge, her mother had never used them. She suspected they were there in case someone accused them of witchcraft or sought to cause them harm. At least she hoped that was the case.

Jem had been tidying up the kitchen and putting the pan on the range to boil water, but now he stopped and stared at her. "I didn't think you did such dark witchcraft."

"We don't. The same cannot be said for others in our family, however. I have heard some curly tales." She couldn't stand that Jem should look at her with such an accusatory glare. "I never would. This is the first time in my life that I am even considering such a thing."

"Me too," Ansel assured him. "Desperate times need desperate measures."

Jem clearly wasn't convinced. "I don't understand why you need to use such a spell if you're binding the poppets with elemental power."

Eliza knew this would happen. The more Jem saw of their witchcraft, the more worried he became, but she desperately wanted him to understand. He was the only man who came close to understanding her and who she really was. For a start he was a valued friend, but she had realised recently that she couldn't even contemplate a romantic relationship with a man who didn't. She pushed aside the implications of that line of reasoning until later.

Seeing as Ansel was looking at her just as expectantly, she said, "There are layers of magic in spells, most of the time. Some are basic charms that require a simple rhyming spell, but this issue requires lots of magic. In fact, the more I have thought about it, the more complex it becomes. We have to save Jacinta. Try to protect her trapped spirit, never mind her body. We must banish the elemental and ensure it cannot return. It has lots of powerful, natural magic and it requires guile and power on our behalf. Hades," she reluctantly admitted, "was right to suggest our current course of action to use parts of the creature. We bind the poppets with the other elements' powers to countermand earth, and then we bind them again once we know its name. And I propose a third option. Thrice the charm."

"And the third binding is?"

"I haven't decided yet." Actually, she had a couple of ideas, but wanted to mull them over more. She gathered the ingredients and her spell book and placed them in her bag. "Right. To the Full Moon Gate."

Ansel felt quite smug once they finished the fire binding spell. It had proceeded better than he expected, not that he should have doubted Eliza.

There was a reason she was Moonfell's guardian and the High Priestess. She was an instinctive witch, knowing when and how to use her power for maximum effect. Ansel had his own skills that were considerable, but Eliza's power was something else. And she was still so young.

They had gathered by the moon gate with Jem keeping watch with the axe, but because they left the plants alone, they had not alerted the elemental creature to their business. Maybe it didn't recognise the magic they did there, although Jem expected it would feel the effects of the binding. *Maybe it was too preoccupied with its attempt to escape.* He suspected Moonfell's magic ran deep underground, or else why didn't the creature just escape that way?

"You know, I've had another idea," Ansel said as they walked through the orchard to the east garden and the Waxing Moon Gate by the parterre, having just placed the finished poppet in the house. "Perhaps even though Jacinta has given it form, her connection to the garden also binds it here—or else why hasn't it burrowed its way out?"

"That's an excellent point," Eliza conceded.

"Or," he added before she said another word, "the bees' bond with Jacinta is also serving as anchor."

Eliza stopped dead, looking at him wide-eyed. "Of course! Why didn't I think of that? I've been so preoccupied on how the bee ritual could help with securing Jacinta's safety that I didn't consider the effect on the creature. By the Goddess. Another level." She grinned at Ansel and Jem. "And I bet it doesn't even know! The ritual was performed before it even arrived."

She looked around at the orchard as if she'd never seen it before, eyes narrowed as she plotted. He could see it written all over her face. Eliza looked swashbuckling dressed in Ansel's shirt and breeches, tucked into Eliza's sturdy leather boots, and he had the feeling that she would wear them more often after this. Her hair that had been so neatly plaited earlier, was now escaping in swinging tendrils. Jem looked besotted, and even though he was trying not to stare at her obvious figure, he was failing miserably. There were worse people who could love Eliza. Ansel actually quite liked the idea of them together. At least Jem was a hard worker, and not some high-minded fop.

The orchard once again basked in the summer heat, and Ansel wanted to lie down in the long grass and fall asleep, only waking when all of this was over. Golden light suffused the deep green shade, and bee song provided a melodic backdrop. Many other animals that normally lived in the main gardens were here too, retreating from the creature's onslaught and gross manipulation of nature. Even their two cows had come here. He felt how safe they were, how it provided an oasis of calm. *How was it resisting the elemental?*

Eliza broke the mood. "Come on. We can think about this latest development later."

The paths to the gate were tangled and overgrown, and it took twice as long to reach it as it should. The air element commanded the Waxing Moon Gate. It was made from an enormous yew hedge, probably trained over a frame that had long since rotted away. They clipped it regularly to keep its shape, but the hedge grew high around and above the gate, offering a deep walkway to the parterre garden beyond it, like a portal to another world—one of the many magical properties that yew was said to have. Now, of course, the bright red hips were growing far too early in the season. Still, the way through was just about clear, as if the yew's years of training had instilled memory into it.

Jem once again protected them, axe resting on his shoulder with easy grace as they set up in the late afternoon shadows. Hades's feathers, beautiful shades of gold and tawny browns, lay ready, along with a collection of other feathers from the garden's birds and insects—raven, pigeon, dove, blackbird, swallow, a tiny wren, and a dragonfly's wing. They regularly collected fallen feathers on their travels, as well as the shells of hatched eggs. All were useful for spells, and thanks to Ansel's magic, he knew just where to look. The other main ingredients were the herb bundle, beeswax candles, and a metal dish.

"So, you'll bind with the smoke?" he asked, to make sure he understood correctly.

She smiled. "A smoke rope."

"Ingenious."

"I thought so. We'll tuck the feathers into the poppet, binding as we work."

"I'll do that."

The poppet had dried in the heat of the day, the soft, supple twigs and cool, slippery roots hardening. He gripped it in one hand, and once Eliza had lit the herb bundle and candles, she started to chant the spell. Ansel tucked the feathers into the poppet, weaving them into the twine that wrapped the twigs into limbs. He tucked them into the head too, repeating the words with Eliza, and filling the poppet with elemental air. Eliza then changed the spell, weaving the smoke into sinuous, silvery ropes. Magic built around them, filling the space beneath the gate, and Ansel's skin tingled with it.

And then the twigs twitched in his hands. "Eliza!" He was so startled that he stopped spellcasting.

Eliza's eyes widened with horror that quickly turned into a ferocious glare that told Ansel not to stop. Her voice rose, power magnifying as she drew on the magic of the moon gate and the magic that bound it to the house. Decades of power that belonged to their ancestors. Stumbling over his words, Ansel rejoined the spell. Jem stepped closer, hands tightly gripping the axe. Ansel could not fail them now.

The smoke binding thickened and hardened into something more tangible as it multiplied. Ansel moved his hands, allowing the binding to wrap around every inch of the poppet, and air tickled the feathers within it. Everything about the poppet was moving, from the feathers to the ends of the branches and roots, to the smoke itself. It was like a living, breathing thing and he longed to throw it to the ground. But they were almost done now.

Suddenly, a piercing shriek echoed across the garden, and Ansel prepared for the worst, expecting strong hands to grip his ankles as the creature manifested beneath him. Instead, however, the furious elemental appeared on the far side of the gate.

It was hard to keep focussed with the guttural screech of the creature in the background, but finally, it was done. The poppet was wreathed in smoke, bound from head to foot, and it now felt limp in Ansel's hands. No one spoke. The elemental stared at them, and they stared at it. Murky green light kindled in its eyes, and then it vanished.

Ansel took a deep breath of relief. "It's working. But the sun is setting. We need to move to the next gate quickly. Do you think it knows what we're doing?"

"Even if it does, we can't stop now, and we have to keep the ones we have completed safe." Eliza stepped to the threshold that faced the house, determination stamped through every muscle of her body. "Run to the house—now!"

Twenty-Four

Present Day

"Do you really think it's possible?" Birdie asked, both excited and worried. "I mean, I'm prepared to believe many things. I have *seen* many unusual things, but could Hades have found Jacinta's spirit?"

All five witches were in the library, studying Moonfell's old plans. These ones were rudimentary, as if done for a project on a lazy afternoon, rather than officially filed plans. They were distinctly childlike.

Odette shrugged. "I don't see why it couldn't be possible. If they are all spirits, then surely they inhabit similar planes of existence." She tapped the plan. "I suspect this was drawn by Jacinta herself. Look at the details of her room. It's actually quite charming. She was an inquisitive child—a teenager, perhaps, at this stage. Wilful, even. I just know it. Look how far she is from Eliza and Ansel's rooms. She's on her own."

Eliza and Ansel were both on the first floor in very grand rooms, but not ones the current witches were in. Birdie pointed at one of the towers. "That's where Virginia is, quite a distance from everyone, too. Do we know much about her?"

"Apart from the fact she seems batshit crazy, based on her spells?" Como said. "No. But I aim to rectify that."

"Perhaps," Lam suggested, "we should have a séance. Or use a Ouija board?"

"We shall do no such thing," Morgana said forcefully. "Oujia boards are notoriously fickle and unreliable. You don't know what you're inviting in. As for séances, I think Jacinta has already made her presence known."

"If it is her!" Birdie said.

"Of course it is," Como exclaimed. "I'm in her room. She dumped a poppet on me!"

Odette cleared her throat. "Actually, I think a séance might be a good idea. If Jacinta is here, she could be instructive."

"Or destructive," Morgana said. "What if the elemental is hanging around?"

"Wow." Lam looked ridiculously excited. "Their spirits could be locked in an eternal fight, and Hades is in the middle of it."

Startled, Birdie almost dropped her reading glasses—the Goddess hadn't fixed *everything*. "What has he got himself into? However, this is progress! I feel we're actually making headway. Admittedly, we're missing details…"

"And have made massive assumptions," Morgana added darkly.

Birdie tutted. "Based on things we know. But we need more. I agree with Odette. Let's have a séance."

Morgana regarded her with pursed lips. "I think it's reckless. We should do more research first, like searching the Wildblood grimoires, including Jacinta's. We might not need to do a séance. That poppet was buried for a reason. It sprang to life! We could gather more information first, and find out about the miasma it gave off."

Birdie was sick of waiting. "Hades is lost, possibly endangered by a vengeful elemental."

"Or a vengeful Jacinta," Morgana pointed out. "She might be as 'batshit crazy' as her mother."

Morgana was frustratingly stubborn sometimes, and overly cautious. Birdie normally appreciated caution, but not now, especially with the boys looking at her expectantly. "I think you're outvoted. We'll do it here in the library."

"Yes!" Como punched the air.

"I thought you didn't want to encounter ghosts?" Morgana said.

"That was before all of this happened. It's exciting!"

Lam looked confused. "Isn't it better to use Como's room?"

"If she's here, she's here," Birdie said breezily, refusing to look Morgana in the eye. "Boys, carry the small round table closer to the fire. We'll use candlelight and the fire. No electric lights. We also need incense and something of Jacinta's. The grimoire is the most powerful object, but let's throw the plans in for good measure, too."

While the boys ran around moving tables and chairs, and then placing the required objects in the centre of the table, Morgana cornered Birdie. "You're being reckless."

"I am not."

"Yes, you are."

"It's just a séance!"

"Now, now," Odette said, intervening. "I think you are worrying too much, Morgana."

"Am I? Then I will sit this one out. I'm sure you don't need me." She gathered up the glasses and walked across the room.

Birdie wasn't sure whether to command her to stay or shout with rage. *Why did Morgana have to be so staid sometimes?* "Morgana! This is important to me."

She turned at the door, fixing her calm, annoyingly rational gaze on Birdie, which infuriated her even more. "Hades is important to me, too. I will do my own research. You don't need me. You are the High Priestess, after all. Please make sure my son escapes unscathed." And then she walked out, shutting the door softly behind her, which made Birdie even crosser. *Always so contained!*

Birdie found Como and Lam staring at her. "Four is excellent for a séance. Cardinal directions, please."

Morgana had no intention of just leaving them all to it. She was genuinely worried about them conducting a séance, but not because she was afraid of ghosts.

Moonfell's energy had changed, and Birdie, normally so level-headed and wise, seemed to have taken leave of her senses. Of course she was worried about Hades; they all were. However, it didn't excuse what Morgana considered risky behaviour. Jacinta had been caught up in something terrible, so terrible that it still had consequences 400 years later. So terrible, in fact, that Hades had vanished because of it. And Hades was stronger than all of them. Aloof, mysterious, and unknown to her other than what she had learned through Birdie.

Unfortunately, that was Morgana's problem. Hades was a constant presence at Moonfell; seen by all, and yet utterly unknown except to Birdie. He wasn't a cat to be petted, and the other cats actively avoided him. Morgana often spotted him hunting mice and birds, or just sauntering through the undergrowth, lying in patches of sun or shade as his urges dictated. He witnessed rituals, watched spells, and had even kept an eye on the demon. He was undoubtedly on their side, and yet he was more unknown to her than the two house cats that generally went unnoticed by their visitors, mainly because when they weren't skulking about the garden avoiding Hades, they were in Morgana's rooms. Abbot and Costello, her two furry friends.

The corridor on which the library was situated was very long, and ran around the inner courtyard, although not anywhere near as linearly as one would expect. There were unexpected steps up and down the slightly different levels, twisty passages that ran off it, odd little rooms as well as numerous large bedrooms, sitting rooms, another billiard room, and bathrooms in varied places. Her own bedroom was on this floor, as was Birdie's and Odette's, all spaced well away from each other. There were also stairs that led to the second floor, much narrower ones than the main staircase, and Morgana accessed the closest set and headed up.

As a child, Morgana adored the second floor. It was quirkier than the first. Quieter. More mysterious. She had spent hours reading in small nooks, chasing the cats that were around long before Abbot and Costello, and practicing spells out of sight and mind. Previous inhabitants had unusual collections, and those were generally displayed up here, too. Part of that particular second floor corridor was just one long wall to accommodate the double height of the library on the floor below. During the course of her explorations, she had discovered panels that unlocked to reveal hidden passages and cupboards. One such panel between two bedrooms led to a narrow passage that ran between the walls and around two rooms, leading to a door that opened on the mezzanine level of the library. She had never told anyone about this door, and seeing as no one had mentioned it to her, she presumed it was her secret.

The panel that hid the access was ornately carved, much like the rest of the panelling, and depressing a carving of an acorn, the hidden door opened on well-oiled hinges. Morgana slipped inside and shut it behind her. She conjured a dim witch-light, and progressed slowly but surely, fingers tracing the wall. She turned right along the back of the mezzanine that rose well above the main library, and after dowsing the light, fearing to be seen through chinks in the panelling, she counted her steps, and then stopped and listened. After hearing nothing exceptional, she slid aside a small piece of wood to reveal a hole that was the size of her eye and peered through it. A golden glow from the candles and fire were the only light beyond. She whispered a spell to muffle all sound and one to drape herself in shadows, depressed the mechanism to open the panel, and eased through silently. The panel was between two display cases, decorated with a painting of a forest scene of witches around a bonfire. It was wonderfully fanciful and Gothic, but she liked it. Leaving it open behind her, she stepped to the balustrade and looked down.

The remaining four witches were seated around the table, all holding hands, the fire crackling close by. A candle burned next to the spell book and plans in the centre of the table. Only four other candles provided light, all on tall brass candleholders. Unexpectedly, Birdie was leading them, rather than Odette, eyes closed, urging the others to silence. They hadn't long begun.

So far, nothing stirred, and Morgana wasn't sure what she expected, or what she'd do if something untoward occurred. All she knew was that she didn't want to take part. Perhaps it would be successful, secrets would be revealed, and Birdie would crow about being right. She'd known it was pointless to dissuade Lam, too. No doubt he would roll his eyes if she was wrong. *One point against her.*

Birdie's clear, commanding voice carried across the library, calling on Jacinta to join them. "You are restless, Jacinta, and clearly troubled. Share your troubles with us. Share your pain, for then we can help."

The air remained still, and it seemed the library listened as she did.

Birdie continued. "Hades, my familiar, has vanished. I fear for his safety and wonder if you know him, Jacinta? I believe it was you who led us to the poppet and your grimoire. Is this so that we can help him, and in doing so help you?"

The air stirred, feeling like a brush of cobwebs across Morgana's face, just as the candles flickered below.

"Is that you, Jacinta?" Birdie's voice was strong and commanding. "You are amongst friends. Show yourself!"

Morgana's skin prickled as a shadowy figure manifested to her left, just visible out of the corner of her eye. Barely daring to breathe, she turned her head slowly, and saw a young girl dressed in an old-fashioned gown, with long hair that fell to her lower back. She was in profile, looking down at the scene below, just like Morgana, and the mezzanine level was clearly visible through her ghostly figure. And she looked sad, so sad. Everything about her screamed it - her dipped head, rounded shoulders, and grim stare.

Birdie continued to call her, and the candles flickered wildly, but Jacinta, if that's who it was, didn't budge. Morgana now noticed details she had missed. Her torn gown, her matted hair, the dirt smeared across her skin. Was it dirt? Or was it bruises?

Then she turned, staring back at Morgana, her face ravaged with scratches and scars, a dark green gleam in her eyes, and it was a miracle Morgana didn't scream. It stuck in her throat. "Jacinta?" she asked, her voice a murmur.

The ghost's eyes widened in horror, and she mouthed a single word. *Help.*

Her features suddenly morphed into a horrific caricature – all hard angles, angry, spiteful and elemental, enveloped in a thick black mist that was full of must and rot. She careered over the mezzanine, straight at the gathering below. The candles guttered out, leaving the room lit only by firelight, and a piercing wind ripped through the library as shouts erupted below.

They had summoned the elemental.

Morgana was pulled into the balustrade at great force, breath knocked out of her, and she clung on, arms wrapped around it. A long tendril of what appeared to be a root lassoed her foot and tried to pull her over the balcony.

Instinctively, she blasted it with fire and blended it with a destructive spell designed to cut and maim. The root shriveled and vanished, and she staggered to her feet, casting a flurry of witch-lights over the scene below. Spells crackled as her coven battled the spirit.

Rather than try to banish the ghost, Morgana cast a barrage of air spells designed to unseat the earth elemental. She bellowed, "Jacinta! Come to me!"

She had no idea if she could lend her power to the ghost of a witch, but she'd try.

Jacinta appeared next to her, contorted and grimacing, her features morphing between her own and the creature that was trying to possess her. Morgana reached for her, sensing her humanity beyond the wild elemental. For a moment, it seemed they had won. Then the tormented girl vanished, and a window broke below, leaving Morgana with the residual taste of chaotic energy and despair.

But something glittered at Morgana's feet. Bees' wings and a tawny feather. She picked them up, sealed the passage, and made her way downstairs. The four séance members looked surprised to see her, not surprisingly, and Lamorak was breathless and scared witless and wasn't ashamed to admit it.

He glared at the coven. "What the hell was that? And where did you come from?" he asked his mother abruptly.

Morgana had no intention of revealing her secrets. "I was trying to avert disaster. I failed."

Como righted the fallen chairs, clearly shaken but trying to hide it. "We're alive, that must be worth something, but I don't understand what happened. Did Jacinta attack us?"

Morgana didn't answer, instead looking at Birdie. "Perhaps Birdie could explain."

"Yes, all right!" Her lips were hard lines, her eyes narrowed with fury. "It was the elemental we talked about. Couldn't you smell it? And yes, Morgana, that's a damn good question. Where did you come from?"

Morgana smirked. "Shadow spells hide many things. I had no intention of leaving you to be foolish!"

"It was both of them," Odette corrected her grandmother. "They were battling each other. It seems our earlier assumptions were right. And now they're in our garden. Again."

"I found these," Morgana said, holding out her hand.

Lamorak picked the feather up. "That's big! It looks like an owl's feather." He looked up at the mezzanine. "You found it up there."

"Yes, left behind after Jacinta fled. I think I managed to help her control the elemental for a moment, but then it came back and they vanished together. Unless, of course, Jacinta carried the elemental away to help us. It's possible."

"So, we're sure it's Jacinta?" Como asked.

"I think so. Ninety-nine percent sure." Morgana relayed what she'd seen.

Lamorak shuddered. "She asked for help?"

"Yes. She was ravaged. Scared. Now more than ever I think the bee ritual did this. It's kicked up something and Hades is in the thick of it." She calmed down, relieved that everyone was okay, but still angry with Birdie. *Bloody Hades. Causing everyone to run around like idiots.* "I suggest we repair the window, reinforce the protection spells, and go to bed."

"Now?" Lamorak asked.

"Yes. We're all exhausted and not thinking clearly." She directed this at her grandmother. "Perhaps with clarity we will find a way to deal with this tomorrow."

Twenty-Five

July, 1664

Eliza knew that everything hinged on their next actions. They had to complete the third binding at the moon gate, or banishing the elemental would be so much harder.

"It knows what we're doing," she said once they were back in the kitchen, the second poppet safely stowed away. She was scared but tried not to show it. The journey through their overgrown garden in the growing twilight was terrifying. She had expected the creature to block her at every step.

"Does it?" Ansel looked doubtful. "How?"

"I just know it. It was the way it watched us. It obviously knew we were binding it, which means we affected its power. It will try everything to stop us."

"The poppet moved in my hands constantly until the binding was complete," he admitted. "It was horrible."

Jem shrugged. "But does it know the moon gates are important? Does it know that the west one relates to water? I doubt it."

"If it can access Jacinta's thoughts and memories it might," Ansel pointed out. "We have no idea how it has taken over Jacinta. Her magic might be aiding it."

"I don't think she's capable of aiding or resisting anything right now," Eliza said. "There is nothing of our sister there. Either her consciousness has been consumed, or it's buried deep inside her ravaged body."

"This is no time for debate," Jem said. He drank some water, and then threw some over his face to wash the sweat from it. "We have to get to the gate now, and it won't be easy, because we must get around the pond."

The sun was already sinking low in the west, and long shadows spread across the grounds as they progressed with the next spell ingredients. It was like a tangled garden from a fairytale, abandoned by their bewitched owners. Eliza half expected goblins to leap out of the undergrowth.

But witches lived in fairytales, and she was one of them. If the elemental thought she was going to give up without a fight, it had no idea of her resolve. As they advanced towards the pond, Eliza gathered Moonfell's magic to her. With every step she felt her ancestors walk beside her, previous High Priests and Priestesses all the way back to Sibilla Selcouth, the first Moonfell witch. She detected what she had missed in her earlier panic and horror at the circumstances. Although the elemental had undoubtedly used its own natural magic to make the chaotic growth, it was rooted in Moonfell's magic, too. That was the shift she had felt and couldn't resolve.

Half of the pond already lay in deep shadow, the sky flaming rose-gold beyond the summerhouse, the bronze moon gate aflame with the last rays of the sun.

"Careful now," Jem warned.

They were halfway around the pond when the elemental attacked. Enormous rose trees erupted from the ground bearing huge, thorny branches, forming an impenetrable wall all around them. The roots tangled around their feet, and the thorns threatened to impale them. Eliza acted instinctively and thrust her hands out, commanding the growth to stop. Nothing happened.

The roses grew taller and thicker until it was as black as night around them. Ansel threw witch-lights above them, and while Jem hacked with his axe, Ansel joined her spell.

"This is useless," Jem shouted. "There is no way we can get through this. It will kill us."

The sharp thorns jabbed at them, slicing through Eliza's shirt and grazing her ribs. One impaled Ansel's arm.

She had to focus. Had to remember her earlier insight.

"I am Moonfell!" she shouted, voice resounding with power. "I am the witch in the fairytale garden. Its power is *mine*!"

Rather than resist the hedge's growth, she sensed her ancestors' magic in it and drew it to her, letting it fill her from her toes to her head, and then she released it, throwing her arms wide, not caring about the thorns and the branches. Light flashed and the branches exploded outwards, splinters of wood flying in all directions. Ansel gripped her hand, lending his magic to hers, and together they sent out a second powerful wave, their male and female energies combining with generations of witches.

But her exultation at their success quickly vanished. They may have destroyed the first barrier, but the path ahead was entirely consumed by the thorny roses, and they completely encompassed the moon gate. There was no way they could get through.

Jem grabbed her free hand. "Back to the house. Now!"

There was no sign of the elemental as they ran, but its influence was everywhere. Roots and branches leaped out to grab them, obliterating the paths. It was only the fact that they knew the house so well that they could navigate the terrain at all. They virtually threw themselves through the front door into the hall. The stone steps rumbled as they cracked into pieces, and a thorny hedge exploded out of the ground, blocking their exit, and from what they could see, it encompassed the house. Fortunately, that's where the destruction stopped. The house remained impenetrable.

They lay winded on the floor, Eliza half tangled in Jem's warm embrace. It felt so comforting that she pretended to be far more winded than she was, but then propriety won out and she sat up, staring at the scene of devastation ahead.

"Well," Ansel said, still clutching the poppet, "it has certainly made its presence known now. I guess its decided that if it can't get in, we can't get out."

Jem stood up and pulled Eliza to her feet. "We should check the upper levels."

The house was dark, and the slithering ivy whispered outside every room. Eliza and Ansel used magic to light the candles and lanterns, banishing the gloom, but there was no denying that the house felt creepy.

There was some good news, however.

"At least the hedge only rises to the first floor," Ansel said with a sigh of relief. "I'd feel as if I was sealed in a coffin otherwise."

"For now," Eliza replied. "If we don't get this sorted tonight, it might well be our coffin. I am not giving up yet, though. That creature thinks it has bested us, but it still can't get out of the grounds, and we still have options. Is the poppet intact?"

"It needs to be tidied up, but is otherwise fine."

"Why?" Jem asked. "We can't get to the moon gate."

"We can still bind it with water. In fact," she smiled smugly as another idea struck her, "we can use the well. That water is drawn from the heart of the grounds." The well was in the centre of Moonfell's inner courtyard.

Jem smacked his forehead with the heel of his hand. "Of course! What are we waiting for?"

They raced down the stairs and along the twisting passages that led deeper into Moonfell's warren of rooms: small sitting rooms that caught the sun at differing times of the day, reading rooms, a games room with a billiard table, rooms lined with tapestries, a music room, dining room, and a room that had once been a chapel—and theoretically still was, but the household never used it. They burst through the door and out into the fresh air, the courtyard gloriously untouched by the elemental. Hercules munched hay in the corner, whinnying at their appearance.

The inner courtyard was comprised mostly of stone-slabbed ground, but there were also a few shrubs and some pretty borders filled with lavender, roses, and lady's mantel. It was the place to go if the wind blew strongly, because it was sheltered. The downside was that for large parts of the day, portions of it lay in shadows. The well was deep, edged with a stone wall and a pitched roof, and equipped with a bucket they could winch down. A pipe also led to a pump in the corner of the yard, and one outside the kitchen door. A few years before, they had taken advantage of The New River that brought fresh water into London, so that they had running water in the kitchen for a part of the day. Consequently, the well wasn't used as often as it once was, but the water was still fresh. It had long been believed that a river ran under the house and grounds, but no one could confirm the direction.

Jem soothed the horse, while Eliza took deep, cleansing breaths and offered up thanks to the Goddess and Moonfell's ancestors for keeping the house safe.

"At least everything here is fine," Ansel noted, looking up at the sky. Twilight had passed, and it was now fully dark, the stars winking above them. "The ivy hasn't reached this far, either. I presume we go ahead with the same spell?"

Eliza nodded. "We can still draw on the house's magic and protection spells. Part of me worries that if we cast the spell, we'll draw the elemental here. I can't bear the thought of it. We'd have invited it to the heart of the house."

"But if it could get here, it already would be," he reasoned. He winched the bucket down the well, and after hearing a faint splash, pulled it up again. He dipped a wooden cup into it that they always kept on the well wall and sipped it. "Tastes perfect, as usual."

While Ansel poured it into a large silver bowl, Eliza rummaged in her pack and pulled the bag of mixed seaweed out. It had all dried out. Some had been ground into powder and put into pots, but most had been left in long strands. She threw it all into the water, casting a spell as she did so. The seaweed immediately started to swell as it absorbed the water, a shimmer of turquoise green illuminating the bowl.

"How's Hercules?" she asked Ansel. He looked calm enough, nuzzling Jem's hand as he stroked his nose.

"Settled. It's as if he can't even feel what's happening out there. Look at how he is with Jem! The house cats are the same. They've found their favourite corners and are sleeping as usual."

"That's excellent news. There are limits to its powers, and it hates that we're binding it, which means we are on the right track." She assembled the ingredients, anxious to complete the final binding in the first part of the spell. "Shall we?"

An hour later, the third spell now successfully completed, Ansel headed up to the roof with a large glass of ale and a platter of cheese and bread, needing to relax, if only for a moment, after the strenuous day.

He was battered and bruised, mentally shattered, and yet exhilarated, too. He had left Jem and his sister in the tower spell room, tidying up and flirting as they celebrated their success. They knew they still had more to do, but for now, like him, they enjoyed the respite.

Ansel was on the roof of the eastern tower. It was flat and edged with crenelated walls, and was no doubt used as a lookout spot in the past. He could see over the boundary walls into Richmond Park, but he barely noticed it, focussing only on the garden. It looked innocuous from up here, a dense mat of greenery, hiding its dark master.

Placing his food and drink aside, he lay flat on his back, the stone warm beneath him, and gazed at the stars. A sliver of crescent moon rose in the sky. He let his mind drift, practicing the techniques that Hades had taught him, and slipped into spirit-walking. Within moments he soared above the gardens, seeing everything in auras. It took a few moments to locate the elemental, but he eventually saw it on the northeastern boundary, attacking the wall. The protective spells held, but the fractures he had seen earlier were spreading. But what was heartening was that the creature's aura was duller than it had been, and its attacks on the boundary looked weaker. It had to be the success of their binding spells.

But how to finish it off for good? Hopefully Hades would return soon with its name, but thrice the charm...

As Hades had advised, he kept his distance from the creature, instead hovering over the orchard, drawn by the golden light. It held strong still, an oasis in the dark. The orchard was the answer, but how could they get there? The routes out of the house were impenetrable.

And then he had an idea.

He dropped into his body and sat up, reaching for his beer and some cheese to fortify himself, hoping his theory was correct. Just as he was about to run down the steps, Eliza and Jem arrived. He grinned at them.

"What are you smirking at?" Jem asked, confused. "We're trapped."

Eliza leaned against the parapet. "Look at it! It's a disaster. How can you smile?"

"I have had a brilliant idea. You talked about thrice the charm, and I know the thrice! The final spell must be cast in the orchard. We will bind the three poppets together using a combination of our magic and the bees'. When it's done, the creature will be so weak that we can banish it."

Jem rolled his eyes. "All well and good, except we cannot get to the orchard! And don't you dare suggest we try to access it via the well."

"Of course not! I don't want to drown! I have another idea." They both looked at him expectantly. "We have extensive cellars, and rumours are that we also have underground passages. We know there are passages in the walls, because we've found a couple of them, as well as hidden panels that reveal inner staircases and secret cupboards. What if there's one that runs to the orchard?"

Eliza frowned. "What on Earth makes you say that?"

"There's a stone building in the orchard where we keep the baskets for fruit picking and the pruning tools—"

"We all know about that!" Jem huffed, interrupting him.

"It has a stone floor, huge flagstones, and it's always been well-maintained. While I was spirit-walking just now, I flew low over the orchard, and noticed that there is a dark space beneath it. I can see auras when I spirit-walk. The orchard is golden, and the bees are like stars. The house has its own glow too, despite the mass of ivy over it, and I can see silvery lines of protective magic all over the house and grounds. I also saw a faint line from the building to the house. A trace of silver, like faded magic."

Jem and Eliza stared, open-mouthed, Eliza finally saying, "You're sure?"

"Reasonably. Enough to warrant investigating. And it makes sense. These old houses would have escape routes in case of attack. Why not one to the orchard? I bet there are more, if we have more time to look. There are really old outbuildings in the grounds, particularly the stable block." He rose to his feet, dusting crumbs off his shirt, and wiping beer foam from his lip. "I think we need to investigate."

"Could you see where it led to in the house?" Jem asked, ever practical.

"No. The bulk of the house hid it. But let's start in the east."

Twenty-Six

Present Day

Maverick arrived at Moonfell at just after nine on Tuesday morning, eager to explore Moonfell's grounds and continue the search.

The clouds were low and heavy, promising rain, and a brisk northern wind lifted his hair, placing icy-cold fingers on his neck. He enjoyed hunting in the rain, as did his pack. It made them feel alive, at one with the elements, and hopefully they would arrive soon.

He already sensed something different. Another shift in energy. He took a moment to absorb it, lifting his head to inhale the new scents, and found something he couldn't place. It was wild. Chaotic. Unfettered. *Interesting.*

Just as he was debating whether to inform the witches of his arrival or hunt regardless, Birdie threw open the front door and marched down the steps to meet him. Her normal vivacity had vanished, and she looked pale and drawn. "I've made a foolish mistake."

"Are you all right? Is everyone else okay?" He looked over her shoulder to the house, but no one else was there.

"I'm fine, physically, and so is everyone else—at least, I hope so. Mentally, I'm clearly a senile old fool."

"I doubt that very much."

"You feel it already, don't you?" she asked, eyes darting around. She was much shorter than him, fine-boned, and a beauty, no doubt, in her youth. Now she was regal and stately, and still a good-looking woman, even with dark shadows under her eyes and unbrushed hair.

"I feel *something*. What's happened?"

"I held a séance last night, and inadvertently invited something unpleasant into the house. Now it's in the garden."

He leaned against his car, arms folded across his chest. "A séance? I thought you were all going to bed."

"The boys discovered that Jacinta used to sleep in Como's room. We reasoned she was the source of the poppet, especially considering it was buried with her spell book." She shuffled, unable to meet his eyes. "I thought she'd have answers, so we called her. She came with baggage."

"Don't tell me there's a demon here!" The last thing he wanted to do was face one of those again.

"No! Nothing as bad. Well...maybe it is, actually. You know the poppet moved last night."

"I'm not likely to forget, or the scent of pain and the vile miasma that manifested. I've been puzzling over it ever since we left."

"We think Jacinta accidentally summoned an elemental creature of earth when she was searching for a familiar, and we also think it returned with her last night." She summarised their thoughts and what had happened. "I don't think the elemental has full power, though.

I think it's a shadow of what it was because our ancestors dealt with it all those years ago. This place wouldn't be standing otherwise, I'm sure. But I don't understand the details. Not how they got rid of it, or the damage it caused. Although, we suspect some of it."

"The overgrown garden. Como's dreams of running in a wild wood."

"Exactly. But it escaped last night. Burst out of the library window, which means it's here somewhere, and I think Jacinta is hanging on to it by a thread."

"Or vice versa."

"Or that, yes."

"What does Odette think?" Maverick knew she had uncanny insights.

"I haven't seen her yet this morning. Or Morgana. We needed to sleep on it."

"You didn't search last night?"

"We were too tired, and I risked the boys' wellbeing enough as it was. It would have been foolhardy going after it in the dark, especially as we still don't know what we're up against."

He nodded. "Good. That was sensible."

She met his gaze finally. "I don't like getting things wrong, but I did last night, and I'm furious with myself. So is Morgana."

Ah. So there it was. Maverick knew something else was going on. "Was she hurt? Or Lam?"

"No. But she warned me not to do it, declared she wouldn't participate, and then snuck back in to watch me, as if she knew I'd fuck it up!" Birdie hardly ever swore, so it indicated how annoyed she was. She paused, taking a breath, considering her words carefully as she looked at him. "I think I'm too old to be the head of this coven. I thought I was young enough because of what the Goddess gifted me, but clearly—"

He cut her off. "Don't be ridiculous. We all make mistakes. You're human. It happens. And you're worried about Hades."

"It doesn't excuse my stupidity. I invited this elemental in! I bet you don't make mistakes like that."

"I've made plenty. Besides, Jacinta's ghost was already here, so likely the elemental was already piggy-backing, or whatever you want to call it. Perhaps you did the right thing by exposing it."

"You're being kind."

"Just realistic. Let's go inside, Birdie. You'll freeze out here. The weather has turned, and we'll have rain soon." He looked up at the cloud-laden sky that was getting darker by the second. *A dark day for dark deeds.* "I guess we're looking for the elemental, too, then?"

"Yes, but I should warn you of how dangerous it is."

"No warning necessary." He grinned. "We like the risks." He turned as the sound of other cars approached. "And here they are. Personally, I can't wait to start. Hunting something new is always fun."

She laughed, finally. "Only you would say that. Coffee before you start? And perhaps some tips. Forewarned is forearmed."

"Yes, please. To both."

Odette stepped back from her easel, horrified by the creature she had painted.

The elemental.

Actually, not just the elemental. There was a young girl in there too, with dark, hollow eyes that were devoid of humanity. She recognised her long hair, fine features, and high cheekbones from the attack in the library, but they were contorted, warped by the earth elemental that had consumed her body and caused her scarred skin, torn nails, ripped dress, and tangled hair. Not to mention the moss and dirt that caked her body until there was barely anything human left.

Odette had seen the truth of it, finally. The encounter with the spirits had torn the veil of illusions aside, allowing her to see the horror of what had occurred. Jacinta had been possessed by the creature after seeking a familiar. Her spell book suggested this was her course of action, but it had gone very wrong. This horror was the result. *No wonder Eliza was crying, and the grounds had erupted into verdant, tangled growth. The creature had done it.*

Fortunately, Moonfell had survived, as had the family, so they must have won, but it seemed they had not saved Jacinta. Odette's thoughts drifted to the bees' wings and the feather she'd placed on the surface close by. *What had the bees to do with this?* The ritual bound the witches and the bees, twisting their fates together. *Fates? Perhaps not the right word. Safety, maybe?* An assured connection to the house and grounds. Perhaps it marked them as belonging. *And the feather...* She picked it up, closed her eyes, and stroked it absently. Large amber eyes filled her vision, calm with wisdom, but also sorrow.

She moved her canvas aside, chose a blank one, and started painting again.

Lamorak had hoped that when he woke up on Tuesday morning, he would find that the weird events of the night might have been a dream.

He had slept poorly, dreaming of spirits and strange elemental energies that were trying to attack him. He'd also hoped that his new magical powers had also evaporated, but as cold, hard reality dawned, and he saw his clothes in a heap on the floor, he knew they wouldn't have.

Maverick and his pack would be back this morning, and he would no doubt have more questions that Lamorak had no idea how to answer. Pausing only to clean his teeth, he went to make coffee in their private kitchen and found Como at the same time. He looked as dishevelled as Lam was.

"Any more poppets?"

"No, thank the Gods. Any more powers?"

"Not that I am so far aware of." Lam edged past him to reach the coffee machine. "I had bad dreams, though. You?"

"So-so. I drank a stiff whiskey before bed, so it helped." Como carried his coffee to the window and looked down at the grounds. "It's colder today. I think we'll have rain. And the wolves are already here. I suppose we are up late."

Lam carried his drink over and spotted two wolves prowling below. "Any idea who they are?"

"No. I suppose we'll get used to them, though. Morgana was not happy with Birdie last night. Do you think they argue a lot?"

He shrugged. "My mother seems a stickler for some things, so who knows."

"She was right, though." Como gave a twisted grin. "She totally said we shouldn't do it, and then she swept in to help. Do you really think she passed us with a shadow spell?"

"She got on to the mezzanine somehow." He rubbed his temples, feeling like he had a hangover. "What do you think those spirits were trying to do to us?"

Como sipped his coffee while he watched the wolves. "I think that Jacinta genuinely came to warn us. After all, she brought the poppet, and could have harmed me but didn't. Which means that the elemental thing or whatever it is wasn't with her then, right? That would have hurt us—*me*—if it could."

Lam nodded. "That's logical. So, Jacinta's spirit was disturbed—perhaps by the weird ritual in the orchard—and she was able to warn us before the elemental arrived. Interesting. That suggests they weren't connected for a while."

"How long is a while? Years? Centuries? Minutes?"

"No idea. It depends on what they did back then. If they saved her, then in theory they have been separated for centuries."

"But all the while it's been plotting its revenge!"

Lam grimaced. "Very Machiavellian. How awful to think that you're not even safe in death." Lam considered his efforts to repel it. "I got a couple of fire balls in, did you?"

"Blast of pure power. I felt ineffectual compared to Birdie and Odette, though. We still have a lot to learn."

"That's why we're here." Lam turned back to the living room. "Whose spell books have we got here?"

"Virginia's and Ansel's. You know, I noticed some interesting spells in his, and I'm wondering if he had your ability to understand animals' emotions. And don't forget Beth, Sibilla's youngest did, too."

"You've got a good memory."

"I like history, especially Moonfell's."

Lam came to a decision. "I hate feeling out of my depth. The others will call us if they want us. Why don't you study Virginia's book and I'll study Ansel's? If that bee ritual has stirred up events from their lifetime, maybe Ansel's powers affected me. When Maverick questions me later, I want to know what I'm talking about."

"Sounds good. We need answers, and I like batshit crazy woman."

"Maybe you shouldn't call Virginia Wildblood that so often," Lam suggested, heading to the couch. "We don't want her manifesting, as well."

Morgana couldn't forget Jacinta's ravaged face and body. They had plagued her dreams all night. The elemental's spiteful features, although horrific, hadn't seemed as bad.

Nevertheless, she had slept badly, and part of that was down to her argument with Birdie. She hated arguing, and yet Birdie had been stupidly reckless. Now, not only did they need to rescue Hades from whatever predicament he was in, but banish the elemental, too. Hopefully, Jacinta would rest easy after that. At least Morgana knew Lam and Como were okay. She had texted her son, unable to face his possible censure either, and he'd reported them both well.

She paced her bedroom, unsettled and annoyed with herself, knowing she must face Birdie at some point, and be civil, too. Arguments were not productive. She should have been more insistent the night before, after all, she would be High Priestess eventually. That carried weight. Her annoyance carried over to her surroundings. Her bedroom that she'd had for years was suddenly unsatisfactory. It's high ceiling and spaciousness were all well and good, and it was furnished beautifully, but her tastes had changed over the years, and what had suited her as a young woman did not suit her now. All the main residents slept on the first floor, but not anymore, Morgana resolved. She would return to the second floor and find a suite of rooms there. Not near the guest rooms, either. They had enough regular guests to make it busy.

Her time spent nursing the injured shifters, and then last night's exploration of the hidden passage had reminded her how much she loved the second floor of the original Medieval house. It was cosier, more mysterious, but still comfortable. It also had a more occult flavour and was furnished more ostentatiously, with elements of the Oriental East. Morgana had a flare for the dramatic and knew what she wanted. A suite of rooms in the southwest corner of the house that caught the late afternoon sun. One of the rooms with a small balcony and long windows to allow in plenty of light. A bathroom, of course, but that was easy. Earlier renovations ensured that all bedrooms had their own bathroom. And a small sitting room. A snug, in fact, for cosy rainy days or weekend mornings when she sought solitude from the other residents. To make them perfect, the rooms would be bold in colour—peacock blues would be fabulous.

Happy with her decision, as if she'd shaken her fist at the long tradition that meant all permanent residents were on the first floor, she straightened her shoulders and decided to see Odette. Hopefully she would have some new insights on their current predicament. Closing her eyes, she focussed on finding Odette's unique magic, and discovered she was in her studio in the new wing.

Fifteen minutes later, Morgana knocked on the door, and when there was no reply, eased the door open, knowing it wasn't unusual for Odette to be lost in her work. It took a few seconds to spot her amongst the canvases in various stages of completion, the space vibrant with colour. Odette was working by the windows, attention fully absorbed on the canvas in front of her. She was dressed in her old jeans and jumper, feet in huge, striped slipper-socks, her hair bundled up in a messy bun. The room temperature was ambient, and a fire burned low in the grate. In the time it had taken Morgana to walk there, it had started raining; the windows were slick with water, and the grounds were a blur.

"Can I come in? Oh!" Morgana walked over to a large painting of an ethereal but menacing elemental creature that was also part young woman. "Odette! You saw it properly!"

Odette finally looked over at her, dragging her attention from the other painting. "Yes. I may not have seen it clearly last night, but I can now. The more I paint, the more details are revealed. That creature caused havoc, and tormented Jacinta. Cinta, actually. That's what her family called her."

"You saw that, too?"

"An insight—just a flash. No wonder the shifters scented pain, and that there was blood in that poppet. They must have been desperate."

Morgana felt sick. "They attacked their own sister."

Odette nodded. "But as Birdie said, there's no binding on that poppet."

"Or it was weak and vanished quickly." Morgana gave a dry laugh. "I doubt that, though. We do nothing by halves. Which means there must be more poppets, because they banished the creature somehow." Her attention shifted to the other painting, a striking barn owl with tawny feathers and amber eyes that stared ferociously at the world. For all their beauty, owls were predators. "And that?"

"From the feather. It's Hades."

"*What?*" Morgana looked at her, astonished. "You saw that, too? Just from a feather!"

She nodded, her dark, unruly hair falling over her forehead, and she flicked it back. "Yes. He was Ansel's familiar, and he was involved in the whole thing. But before you ask, I do not know details."

Morgana leaned against the window, slightly incredulous. "So, he was here then. Incredible. I suppose we always suspected. Okay, so we know that Hades was involved in banishing the creature, we have no idea if Jacinta survived at the time or not, but she is clearly still battling the elemental now. Hades is stuck somewhere in the spirit realm..."

"We have to find the other poppets," Odette said, placing her brushes in a glass of murky water. "Can you carry one of the paintings, Morgana? I'll take the other. We'll find the rest of the coven and update the shifters. By the way, I'm sorry about last night. You were right."

Morgana shrugged. "I should have stuck to my guns. I never doubt my gut instincts."

"Birdie is stubborn, and she was adamant last night. We've both seen it before. I admit to being curious. Also stupid. Sorry. The boys could have been hurt."

"You could all have been hurt! This isn't just about Lam!" She sighed. "You weren't, though, so that's the most important thing. Although, I wonder what the spirits are doing now. I hope the shifters can track them."

But if they could, what then?

Twenty-Seven

July, 1664

Eliza rarely went into the cellars. They were dark and damp, comprising of a warren of interconnected spaces, and home to spiders and rodents. Despite their best efforts, the cats never caught all of them.

The area they accessed the most was where they stored the wine. One of their ancestors was particularly fond of it, and had bought cases of it from his travels in France. They also stored their coal down here, as well as wood for the range and fires in the winter.

"Have you ever explored down here?" Jem asked, as they descended the creaking staircase.

"Not really," Eliza admitted. "Even with witch-lights and lanterns, the place gives me the shivers. Some of the rooms have doors with bars set into them. I hate to think what they might have been used for!"

"I suppose a grand house like this would have had a Lord of the Manor at some point. They would have needed a place to keep their enemies, or those who broke the law, perhaps."

Ansel called over his shoulder, "I explored down here when I was younger, but was worried I'd get trapped. Silly, I know, but it's surprisingly large. It runs under most of the house." He paused when he reached the first room, swinging the lantern around to illuminate the space. "I think there must be another way in here from somewhere in the house, but I never found it."

Eliza shivered in the damp, pulling her shawl around her shoulders. The roof was low and heavily timbered with beams and planks of wood, the walls of stone and brick, but the ground was only beaten earth. Racks of dusty wine bottles lined the walls, and Eliza decided she would replenish their supplies when they had more money.

Rooms and passages ran in all directions. The coal store was further along to the left, the barred-door rooms just beyond, but after that, Eliza wasn't sure what was down there. Ansel seemed confident, though.

"This way is east," he declared, setting off down one of the passages.

Everything was shrouded in cobwebs, and Eliza whisked them away with magic. Despite her misgivings, she looked around with interest as they walked through interconnected rooms and corridors. They came across huge, thick walls in places, and areas where it looked as if stones had been loosened.

"Is there anything hidden behind those?" she asked.

"I checked them years ago," Ansel said, "and found nothing."

"Are you hoping for buried treasure?" Jem asked, close behind her.

"Secrets, more like." Small, child-sized breaks in the walls caught her eye, and she headed towards them, ducking to see into the space beyond. "Why are they so low?"

"To avoid support beams, I expect," Jem said, close on her heels.

A witch-light revealed broken furniture and old barrels, and disappointed, she turned away.

Ansel had waited for them, and he grinned. "It's addictive, isn't it? Now that I'm older, I don't feel as scared. I'll come down here more often. Time for a spell, I think."

"A revealing spell? They don't always work upstairs." She knew because she'd tried, and had found some secret panels by manual searching alone, as if warded against magic. It was almost like the house was playing games with them. The more effort they put in, the greater the reward.

"May as well try. We haven't got time for this. It's bigger than I remember. *Hidden pathways, come to light, show your secrets, clear and bright.*"

A grating noise resounded down the corridor, coming from behind them, and then more and more, all from different directions.

Jem looked astounded. "Gadzooks! That's a few of them!"

Ansel grinned. "I knew it!"

Wide-eyed with excitement, he led the way to where they thought they'd heard the closest noise, and found a portion of the wall had shifted in one of the central rooms, revealing a narrow set of stairs that ran up into the house. Ansel bounded up them without a second thought, and within moments, he shouted, "It leads into the east parlour!"

"Actually," Eliza admitted, "this is both exciting and odd. I feel as if I could be spied upon in my own house!"

Ansel reappeared, a cobweb draped across his hair. "Well, this is great, but it's not finding us the orchard."

"Another spell, perhaps, to narrow it down?" Jem suggested, amused. "The other passages can wait!"

"Let me," Eliza said, deciding to appeal to the house at the same time, hoping that such a passageway existed. "House! Do not obstruct us. This is life or death! *Path unseen, now be found, guide me to the orchard's ground.*"

A golden orb appeared in front of Eliza, slightly smaller than a witch-light, and it floated down the corridor. They followed it through the rooms and along several corridors, until Eliza knew they must be at the far end of the house. The sturdy stone foundations lay ahead of them, but a dark edge marked where a doorway had opened. It would likely have been impossible to see, as it was made to blend into the wall, and was covered in dirt and grime.

Jem reached it first and pulled the stone door back, revealing a dark passageway beyond. A flurry of witch-lights revealed a rough, brick-built passage, and the golden orb bobbed along it.

Eliza took a sharp intake of breath. "Od's bodikin's! This must be it."

Ansel pushed past both of them. "I knew it!"

"Be careful," Jem called after him. "It could be unstable."

Despite his words of warning, Jem followed just as quickly, checking on Eliza to make sure she was behind them. The passageway ran narrow and straight, and was in reasonably good condition, other than the odd crumbling brick and cobwebs. Pungent damp and must made breathing unpleasant, but Eliza was too excited to care, and within a few minutes they reached the end where a set of ladders was set into the wall. The orb bobbed against a trap door above them.

Jem was the stronger of the two men, and after testing his weight on the ladders, climbed up and set his shoulders against the trap door. After a few grunted mutterings, he managed to lift it an inch. "Wedged tight. I think something's on top of it."

"Any clue where we are?" Eliza asked.

"No. I couldn't lift it high enough."

"More magic, then," Ansel said, wiggling his fingers. "Something subtle, or brute force?"

Eliza glared at him. "Subtle! We need to seal it again!"

"Spoilsport," he muttered.

He directed a spell at the trap door, and as Jem lifted it with ease, they heard a thud. "Just a crate," Jem called down. "You were right, Ansel. We're in the storeroom in the orchard."

Within moments, they were all standing outside the old stone building, breathing in clean, warm air. Only a short walk away were the beehives.

Jem slapped Ansel on the shoulder. "Well done! Brilliant, in fact."

"I have my moments. So, back to the house to grab our equipment, and then set up for the next part of the spell?"

Eliza nodded, wishing she felt more confident.

Ansel tried and failed to find Hades again, and sighed with disappointment. "No, I can't find him. Can we do this part of the spell without him?"

They were in the centre of the orchard now, close to the hives, after collecting the three poppets bound with fire, water, and air, and the ingredients for the next part of the spell. The ability to pass to and from the house without fear of being attacked had elevated all their spirits.

"Of course," Eliza said, lighting candles and lanterns with magic. "This second binding doesn't require its name at all. In fact, if we do this well, even if Hades isn't successful, we should still be able to banish it." A flicker of doubt flashed across her face as she turned to Ansel. "But its name would be ideal. To fail would be a disaster. It might even strengthen it. I have visions of it hanging around the garden forever, a malevolent spirit that has little power but can't be banished. It would be like a hideous haunting. And Jacinta would be lost forever."

Like Ansel, Eliza refused to say the word 'dead.'

Jem had accompanied them, still carrying his axe—just in case of emergencies. "I'm not sure how burying the three poppets will help. You'll be putting them in the earth—its natural environment."

"But they will be in the orchard," Ansel said, thinking Jem must not have listened earlier. "The orchard is immune from its magic."

"I still don't like it. I think you should place them in a tree or something. Or burn them. Bury the ashes instead."

Ansel cocked his head at Eliza. "That's an interesting idea."

"No. We'd destroy all the bindings. Trust me. All will be well. Besides, I am also going to douse them in honey. Lots of honey." She rubbed her hands together with glee. "And we'll do it at midnight. Earth's strongest hour, which should be counterintuitive, but it's not. Right. You two, bring the cauldron over."

They were in a clearing where they had made a fire pit in the centre, a tripod constructed around it. In seconds the cauldron was suspended from the chains, and Eliza lit the fire with a word of command. She then added water from the well and a large jar of honey, stirring it widdershins. The poppets were propped against the base of a tree.

"I think they're watching us," Jem said, eyeing them nervously.

"I can assure you, they're not," Ansel said, but he knew what Jem meant. Poppets were always unnerving. He finished laying out the rest of the ingredients and asked Eliza, "Anything I can do?"

"Tell the bees. I don't want them upset."

Ansel rarely visited the orchard at night, just because he didn't need to, but now he found it had a quiet, contemplative quality that was slightly unnerving. He felt watched. The beehives were silent, yet still emitted a compelling power. After sitting quietly for a few moments to attune to their energy, Ansel explained what they were going to do.

"It doesn't seem fair," he finished, "to bury such things in here, but we feel it's the safest place for them. We think your magic will weaken the creature further. Whatever you do here is very effective."

He wished he could properly converse with animals; it would be hugely helpful. Perhaps Hades could help him with that, too. Surely it was magic that he could grow with time.

"Anyway," he concluded, "please don't be alarmed. And please help Jacinta, too."

He closed his eyes, weariness washing over him, and he wished he could sleep for days. In fact, when this was all over, perhaps he would. His earlier elation at finding hidden passages faded into insignificance now. Jacinta would be so excited to explore them, and she might never have the chance.

Suddenly, an image filled his mind, and he saw Jacinta's broken body lying in front of the hives, the bees weaving a golden dance over her, but it was quickly replaced by a murky green cloud of miasma. *What did it mean? Were the bees helping to save her, or saying their goodbyes? Were they already predicting the outcome?* He squeezed his eyes tightly shut, hoping to see more, but the vision faded, and when he opened them again, the hives remained silent in the dark. He sighed. *Time to help Eliza complete the spell and bury the poppets.*

An hour later, after a long and complicated spell that bound the poppets in a honey gold liquid that shimmered with banishing and binding spells, fortified with the strength of fire, water and air, they buried the poppets in a deep hole lined with salt, poured the last of the mixture over them, and Jem threw the earth over the top as Eliza chanted the final part of the spell. She ended it by clapping her hands together, the sound echoing across the grounds, as she cried out, "As I command it, so shall it be!"

A shudder ran through the orchard, and Ansel felt a distinct shift in Moonfell's magic, just as a bloodcurdling shriek split the air. The ground over the poppets cracked and sank, before finally shuddering to a halt.

"Is that a good sign or bad?" Jem asked, stepping back from the site.

"Good, I think," Ansel said, looking to Eliza for confirmation. "The garden's magic feels lighter, as if the balance has swung back in our favour."

Eliza's eyes shone with power as she nodded. "I agree. We have weakened the elemental's power—by a lot, if that shriek was anything to go by. Now to banish it for good. Thrice the charm." She gathered their belongings and doused the fire with a word. "We'll leave the cauldron here and collect it later."

Ansel felt the urgency of time, fearing the creature may either make good on its escape now, while it still could, or try to hide. "We need to try to lure it to us and trap it, otherwise we'll end up chasing it all over the garden."

"Or it will chase us," Jem pointed out. "Is there a place in the garden that is the most logical place for us to be?"

"Perhaps the place it first appeared?" Ansel suggested. "The summerhouse. But there's something I should tell you. The bees sent me a message when I spoke to them. A vision."

Eliza's excitement at successfully completing the spell vanished as he recounted it. "They must have given you that for a reason. We'll bring her body here and they will save her."

She turned away, unwilling to discuss it further, and Ansel exchanged a worried look with Jem. He admired her positive attitude, but wasn't sure he agreed with it. And they still had to banish the elemental.

Twenty-Eight

Present Day

Hunter tracked the unusual elemental creature through the undergrowth, hackles up, belly low, nose to the damp earth.

Three pack members were close by: Domino, Monroe, and Tommy. For now, their instructions were to find and track it—if possible—just to learn more about it. Maverick had warned them, however, not to get too close. Its powers remained undetermined. So far, the creature was proving elusive. Its scent was distinctive, even with the rich smell of damp earth all around them, but just when they were close, it flitted away, darting between the plants.

Its wild, elemental magic was intriguing, as was its form—all twisted roots and branches, moss-clad and misshapen, making it hard to discern from the shrubs. For something that was supposed to be spirit, it seemed physical. Tangible. And so far, it seemed to be keeping a wary distance from them, too. Hunter reached a clearing by the west moon gate and shifted to human, his companions following suit. The fine rain was cold but refreshing, and he slicked his hair back, blinking water from his eyes.

"That damn thing is not going to be easy to trap," he complained.

Tommy grunted in agreement. "I want to sink my teeth in it, just to see if I can."

"It's hard to know, isn't it?" Domino said, attention on their surroundings. "It feels real. It has substance, and yet it shouldn't. It arrived through the séance, and years ago had to use Jacinta to give it form—well, that's the impression I got."

Hunter was used to seeing Domino naked, but he had trouble concentrating on her words. Shifters had little modesty, and saw each other naked all the time, but no one stared; that was just rude. However, he wasn't blind, and Domino had a great figure. Besides, it was more than that. They made each other laugh and had similar tastes. And he and Domino had too much unsaid between them. Too much sexual tension. Too much desire. Too much of her keeping him at arm's length. Partly because she was the Head of Security for the Storm Moon Pack. *The other part?* He wasn't sure. *Uncertainty, perhaps, about a relationship with a pack member. If it went wrong, things could be awkward.* He understood that, but he didn't share her fears. He wanted her, plain and simple, and if the others weren't around, right here and now in the rain and the wild would be the perfect time to get intimately acquainted, their bodies slick with water and desire.

"Hey, Fly Boy." Domino clicked her fingers in front of his face. "Hear me?"

He gave her a slow, knowing smile. "I was thinking of other things."

Monroe huffed. "Fuck's sake you two. Just do it already."

Domino flipped him the bird. "Piss off! I was saying, Hunter, that herding it to a prearranged spot would be a good move. If we can corner it, we could provoke a response. See how powerful it is. I'm with Tommy. How real is it?"

"Which is not what Maverick wanted," Hunter reminded her.

"When did you start following all the rules?"

"When did you start breaking them?"

"Yeah," Tommy scoffed at him. "Sissy."

Monroe laughed. "Much as I want to know what this is, risking Maverick's wrath is stupid. We should collaborate."

"We also need the witches," Hunter pointed out. "If it is a spirit, us trying to chew up the damn thing won't work. I want to know where Jacinta's ghost is, and why they aren't together."

Tommy had become unusually still, staring at the summerhouse. "I think I see her."

Tommy shifted to his wolf, and the others joined him. With his acute wolf vision, Hunter saw Jacinta's ghost in front of the summerhouse, staring at where they had dug up her spell book a few hours earlier. He was suddenly struck by how sad she was. A spectral figure haunted by her past...and maybe the manner of her death. With unexpected speed, the elemental appeared out of seemingly nowhere, and Hunter caught his first clear view of it and growled, unable to stop himself.

It had looked wizened before, twisted in on itself like an ancient twig creature. Now, however, it changed shape, towering over Jacinta, with limbs of corded wood, bristling with greenery, and glowing red eyes. Far from being afraid, though, Jacinta made a peculiar gesture in the air—a sigil of some sort—and with a visceral hiss, it vanished again.

"I'm sorry," Birdie said to Morgana, trying not to grit her teeth as she was still smarting about her decision and hated to admit it. "I was wrong last night. Hot-headed."

"Yes, you were. As I said to Odette, at least no one was hurt."

Birdie should have known not to expect any contrition from Morgana. No, *well, it might have worked*. Just a plain, *you were wrong*. And she was, so she better suck it up. "I let the elemental in."

"Maybe that was inevitable."

"Perhaps." She shifted her attention to the two paintings that Odette had propped on the mantlepiece. "So, my darling Hades was an owl, and *that* is the creature. Well done, Odette."

She shrugged. "It's what I do. Interesting, isn't it? He was a predator then and is one now—as a cat, I mean."

Birdie blinked, startled. "I hadn't considered that."

"It was all I could think about as I painted him."

Why did that seem ominous? Hades had been nothing but kind to her.

Morgana made a noncommittal noise that smacked of withholding judgement.

Odette continued, tapping the portrait of the elemental. It was painted with big brushstrokes; bold, forceful, and dramatic. "As I painted this, I felt its malice. It seized Cinta like she was nothing, using her for its own ends."

"Which were?"

"To relish getting out of its natural element and being unleashed in the garden. It wanted to escape, explore, and wreak havoc. I caught only broad intentions, of course, but it was determined. Nasty, spiteful thing. Not at all how I presumed an earth elemental would behave. Earth is so grounding, normally. Calm. I still haven't had a chance to really study Eliza's grimoire yet, which is remiss of me. This compulsion took over."

"And is very useful," Morgana told her. "We need to summon the shifters and make a plan. I suggest the glasshouse. It's big enough to accommodate a pack of soaking shifters. I'll find some towels. Can someone summon the boys?"

"I'll call the shifters," Odette said, "and take these into the glasshouse, too."

Birdie nodded, bristling at being given orders, but trying not to show it. She was still the High Priestess of Moonfell. *For now.*

Ten minutes later there were two jugs of coffee, a tray of mugs, and a plate of home baked cookies on the table in the glasshouse, and eight wet shifters and five witches gathered around it. The shifters had towelled off and pulled on jeans and t-shirts. Well, Cecile and Domino had. The men remained bare-chested.

Tommy rubbed his hair dry with one hand, while reaching for a biscuit with the other. "You ladies are bloody amazing! Morgana, are these yours?"

She smiled. "Freshly baked yesterday. I've just warmed them up."

"Fantastic!"

Birdie called over to Maverick, who was talking with Domino and Hunter. "Any luck with the elemental?"

He rolled his eyes. "Plenty. Too much, in fact. It's everywhere and nowhere."

Monroe grunted in agreement, his pecs popping as he picked up a mug of coffee. "It's leading us in a merry dance across the grounds, and the rain isn't helping. However, it has a distinctive, strong scent."

Lam frowned. "So although it's a spirit, it has a scent? Crazy!"

"Ghosts that are strong enough bring all sorts back with them," Morgana explained. "Besides, the elemental isn't a spirit as in a ghost. It's an elemental being that is spirit by its very nature, and is still bound to Jacinta."

"Not right now, it's not. We found her, too," Hunter said. "Round by the summerhouse. Alone."

Birdie looked at him, startled. "They aren't together?"

"No. She looked as if she exerted some sort of control over it, too."

"*What*?" Birdie was shocked, slow to process his words. "You saw Jacinta's ghost? She's manifesting strongly, then."

Hunter shrugged. "I guess you could say that. We see differently in our wolf, though. Animals sense things that humans can't. Our sight has a different spectrum. For example, we don't see colours as well, and we see far better at night. But, seeing as we're paranormal too, we see spirits more clearly. However, Tommy saw her shade first, when we stopped to speak by the west gate. As for the elemental..." He trailed off, looking at the other shifters. "Well, it changed shape. It was huge and towered over her. I think we must have seen its natural form."

Domino shook her head, clearly perplexed. "We're missing something, I am sure of it."

"Hold on," Morgana said, frowning. "You said Jacinta had some kind of control over it? How?"

"She made a shape in the air with her fingers," Hunter lifted his hand to mimic her. "A sigil, I think. It fled, but not far. It's still in the grounds. And that's the wrong shape I made, so don't get excited about that."

Morgana smiled, tension dropping out of her shoulders. "That's excellent news, and most intriguing. I wonder if Jacinta remembers how her siblings banished it."

"Maybe they didn't," Maverick suggested. "Maybe *she* did."

"Not from what I saw," Odette said with conviction. "Did *you* see Jacinta?"

"No. We," Maverick's glance encompassed Arlo, Cecile, and Vlad, "were by the orchard. We saw the elemental, but not Jacinta. Same experience. It flitted about, evading us."

"It didn't enter the orchard, though," Arlo added. "It skirted its edges."

Birdie exchanged glances with her coven. "The bees again. What is it about that orchard? Never mind for now." Birdie looked at Odette. "Tell them what you've found out."

Odette ran through her visions as everyone examined the paintings. "I think Hades was involved in the spell to bind the elemental, and we also think that the ritual we did to welcome Lam and Como was done back then, too."

Maverick nodded. "It's the trigger for a chain reaction."

"Exactly. When we repeated the bee ritual, he was somehow catapulted into the spirit realm and trapped there. We think there are more poppets that we must find to free him."

Cecile frowned. "What makes you think that?"

"Because they banished it somehow by using its own body—if that's the right word. Its roots and twigs that bleed seem to be the best way to do it. The poppet we found isn't bound. That means others are."

"Doesn't that mean breaking the binding?" Hunter asked, as usual, very familiar with magic.

"We don't know," Odette said. "In fact, there's still lots we don't know."

Lamorak spoke up, addressing Maverick more than anyone. "I think I know where my magic has come from. My new magic, that is. I've been reading Ansel's spell book, and it seems Ansel could detect animal's emotions from a young age. He acclimatised to it over time.

His spell book lists all kind of spells to hone his skills and shape it, I suppose, is a good word."

"And block it," Como added.

"That, too. Plenty of things for me to experiment with."

Birdie smiled encouragingly. "That's excellent news. We'll help."

"I," Como said, "have found lots of weird and wonderful spells in Virginia's spell book. As we first noticed, Odette, her writing deteriorates at the end of the book, and she seems to have become more paranoid, writing darker and darker spells. I found a heavily marked spell, and tucked next to it was a stained piece of paper that looked like it was torn from another grimoire. I think it's the one that Jacinta used to summon the elemental in the first place."

Birdie was hearing many things that gave her hope of finding a solution, but this was the best yet. "Can you fetch it?"

"Of course."

He vanished in a whirl of air, and Tommy swore. "What the fuck?"

"He's an air witch, you pillock!" Hunter informed him, looking cocky. "I knew a couple."

Como must have had the book ready, because he returned in seconds. "Here you go." He placed the book on the table, turning it to a marked page. "The damaged one clearly warns that it's a dangerous spell."

"And yet she used it anyway," Birdie said with a sigh. "I wonder what made her so desperate." She fell silent as she read the spell, the others beside her, and finally said, "Damn it. There's little to hang a reversal on."

"Which is probably why they chose to bind a poppet," Morgana suggested. "They did well to even manage to get a part of it, if it's evading you shifters so successfully."

"What now?" Maverick asked. "It's out there with Jacinta, and still no Hades. Are you really sure there are more poppets?"

"No, but it seems logical," Birdie said. "If only we could find Hades and speak to him. He would tell us everything, instead of us fumbling around in the dark."

Cecile said, "If you used a séance to speak to Jacinta, can't you use one to speak to Hades?"

"I must admit that I haven't considered it," Birdie said, wondering why she hadn't. *Idiot. Old and senile.* "I tried scrying, but that's quite different. There's no harm in trying, I guess. The elemental is already here."

"We'll help," Como said eagerly. "Me and Lam."

"We should help the pack," Morgana suggested to Odette. "Try and work out a way to corner the creature. Or Jacinta." Her expression softened. "I'd like to talk to her."

"Good," Maverick said, "because we want to capture it, too."

Lam shuffled, looking awkward. "Actually, I'd really like to help the pack, too, but if you need me, Birdie?" He trailed off, looking hopeful that she wouldn't.

"No, Como and I will manage fine," Birdie said, resigned to leaving things unsettled between her and Morgana, who she knew would appreciate spending time with her son. "We'll use the library again. However, before you all head off into the garden to look for the creature, we need to decide what we're doing with it. How are we going to capture it? We have one poppet and the green miasma we kept from last night. Can we use them somehow?"

Odette exchanged a questioning glance with Morgana. "I doubt the miasma will be of any use, but the poppet could be. They might not have bound it, but surely we can?"

Birdie groaned. "Of course. Why the hell didn't I think of that? I swear, I'm losing my marbles. In theory, it's already weaker than it once was. Another binding would add to that."

"But," Hunter suggested, "the miasma is part of it, right? Like some of its essence—kind of like our blood. If you put that in a jar, can't you bind the jar?" His face wrinkled in confusion. "Is that even a thing?"

Birdie didn't speak as she mentally ran through the various binding spells she knew. They were many and varied, but you could of course bind anything. "Of course we could. Like using hair, skin, or nails. It's part of the elemental. Thank you, Hunter. That should have been obvious."

"It wouldn't have been to me," Tommy pointed out. "It's different, isn't it? It isn't flesh and blood. It's an elemental, or whatever you call it. Not like us at all! Bloody thing gives me the creeps. It did not like whatever Jacinta did, though. That weird, squiggly gesture she made."

Birdie, Morgana, and Odette spoke as one. "Sigil magic."

Morgana cocked her head at Birdie. "Perhaps there was another reason they put sigils and runes on that metal box. Runes are some of the oldest types of magic we know. They go back hundreds, if not thousands, of years. Perhaps they are the perfect things to use on an ancient, elemental creature. I will tackle the binding spells on the poppet and the miasma, Birdie, while you continue to look for Hades. And perhaps, Lam," she looked at her son, eyes narrowed speculatively, "before you hunt with the shifters, maybe you should see if your newfound powers work with the bees. Politely, of course."

Lam froze. "Is that wise? They seem kind of scary."

"They accepted you to the house and grounds, and the ritual reaffirmed our connection to them. I doubt they would hurt you."

He nodded, squaring his shoulders as if going into battle. "Of course. I need to get used to this, anyway. May as well start with them."

"Which leaves me," Odette said. "I'm going to find Jacinta. We need to chat."

"Not alone, you don't," Arlo said, his tone brooking no argument. "I'll come, too."

Birdie sighed with satisfaction. "Excellent. If anything significant happens, summon us with a howl. Come, Como. Let us find Hades."

Twenty-Nine

July, 1664

"I have an idea," Eliza said, brandishing Jacinta's spell book like a weapon. "We lock this in a spelled box, along with Jacinta's favoured things, as a way of binding her magic. Perhaps the elemental will decide to abandon her."

Ansel's brow creased with confusion. "We bind her, too? Surely that will weaken her defences. I don't like that at all."

"Me neither," Jem said. "It could be a disaster."

Eliza huffed with impatience. "It is already a disaster." They were back in the tower spell room after once again using the underground passage, planning their final assault. There was no time to waste. "And we use the New Moon Gate."

"But it's in the north. In theory, the strongest place for the elemental," Ansel pointed out.

"And therefore, the place best to bind it. I am sending that thing back today, if it kills me to do it!"

Jem inhaled in horror. "Don't say that!"

"I will not allow that creature to leave or continue unchallenged any longer. We have struck back now. The balance is in our favour. Ansel, don't argue with me." She could see him ready to start, and she hadn't got time. "Bring me hair from Jacinta's brush, and anything you think useful from her room. You know what I mean. And a doll. Her favourite that she played with as a child."

Once he'd left, she turned to her shelves, searching for a suitable box to use. She kept many for storage purposes as well as spell work, and reached for one made of copper. "This will do well." She turned to her grimoire, flicking through the pages until she found her list of runes and rune spells. "I know the ones I should use. I just need to etch them into the box."

"What with?"

"Magic, of course. I have the perfect spell for that, too. I estimate it will take me an hour at the most. Then we head back to the garden." She considered her other brilliant thought. "I'll bind Jacinta, too."

"I thought you were already using the book for that?"

"I mean with the twigs from the creature. I'm going to use them to make another poppet." She pointed to the top shelf. "They're up there. I put them well out of the way. Can you get them for me?"

"I don't like the sound of this."

"Just trust me."

While they waited for Ansel, she worked quickly, thinking of Jacinta as she bound the twigs, and imbuing it with her sister's essence. It felt odd to be doing such a thing, but she knew in her gut it was right. When Ansel arrived with her hair, snippets of her clothing, and Jacinta's old toy, she fashioned another poppet from the doll and stuffed it inside the first. When she finished, she admired her handwork. "Brilliant."

"Horrific," countered Jem. "I hate it."

"But it will work. He is bound to her like a weed. We must pull him out. Ansel, where is Hades?"

He retreated to the door. "I'll find him."

Ansel went to the room below, a dusty bedroom that no one had used in years, and sat on the window seat, forcing the window open past the wriggling vines, to let in the warm, humid air that choked the grounds after the hot summer's day. The heat was still oppressive, but on the horizon was a dark band of clouds swallowing the stars. A storm was coming.

He sat quietly, eyes closed, letting the wriggle of vines lull his mind to somnolence, and feeling for Hades's distinct energy signature. *"Hades, we're running out of time. We need you now! Do you have the creature's name?"*

He sat for what seemed like a long time, and just when he was giving up hope, thinking that perhaps Hades wasn't going to return at all, he felt his presence. Opening his eyes, he saw Hades perched on the windowsill regarding him solemnly.

Ansel sighed. "You didn't find it, did you?"

Hades shuffled and screeched, the noise surprisingly loud, before his voice resounded in Ansel's head. *"No. It is frustrating. For all of my many, many contacts, elemental creatures are not well known on my spirit plane. It is impossible for me to find its name. I'm sorry."*

A huge swell of disappointment filled Ansel until he feared it might suffocate him. He took deep breaths, regaining control of his emotions. "We'll do it regardless. We have plans."

"*I can still help. Grasp it like I did before, perhaps.*"

Ansel nodded, taking in Hades's large form and predatory gaze. "Why now?"

"*What do you mean?*"

"Why are you here now?"

"*I told you. I tried to get through before, but couldn't. And then you summoned me.*"

"You know, I've been thinking about that. I block the emotions and feelings of other animals a lot, but not all the time. Not in the house. The scurry of mice and their obsession with nests and food doesn't bother me, nor the cats who hunt them. Or even the many spiders who weave their webs. If anything, they're a comforting background to hear around the house. It feels less empty. But you have never contacted me here, and you could have, many times. You only came after we did the bee ceremony. Did they call you?" Hades didn't answer, but Ansel refused to look away. He felt he might drown in those amber eyes, or that Hades might strike with one of his huge, taloned claws, but he didn't budge. "Your silence speaks volumes."

"*Does it matter?*" Hades finally asked.

"It does to me. I would like the truth. To know that I can trust you. If I can't, you may as well leave now. I have managed without a familiar for years, and so has my family. Searching for one has cost Jacinta her life."

"*You don't trust me?*"

"Not entirely. And stop answering my questions with more questions."

Hades's claws contracted, scratching against the stone sill. "*I am trustworthy, and your wellbeing is most important to me. But yes, I*" *admit you caught me in a lie. I have never sought you out. The bees asked me to, considering the circumstances. We go back many years, and they thought I would be able to help. I fear I have not.*"

"Why did they think you could help? Because of your association with my family?"

"*Yes, that and my vast well of knowledge.*" Hades had answered far too quickly, and Ansel cursed himself for offering up an explanation. "*That is as much as I can say.*"

"Or are willing to say." Ansel tried to probe his mind as he did with the animals, but all he encountered was a void, and he feared what that meant. "Perhaps you should leave, Hades. You would rather not be here, obviously, because the bees made you come. I summoned you to help Jacinta. It seems that we have a solution for that." He stood up, feeling a sense of loss, but deep resolve. "I absolve you of any obligations you might feel, or of the lessons you said you would teach me. Return from whence you came."

"*The bees have commanded that I see this through, so I will.*"

Ansel laughed dryly. "The bees command you? Well, that's the first thing you've said that I believe, but it's too little, too late. Go, I insist."

"*There is much you don't understand.*"

"Enlighten me."

"*I cannot.*"

"We are at an impasse then."

Hades regarded him for long, unblinking moments, and then vanished.

Ansel released a long-held breath, and felt tears prick his eyes. He had put so much store in Hades. He turned up just when he needed him, and Ansel knew he was ancient and wise, but once caught in a lie, he wasn't sure he could ever trust him again. And it was the matter of the lie. *Why pretend to have been searching for him? To forge a deeper connection? And how could bees command him?*

These were all questions that could wait. They had an elemental creature to banish.

Eliza cast a shadow spell over their small group, muffling all sight and sound, and they crossed the garden with a great deal more ease than they had earlier.

Of course, they used the hidden passage again, and then crossed to the north from the orchard. The garden felt threatening in the day, but seemed far worse at night, especially compared to the previous evening when they had returned from the theatre. When she turned to look back at the house, her heart ached to see it walled with thorns. It reminded her of the fairytale, *Sun, Moon, and Talia,* in which poor Talia is put into a magical, deep sleep by a cursed splinter and the house locked up around her. However, Talia was not a witch like Eliza, and the creature's powers had waned. The prolific plant growth had slowed, and no longer was fresh growth wriggling across the path. Unfortunately, a wounded creature could be more dangerous. Desperate.

Ansel was dispirited after his conversation with Hades, but Eliza was relieved. Of course, having Hades's help was useful. He had helped her and Jem escape the creature, after all, but he unnerved her, and she couldn't explain why. Not knowing the creature's name was a blow, but Eliza felt sure that her latest plans would work regardless.

The New Moon Gate loomed over them, and it was clear the promised storm was almost upon them. As soon as they were beneath its broad arch, Eliza dropped the spell, and Jem and Ansel used a combination of spade and magic to dig the hole and complete their other preparations.

"You know," Eliza whispered, "this all started with the new moon. It's appropriate we finish it here."

"I admire your confidence," Jem said.

"Intention is the first rule of witchcraft. I have complete faith." She stared at the poppet fashioned after her sister and her gut churned. "Forgive me, Jacinta. I mean this for the best."

"When do you want the fire lit?" Ansel asked her.

"As soon as the creature arrives."

While fashioning the poppet, Eliza had refined her plans even more. She felt like a monster for what she was about to do, but could see no other way to banish the creature. She checked for the bucket of well water at her side, the metal bowls, the candles and herb bundle next to them, and some of the remaining roots they had salvaged. All she had to do now was summon the creature.

"Jem, you must stay behind me, regardless of what you see or hear."

"I'll try, but if you're in trouble…"

She vowed that when this was over, she would explore her feelings for Jem properly. "Don't risk yourself for me. Or you, Ansel."

He gave a non-committal grunt.

Grasping the two entwined poppets in her left hand, she pulled tendrils of the creature's roots from the bucket and wound them around the poppets and her hand, and raising her voice, commanded Jacinta to her side.

"*Sister mine of blood and flesh, our bond was cast at birth, by moon's light and stars above, come to me, dear love on earth.*" A rumble of thunder punctuated her words and the roots tightened about her wrist. She continued to bind. "*Sister dear, hear my plea, through night and mist and storm, bring the creature to my side, who has so wickedly seized your form.*" A guttural roar resounded across the grounds, mixing with another rumble of thunder, and the earth trembled beneath her feet. Eliza shouted to be heard above the gathering storm as the wind whipped up the thick growth around them. "*Wildblood with power grand, Jacinta, heed my plea, come to me now across our land, as High Priestess I command thee!*"

With a crackle and flash, her sister's possessed and defiled body appeared before them, writhing and twisting in pain. Her eyes glowed with a sickly green light, and her lips were pulled back in a ghastly grimace. As soon as she arrived, Jem ignited a ring of flames around the entire gate, trapping them all inside.

Eliza stopped binding the poppet to her and cast the roots she'd used into the fire. The elemental shrieked in pain, but she hardened her ears to it, instead shouting to Ansel to light the candles and put the bucket at her feet.

Then she started to pull apart the poppet wrapped around her sister's doll, casting her spell as she did so. The words tripped from her tongue as she dismantled the poppet piece by piece and Ansel took them from her, passing them over smoke, before burning them to ashes in a small metal dish, and then throwing the ashes in a small bowl of water. It took a long time. The creature tried to attack, but it was a feeble attempt after already being bound, and it screeched with impotent rage. Her sister's face became more distinct, and Eliza's heart thudded with every crack of thunder. Lightning was forking around them now, huge flashes that lit up the night sky. Eliza wanted to hurry. She knew that although she was destroying the creature, she was harming her sister too, but she must be steady. *She must be sure.*

And then it was done. One last piece of the elemental remained wrapped around Jacinta's doll poppet. Her sister's body lay curled and broken on the ground, bathed in a mass of writhing shadows caused by the ring of fire that she dared not approach yet. Eliza plucked the final root off, leaving only her sister's limp doll in her palm.

"*Elemental creature of earth, I banish you from this garden forevermore. There is no rest for you. No earthly place that will accept you. No place for spirit, no water that will replenish you, or fire that will warm you, or air that will caress you. I cast you into the endless void. There you shall wander for eternity. A creature of smoke and shadows, without will, without power. So I command it. So shall it be."*

Ansel cast the silty mix of ash and water into the salt-filled hole, and Jem filled it in with earth. Only then did Eliza rush to her sister's side. She fell to her knees, soaked and freezing, but mostly terrified.

Her sister's body was so still and limp, and she leaned forward, and then stopped abruptly, horrified at what she might see.

"Let me," Ansel said, edging her out of the way. He turned Jacinta over, rolling her gently onto her back, and almost whimpered. "Jacinta, no!"

Although Eliza thought she'd prepared herself, she hadn't.

Jacinta's face was ragged with cuts and bruises, her eyes swollen shut and almost black, her lips dry and cracked. She was barely recognisable from the pretty young woman she had been. The rest of her body hadn't fared much better. Deep welts and cuts scored her skin, ragged wounds were filled with dirt and stones, and she was horribly still.

Thirty

Present Day

Lam stood in front of the hives, noting that the orchard continued to be slightly warmer than the rest of the grounds. Nevertheless, it still drizzled here, and he pulled the hood of his coat further over his head, feeling foolish and out of his depth.

Not that he would let on to Maverick, though. The shifter had insisted on remaining with him, to protect him—or so he claimed—and paced around as Lam prepared himself. The other five shifters, all in their wolf, had spread across the orchard. Arlo was with Odette as she searched for Jacinta, and Monroe had opted to help Morgana with the binding spells.

Lam took a few deep breaths to settle himself and opened himself up to the sounds of the animals around him. The birds were busy with their nesting, their excitement obvious even in the hush of the orchards. Insects scurried, and not too far away, a nest of dormice slept. Maverick bristled with aggression, hyper-alert for any sign of the creature, and he tried to shut that out. Not before he felt a tentative connection to him, and Lam quickly shut that down, too. But bee song was stronger than any of them. They were watchful and alert, curious at the shifters who searched the orchard, but not afraid.

Lam spoke aloud. "Good morning, bees. I trust you are well. I have brought a small amount of sugar as a gift." He placed the small bowl he carried on the closest hive and stepped back again. "It's for all of you, of course. I bring news. You might not be aware, but an old problem has returned to Moonfell. An elemental creature that we believe caused Eliza Wildblood trouble over four hundred years ago is now back, as is Jacinta's ghost. She gifted us a poppet that we believe is a clue. She wants to help us. Actually," he said, following his thoughts to their natural conclusion, "she needs *our help*. Her spirit and the elemental are still tied together somehow, even now. It seems, though, that she has some control of it, although it's confusing. So far, the elemental does not have the power it once had. The garden is fine. There isn't the rampant growth that Odette saw in her vision. But worse, Hades has vanished, and we think they are connected. His disappearance has upset Birdie. If you know something, we would appreciate your assistance."

The bees had been tolerant of him up until now. Polite, but barely acknowledging him, as if he'd dropped in for afternoon tea with an absent-minded aunt. Now, however, he felt their collective consciousness switch to him, and it felt so powerful that he almost stumbled back. Mentally he added, "*Gently, please. You are all so strong. I am unused to this. I think my new powers are Ansel's gifts. I'm sure you must remember him.*"

An insistent hum vibrated through him, starting in his head, but it swept down until his entire body tingled and he felt as if he'd been filled with golden light. *Was that the bees' warm response to Ansel's name? Or was it to Hades's?* His connection now felt stronger. He could see the bees in the hives in his mind's eye, and had a startling awareness of them spread across the orchard and the garden beyond, connected like golden threads.

They were searching for something.

Thousands of rapid images fired through his synapses—snapshots of the garden, close-ups of leaves and spring flowers as the bees collected nectar, micro-images in vivid blue, green, and ultraviolet light. It all happened so fast that he could barely comprehend it. And then Maverick was in his head, too, piggybacking as the bees searched.

Lamorak clung on to the experience as if he were on a roller coaster, until the shuffling of images stopped, and he saw a twisted form lurking in the huge yew hedge close to the Waxing Moon Gate. *The elemental creature.* It was all shades of blue and green, natural but unnatural, and vivid with his bee vision. Then he was once again in the orchard, seeing himself through their eyes, before he was firmly back in his own body. *What the actual fuck had happened?*

But the bees hadn't finished with him, and they directed his attention to the right. The orchard, much like they had seen it after their ritual, appeared to have golden glitter shot through it, but a brighter pulse of light drew his eye. Something in the ground. The buzzing became insistent, shaping itself into a command.

Dig.

"What about Hades?" Lam asked, far louder than he meant to.

Unfortunately, their connection was broken, and he turned to Maverick. "Did you see what I did? The elemental by the yew hedge?"

Maverick shifted back to human, eyes boring into Lam's. "Yes. How did you do that?"

"I don't know. The bees did it. I felt them nudge themselves into my brain, and the next thing I knew, I was seeing what they did through their collective mind! At least I presume that's what it was. And then you arrived. How did *you* do that?"

"Just like the other night." He smirked. "It seems it works both ways."

"Maybe some warning next time!"

Maverick's smirk vanished as he weighed Lam up. "I don't even have that connection with my pack."

"I'm not exactly thrilled about it, either! But we haven't got time for this. What are we doing about the elemental?"

"Nothing, for now. We know where it is, and the bees have satisfied themselves that you're not lying. They were perturbed enough to point us over there."

Maverick walked through the orchard to the spot the bees had indicated, and Lam, equally long-legged, fell into step beside him. They reached a small clearing ringed with wizened apple trees, and a short distance away was the old stone hut used to store garden tools. Lam closed his eyes, trying to see what the bees had shown him. The golden glow that must lie in the centre.

Lam sighed, head still fuzzy from his bee encounter. He should have felt victorious, but instead he felt confused. "Everything looks completely normal, but they said 'dig,' so I guess that's what I do. What do you think is down there?"

"Only one way to find out. Grab a spade, and I'll use my paws."

Morgana was glad of Monroe's company. They had fallen into an easy friendship since they had fought the demon, and an easy flirtation, too. *Well, Monroe had*. She accepted his teasing flirtations graciously, not entirely sure how serious he was, and terrified of making a fool of herself.

"You know, you don't have to help me," she said as she searched for the herbs in the stillroom. "I'm sure you'd have more fun hunting."

He grinned. "I am hunting, of sorts."

"That sounds predatory."

"Only in a good way. I mean, I'm helping you hunt with magic."

"Oh! Of course you are." She laughed. "In that case, be useful and grab me the large jar of belladonna off the top shelf. Save me fetching the ladders."

Monroe reached it easily and handed it to her with a flourish. "My lady."

"Thank you." She consulted her list. She was planning on a simple binding for the poppet. Something to restrict its movements rather than its powers, which right now seemed negligible. She would also need thick twine, and she had just the right potion to soak it in. "Could you get the jar of saltwater on the second shelf?"

"Just saltwater?"

"Salt in full moon water."

"Ah! So," he said, once he'd placed that down too, "you're a hard woman to get alone."

"Am I?" He moved closer, thrumming with his tightly-leashed shifter power. She made herself stand her ground. "But I'm here all the time, alone, in this kitchen, cooking up potions and magic."

"I'm not here then. I'm only here with the rest of the pack, while you and your coven plot."

"I think you wolves do plenty of plotting, too."

"I like plotting. I'm plotting right now."

Monroe stepped closer. He'd put his shirt on, thank the Goddess, or she wasn't sure she'd be able to concentrate. She'd seen him naked, so she knew what those clothes concealed. Monroe was tall and broad-shouldered, bristling with muscle and zero fat. A perfect physique, like all shifters. He had shaved his hair so that only millimetres showed, and his black skin was burnished like a plum. And yes, he looked good enough to eat.

He backed her against the counter, not touching, but close enough for her to feel his heat. "Come to dinner one night. Your choice. Anywhere in London."

Her breath shortened. "Just us two?"

"Just us two. As long as it's not a vegetarian restaurant." He grinned, showing his perfect teeth with two slightly pronounced canines. His wolf was simmering just below the surface, and she found that she liked it.

Her brain, the rational side, was telling her to say no. He was younger than her, surely. She, meanwhile, had a son, and was considered serious. *What did he see in her?* She needed to know. It made her feel excited and young again. Attractive and desirable. "You choose. I'll enjoy being surprised. As long as it's not a burger joint."

"Deal. No vegetarian, no burgers. As if I would, by the way!" He rolled his eyes dramatically. "I have just the place in mind. Pick a night."

He was still intoxicatingly close, and she plucked a night at random, terrified she'd back out if she didn't commit now. "Friday—as long as you're not at work, of course."

"Perfect. I'll pick you up at seven." He eased backwards, leaving her with a dry throat and a grin so big her face ached. "Would you like another jar?"

"Just the bundle of roots in the basket."

He lifted them down, and then scanned the book over her shoulder, breath warm on her cheek. He was deliberately not touching her, and her body screamed for him to. It was as if he'd unleashed an unknown hunger in her, but if he could wait, so could she. *What? Wait?* Her mind was already racing ahead. *Stop.*

"How does this binding work?" he asked.

She reached for a bowl, poured the mixture of saltwater and belladonna in, and then dropped a coil of twine in while she weighed the roots to grind into a powder. "We will ensure that wherever it is in the garden, it cannot move."

"Smart." He picked up the poppet and examined it. "Ugly thing. What if you put this in the potion?"

"I'm not sure I want to. It's brittle now. Breakable. I don't want to feed it with a potion, even though it's poisonous."

"And the jar of miasma?"

She fell silent, considering her options. "Let's bind them together. Jar and poppet. I feel I'm working in the dark, but that strikes me as the best option. The simplest. Best not to overcook it."

"You've been doing this a long time."

"My entire life. When Birdie dies—not any time soon, I hope—the responsibility for this place will fall to me."

"That's a lot to deal with."

She smiled. "Like I said, I'm used to it. Even dealt with much of it when Birdie was ill. Well, old."

"You two have argued, I can tell."

"Can you?" Morgana looked at him, alarmed. "It was nothing. She's stubborn sometimes, and while she makes many good decisions, right now her worry for Hades is skewing her judgment. I hate saying *I told you so*, but, well..." She shrugged. "Jacinta was already here, it seems. Best it's out in the open."

"You're loyal."

"So are you, to Maverick."

Monroe nodded. "Of course. He's a good alpha. That's what I like about you. Well, that and other things," he said, flirting again. "You're not worried about Birdie now? Alone with Como?"

"No. She won't make the same mistake twice. I trust her." She forced a smile. "Anyway. Time to bind."

Como was getting bored, despite his best efforts, because Birdie was having far from an easy time of it.

The library's enormous curtains had been shut, plunging the room into darkness. The only light came from the fire and the candles, just like it had during the night, and Birdie had dropped into her trance-like state quickly, a candle flickering between her and Como. Her hands were warm and small, and they gripped his tightly.

It was fair to say that communing with spirits was not one of Como's strengths, and according to Birdie, not one of hers, either. Odette was much better suited to the task with her ethereal ways and uncanny abilities. But this was Hades, and Birdie was sure that he would come to her and only to her. However, despite almost an hour of searching for him, reaching out beyond the here and now, Hades remained stubbornly absent.

Como found it hard to relax. His eyes kept jumping to the mezzanine, hoping nothing manifested in the darkness, or that Hades wouldn't appear on the table with a hiss and a howl.

Birdie finally released Como's hands and sat back in the chair. "It seems I have failed."

"He's trapped, that's the only explanation," Como said valiantly. "He would never abandon you otherwise."

"You're a very dear, sweet boy."

"It's true." Como leaned forward. "Why live here with you for decades and then just vanish? Perhaps something has bound *him*."

She leaned on the table, fingers twirling with her hair as she considered his words. "That's a very interesting suggestion."

"Well, there's a lot of binding magic going on, isn't there? Clearly there are repercussions, because Jacinta is here."

"Who is still bound in some manner to the creature. Como, I think you're right."

"I am?" His eyes widened with surprise, and Birdie smiled. "You are just like your grandmother, you know. She was so excited to be a witch, and loved learning everything. I see that in you. We must call her and make sure she visits while you're here."

"I think she's already planning to! Am I really like her?" He was both pleased and horrified. He was very fond of her, but she was such a battleaxe sometimes. A small, round one.

"Yes, but far less petulant. Although, your swearing earlier reminded me much of her. You'd be surprised at what she comes out with when riled. Now, back to binding."

The fire crackled and the rain battered against the windows, cosseting them in a cocoonlike embrace. The poor wolves were out there, as was Odette, getting soaked, no doubt. Como wasn't sure whether he'd rather be inside, warm and dry, or outside with the others, battling the elements. Either way, he was sure he'd feel out of his depth, baffled by the many layers of their current conundrum.

"We need answers, Como," Birdie continued. "The ritual must link the past with the present. Hades was involved. Have we sent him to the past again? That can't be right. And if he hasn't been bound for all these years, and he can't have been because he's been here with me, and no doubt has been up to many other things, why now?"

Como shrugged, looking for the simplest solution. "Because you've activated it. It's like a reset button. I bet he didn't even know."

Birdie stood, the chair scraping across the floor. "In which case we might need to start undoing bindings. Except that might not be wise."

"Plus, we don't know how Eliza did it." He rose to his feet, too, alarmed at her suggestion.

"Yet."

Birdie marched towards the door, and Como ran after her. "But Birdie, if you undo the binding, won't that make the elemental powerful again?"

"It might, but we can't leave Hades locked up and bound forever. Our spirits are eternal, Como. Would you like it?"

"No! But do we want an elemental spirit roaming the grounds forever, locked with Jacinta? Consider what she's been through!"

"I am not abandoning Hades. I will tear every binding spell down if I have to."

Her fierce expression in the flickering half-light was terrifying, and the power that she normally kept so close, veiled even, crackled from her as she flung the door wide with magic. A spectral wind appeared out of nowhere, guttering out all the candles and whipping open the curtains to reveal the rain lashing down outside.

Birdie threw her shoulders back, jaw set. "If the elemental thinks it was in trouble before, it hasn't seen anything yet."

***

Odette could not get to the summerhouse or the Waning Moon Gate. Instead, the garden thwarted her and Arlo at every step, and the weather made it so much worse.

By the time they arrived at the New Moon Gate in the north, they were both soaking. Sheltering beneath the huge gate made of stacked slate, Odette cast a warming spell, and took most of the water from her hair. Arlo shook water from his coat and shifted to human, but his skin and dreadlocks were still damp.

"Why here?" he asked, looking completely unperturbed by the cold.

"It seems this is where we must be. North is the direction associated with earth, and that must be significant."

Arlo nodded. "I remember you telling me about elemental correspondences."

"That must have been riveting for you. Sorry."

He shrugged, lips twisting into a half-smile, his eyes never leaving hers. "Don't be sorry. I asked. I wanted to learn more about what you did. It was important to me. It still is."

"Really? After all that has happened between us? Let's not lie to each other, Arlo."

"I'm not lying. We might not be lovers, but we are friends. We agreed to a truce."

"We did, you're right." Arlo's close proximity still did odd things to Odette's nerves. She wanted to pull him close, lose herself in him as she once had. "Sorry. This situation has me all at sixes and sevens. Let's hope I can call Jacinta without summoning the creature."

"It's nowhere near us at the moment."

"Good." She considered her options. "I normally see things in the moon gates, or through them. I'm not sure standing in it will do us any favours. I could cast a spell over the bench next to the hostas. That's close enough to see well. Although..." she trailed off, examining the moon gate. *What had happened here at that time?*

"Speak to me, Odette. Talk it through."

"The new moon is embodied in the New Moon Gate—this one we're under right now—and it represents new beginnings, plans, introspection, and planting the seeds of our future endeavours. It also represents elemental earth, strongest in the north, in winter, and at midnight—at least according to the correspondence we use. Some associate earth with late summer. In theory, the earth elemental is strongest here, or at least in this part of the garden. It seems an odd place to do any magic where the elemental is strongest."

"But maybe that's the point," Arlo reasoned. "Hit it hard. And perhaps they'd already weakened it."

She nodded. "That makes sense. Perhaps the other binding spells did the trick. But what went wrong? Why is Jacinta here now with the elemental? I must try to speak to her, or at least see her. See what happened. You know, rather than watch, I'm going to call her. Just stay silent, please."

"Sure."

Odette steadied herself with deep breaths, and then decided to ground herself even more by slipping off her boots and wriggling her feet in the earth. It was cold, but she felt the power of the gate surge through her. She called the magic close, feeling her coven's magic woven within it, and years and years of history. Her family's magic that went back centuries. That meant Eliza's, Ansel's, and Jacinta's magic, too. And Jacinta was still here, her spirit summoned from wherever it had been.

"Jacinta," she said, voice loud and clear. "I know you're here. We met briefly in the library when you arrived with the elemental. Tell me what you need!"

For long moments, nothing happened, except the rain continued its insistent drumming on the moon gate, pooling in the stones that mimicked a streambed running through it. The weather was getting wilder too, the wind gusting strongly, and battering the spring plants and fresh, green shoots. It whipped her hair around her face, temporarily blinding her, and the sky darkened as lightning forked across the sky. With a startled intake of breath, Odette realised it was night, and the air was hot and muggy, and a body lay crumpled at her feet.

The vision vanished as quickly as it had arrived, but it left Jacinta's ghost standing in front of her.

She was barely older than a child, mid-teens at the most, slender-limbed and short, her long dress in rags, her skin ravaged by cuts. Looming behind her was the shade of the elemental, twisted and misshapen. Three wolves surrounded it in moments, but in a blink it had gone, and was instead a gnarled tree curled over Jacinta like a bent old man.

Odette swallowed, barely daring to breathe. "Jacinta, I'm so sorry for what happened to you. We think we understand, but the truth is, we know so little. How is the elemental still with you if your family banished it? How can we help so that you can truly rest?"

Jacinta's mouth moved urgently as if she was trying to tell Odette something, her eyes wide and imploring.

"Again, Cinta, but slower. I can't hear you."

Cinta stepped closer, lips moving just as rapidly, and Odette was so intent on watching her lips, it was only at the last moment that she saw the gnarled tree branch reach forward to clutch Jacinta's shoulder as if to pull her away. Arlo was instantly back in his wolf, snarling ferociously. However, before anyone could do anything, a flash of magic, blindingly white, enveloped the creature, and it froze mid-movement.

Jacinta leapt at Odette, face etched with anger and frustration. The cold, sharp shock of the ghost's touch was like being doused in a bucket of ice-cold water, but Jacinta's strange mutterings became crystal clear, the words thrust into Odette's head by sheer force of will. Odette crashed back into the wall behind her, her shoulders scraping against the ragged slate, and she swore in shock. But Jacinta had already gone.

Arlo's warm hands were on her arms. "Odette, are you all right? What did she do?"

A strange name tripped off the tip of her tongue. "*Heathgrim Barrowdwell.*"

"What the fuck?"

Before she could answer him, Maverick's commanding howl had them both whirling around, looking in the direction of the orchard.

Thirty-One

Present Day

"You found them," Birdie said, crouching to examine the strangely well-preserved poppets that Lam and Maverick had dug up.

"Thanks to the bees," Lam said. He looked wet and miserable, despite the shelter spell that he'd cast over the clearing to protect the hole and the gathered group of witches, Maverick, Arlo, Domino, and Monroe. "They pointed us in the right direction."

Birdie bit back on her wish to say something uncharitable, and instead said, "Well, it's good they decided to get involved."

"I'd say they've been involved all along," Maverick quipped, cocking his eyebrow. "Should we shelter in the stone hut? You look cold, Birdie, regardless of your spells."

"Not yet." She studied the poppets again. Funny, wizened things, coated in honey and herbs, buried in salt, and bound with strong magic. "Air, fire, and water. Still here after all these years. Most intriguing. Especially this." She pointed out the bunch of feathers in the middle of one poppet, bedraggled, the burnt honey colour of wings barely visible. "Hades, I presume, to represent air. I think I see it now."

"You do?" Como asked, looking utterly baffled.

"So do I," Odette said, face still flushed from her race across the garden. "I have a way to banish the elemental completely."

Birdie stood, her knees creaking in protest. "How?"

Odette grinned. "Jacinta gave me the creature's name. *Heathgrim Barrowdwell*. She must have found it out somehow."

"Clever girl," Birdie said, nodding with approval. "That will work. Names have power. I have just the spell, although it's been years since I used it. We just need to find the elemental."

"Already done," Arlo informed her. "It's at the New Moon Gate. Cecile, Vlad, and Tommy are watching it."

"Thanks to your spell, I presume," Odette said, addressing Morgana. "Your binding worked at the nick of time."

Morgana sighed with relief. "Good. I thought it was the best type of binding to use." She gestured to the bag that Monroe carried. "We've brought them with us, just in case, so now we'll head there and get rid of it. But what about Hades?"

"I'll find him later," Birdie said thoughtfully. "Alone. I thought I would have to rage and storm about, breaking all the binding spells, but it seems just one will suffice."

Lam frowned. "It won't bring the elemental back?"

"Not once it's banished using its name. I'll know more about this entire event when I speak to Hades." She hoped. Birdie still wasn't sure how the ritual had triggered his disappearance, but presumed that he would know. Whether he'd tell her, however, was another matter, but it was more likely if they were alone. He would not relish being returned to a circle of curious onlookers. "Well, we can only get so wet, so I suggest we just get on with it and banish the creature now. We'll leave the poppets here, protected by the shelter spell."

"You don't want me to guard them?" Maverick asked.

"I have a feeling the bees will do that." The bees were already gathering, the thrum of bee song mixing with the steady patter of rain on leaves. "After that, Lam, you and I must chat. Perhaps with Maverick, too." As High Priestess, she should be helping him deal with his new powers, and so far, she had failed completely.

Without waiting for argument, Birdie set off across the orchard, staff in hand, clad in Wellington boots and a thick wool skirt and jumper, all covered with a cloak that made her feel dramatic. The others trailed behind her. She cast a spell to make sure they couldn't catch up, wanting to be alone with her thoughts as she crossed the garden. Her coven followed her, talking amongst themselves, but the shifters raced away to join the rest of their pack. She didn't need her grimoire for this spell, nor would she risk it in the rain, anyway. In fact, she could probably cast this spell from anywhere in the garden now that she knew the elemental's name. But that wouldn't do at all. She wanted to look it in the eye and see it leave.

Birdie had doubted herself over the last twenty-four hours, and still did, deep down. Hades's loss had shaken her, and her reaction had surprised her even more. She was a silly, sentimental old woman to be so upset by his disappearance, and she needed to think on her next plans. She would rather pass on her mantle than have it ripped from her. By the time she reached the New Moon Gate, the garden opening up before her so that the most straightforward path revealed itself, she was thoroughly seething, both at herself and the elemental. However, as soon as she saw it, that all vanished in wonder.

The elemental had taken the form of a gnarled old tree overhanging the New Moon Gate. Its many branches, clad in moss and fungi, were spread wide, casting the gate in deep shadow. One branch reached towards the gate like a clutching hand, frozen mid-movement, and its roots were visible in the earth, clutching the ground like claws. However, the tree looked as if it was carved from stone rather than made of wood, and smelled like damp stone, too. It was bathed in bands of white light—the binding spell cast by Morgana—but despite that, it still exuded raw power that spoke of growth and rest, the long, slow movements of time, and deep earth that seeded the world. She felt the strength of ancient rock, the roots of mountains and seams of continents that moved the Earth itself.

And yet for all that, it had wanted more, so much so that when Jacinta had dragged it to her, it had seized her with malice. It looked nothing like the elemental creature that Odette had painted. That was when it possessed Jacinta. Birdie wondered how many other faces it might present to humans.

The wolves wisely kept a healthy distance from it, and no wonder. Despite the binding, it looked as if it might tear itself free at any moment and rampage about the garden as it once had. It was magnificent. However, knowing what it had done, and still would had it not been bound, she couldn't admire it.

Birdie dropped her spell and Morgana and Odette immediately stepped to either side of her, Morgana asking, "Do you need our magic?"

Birdie was about to refuse, wanting to exert her authority, but realised that would be churlish. "Yes, please, and the boys'. They should be part of this. It's not often we get to banish an elemental, or even see one, and while it's bound now, I can feel it straining like a dog at a leash." She watched what she presumed was its face, the huge knots in the trunk like eyes boring into hers. "It has more substance than I expected. Perhaps the latest binding spell has made it so."

"Most likely," Morgana nodded in agreement. "How do you want us, Birdie?"

"In a line, please. You and Odette on either side of me, the boys at each end, but I need my staff in hand. Morgana, I suggest you take the poppet and jar from the bag. At the opportune time, destroy the binding. I will tell you when." The boys looked nervous but determined, and she tried to reassure them. "Just follow me, you'll be fine." Then she addressed the shifters, all back in their wolf. "Stay back. I suspect this will be messy."

Birdie felt the garden's energy ebb and flow around her, a silent battle with the elemental it recognised from all those years ago, and she thought how strange it was that those events had such a lasting impression, and how devastating it must have been at the time. She didn't waste time with introductions and pleasantries. "You have caused much heartache, Heathgrim Barrowdwell. You have scarred this garden and the family who lived here then. I feel their memories and their pain. Have you anything to say for yourself before I banish you for good?"

The elemental groaned through every infinitesimal movement of its branches, and rough-hewn lips creaked out a reply. "I did what is my nature."

Furious, Birdie cracked her staff on the damp ground, and it boomed with power. "That is a lie! Earth can be nurturing, supporting, and grounding. It cradles life as well as destroys it. You chose to show only one side of your nature. You were unbalanced and vindictive. I do not know how you managed to cling to Jacinta all these years, but it ends now! You will not violate this house or Jacinta Wildblood any longer."

Birdie opened her heart and mind to the garden, drawing first on the power of the New Moon Gate as she started her spell, and then as her voice swelled and the spell grew in strength, drew from the coven and the rest of the garden. Her coven's voices rose with hers, and Birdie was assailed with nature's memories of that terrible time. The turbulent growth, the assault upon the house, and destructive malice. Another spell weaved itself with this one, and Birdie heard another voice, bright like the keening wind, or water over stones. She knew exactly who it was.

Eliza Wildblood.

The garden was lending her voice to the spell, too.

Hunter danced out of the way of the ancient elemental being, scarcely able to believe what he was seeing.

The creature was trembling all over, groans and creaks filling the air as the spell took hold. The earth cracked beneath it as the roots thrust up, and plants and stones went flying. He and the pack edged back even further, but it was hypnotic to watch.

Hunter might not be a witch, but he could feel the raw power surging around him, both the witches' and the elemental's. If the creature was weaker because it was bound, Hunter was horrified to consider what it was like before.

Over and over Birdie chanted the name "Heathgrim Barrowdwell," weaving the ancient banishing spell that forced the creature out of the garden forever. The other witches were lined up next to her, all chanting the repetitive spell that looped and circled back on itself, seeming to tie the name Heathgrim Barrowdwell in knots. Hunter couldn't see it, but that's what it felt like—as if a noose was being drawn incrementally tighter. The elemental creaked and groaned, the sound turning from low-pitched rumbles to ear-splitting screams. Its branches started to shatter, chunks of stone and wood exploded into the air and across the ground, forcing the wolves to retreat even further. But at this point, it was clear the binding was stopping it from deteriorating further.

Birdie shouted, "Now, Morgana!"

Morgana had been readying herself, and with deft fingers shattered the binding spell on the poppet and jar. The thick bands of white light that had circled the elemental vanished.

Birdie rejoined the others in the spell and cracked her staff upon the ground. The earth buckled, opening a huge chasm under the elemental, and with an Otherworldly, earthshattering groan the elemental fell into the deep, ragged hole. Morgana threw the poppet in after it, and Monroe, swiftly changing shape, took the large jar from her and hurled it in, too.

A few ragged branches and roots clung to the lip of the chasm, trying to claw itself out, but Birdie and the witches were relentless, and Birdie crashed her staff upon the ground again. "You are banished from this world forevermore, Heathgrim Barrowdwell, destined to live in the roots of the world, forbidden from ascending to light. Forever shall the earth hold you in its deep embrace. Forever shall seams of rock trap you. You will relinquish your hold on Jacinta Wildblood, and no more will the halls of the spirits be open to you. So I command you, so shall it be."

The last fingers of rock and wood vanished with a guttural rumble that Hunter felt through his entire body, and with a series of what sounded like thunderclaps, the ground sealed itself shut. For the next few seconds, the surface rearranged itself; ripples of earth smoothed out, stones rolled flat, plants shuddered as they settled, before everything finally fell silent.

It was over.

"Fuck me," Lam said, standing at the edge of what had just been an enormous pit. "That was epic!"

He was cold and wet and had long abandoned the spell to keep himself dry, but he didn't care. It was the most alive he'd felt in years. *Perhaps ever.* Magic still coursed through him like jolts of lightning, his hairs still standing on his arms.

Como stood next to him, equally shocked. "I feel as if several thousand gallons of caffeine were injected into me. That was unreal."

Tommy, the huge, hairy shifter, grinned next to them. "That were fucking brilliant. Not quite as much fun as laying dynamite charges and blowing up an entire valley, but close."

Lam stared at him, slightly deflated. "You did *what*?"

"We had some trouble a few months back. It got messy. It was on the news, you know. In Wales."

Lam's mouth fell open. He remembered reading about a collapsed valley that was blamed on old mine workings in North Wales. "That was *you*?"

He nodded, clearly very pleased with himself. "Demolition is my thing. The girls were there," he said, nodding towards the three witches. "Petrified forest and all sorts. Never a dull moment, right?" He sauntered off, shifting to join his pack who were running around the garden with unbridled enthusiasm.

"What the hell else don't we know?" Como asked, face wrinkling with annoyance. "The sooner we move in here, the better."

Lam slicked his hair back, smiling at him. "This hasn't put you off?"

"No! Has it you?"

"No, but I would like a bit of peace to finish my revision."

"Bollocks to that. It can wait for another day." Como shivered. "I'm freezing, and I need a drink."

"I wonder if Jacinta has gone?"

"I hope so, but that can wait, too. Coming?"

"In a minute."

Como left him to it, and Lam took one final look at the area. It was uncanny. Apart from a patch with no plants, it was hard to imagine what had happened. And bizarrely, the moon gate had remained undamaged, despite the earthquake-like rattles in the area. Lam didn't feel he was quite ready to leave yet. There was still so much to absorb that he thought he'd be processing it for days. He was so lost in his thoughts that he jumped when his mother appeared next to him, laying a hand on his arm.

"Are you okay, Lam?"

"Just soaking it all in."

"It's a lot," she admitted, her attention not on the garden but on him. "You did well."

"I didn't know what I was doing. I just followed you three."

"That's as good a way to learn as any. You'll find your way." She smiled. "You already are."

Morgana came barely up to his shoulder, and he suddenly felt very protective towards her. "You three take on a lot."

"It's what we do when we have to. We don't seek it out. This thing could not continue. I feel for Eliza, Ansel, and Jacinta. I think they had it far worse. Especially Jacinta."

"Has she gone?"

"Odette thinks so, but it's all a bit raw now." She put her arm through his. "Come on, to the house now, before we all freeze. I want a steaming hot toddy and chocolate cake."

He allowed her to pull him along the path. "Do you think we'll ever know what happened to Jacinta back then? Whether she survived, I mean? We don't at the moment, not really, do we?"

"No, we don't. Perhaps Hades can tell us. Or Odette."

Birdie, despite everyone's objections, returned to the orchard alone, surrounded by a crackling shield of swiftly conjured summer sunshine to warm her and the umbrella spell to shield her. She was not prepared to wait to find Hades.

Besides, this was the best time to do it. The garden's magic was still coursing through her, and her ancestors felt close. It would all ebb away soon, and she wouldn't have the energy later. Best do it now.

However, when she reached the clearing in the orchard where Lam's spell was still in place, she realised the energy had shifted again. The bees were buzzing around and crowding on the trees' branches, and it felt as if they had formed a mini amphitheatre to watch. As she stepped into the circle, she realised why. Hades was sitting in the middle, cleaning himself nonchalantly.

"Hades! You're back!" She rushed towards him, and regardless of the fact he was not a cat that loved cuddles, swept him into her arms and cuddled him anyway. "How are you here? I haven't done anything!"

Hades purred contently in her arms, and unexpectedly licked her face, his rough tongue like sandpaper across her cheek. His voice, as rich and velvety as cream, rumbled in her head. *"I disagree. You did quite a lot. As did the bees."*

"I saw your feathers in the poppet."

"*Ah, yes. My old form. I gave them those to help them bind the elemental. It seems there were unexpected consequences. However, the bees extricated them. Could you put me down, please? This is most undignified.*"

Birdie kissed his head. "Old curmudgeon. What do you mean about the bees?"

However, as she crouched to look at the poppets, she saw exactly what they'd done. The poppets were laid in a line, the binding that had held all three together removed, and Hades's old feathers were now out of the poppet that had been bound by air. They looked bedraggled and soggy, but she lifted them all anyway, feeling the residual magic that had preserved them.

"I didn't know bees could do this." Birdie studied the bees, and they studied her, the weight of their gaze surprisingly intense. "Thank you, bees. It seems you have a lot of surprises hidden away. I am most grateful for your help."

Hades said, "*They thank you for finally and properly banishing the elemental. Eliza did well, but I failed them at the end.*"

"I doubt that."

"*It's true.*" He sauntered out of the clearing. "*Let's talk in the fruit shed.*"

Within a few minutes they had settled in the old stone building, Birdie seated on a rickety old cane chair and Hades on the bench top facing her. He looked none the worse for his entrapment, but neither did he seem as he normally did.

"This has the air of a confessional, old friend."

"*It is, of sorts, but in case you're getting very excited, I'm not going to divulge my deep, dark secrets.*"

"At least I know you have some."

He gave a rumbling laugh and blinked his large, amber eyes.

"Odette has painted you in your owl. You looked large. Magnificent, in fact."

"*I liked being an owl.*"

"Be one now, then...although, you're cuddlier as a cat."

"*No, I have moved on from that. After Ansel told me he couldn't trust me, I only ever used that form once more.*"

"Why didn't he trust you?" She felt aggrieved on Hades's behalf.

"*I lied. I told him that I had sought him out to be his familiar, but it wasn't true, and he discerned that. But I was trying to help.*"

"You're confusing me. You have to give me some context, Hades. And I want to know more about the bee ritual, and how you vanished, and where you went! And Jacinta! Did she survive the elemental's attack?"

"*You don't know?*"

"No! I'm not a time traveller, and Odette sees only glimpses, although perhaps she has found Jacinta's ghost. Or rather I hope not, actually. I want her to have moved on without Heathgrim Barrowdwell causing her grief."

"*Settle in then, Birdie. It's quite a tale.*"

Thirty-Two

Past and Present

It had been a whole month since the elemental creature had attacked Moonfell, and Eliza had barely left Jacinta's side the entire time.

Ansel, of course, took his turn, as did Jem's mother, but Eliza had borne the brunt of the care. She felt it was her responsibility. Although her sister had survived the attack, she had been horribly wounded. On the first day, they weren't sure if she would survive at all; she was so pale and sickly after losing so much blood, her wounds grievous, and they cleaned them meticulously. As Ansel had seen in his vision, they carried her to the bees, and they danced over her, weaving a golden light to cocoon her, and Eliza hoped that it would prove miraculous. As the day progressed, her breathing deepened, and she slept properly for hours. But after that the nightmares started, and she screamed and screamed until she was hoarse.

Despite all of Eliza's and Ansel's healing skills and spells, it seemed that Jacinta would never fully recover. They had removed the binding from the box and doll, so that her own magic would once again flow freely, and made her as comfortable as they could in her bedroom in the tower, but she didn't speak and didn't look at them. The bruises around her eyes had slowly faded after the first week, and she could at least open her eyes, but they remained bloodshot for another week, and her gaze was often vacant. As for her skin, most of the wounds had healed, but she had scars that Eliza doubted would ever truly fade.

Eliza sat back in her chair that was positioned under Jacinta's window, putting her embroidery aside, her fingers and eyes aching, and instead looked at the gardens sprawling below. Within days of them banishing the creature, the gardens had slowly returned to normal. The thorny hedge that had surrounded the house vanished virtually overnight, the wriggling ivy had retreated, and the verdant growth had disappeared; what hadn't left was hacked back by Jem and Ansel together.

July had slowly become August, fruit was ripening in the orchard, and the bees were busy in the garden, providing more honey than they ever had before. It looked so peaceful, and yet Eliza hadn't felt at peace in weeks. Her plans to make money were now dreams. She felt stuck. Impotent. Jacinta was sleeping, tossing and turning as she often did, sleeping more than she was awake. She sipped on water and soup, and consented to being walked to the privy and back, but she moved like a stiff old lady, and she didn't speak.

Eliza opened the casement window, allowing in a fresh breeze to air the room. The weather had turned after that hot July, and thankfully the oppressive heat had not returned, but today was bright and blue once more. She was just easing back in her chair, wondering whether there were more spell books she could study to help Jacinta, when a large bird flew closer to the window, its wingspan filling her vision. In moments, the large barn owl with tawny wings and amber eyes alighted on the windowsill.

"Hades," Eliza hissed, unable to hide her annoyance. "You seem remarkably more solid since last I saw you. I believe Ansel asked you to leave, and yet you are still here. I hope you do not bring more lies."

His voice resounded in her head, deep and melodious, and she jumped. "*I come to help.*"

"With what?" She fought to keep her voice low, not wanting to disturb Cinta. "It is already too late. We banished the elemental without you, and Cinta exists in a half-state. Neither here nor there. It haunts her still. She is lost!"

"*I could not find the elemental's name. I apologised to Ansel, and I apologise now to you. These creatures are not of my spirit plane. They are altogether different. But I come with another proposal.*"

"Unless you can restore Jacinta, there is nothing you can do for me."

Hades had been staring at Cinta, but now he turned his huge amber eyes on her. Close up, she saw gold streaks in them and flashes of green, like spring leaves. She tried to look away but found she could not. "*I wish to be her familiar.*"

Eliza laughed. "You jest, surely. You refused her."

"*No. She sought a familiar, but not me. I was otherwise engaged.*"

"So I gather. The bees dragged you to help us. As Ansel said, either help willingly or not at all." She blinked, finally breaking his intense stare, and looked at her sister. "Besides, I fear there is too much in her head for you to be there, too."

"*I can help her find peace. Joy, too, I hope. She is lost right now, her spirit is trapped within mazes of the creature's making, and she needs help to find her way out.*"

"Mazes?" Eliza frowned. "How do you know?"

"*While I have been away, I have asked questions and I have found answers. I pride myself on helping, but failed before. I will not do so again.*"

"An instruction from the bees?"

"*No.*" Hades shuffled on the sill, his talons loud on the stone. "*I have been on this land for as long as the bees. Together we guard this place—the moon gates and the orchard especially. They are custodians, here forever. I come and go as is needed or wanted. Now I am needed. She searches still, you know. Cinta needs a light in the dark, tangled forest that is her mental maze. Someone to guide her home. I will be that light.*"

"Can you really do that?"

"*I can—if she will follow. But it may take time.*"

"And you seek my permission why?"

"*Because you are Mistress of Moonfell.*"

"You didn't before. You went straight to Ansel. Why now?"

"*Because Jacinta*," he pronounced her name carefully, "*cannot speak for herself.*"

Despite her earlier antagonism, Eliza softened her stance. "Thank you. That is thoughtful. If you really think you can help, then I gratefully accept. She is so young, I cannot bear to think that this is her life from now on."

"*Good. Then I will start now.*"

"You will keep me informed." It was not a question.

"*Of course, but you will be busy with your own business. A carriage is traveling along your drive right now.*" Hades seemed to twist his beak into a smile. "*You must hurry, and wear your best gown.*"

Eliza shot to her feet. "Who calls? No one has sent word!"

"*I fear Miss Nell is impatient. She brings Villiers to see you.*"

"*Now?*" Eliza almost shrieked.

"*Now. Run along. I have work to do, and so have you.*"

"But I'm not ready! Not for lords and ladies. It's too much. It was a dream. A silly dream."

"*The best things start with dreams. Go and make yours a reality.*"

Present Day

Odette listened as Birdie related Hades's story, suspended in a dreamlike state as the strange tale unfolded.

The large, green living room was full once more, the eight shifters and five witches spread across sofas and chairs, all listening attentively. It was mid-afternoon, and the spring rain had continued unabated, but no one cared. The fire blazed, lamps provided puddles of warm light, and hot drinks, chocolate cake, and cookies sustained them. Hades was outside, hunting again, seemingly unperturbed by being locked in the spirit realm.

"How was he locked in?" Como asked, a rebellious twist to his lips. "I don't understand!"

"As we thought," Birdie explained, "the bee ritual was last performed by Ansel, Eliza, and Jacinta. The bees had suggested it as a way to give the three good luck, especially Eliza in her endeavour to make more money. A sort of charm. Hades wasn't there for the ritual, but he appeared later, and offered his feathers to use in the binding spell. He thought it would be more potent, and it was. But when we did the ritual, it triggered a link to what had happened back then. The magic not only bound us to the bees, but also to the events that immediately followed the ritual—when Jacinta accidentally summoned the elemental. Hades describes the bees as guardians of the grounds.

He is their friend – for want of a better word – whom they call on in moments of need. They were here long before our family owned Moonfell, and their magic is deeply woven with that of the grounds. The ritual made a bridge between our time and Eliza's, just briefly. Enough to have strange repercussions."

Odette leaned forward, adjusted her legs that were folded beneath her. "Why? What is so special about this land?"

Birdie shrugged. "I have no idea. Hades continues to keep secrets."

Tommy huffed. "Or maybe he doesn't know!"

"I suspect he does," Birdie said softly.

"Forget Hades," Morgana said, "although, obviously, I am glad he is okay. What about Jacinta? Has her ghost gone?" She looked to Odette.

"Yes," Odette confirmed. "I have tried to find her, but she isn't here anymore."

All eyes turned to Birdie, who said, "I am pleased to say that Hades eventually led her mind back to reality, but it took months. She was never the same again. When she did recover, she didn't want to remain at Moonfell any longer, or practice magic."

"I can understand that," Lam said. "I don't think I'd trust myself either."

"At her request, they placed her spell book in the box again, cast in rune spells, and then buried it where she first encountered the elemental, with the final roots that remained bound into a poppet above it. It was a sort of funeral for her magic that I find quite chilling," Birdie mused. "Then when Jacinta was strong enough, she joined her uncle in Lisbon, and that's where she stayed. I am very pleased to say that she married, had a long and happy life, and had three children, who all at some point found their way to Moonfell."

Odette hadn't realised she had been so tense about the outcome, but as soon as Birdie said she'd survived, she sighed with relief. "I'm so glad! I'd hate to think the elemental had won. And Eliza and Ansel?"

"Well, as we know, Eliza finally made her connections, and eventually met King Charles II. He was very scientific-minded, but was also intrigued with many occult things, too. He consulted Eliza on many occasions. He wished to become her lover at one point. He had many, you know, including Nell. Eliza, however, married a man named Jem, who was the gardener and general handy man. Apparently, his family had worked at Moonfell for years and knew all about the residents being witches. They had six children, and the house was full of laughter. Rather lovely, I think. As for Ansel, he had quite the hedonistic time in London for a while, enjoying the delights of the theatres." Birdie had a twinkle in her eye. "After that he travelled widely, finally returning to Moonfell in old age where he became a doting uncle to his nieces and nephews."

Odette had been puzzling over how the elemental attached itself to Jacinta's spirit, and thought she had worked it out. "Eliza bound and banished the elemental, weakening it significantly, but it was never truly gone, was it? It found Cinta after her death. That's horrible!"

"But it had no power over her," Birdie said. "It followed her like a dog. Jacinta was a smart one, though. She found its name out. It's definitely gone now."

"Couldn't Hades have helped?" There was a note of reproach in Morgana's voice.

"He didn't know. Once he had helped Jacinta leave the maze planted in her mind, Hades left the family for years. He comes and goes. Always has."

Odette realised that Birdie was still unsettled, although she was putting on a good show for them. She was still cross with Morgana over the séance, and even more annoyed with herself. She was mulling things over, and so was Morgana. There was a shift in both of them, although Morgana's energy was distinctly lighter. She was sitting close to Monroe, with an air of expectation and hope. That was down to both him and Lamorak. Odette realised that Morgana had made a decision, but about what she wasn't sure. And perhaps so had Birdie.

When Birdie ended her story, the group broke into lots of different conversations, but the shifters were making moves to leave, with an open invitation to run in the grounds on occasions. Odette looked at Arlo who sat next to her, relaxed and smiling, his eyes hooded though, hiding his thoughts.

"You'll be back to run in the grounds, I presume," Odette said.

"If you have no objections. Not often, of course. We wouldn't intrude."

"We wouldn't have offered if we thought it intrusive."

"But *you* don't mind."

She shook her head. "No, I do not."

"Good." His smile broadened. "That's absolutely fine, then."

It was late when Morgana entered Birdie's sitting room on the first floor. She had closed up the house for the night, turned out the lights, dowsed every candle, and had said goodnight to Lam and Como who were in their own sitting room.

Birdie and Odette were waiting for her, and she sat in the large, squashy armchair that flanked the fire, facing the other two. They looked expectant, wary perhaps, and it needled her.

"The house is at peace again, which is a relief. You two, however, are not. Is something wrong?"

"I'm just aware," Birdie said, "that you did not like my decision the other night. You were very vocal on the matter. I was shocked. We have not put the matter to bed."

"I hope you don't expect an apology, Birdie. I'm not going to blindly agree to everything if I disagree. You were wrong."

Birdie clucked, lips pinched. "I know. I was worried about Hades, and have already said it wasn't a great decision. Did you have to be so dramatic, though? Especially swooping in as you did. Sneaking back in the room, in fact." Her eyes flashed. "Were you trying to undermine me?"

"Don't be ridiculous. I was worried, and I wanted to be close to help. But neither did I wish to have you glaring at me the entire time. Honestly, Birdie, this isn't always about you! Lam and Como were there. Besides, does it matter? I couldn't stop it, either. We all failed. At least no one was seriously hurt."

"You think I'm too old for this job. To be High Priestess."

"I think nothing of the sort." Morgana had a short temper, and it was rising now. "You are excellent at your job, but you were sidetracked by Hades, and you know it! Do not deflect your self-doubt on me." She glared at Odette. "I hope you're not encouraging her in this idiocy. We've already discussed this."

"I know." Odette tried to be conciliatory. "I suppose you were more abrupt than normal on such matters."

Morgana was about to retort, but instead sat back, legs crossed, far too tired to be sparring. "Things are changing here. The boys are moving in. My son is here! For the first time in years, I have the chance to know him properly. I don't want him endangered merely to serve someone's ego."

"Mine, you mean," Birdie said.

"Yes. Or anyone's, in fact. You're Moonfell's High Priestess, Birdie. You don't need to prove yourself to anyone."

"I was not!"

"Oh, stop it! You have an ego, like anyone. And I'm changing, too. I'll be the next guardian of this house. I will not sit back if I disagree. Disagreement is healthy. Same goes for Odette. We are all very different. Our differences work."

"They do," Odette said, nodding. "That is very true, and the boys will have different opinions, too. It would be very boring if we all agreed—or meekly followed everything you did, Birdie." Odette's gaze slid to Birdie and then back to Morgana. "So, you don't think Birdie is too old for the role?"

"No! How many times... Birdie," Morgana said, staring at her grandmother pointedly, "is having her own doubts as to her abilities. I do not think that. I disagreed with *one* decision. Get over it!"

Birdie shuffled in her seat, pulling her cardigan around her, and her expression changed from annoyance to doubt. "I did wonder if I was too old. My body is young, but I'm still an octogenarian."

"Who still has all her faculties," Odette pointed out.

Morgana huffed with annoyance. "Oh, good grief, Birdie. We all make mistakes. You banished the elemental perfectly well. I'm not impatient to become head of Moonfell, so put that right out of your mind. Neither will you relinquish it. I'm impatient to get to know my son, to change the pace of my life, and," Morgana wondered whether to tell them her news, but figured they'd know soon enough, "to go on a date with Monroe. I'm rather excited about it, actually."

Odette squealed and shot upright in her chair. "Are you? How brilliant! I knew he liked you. He was just taking his time. And he's so yummy! He's just perfect for you."

"It's just one date."

"The first of many, I'm sure." Odette was beaming. "How exciting."

Birdie looked more circumspect. "That is lovely. Those days have gone for me. I hope you have a lot of fun, Morgana. And I'm sorry. Hades's disappearance shook me more than I expected. Silly."

"Not silly. You care for him. He's been your companion for years. And you, by the way, are still wonderful. It's never too late for a little romance. Can we move on now?" She gestured between them all. "Are we all okay?"

They both nodded, and Birdie said, "Of course."

"Good. Then you should know I'm also moving rooms. I'm heading to the second floor. I've always liked it upstairs. It has an air of mystery. All those twisty passages and wonderful carvings. I may have to get the decorator in, too. We shall see. I'll probably move some furniture around. I have an idea as to where, but I shall decide over the next few days."

Birdie's mouth fell open in shock, but Odette nodded her approval. "New energy. Yes, I see it. Perhaps I should, too. Another tower room, maybe. They're too lovely not to use all the time."

If Birdie disapproved, she didn't voice it. Now to tackle the next subject.

"Perhaps," Morgana suggested, "we should now talk about the bees. According to Hades, they are the guardians of this land. We've always suspected their long connection to this place, but this casts a different light on it. Why are they? What's so special about this place? And does it have anything to do with the moon gates?"

Birdie settled more comfortably in her chair. "I admit I'm interested, but I'm not sure how we will find out, or whether it will change our relationship with Moonfell. Perhaps one of our ancestors found out and hid the knowledge."

"Or maybe," Morgana countered, "no one has bothered to investigate. I think we should."

"That could take years," Odette pointed out, "but I'm intrigued enough to help."

"Good. Thank you."

Something was important about this land, and Morgana had every intention of finding it out – whether she had the bees' blessing or not.

Thanks for reading *Triple Moon: Honey Gold and Wild*. Please make an author happy and leave a review.

My next release will be *Sacred Magic*, White Haven Witches Book 13.

Newsletter

If you enjoyed this book and would like to read more of my stories, please at tjgreenauthor.com. You will get two free short stories, *Excalibur Rises* and *Jack's Encounter,* and will also receive free character sheets for the White Haven Witches and White Haven Hunters series.

By staying on my mailing list you'll receive free excerpts of my new books, as well as short stories, news of giveaways, and a chance to join my launch team. I'll also be sharing information about other books in this genre you might enjoy.

Ream

I have started my own subscription service called Happenstance Book Club. I know what you're thinking! What is Ream? It's a bit like Patreon, which you may be more familiar with, and it allows you to support me and read my books before anyone else.

There is a monthly fee for this, and a few different tiers, so you can choose what tier suits you. Some enable you to receive new release signed paperbacks and hardbacks. All tiers come with plenty of other bonuses, including merchandise, but the one thing common to all is that you can read my latest books while I'm writing them – so they're a rough draft. I will post a few chapters each week, and you can read them at your leisure, as well as comment in them. You can also choose to be a follower for free.

You can comment on my books, chat about spoilers, and be part of a community. I will also post polls, character art, share rituals and spells, share the background to the myths and legends in my books, and some of my earlier books are available to read for free.

Interested? Head to

https://reamstories.com/happenstancebookclub

Happenstance Book Shop

I also now have a fabulous online shop called Happenstance Books and Merch where you can buy eBooks, audiobooks, hardbacks, and paperbacks, many bundled up at great prices, as well as fabulous merchandise. I know that you'll love it! Check it out here: https://happenstancebookshop.com/

YouTube

If you love audiobooks, you can listen for free on my YouTube channel, as I have uploaded all of my audiobooks there. Please subscribe if you do. Thank you.

Read on for a list of my other books.

Author's Note

Thank you for reading *Triple Moon: Honey Gold and Wild,* the first full-length book in the Moonfell Witches series

I love my new coven and their wonderful Gothic house, and it's been fun to see more of their past ancestors. There will be more books in this series, and I'll continue to explore past lives, but no doubt in a slightly different way. I have a kernel of an idea for the next book. Of course, I'll continue to have the Storm Moon shifters as part of the story, and other favourite characters will drop in too, such as Harlan Beckett and Maggie Milne.

The history of bee lore is long and varied, and I will explore more of that in a post I'll share with my Ream subscribers, or maybe in a blog post. I haven't quite decided yet, but it will happen. As far as King Charles and Nell Gwyn's history goes, their relationship is true. Nell was one of his many mistresses, and is a very colourful character. She did start life as an Orange Girl in the theatre, and went on to become a celebrated actress. The Playhouse Theatre was also known as the Theatre Royal, and the original burned down in 1672. It was consequently rebuilt.

If you'd like to read a bit more background on the stories, please head to my website www.tjgreenauthor.com, where I blog about the books I've read and the research I've done for the series. In fact, there's lots of stuff on there about my other series, too.

Thanks again to Fiona Jayde Media who keeps producing such fabulous covers, and thanks to Kyla Stein at Missed Period Editing for sorting out my knotty sentences.

I must also thank my wonderful Happenstance Book Club members who read an unedited version of this book before anyone else. I loved hearing their feedback as I was writing it. Please join one of the tiers if you want to read early versions of my work, as well as receive other goodies!

Thanks also to my beta readers—Terri, and my mother. Their reassurance as they read each new book always soothes my nerves. Also, thank you to my launch team, who give valuable feedback on typos and are happy to review upon release. It's lovely to hear from them—you know who you are! I also love hearing from all of my readers, so I welcome you to get in touch.

I encourage you to follow my Facebook page, TJ Green. I post there reasonably frequently. In addition, I have a Facebook group called TJ's Inner Circle. It's a fab little group where I run giveaways and post teasers, so come and join us.

About the Author

I am a writer, a pagan, and a witch. I was born in England, in the Black Country, but moved to New Zealand in 2006. I lived near Wellington with my partner, Jase, and my cats, Sacha and Leia. However, in April 2022 we moved again! Yes, I like making my life complicated... I'm now living in the Algarve in Portugal, and loving the fabulous weather and people. When I'm not busy writing I read lots, indulge in gardening and shopping, and I love yoga.

Confession time! I'm a Star Trek geek—old and new—and love urban fantasy and detective shows. Secret passion—Columbo! My favourite Star Trek film is the *Wrath of Khan*, the original! Other top films—*Predator*, the original, and *Aliens*.

In a previous life I was a singer in a band, and used to do some acting with a theatre company. For more on me, check out a couple of my blog posts. I'm an old grunge queen, so you can read about my love of that on my blog: https://tjgreenauthor.com/about-a-girl-and-what-chris-cornell-means-to-me/. For more random news, read: Read Self Published Blog Tour. To read about my journey as a witch, read: https://tjgreenauthor.com/leaning-into-my-witch/.

Why magic and mystery?

I've always loved the weird, the wonderful, and the inexplicable. Favourite stories are those of magic and mystery, set on the edges of the known, particularly tales of folklore, faerie, and legend—all the narratives that try to explain our reality.

The King Arthur stories are fascinating because they sit between reality and myth. They encompass real life concerns, but also cross boundaries with the world of faerie—or the Other, as I call it. There are green knights, witches, wizards, and dragons, and that's what I find particularly fascinating. They are stories that have intrigued people for generations, and like many others, I'm adding my own interpretation.

I love witches and magic, hence my second series set in beautiful Cornwall. There are witches, missing grimoires, supernatural threats, and ghosts, and as the series progresses, weirder stuff happens. The spinoff, White Haven Hunters, allows me to indulge my love of alchemy, as well as other myths and legends. Think Indiana Jones meets Supernatural!

Have a poke around in my blog posts and you'll find all sorts of posts about my series and my characters, and quite a few book reviews.

If you'd like to follow me on social media, you'll find me here:

facebook.com/tjgreenauthor/

pinterest.pt/tjgreenauthor/

tiktok.com/@tjgreenauthor

youtube.com/@tjgreenauthor

goodreads.com/author/show/15099365.T_J_Green

instagram.com/tjgreenauthor/

bookbub.com/authors/tj-green

https://reamstories.com/happenstancebookclub

Other Books by TJ Green

Rise of the King Series
A Young Adult series about a teen called Tom who is summoned to wake King Arthur. It's a fun adventure about King Arthur in the Otherworld!
Call of the King #1
The Silver Tower #2
The Cursed Sword #3

White Haven Witches
Witches, secrets, myth and folklore, set on the Cornish coast!
Buried Magic #1
Magic Unbound #2
Magic Unleashed #3
All Hallows' Magic #4
Undying Magic #5
Crossroads Magic #6
Crown of Magic #7
Vengeful Magic #8
Chaos Magic #9

Stormcrossed Magic #10
Wyrd Magic #11
Midwinter Magic #12
Sacred Magic #13
White Haven and the Lord of Misrule novella

White Haven Hunters
The fun-filled spin-off to the White Haven Witches series!
Featuring Fey, Nephilim, and the hunt for the occult.
Spirit of the Fallen #1
Shadow's Edge #2
Dark Star #3
Hunter's Dawn #4
Midnight Fire #5
Immortal Dusk #6
Brotherhood of the Fallen #7

Storm Moon Shifters
This is an Urban Fantasy shifters spin-off in the White Haven world, and can be read as a standalone. There's a crossover of characters from my other series, and plenty of new ones, too. There is also a new group of witches who I love! It's set in London around Storm Moon, the club owned by Maverick Hale, Alpha of the Storm Moon Pack. Audio will be available when I've organised myself!
Storm Moon Rising #1

Dark Heart #2

Moonfell Witches
Witch fiction set in Moonfell, the Gothic mansion in London. If you love magic, fantastic characters, urban fantasy, and paranormal mysteries, you'll love this series. Join the Moonfell Coven now!
The First Yule - Novella
Triple Moon: Honey Gold and Wild

Printed in Dunstable, United Kingdom